FALCON DOWN

C. H. COBB

Published by Doorway Press,
Greenville, OH, USA
doorwaypress.com

Signed copies are available by ordering from
chcobb.com.
Print version is also available on Amazon.com.
E-versions available from Amazon for the Kindle, and
from Barnes and Noble for the Nook

ISBN: 0-9848875-1-2
ISBN-13: 978-0-9848875-1-4
Library of Congress Control Number: 2013941671
First Edition, 2013

Cover design by Dani Snell,
www.refractedlightreviews.com.
Cover photo © Kris Klop / Clear Sky Photography, used
by permission.

Acknowledgments

It never ceases to amaze me that (a) my wife not only allows me to spend the vast quantities of time necessary to write a book, but (b) she actually expects them to do well on the market. The first demonstrates grace, the second faith. I'd put the second in the category of "miracle." We shall see. In any case I am indebted to Doris, and it is a debt I have been happily paying since 1978.

Another amazing person involved in the creation of this book is my sister Elizabeth. She's my editor extraordinaire. Elizabeth is one of those truly gifted people who doesn't realize it. She patiently and carefully edited *Falcon Down*, corrected my attempts at Russian (the Internet is wonderful, but not always reliable for translation), and provided me a terrific resource for understanding Russian culture. My writing, and this book, is much improved because of her input.

Lou, my big brother, is the reason I am writing. His encouragement has convinced me that I can spin a tale others might be interested in hearing. He read the manuscript numerous times in its various incarnations and made multiple helpful suggestions as to story structure, pacing, and consistency.

Thanks also to Mike Hohler, who gave me an Army Ranger's perspective of chapter one, and provided many helpful suggestions.

Any errors of fact or grammar that remain are mine.

Soli Deo Gloria!

Dedication

In memory of Cdr. Lewis Milner Cobb, USN (Ret.)

In every generation there are those men and women who simply do what needs to be done, even at great risk to themselves. My dad was one of those men. He was pursuing an engineering degree at Georgia Tech when World War II reprogrammed his future. Dad joined the Navy and became a fighter pilot, flying Grumman Hellcats off the pitching decks of carriers in the Pacific. He married mom in August, 1945, expecting to return to the Pacific for his third tour after their honeymoon, but by the time their honeymoon was over the war had ended. He stayed in the Navy, eventually retiring as a commander in 1966. From there he went into the Episcopal ministry, still serving people, but in a different way.

He died a couple of years ago. He was faithful to his wife, his family, and his country: a good man, with a life well-lived. He was a great father. This one's for you, dad.

Cast of Characters

Anatoly Geredin: General of the Army, head of the KGB.

Boris Toporov: Co-director of Sidima Timber Cooperative, brother of Galina Toporova.

Galina Toporova: Co-director of Sidima Timber Cooperative, sister of Boris Toporov.

Jacob Kelly (aka. Jake, Falcon, Yakov Sokolov, Sergei Primakov): Major, USAF. Test Pilot for Project *Hydra*.

James Franks: General, USAF. Head of Project *Hydra* at Edwards AFB.

John Smith: Major, USAF Special Operations. Combat Control Team leader. True identity unknown.

Nikolai Pavlovich Chernikov: Colonel/Major General GRU, Commandant Prison 87, director of Project *Krasnyy Voskhod*.

Oswald Simmons (aka. Oz): Scientist working on integrated circuit miniaturization.

Roman Romanovich Nikitin: Major, GRU. Aide to General Chernikov.

Sam Bergman: CIA Counter-intelligence analyst, Soviet Department.

Sevastyan Zavrazhny: Founder of Sidima Timber Cooperative. Former Soviet navy corpsman.

Valeriy Ivanovich Patrikeyev: Lieutenant General, head of the Ninth Directorate of the GRU.

William Jensen: Professor of Political Science, Georgetown University.

Chapter 1

Tuesday, April 15, 1986: 0015 local
Tripoli, Libya

The chill night air was thick with a sense of foreboding danger; but Major John "Smitty" Smith couldn't tell whether it was intuition or imagination. He didn't linger on the question, as he watched Lieutenant Gordon Blake using hand signals to deploy four of his combat control team (CCT) operatives around the base of the old water tower. They disappeared into the gloom, taking up positions to establish perimeter security. A dog began barking somewhere nearby. Every member of the team froze in position. The sound of a slamming door was followed by a furious shout in Arabic, then the door slamming again. The dog gave one last defiant bark and grew quiet.

Smith motioned to Blake, *follow me*. The two men ran lightly from the thicket where they had been hiding to the tiny pump house at the bottom of the tower, and melted into the shadows. The major scrutinized his surroundings one final time then slung his weapon over his back and began climbing the rusty ladder, followed by the lieutenant. When they reached the top both men lay on the flat roof, facing their target.

Major Smith was just minutes from calling down fire from heaven, only it wasn't the wrath of God but the retribution of an angry civilized world, and it wasn't going to be brimstone but 8000 pounds of laser-guided high explosives. Ten days earlier a nightclub in West Berlin had been bombed by terrorists, and all available intelligence pointed to the Libyans. The President of the United States had come to the decision that just *carrying* a big stick was not making an adequate impression on the world's troublemakers. He was going to swing that stick, and hard.

The USAF combat control team was about six kilometers south of the perimeter fence surrounding the Tripoli International Airport, a facility that was shared with the Libyan Air Force. *They're just about to regret that decision to colocate,* the major thought to himself. He could see the rotating beacon on the airport control tower from where he lay. Two hours earlier the final civilian flight for the evening had landed, and the night had grown quiet. The only sounds were the creaks and groans of the steel in the old water tower as it adjusted to the cooling evening temperatures. A moist chill was blowing off the nearby Mediterranean, but Smith ignored the cold. The pleasant scent of nearby citrus groves wafted on the breeze, mixed with the salty aroma of the sea.

Three hundred meters west of him was the compound that served as the Libyan headquarters for *Fatah*. An intelligence intercept had indicated that the leaders of the organization from Gaza, Lebanon, Syria, Iran, and Yemen were to be in-residence this week. Planning had already been underway for the retaliatory bombing of Libya, known as *Operation El Dorado Canyon*, when the CIA Deputy Director of Operations (DDO) had suggested that as long as they were going to break things and kill people, they might as well take the opportunity to degrade Abu Nidal's *Fatah* terrorist organization. It was a unique opportunity to even the score, and the President had jumped at the chance.

"I see three possible entrances, Smitty. There's what looks to be a recessed underground entrance just beyond that deuce and a half, to the left of it. To the left another 40 meters are some vents on some sort of revetment, with what looks like another entrance. And there is the very obvious one, beyond and to the right of the truck. That's all," whispered Blake, as he studied the target through night vision binoculars. Somehow Blake had earned the nickname, "Fat Boy," or more often, "FB." He was squat, built like a tank, rock-hard, and did not carry an ounce of fat on his short, broad-shouldered frame, despite his nickname.

"Yep. I agree, FB." The major topped out at a lanky six

feet two inches. Like the rest of the team, his face and exposed skin were blackened. Between the darkness of the night and their battle dress uniforms, the operators were virtually invisible.

Major Smith flipped the switch on the secure satellite uplink, and said quietly, "Goldilocks is green." He checked his watch, and began setting up the tripod for his laser designator. "Showtime in five minutes, Blake. Let's get the stage lighting set up."

Operationally, Major Smith knew this mission was a nightmare: insufficient planning based on inadequate intelligence, and no training. The CIA had the proper address for the headquarters complex, but had not been able to discern the floor plan, so to speak. The DDO's plan was simple: insert a CCT with laser designators, start the air raid, and let the boots on the ground watch which hole the rats disappeared down. Light it up with laser designators, send in the F-111 Aardvarks with their GBU-10 Paveway bombs, and, poof! One layer of terrorist leadership incinerated. The extraction plan was equally simple. Since the US was going to be delivering a rather obvious message, if the covert extraction went sour just go in fast, hard, and hot with a few elements of an Army Ranger unit attached to the Carrier Strike Group presently floating off the coast, and rescue the combat control team with overwhelming force. Simple for everyone except the members of the CCT, who felt like they were strapped to the front bumper of a New York cab in rush hour.

****

Fourteen inbound F-111s swept over the coast at 100 feet. The first flight divided into three sections, popped up, and began hammering their targets. The Libyan air defenses responded immediately, and surface-to-air missile (SAM) sites around Tripoli began lighting up the intruders. As soon as the Libyan targeting radars began to paint the incoming aircraft, a flight of Navy A-7s unleashed a volley of high-speed anti-radiation (HARM) missiles. Each rocket followed the enemy's radar beam directly to the installation and blew it to pieces, destroying the eyes of the air defense network.

Air raid sirens screamed at military installations all around Tripoli. Within minutes, the combat control team could hear and feel the detonation of bombs cratering the runways on the nearby airport. Smith and Blake ignored the distraction of the attack, and concentrated on their target. The door on the enlisted barracks was flung open, and a stream of men began sprinting for the right-most bunker entrance. Immediately after, a line of running men emerged from the officers' quarters, headed for the entrance farthest on the left.

"Bingo," muttered Smith, as he focused his laser designator on a vent pipe of the left-most air raid shelter.

"Sure wish we had enough stuff to take 'em all out, sir," whispered Blake, as he locked his laser onto the same target. The Paveways would pick up the sparkle of the lasers reflecting off the target and drop right on it, so long as the F-111 strike team released the weapons in the proper trajectory window.

"Me too, FB. But cut off the head and the snake can't strike. We've got this opportunity, let's make double sure we cut off the head." He keyed the satellite link once more and spoke into the mic, "Goldilocks says the fox is Alpha-Whiskey-Romeo."

The encrypted signal was received by a geostationary satellite locked in orbit 22,236 miles above the equator, then retransmitted from satellite to satellite, until it was beamed down to Langley and routed to Washington. After a 500-millisecond delay, Smith's voice came over the speakers in the Situation Room below the West Wing of the White House. All heads turned to look at the President.

"Do it," he ordered without hesitation.

His Chief of Staff, Ralph Kepplehof, was standing behind the President with a puzzled look on his face. He motioned to one of the officers present, and whispered, "General, what does 'Alpha-Whiskey-Romeo' mean?"

The man chuckled, and then replied quietly, "It's a bit of

black humor, Ralph. It means that the tangos have entered 'Allah's Waiting Room'. We're about to usher them into his presence, if you get my drift."

One minute later four more Aardvarks crossed over the Libyan coast. Two of the aircraft were armed with HARM missiles and electronic counter-measures. The other two were each carrying a pair of GBU-10 2000-pound Paveway laser--guided bombs. The first two F-111s popped up and drew the attention of the remaining Libyan air defense systems. The second two entered into the flight profile that would enable them to put their bombs on target.

As soon as the F-111 flight leader heard the Paveway's laser acquisition tone in his headphones, he released the bombs then transmitted, "The package is delivered, Goldilocks."

Smitty alerted his team, and each dropped to a prone position, covering their heads. A few seconds later, four tons of bunker-busting ordnance sent fourteen men to an appointment that did *not* include seventy-two virgins.

Smith and Baker dismantled their equipment, and then clambered down from the top of the water tower. Flitting through the darkened fields and orchards like shadows, the team headed north for the airport security fence. The air raid sirens continued to wail into the night but the bombs had stopped falling. Portions of the skyline to the north were illuminated from fires caused by strikes on other targets. The smell of acrid smoke and cordite lay heavy on the night air.

Ironically, the primary extraction point deemed safest was at the airport. The south apron of the main north-south runway was farthest from the terminal and the airport security forces and had been designated as the landing zone. As mission planners had predicted, the Libyans had extinguished the runway and taxiway lights as soon as the air raid began. The darkness worked to the team's advantage and they arrived at the extraction point without incident.

"Goldilocks is at grandma's house," Major Smith informed the mission controllers. His small team secured the LZ and set up an infrared beacon. At this point things began to unravel.

An armed Libyan patrol dispatched to evaluate the damage to the runways was approaching rapidly.

"Hey, boss, we got visitors. Two armored personnel carriers approaching from the north. Both vehicles have a weapon mounted." Blake paused, studying the approaching vehicles through his night vision binoculars. "Looks like they're both fifty-cals."

"Okay, listen up!" Smith said into his whisper mic, addressing the whole team, "Stay out of sight and hold your fire. Maybe they'll go right by without seeing us."

The six members of the CCT hunkered down. Equipped only with light weaponry, they had nothing that might take out an armored personnel carrier (APC), much less two of them. The major contacted the controllers to let them know the landing zone was compromised. Too late! He heard the incoming Pave-Low chopper just as he keyed the mic.

The MH-53J came in fast and low, its door gunner concentrating fire on one of the APCs, setting the vehicle on fire. But the second APC was scoring hits with armor-piercing rounds and the helicopter began to fly erratically. The door gun was silenced. The chopper smacked roughly onto the tarmac and the combat control team sprang from their hiding places and raced toward it, screaming the running password, *"GRANDMOTHER, GRANDMOTHER, GRANDMOTHER!"* As they ran they sprayed the second APC with small arms fire, suppressing its gunner and causing him to duck into the vehicle for cover.

As they raced up the ramp into the chopper, Major Smith shouted forward to the cockpit, "GO, GO, GO!" But there was no response. The inside of the helicopter was spattered in blood. Both door gunners were hit hard, the flight engineer was dead, and Smith dreaded what the situation might be in the cockpit. Assessing the situation instantly, he barked out commands. "Santini," he shouted, addressing one of his team members, "as soon as we lay down suppressing fire, get on the door gun and destroy that vehicle! Atkins, Morris, see to these wounded! Lieutenant, check on the cockpit. Jonesy, grab your rifle and follow me."

Smith rammed a fresh magazine into his CAR-15 rifle, lay down on the ramp and began peppering the gunner on the APC to give Santini a chance to set up. Jones laid down suppressing fire on the troops that had disembarked from the first APC. Soon the chopper's door gun was chewing pieces out of the second Libyan vehicle and it too finally caught fire.

"Jones, go forward and support Santini. You! What's your name?"

"Reed, sir, crew chief," replied the only uninjured airman from the chopper's crew.

"Well, Sergeant Reed, raise this ramp and get us buttoned up. I'm going forward to the flight deck."

"Major?" Lieutenant Blake called from the cockpit, speaking into his whisper mic. "We're hosed. Gotta go to plan B. Pilot and copilot both bought it. Without a stick jockey, this crate isn't going anywhere."

"I'll see what I can do, Blake. Get everybody settled back here, then come back to the cockpit. I'll be needing you."

"Unless you can raise the dead or fly, boss, not much you *can* do," Blake muttered.

The firefight had slowed down, as most of the attackers were dead or injured. Smith knew that Libyan reinforcements would show up soon so he moved quickly to the flight deck. A grisly scene confronted him: both pilot and copilot were dead and blood was everywhere. He muscled the bodies out of the cockpit, sat down in the left-hand seat and buckled in. The instruments seemed to be intact but the radio was dead. Scanning the gauges, the major increased power and lifted the craft off the ground. Ignoring the shouts of surprise and fear coming from the back, he verified that the helicopter was responding properly to the flight controls, then throttled up to cruise power. Soon they were racing over the ground headed for the coast.

Blake came into the cockpit soon after and squirmed into the right-hand seat. "Who taught you how to fly, Smitty?" he asked nervously.

"My momma, Fat Boy. Now shut up and listen! The radio is shot to pieces. Get on my satellite link, explain our comm situation. We need an escort back to the carrier. Let 'em know we're bringing casualties. Don't mention anything about the pilots or what I'm doing. Nothing! Got it?"

****

Four hours later the combat control team was on an Air Force transport bound for Fort Bragg, outside of Fayetteville, North Carolina. Gordon Blake put a mug of hot coffee in John Smith's hands and then strapped himself into the webbing seat next to him. The rest of the men were snoozing back toward the tail.

"You don't have any kids, do you, Major?" Blake said. It was more of an observation than a question.

"No, Lieutenant, I don't. I'm not married. But I'm curious; why are you asking?"

"Well, sir, you chose the passwords and unit names for this mission, didn't you?"

Smitty nodded.

"You butchered a couple of fairy tales, sir. You confused *Goldilocks and the Three Bears* with *Little Red Riding Hood*. Any self-respecting four year-old would have taken you to task, sir." Blake laughed. "My daughter would be highly offended that you confused her favorite bedtime stories."

"Just tell her it was for operational security."

"Oh, yeah. Right." Blake looked at the crude webbing seats across from them, and grunted. "Once, just once, I wish they'd fly us first class," he groused. Smith smiled but didn't respond, so Blake continued, "You've been holding out on us, boss. When did you learn to fly? When you set that big Pave Low on the deck of that carrier I got the distinct impression you'd done it many times before."

Major Smith nodded, "I guess we all have our secrets, Gordon."

Blake stared at him thoughtfully for a moment before responding, "Maybe some more than others. Major, you've deployed with my team three times. You've clearly been trained for special-ops. General Reynolds tells me that you're attached to some weapons development project at the Pentagon. Well, okay, I can buy that: all three deployments have involved airstrikes with Paveways. Maybe you're doing some sort of work with the laser designators, or another part of the guidance package. Except for one big problem."

"What's that, Lieutenant?"

"After our last mission I wanted to send you a case of Corona; you really pulled our butts out of the soup when the insertion got so screwed up. So I called a buddy of mine at the Pentagon, asked him where I should ship the beer." Blake paused and slurped his steaming coffee.

"And?" Smith asked, knowing what was coming.

"He'd never heard of you. In fact, no one at Fort Fumble knows anything about you. So I got to thinkin' . . ."

"C'mon, Fat Boy," Smith interrupted, trying to redirect the conversation, "You know what they say about that!"

"No, sir. Enlighten me," the lieutenant responded.

"'You don't get paid to think, soldier!'" Smith rasped, with mock harshness.

"Oh, right," Blake replied sarcastically, "Ours is not to wonder why, ours is just to do and die."

"There you go."

Unsatisfied, Blake continued. "Are you really a major in the Air Force, sir?"

Smith laughed, "Yes, Gordon, that I really am."

"Why are they sending a field grade officer on these missions, sir?" When Smitty did not respond, Blake tried again, "Is your name really John Smith?"

Smith just smiled, but still didn't answer.

"Well, who are you, Major?"

"Gordon, I need you to do a couple things. First, make sure nobody talks about the fact that I flew the chopper. It wasn't supposed to happen and I don't want to lose my day job. Remember the story: *the pilot was gravely wounded, but managed to fly it back to the ship, dying just after he set it down. The man deserves a medal.* Make sure the other men have the same story. Got it?"

"Yes, sir, if you say so."

"Second, don't be asking questions about me. Unpleasant people might start knocking on your door and I don't want that to happen. We're both on the same team, playing for the good guys. That's all you need to know. And you don't need to tell anyone what you might suspect. If all goes well, maybe in a couple of years I can tell you where to ship the beer."

Chapter 2

Two years earlier
Monday, April 16, 1984: 0837 local
Edwards AFB, CA, USA

Edwards Air Force Base air traffic control (ATC) gave the incoming F-16 Fighting Falcon a straight-in approach for runway 22L, as it was a slow day and there was no traffic at the moment. The pilot adjusted his glide slope to 2.5 degrees, throttled back, and allowed his speed to bleed off as he raised the nose of the sleek fighter, increasing the angle of attack.

Major Jacob "Jake" Kelly had wanted to be a fighter pilot since his tenth birthday, when his dad had given him a picture book of military aircraft. The dream not only persisted, but grew in intensity and sophistication. By the time the young man entered his junior high years his goals were cast in stone: he wanted to snag an appointment to the Air Force Academy in Colorado Springs. He pursued the dream with a single-minded intensity that pleased his dad and worried his mom. Jake sought to ace every mathematics and science class in school. He began to spend time in the weight room and on the track, and played football all four years of high school. And finally his dream came true. After being nominated by a member of Pennsylvania's congressional delegation, Kelly was accepted into the elite school.

His parents were Clancy and Galina Kelly. Clancy's heritage was Irish. One of his ancestors had been a track layer on the Union Pacific Railroad, and was present at the golden spike ceremony in Promontory, Utah. Galina's parents had escaped Stalin's Soviet Union and immigrated to the United States, settling in Idaho. They never did learn to speak English. Jacob spent every summer with them in his youth, roaming the mountains, fishing and camping. He also became fluent in Russian, a fact he managed to obscure in his Air Force files with the willing complicity of family members. He'd heard that flight spots became mysteriously unavailable to cadets who spoke Russian, while Air Force intelligence positions were wide open. Jake didn't want to fly a desk (or a satellite), so his fluency in Russian remained unknown to the Air Force, even when they vetted him for advanced security clearances.

By the time he graduated from the academy in '77, Kelly was both a skilled athlete and an academic star. He got the pick of the litter in flight slots, eventually winding up with the 34th Fighter Squadron. Within five years, he was a two-time alumnus of the Air Force's Red Flag exercises, where he'd gained near-perfect ratings.

But the young man had experienced his share of sorrows, too. His dad, Clancy, had passed away from an aggressive form of cancer in 1983, and Galina from a heart attack in 1984. As an only child with neither parents nor grandparents nor aunts nor uncles he felt very much alone in the world.

****

Kelly's F-16 settled onto the runway, the nose wheel dropping lightly onto the centerline. Twenty minutes later the lanky officer was waiting outside the office of General James T. Franks, known covertly by his subordinates as "Captain Kirk," though no one dared call him that in his presence. Franks was a Star Trek fanatic and had the hull number of the Starship *Enterprise*, NCC-1701, tattooed on his right forearm.

"The general will see you now, Major Kelly." It was Kelly's tenth trip to the general's office in two months, and the secretary knew him by name.

The major strode into the office and saluted, and Franks returned the gesture. "Take a chair, Jake," he said. "How was your flight?"

"Good, sir." The squadron insignia on Kelly's flight uniform identified him as belonging to the "Rude Rams," the

34th Fighter Squadron stationed at Hill AFB, Utah. Kelly sat and waited on the general, who seemed to be busy with some papers. Finally he looked up.

"Major, you've successfully passed all of our vetting. Security clearances, duty record, flight proficiency, medical records, the whole shootin' match, not to speak of all the tests and exams we've put you through. You've done quite well."

"Thank you, sir."

"Up until today, you've not been told why your commanding officer has released you on temporary duty to my command. You've just known that we've given you everything but an anal exam. Well, I don't know, I suppose the flight surgeons might have done that, too. Did they?"

"Um, no, sir."

"Anyway, I think it's time to fish or cut bait. Jake, I'd like to offer you an assignment. I'm in charge of a development project here at Edwards, a project involving the F-16. I'm in need of a test pilot. But there's a catch, and it's a big one. The test pilot I need is going to be doing things in addition to flying an airplane. Dangerous things. *Very* dangerous things.

"If you sign on with me, you'll be detached from the 34th for the duration of this project. Now, the difficult thing is, I can't say any more about the job 'til you sign on the dotted line. If that seems unfair, too bad. The Air Force doesn't do fair. So what do you say? Are you willing to take a gamble?"

Kelly hesitated, studying General Franks. The senior officer was built like a weightlifter who'd not spent much time in the gym lately. Franks tended a little to the short side of normal and was a bit heavy. He remained silent under Kelly's studious gaze, his brown eyes giving nothing away. Finally Kelly asked, "How long, sir, do you expect this project to take?"

"Three years, Major, at most."

"It's not going to get me away from flying, is it, sir?" The tall pilot would rather fly than eat. He wasn't about to take on a project that would keep him on the ground, or worse yet, in a lab with a bunch of civilian contractors.

"Not really. It's going to require some extra training in, ah, specialized ground tactics. You'll have some . . . ground assignments, or more accurately, missions. But, no, it won't get you away from flying. It *will* change the kinds of missions you're flying. You've been doing air-to-air stuff. This project involves strike missions, air-to-ground. That's all I can say."

Jacob Kelly was silent for a moment, pondering. On the one hand it was an honor to be singled out. On the other, he didn't want to be out of the air combat milieu.

"Sir, can I ask you this? When your project is complete can you get me back into an operational air combat wing? I don't want to fly a desk, sir, no disrespect intended."

"Major Kelly, I will personally guarantee that you are placed in the air wing of your choice at the conclusion of this project. I think I've got that much pull."

"Then I'll sign up, sir. Thank you for giving me this opportunity."

Franks nodded, and picked up the phone, "Susan, get me the base JAG in here, pronto . . . no, not him, the other one, the one with top security clearance . . . yeah, him. Major Kelly has some papers to sign."

****

After the paperwork was complete, Franks dismissed the military lawyer, rang for some coffee, and beckoned the major over to his conference table.

"Jake, everything I'm telling you from here on out is top secret and is to be discussed with no one, and I mean *no one*. Now, what is your assessment of the relative balance of tactical power between the NATO and Warsaw Pact air and ground forces in Europe?"

"They have more men than we do, but ours are better trained, have better morale, and are more loyal. We have an edge in aircraft and avionics. They have a large edge in armor and probably artillery. We own tactical nuclear. Their supply lines are shorter and simpler. Our manufacturing is better."

"That's a fair assessment, Major. A few years ago the National Intelligence Estimate put the numbers of Warsaw Pact medium tanks at 45,000. That's a big edge. Hitler showed us forty years ago what can be done with a bunch of well-commanded tanks.

"I am leading a project entitled *Hydra* whose goal is to erase that edge. By the way, officially *Hydra* does not exist and I'm not just talking about the project, I'm talking about the name, *Hydra.* You do not use that name with anyone, understood? It never gets written down. It never gets typed into a computer. The only people who should ever hear that term pass between your lips are folks who are *part of the project here at Edwards!* No one else, and *nowhere else.* Got that?"

"Yes, sir."

"Good. You are familiar, Major, with the PAVE systems?"

"Yes, sir, the precision avionics vectoring equipment. We carry PAVE Pennys on the Falcon, sir, for use with our Paveway ordnance."

"Right, laser-guided munitions. Ground troops, including our Air Force Combat Control Teams, illuminate a target with an encoded laser; the PAVE system in the aircraft picks up the sparkle and the bomb locks on. As long as the aircraft releases the ordnance in an acceptable trajectory window, the guidance system in the bomb will put it right on the target.

"What the *Hydra* project is supposed to accomplish, Major, is a cluster release of Paveway ordnance in a target-dense battlespace—simultaneous releases of up to thirty-two Paveway bombs carried on multiple aircraft, each bomb locking on to a separate target. This is, of course, predicated on thirty-two different ground pounders all using laser designators at the same time.

"In the few seconds from release to impact, the *Hydra*-modified munitions will establish a radio network and elect one of the bombs as a master controller, which will then hand out specific target designations from all the currently illuminated ground targets, taking into account the trajectory of each separate bomb. All the intelligence and control will reside in the avionics contained in the bombs themselves. It's a 'fire-and-forget' system; once the bombs are released the pilots can skedaddle.

"If *Hydra* is successful, Jake, just four of my airplanes can smoke three companies of Ivan's tanks faster than you can say 'Mother Russia.' That skews the balance of tactical power in Europe between NATO and the Warsaw Pact forces to where it belongs: in our favor.

"There's just one catch for you, Jake. In order to be the chief test pilot for this project you must be thoroughly familiar with battlefield conditions on the ground, and the difficulties ground troops will face using the targeting lasers in combat situations. That's going to require your participation in some ground missions, Major. I have some rather exotic training in mind for you . . . "

****

Kelly returned to Hill AFB later that afternoon and began the series of tasks associated with his change of assignment. That evening he had dinner at the Officers' Club with his squadron commander and his wing man, then returned to his base quarters and packed up his gear, all of which filled just three duffel bags. He sat down at the table in the tiny kitchenette, popped open a beer, and decided that there was one more phone call he had to make. He wanted to talk to Bill Jensen.

Bill had been a friend of the family since Jake's high school days. Jensen's association with the Kelly family had come about through a mere chance association (Jensen always referred to it as "providential"). The Kelly family owned a summer cabin near the Snake River. Jacob and his dad had been fly-fishing on a tributary of the Snake River one beautiful August day, and had rounded a bend of the river just in time to see another fisherman slip on the rocks. The unfortunate man struck his head on a knot of granite and fell unconscious into the river. The Kellys pulled him to safety, and took him to their cabin. He stayed long enough to recover from the nasty blow on the head. From that chance encounter a friendship developed. Within two years, the families had grown very close. Jake's dad and Jensen discovered a common love of the outdoors, books, military history, and a host of other topics. It was as though the two men had grown up as twins.

When Jacob's father had died in '83, Bill had flown back from a vacation in Australia to be at the funeral. His calm presence and unqualified assistance in every area had been a great comfort to the family. Since those days the major had grown as close to Jensen as his dad had been, and the family friendship had continued, even beyond the death of Jake's mother in '84.

Jensen was an independently wealthy academic, teaching occasionally at Georgetown University. His area of specialty was International Relations. His knowledge of countries around the Pacific Rim in particular was encyclopedic. He was a fascinating conversationalist, and had become something of a surrogate father for Jake.

"Hi, Mr. Jensen, it's Jake Kelly."

"Hello, Jacob! Great to hear from you. What's it been since we last talked, three months?"

"About that, sir. I guess things have just been really busy."

"Yeah, here too. I've had a heavier teaching load this semester, and between that and renovating our basement, I've just not had much time."

"What are you doing to your basement?"

"Remember that big snow that Maryland got in late January? Well, it was followed immediately by heavy rains. Our basement flooded, and I've had to tear all the carpet and drywall out. So I've been remodeling down there, starting with the sump pump."

"Sounds like a mess."

"Got that right. So what've you been up to? Still enjoying driving Falcons on the taxpayers' dime?"

"Love it, Mr. Jensen. As long as you're willing to foot the bill, I'm willing to burn the gas. That's why I'm calling. I've been transferred to Edwards, and I wanted to give you my new address and phone number."

"Edwards Air Force Base in southern Cal'? That's exciting! You'll get to watch shuttle landings, you lucky dog! What will you be working on at Edwards?"

"Can't say, Mr. Jensen. But I'm looking forward to it."

"I'll bet you are. So, how are you doing since your mom died, Jake? Susan and I really miss your parents."

"Okay, I guess. I miss 'em. Don't feel like anywhere is really home anymore. Even though I've still got the house on the Susquehanna, and the cabin on the Snake, they're just empty buildings now with mom and dad gone," Kelly said. He swallowed hard, trying to get rid of the lump in his throat.

"I know they were very proud of you, Jake, and so am I. Look, Susan and I are planning another trip to the Snake River in September. Why don't you come? We'd love to see you again. Besides, I want another chance at our 'largest-trout' competition."

"Love to! If I can schedule the time, I will."

The two men talked for a few more minutes, then Jake signed off and turned in. There was an 0400 transport to Edwards leaving in the morning, and he and his duffel bags had to be on it.

Chapter 3

January, 1986: Two years after Kelly's
recruitment
Monday, January 6, 1986: 2330 local
south of Leningrad, USSR

Aleksei Kozlov was having trouble focusing his eyes. It might, he thought, have something to do with the fact that this was the sixth time that Chernikov had refilled the scientist's large coffee mug with vodka. *By all that's holy, how I hate that man*, Kozlov thought to himself. Thankfully he was still sober enough to not say it aloud. The diminutive scientist stood just under five and a half feet with his boots on, and he was intimidated by the presence of the larger man.

"So, Aleksei, we have missed our development deadline again. That makes three straight months in which you have given me bad news. When shall I have good news to report to my superiors?" Colonel Nikolai Pavlovich Chernikov had not kept pace with the red-faced man's vodka consumption. He was quite sober, the vodka from his first mug untouched.

"Come, comrade Colonel! It's not like making cheese, you know. We've been working hard to create a mathematical model of fluid dynamics," Kozlov slurred, "that approximates the environment of a propeller in sea water. Different depths. Different temperatures. We need it to progress with our design work. It's just not coming. You haven't given me mathematicians, Colonel Chernikov! You have not given me scientists! These men are working hard, but they are only engineers. They can prototype and test a design; they can fix a good design to make it better, but they cannot invent a wholly new one."

Chernikov was neither a scientist nor an engineer. He was

an officer who had originally served with distinction in the Soviet Union's elite 106th Guards Airborne division in Afghanistan. When his commanding officer, General Valeriy Patrikeyev, had been recalled to Moscow and placed over the Ninth Directorate of the *Glavnoye Razvedyvatel'noye Upravleniye*, the Main Intelligence Directorate (GRU) of the General Staff of the Soviet Army, he took Chernikov with him. Because Chernikov had displayed a remarkable ability to accomplish difficult tasks, the colonel had been placed over a development effort aimed at quieting an already dangerously silent class of diesel submarines, the Project 877 boats, known to NATO as the Kilo class submarines.

The colonel knew nothing about submarines. The titular head of the development project was a three-star navy captain who'd been transferred from a promising submarine career because an auto accident had left him heavily dependent upon a cane. On paper the captain ran the show. In actual fact, he was responsible only for the naval outcomes of the project; Chernikov possessed the day-to-day operational authority.

Beyond general administration, Chernikov's duties included ensuring the secrecy of the project, protecting the scientists, and guaranteeing that the scientists were at their productive best, a task that occasionally required firm "persuasion and encouragement." Try as he might, the colonel's team was nonetheless missing the development deadlines and milestones laid out for him by his superiors.

"Always complaining, Aleksei, you are always complaining. Perhaps your wife and children would find Chersky more to their liking? It can be arranged." Chernikov's gray eyes were fixed impassively on the nervous scientist. He'd already decided that this development project would be a success, with or without the little man across the table.

Kozlov paled. Chersky was a tiny outpost on the Kolyma River in northeastern Siberia, and was at one time part of Stalin's gulag. It was not uncommon for winter temperatures to sink lower than fifty below zero. "We are trying, comrade. These men will not be more productive if you add to their worries."

"I do not add to your worries, comrade Kozlov, out of idle cruelty. I take no pleasure in such threats. But you forget, Aleksei, that I have my own masters to please in Moscow. We'll all be spending the winter in Siberia if your team is unable to produce."

Kozlov put his head in his hands. He knew what had to be done, but he detested it with every fiber in his body. He had no religious inclinations, he was pragmatic to the core, but he did have his professional pride and that was what he was wrestling with at the moment. But the threat of Chersky was simply too much. He sighed, looked down at the table, and said, "Robert Alton."

"What?"

"Robert Alton has what we need. He's a British mathematician at Cambridge. He developed a mathematical model to study the flow of water around the turbine blades of high performance hydroelectric generators. I saw his work at a convention in West Germany three years ago. It could be easily adapted to our needs."

"How does that help us? Does this look like Cambridge? We do not have his model," the colonel responded. He knew what the scientist was suggesting, but wanted the satisfaction of hearing the man say it. It would represent a complete victory over the smaller man's pride, and Chernikov was not above occasionally humiliating his subordinates.

"If you can arrange things, comrade Colonel, could you not persuade the KGB to steal it?"

Chernikov studied Kozlov's face, looking for the slightest hint of reproach or sarcasm, but the scientist's visage remained guileless. *And I was beginning to think the mouse had teeth,* he thought to himself, *but, no, the man is too frightened even for sarcasm. And well he ought to be; it would have gone ill for him had he disrespected me.*

"Steal it, Aleksei? How can you even suggest such a thing? Are there no professional ethics among scientists?"

****

It was sleeting when Chernikov left the scientist's quarters. The tightly guarded research compound was about 40 kilometers south of the Admiralty Shipyard in Leningrad. A massive low-pressure system over Finland was scooping buckets of moisture off the Gulf and dumping it all over the Leningradskaya Oblast.

The colonel wrestled with his thoughts as he trudged through the nasty weather to his waiting car. Something Kozlov had said was seeking to burst forth as an idea in his mind, but he could not pin the thought down. It was like awakening after a wonderful dream of which you were unable to recall any details.

Chernikov opened the door and slipped into the back seat of the warm, waiting refuge offered by his Zil-115 armored limousine, one of the many perks he enjoyed as a member of the *Nomenklatura*, the Communist Party-favored upper class of the classless Soviet society. That he belonged to the highly secretive GRU was a fact known only to other GRU members. In years not too long before, were a citizen even to utter the acronym "GRU" they would soon disappear. They would be mercilessly interrogated until they coughed up where they had heard of the organization, and then *that* person would disappear and be likewise interrogated, until the entire chain of the leak was discovered and eradicated. As the existence of the elite military intelligence organization gradually became known over the years, their tactics for preserving their secrets became somewhat less lethal, but it was still spoken of only in whispers and great fear among the population, if at all.

"Take me to my apartment, Yuri, then you can go home. No one should be out on a night like this," he directed, as he pulled off his *ushanka* and beat the icy sleet off of it. Though he was six feet three inches tall with broad, muscular shoulders, he fit comfortably into the back seat of the roomy Zil.

"Very good, comrade Colonel. What time shall I pick you up in the morning, sir?" his driver asked, knowing the answer. Like Chernikov, the driver was dressed in civilian clothes with no military insignia to betray the fact that as the colonel's driver and bodyguard, he was a sergeant in the Spetsnaz.

"Five, Yuri, as usual."

"Very good, sir."

The colonel chuckled to himself as he replayed his conversation with the diminutive scientist. *He wants me to get the KGB to steal the model? Those bumbling fools! Well, at least he does not realize that his lord and master is the GRU.* Still, he was unsettled. Just beyond his mental grasp lurked the answer to the project's roadblock. He simply could not make the thought take shape.

****

His apartment was dark and empty when he arrived. Rather than moving about the country with him, his wife Kira maintained their home in Minsk. Colonel Nikolai Pavlovich Chernikov was the son of tea merchants who, despite the Soviet system (or perhaps, because of it), had managed to accumulate substantial wealth. As a result, the colonel and his wife were easily able to maintain two residences, in addition to their *dacha* south of Moscow.

Nikolai changed into his pajamas then slopped some vodka into a tumbler and sat down at his kitchen table for a nightcap. He noted that his nightcaps had begun requiring about a quarter of a bottle of the fiery liquid lately. *Enough of this, Kolya. You are not going to turn yourself into a drunk!* The self-rebuke turned his thoughts in an unpleasant direction, one that he usually avoided, but a direction he seemed drawn to tonight. The colonel rarely allowed himself to think beyond the immediate physical world; he was quite cynical about religion and those who claimed to believe in a god of some sort. But he was also beginning to realize that he had become just as cynical about his atheism, and it bothered him. *Cynical about religion and disillusioned about atheism . . . so what am I? A nihilist?* He refilled his glass, surprised that it was already empty. *No, not a nihilist. I find my purpose in serving the State, Mother Russia, with all her faults. And I find my pleasure in power. So is that good, Kolya? What is "good?" What is "goodness?" And does it matter any-*

way? After all, no One is watching. He swallowed his drink and poured another. *You're quite the philosopher tonight, Niko. The GRU would not approve. But they do not know, do they?*

He fixed himself a small snack, and began to think once again about his conversation with his chief scientist. The man had reluctantly admitted that the British scientist, Robert Alton, had developed something that Kozlov's small stable of Soviet researchers had been unable to reproduce: a mathematical model that would enable the development of a screw producing greatly reduced cavitation, hence, a quieter submarine. If only they could steal . . .

Suddenly the thought took clear form and shape, like a longed-for friend walking out of the fog. It was what the subconscious portion of his brain had been tugging at all evening, ever since leaving Kozlov. Setting up an espionage operation to steal the model could take four or five months and was fraught with danger, so *why not just steal the mathematician instead?* That could be accomplished in a month's time and with far less expense and trouble. And, it would have the salutary effect of retarding British weaponry development while it accelerated Soviet efforts.

When administered with a sufficient quantity of vodka, any idea can sound like a good one. So it was that Colonel Nikolai Pavlovich Chernikov of the GRU landed upon a plan that would earn him an early promotion to Major General, but which would also purchase a pack of trouble, trouble that would eventually threaten all for which he had labored.

****

Three days later, Chernikov made a trip to the Aquarium, otherwise known as the GRU headquarters located at the Khodynka Airfield in Moscow. His patron and immediate superior was Lieutenant General Valeriy Patrikeyev, commanding the Ninth Directorate of the GRU and tasked with acquiring and exploiting foreign "materials" related to weapons development. It was a fortuitous connection, considering the colonel's idea.

Patrikeyev listened patiently as he explained his idea, but offered no comment at the moment. Chernikov left uncertain of how his superior had received the proposition. But two weeks later, Chernikov was summoned back to GRU headquarters.

****

"Please be seated, Colonel Chernikov," Patrikeyev requested. His tone remained formal, his expression serious. The colonel began to wonder whether his recommendation to kidnap Alton might have been a mistake. Patrikeyev remained silent and held Chernikov's eyes in a stern stare. Sweat broke out on Chernikov's forehead, but he dare not look away or display any weakness. Though quailing inwardly, he managed to maintain his demeanor of outward calm, and met his general's challenge with a cool gaze.

"Congratulations, comrade Colonel," Patrikeyev offered, though his bearing remained stern.

"Sir?"

"Relax, Kolya," the general said, breaking into a wide smile, "your plan has been approved by the *Politburo*. Prepare Alton's quarters and arrangements, and have a selected guard of Spetsnaz available. Security is to be airtight. Impress upon your men, Kolya, and Kozlov as well, that violations of security shall be met with a swift and certain death."

"Very good, sir," Chernikov replied, "what unit do you recommend I task with the scientist's kidnapping?"

"That, Kolya, is out of your hands."

"Sir? I don't understand."

"I'm sorry, but the only way that our dear General of the Army and head of the KGB, comrade Anatoly Geredin, would approve of the operation was if the KGB did the snatch. As a junior member, I did not have enough clout to overcome his objections. Consequently, the KGB will deliver him into your hands in less than three weeks. Be ready."

"A partial victory, then, comrade Lieutenant General."

"Yes, Kolya, partial. But with the KGB in the ascendency right now, I'll take whatever I can get," admitted Patrikeyev.

The Soviet government did not function by trust. As a government of men and not of laws, no single organization outside of the Communist Party itself was allowed to become too strong, lest the October Revolution happen again. The Soviet Ministry of Internal Affairs (MVD), the Committee for State Security (KGB) and the GRU were pitted against one another, enmeshed in an endless series of internal intrigues. The Central Committee first (until it was weakened) and then the Politburo used the various entities as a check and balance against one another. Had there been only the MVD, a secret coup might be planned and carried out. But with *both* a KGB and an MVD, the left hand could not plot without the right hand finding out about it. Fittingly, power in the Soviet Union was maintained by a series of chess moves; the long-suffering citizenry were the pawns, the security services and the military were the bishops and knights, and the Politburo functioned as king and queen. Essential to the strategy was maintaining distrust and fear at all levels.

"But listen, Kolya, when Alton is delivered into your hands, the role of the KGB ends. You are to tell them nothing. They are never to find out of your successes or failures, nor where the bodies are buried. Do you understand?"

****

Robert Alton was in the business of making predictions; ironically it was his own predictability that was his undoing. He was a senior research professor of mathematics at Cambridge and was making history with his sophisticated mathematical models of fluid dynamics. The value of his model, to Alton, was the sheer artistic elegance of the formulas. The value to his benefactors was that his model predicted with uncanny accuracy the flow patterns and turbulence caused by the rapidly turning turbines of hydro-electric power generators.

The applications were myriad: early indications showed that an eight percent increase in efficiency could be made in existing turbine-generators simply by a redesign of the blades. It did not take a genius to realize that there was also an application for the screws of a nuclear fast attack submarine. The Royal Navy, having an understandable penchant for silent submarines, was funding Alton's appointment, plus some, on the premise that they would be the sole beneficiaries of his research. On this day, however, Robert Alton was about to get a new partner.

Immersed in an idea about how perturbation theory might solve a particular anomaly in his model, the slightly-built, clean-shaven Alton did not notice the two men following him as he left his office on the Cambridge campus. Turning on to Benet Street, the scientist made his daily pilgrimage to the Eagle Pub for his regular pint of bitter. Alton's imagination was reserved for his mathematical ponderings; he wasted none of the precious mental energy on his daily schedule. Consequently the bartender at the Eagle always glanced at the clock over the bar whenever the mathematician walked in, to make sure the clock was correct.

While the bartender might have had cause to be thankful for the fact Robert Alton's routine was as unvarying as a solar cycle, it was the KGB surveillance team watching the professor that was really appreciative. They had completed their work in half the regular time.

As Alton walked toward the pub, a tall old woman being helped out of a minivan fell to the pavement, crying out in pain. Her companion, almost as feeble, crouched down to help her regain her footing. He looked up as Alton approached.

"Can I help you, sir?" Alton asked with genuine concern.

"Here's a good bloke, Mary. He'll help you up," the man said to the fallen woman. "Aye, sir, we could use a hand here. Lift 'er up by the shoulder there. That's right. Now help me sit her in the car."

Alton guided the woman toward the minivan. As she climbed in, the mathematician leaned in to get her situated.

Before he could resist or cry out, the "old woman" grabbed his lapels with two incredibly strong hands, and, helped by the tails who had by now caught up, hauled him bodily into the van. Another hand clamped a handkerchief soaked in ether over his mouth and nose. The "feeble" old man slammed the side door of the van shut and jumped into the front passenger side. The whole snatch had taken less than fifteen seconds, and there were no witnesses. Had there been they might have noticed as the van pulled away that it had no license plate.

Meanwhile, the bartender looked at the clock and wondered where Robert Alton was.

Chapter 4

"Get up! They are coming for you in thirty minutes. Be ready!" The guard pulled the door shut with a bang. The sound of the lock snapping shut did not improve Alton's mood. For four days he'd been interrogated, cajoled, bribed, and threatened. They wanted him to recreate the mathematical model he had derived for fluid behavior. They had pushed a pad and pencil towards him as though it was as simple as the Pythagorean theorem, and expected him to write it out in a line or two of pencil scratchings. *The idiots!* Clearly, there were no mathematicians among them, just a bunch of Soviet thugs. He had not cooperated. It seemed to him almost as if his tormentors were waiting for something, though what it might be he knew not.

Everything from the kidnapping to his incarceration in this miserable facility was vague in his mind. He'd been drugged, that much was obvious. When he woke up four days ago he'd had no clue where he was, but he knew that his jailors were Russians; at least, that's the language they were speaking. Alton was quite fluent in Russian and it had not taken them long to figure that out.

The mathematician groaned, swung his feet to the floor, and headed for the cubicle that passed as a bathroom. So far he had been threatened with physical violence, but other than taking a few slaps to the face and being pushed to the floor several times, he was unscathed. Unscathed, perhaps, but thoroughly frightened, thoroughly intimidated.

The bathroom was not much by Western standards. It was all concrete, and rough concrete at that. It was sort of a four-foot by four-foot one-stop shop. In the corner was a small sink; the drain simply spilled its contents onto the floor. Overhead there was a corroded shower head. In another corner was a hole in the floor that served as the toilet, and doubled as the drain for the shower and sink. The stench of sewer gas was awful. The narrow entrance to the bathroom was fitted with a two-inch concrete lip that kept the water on the bathroom floor from running out into the cramped living space. There was one handle for the sink faucet and one for the shower, and only one temperature for the water: freezing. A dim light bulb hung from the concrete ceiling, suspended by the electrical wires that were attached to its socket. There was no light switch, and as the bulb was too high for Alton to reach and unscrew, it remained on.

He'd been issued no towel or wash cloth, and was reduced to drying himself with the blanket on the cot, which he then spread out so that it would be dry by bedtime. Thankfully there was a decent bar of soap. A newspaper, obviously to be employed as toilet paper, completed the inventory of the bathroom.

Thirty minutes later he was eating breakfast: a bowl of oatmeal and cold toast. At least the oatmeal was hot, and not half-bad, he decided. He finished breakfast quickly lest they snatch it away from him like the day before.

****

"Good morning, comrade Alton. Did you sleep well?" Chernikov smiled at the mathematician. It reminded Alton of the cheerless grin of a shark. They were seated at a metal table, opposite one another. Alton was handcuffed to the chair, but it was so flimsy that had he decided to stand it would have simply come up with him. The interrogation room could have been a twin of his cell, Alton observed, except that there was no bed and no bathroom.

"I insist that you take me to the British Embassy immediately. I am being illegally detained. This will probably be considered an act of war, or at least a terrorist act under international law; that makes you a war criminal!" Alton had no idea what he was talking about, but it gave him something to say, a way to vent his frustration and fear.

"I'm afraid that's not going to happen, Dr. Alton. No one knows where you are. If you don't cooperate with us, we'll simply drop you out of an airplane ten thousand feet above the *taiga* somewhere in Siberia. I'm sure you would make nice fertilizer after you thaw out in the spring. Let's get down to business, shall we? You have something we want, we have something you want. I'm sure we can come to an agreement as reasonable men."

"What do you have that I want?"

"Your life. Your formula for your life. I think that's a good bargain, don't you?"

Alton was about to respond when the door of the interrogation cell opened with a rusty groan and a guard entered and whispered something to Chernikov.

"Finally!" he exulted. "Would you excuse me for a moment, Dr. Alton?" The mathematician merely shrugged. When Chernikov returned, he was holding a large brown manila envelope with a Soviet diplomatic seal on it.

"Now, about our bargain—" Colonel Chernikov began, before being cut off by Alton.

"We made no bargain, sir, nor are we liable to."

"Perhaps I can sweeten the deal, comrade Alton. Your formula now buys you four lives, not just one. Four." He placed the envelope on the table, and motioned for the mathematician to inspect the contents.

Alton opened it and choked back a cry. Inside were pictures of his mother, father, and sister.

****

Three weeks later a Kilo, the B-401—more imaginatively christened as the *Novosibirsk*—slid down the ways at the Nizhniy Novgorod shipyard and sailed down the Volga for sea trials in the Caspian. It was sporting a newly redesigned screw, machined at the Admiralty shipyard in Leningrad according to Robert Alton's specifications.

****

The sea trials were successful, so much so that Chernikov's project was officially scored as a victory, and was brought to a conclusion. His engineers were reassigned to other projects, and Robert Alton was taken off his hands by a small team of GRU operatives. Chernikov was instructed to close down his office in Leningrad and report to GRU headquarters to receive his next assignment.

He took a final look around the empty office and headed for the door. Once again the weather had turned nasty with a wet, late-winter snowstorm. He locked the office behind him and trudged through six inches of snow to his Zil where his bodyguard waited to open the car door for him. *That's odd*, he thought to himself, *Yuri seems tense, as though something is wrong.* As soon as the colonel entered the car, he understood.

"*Dobryy dyen'*, Colonel Chernikov."

Chernikov was speechless. Seated opposite him was General Anatoly Geredin, with a small glass of vodka in each hand. Though Geredin was dressed in civilian clothes, Chernikov knew that he was facing one of the highest ranking officers in the country. Head of the KGB, Geredin had attained the rank of General of the Army.

The relationship between the KGB and the GRU was quite simple: they detested each other. They disdained each other. Though the GRU was larger (if you did not count the KGB's volunteer informants) and more lethal, the KGB was better connected, and had more clout in the Politburo at the moment.

"If you are not going to greet me, comrade Colonel, perhaps you could at least close the door. That damp cold is hard on an old man's arthritis."

"My—my apologies, comrade General," Chernikov stammered, quickly shutting the door. "Good—good afternoon, sir! Pardon my surprise, I was not expecting you," the flustered officer finished lamely.

"If you *had* been expecting me, I would not be a very effective director of the KGB, would I?" Geredin did not wait for an answer. "But, then, I suppose the fact that you were not expecting me does not say much for the abilities of the GRU, does it? But never mind that. I come bearing news, comrade Colonel. News and a warning. You have been summoned to the Aquarium. General Patrikeyev expects to see you there at 0900 tomorrow. You are to be given a new assignment that will take you to Tara, in the Omsk Oblast. I know what that assignment is, but I shall not spoil the surprise for you."

Chernikov fought to keep his demeanor calm, but inside he was screaming, *How can he know these things? Patrikeyev communicated with me through an "eyes-only" dispatch!* Evidently Geredin's goons had access to GRU communications at the deepest level, and the old man was so confident of the security of his source that rather than hiding the breach, he flaunted it. Chernikov made no response, for he had no idea what to say.

"You are also about to be promoted. Let me be the first to congratulate you, comrade Major General." Geredin put one of the shot glasses of vodka in Chernikov's hand, held his own up, and made a toast. "To Mother Russia and her fine officers! May they always be courageous, and," Geredin locked eyes with Chernikov, then finished his sentiment, "wise."

Chernikov choked on the fiery liquid, and began to cough hoarsely. Geredin drained his glass and placed it in one of the holders in the back of the Zil. He pulled on his *ushanka*, preparing to get out of the car.

"And my warning to you, comrade. If you dishonor Mother Russia through your new assignment, I will have you shot." His words were spoken in a grandfatherly tone, but Chernikov knew better than to allow the tone to defang the message. Geredin was known as a man who would order the execution of a close friend as dispassionately as he would order a cup of tea. Anatoly Geredin had but one love and one loyalty— Mother Russia—and heaven help the poor comrade who did anything to bring shame upon her.

With that, the old man stepped out into the swirling snow and shut the door of the Zil, leaving Chernikov alone with his thoughts.

****

The ominous portent of his unexpected meeting with Geredin lingered in the back of his mind like the memory of a foul smell, but it did not diminish the sense of elation that Chernikov felt as he entered GRU headquarters the next morning, flush with a significant success under his belt. The building and its occupants exuded a raw power and lethality that was intoxicating. Chernikov allowed himself a brief moment of self-congratulation, realizing that he was probably one of the few citizens of the Soviet Union who could enter the Aquarium without the slightest tinge of fear. This time, at least. As was typical of the secretive organization, he was smartly turned out in the dress uniform of the unit from which he had been recruited into the GRU. To any onlooker, military or civilian, Chernikov would appear to be an active duty officer of the 106th. There was no insignia, nor any other identifying mark to advertise his membership in the elite intelligence organization.

Lieutenant General Valeriy Patrikeyev greeted him warmly, "Comrade Colonel! Congratulations on your great success! I've been reading the reports on the noise reduction achieved by the new propeller design. Our surface ships were unable to detect the *Novosibirsk* during the wargaming portion of her sea trials. You have impressed many people, very important people."

"Thank you, comrade General. I serve the Soviet Union."

"Sit down, Colonel, we have much to talk about."

Patrikeyev rang for tea, and the two men spent the next half hour debriefing on the concluded project. The general questioned him thoroughly about his methods, his management of the personnel assets given to him for the project, and his security arrangements.

"Did the KGB attempt to interfere with your work, Kolya?"

"No, sir. I know that my secretary was a KGB agent. I don't think she was aware that I knew her true identity."

"She was only the distraction, Kolya, the misdirection."

"Sir?"

"She was an obvious plant, comrade Colonel. It was intended that you find her and think of her as the means by which the KGB would keep track of your operation. Geredin knew you would spot her, and he knew you would stop looking for spies once you had identified her," Patrikeyev explained patiently.

"You mean there was another?"

"Of course! The KGB recruited an informant from among your own people. The real spy was Staff Sergeant Yuri Slavin."

Yuri? Chernikov became furious at the thought. He'd been betrayed! Yuri was his bodyguard, handpicked from his staff in the 106th Guards. Of all his subordinates, Yuri was the most trustworthy. *He's the last man I would expect to be turned!*

"Really, Kolya, you must learn to veil your emotions! I can see you've become angry, your face is as red as a beet. You need not worry. Slavin was recruited by the KGB two months ago. He reported the KGB's contact immediately, directly to me rather than you. It was the good sergeant's opinion that it would be profitable for us if the boys from Lubyanka thought they had recruited someone right next to you. He told his recruiter that I had assigned him to spy on you—a brilliant move on his part! This gave him perfect cover to make clandestine reports to me without his KGB handler suspecting anything. Slavin is our own little misdirection ploy. He's a very intelligent man; Sergeant Slavin will go far in the GRU."

"So . . . my own bodyguard has been spying on me?"

"He has been spying on you for me, Colonel Chernikov, for as you know we all watch one another. Geredin believes that Slavin is spying on you for the KGB. I allow comrade Slavin to report little tidbits to his handler, and the occasional big piece of news, just to keep the fish on the hook. But you may be assured, Kolya, that Slavin is utterly loyal to you. It was necessary that you know nothing of this, ah, arrangement, in case the KGB had put a wire in your car, apartment, or office. The only reason I tell you of it now is so that in your next assignment you place Slavin in a position in which he will be able to contact me covertly. We must maintain his cover in the eyes of his KGB handler."

Chernikov nodded reluctantly. He was still angry—angry with himself that he had been outfoxed by the KGB's decoy plan with his secretary. He was also irritated because he had not spotted Yuri himself. It was humiliating, especially since he took great pride in his own field craft as a GRU operative. It was necessary for an intelligence officer to develop a finely honed sixth sense about these matters, not only for his own success but more importantly for his own survival. Chernikov saw his failure not only as a professional lapse, but as a matter of potential personal danger. He paused for a moment, getting his emotions under firm control.

"I shall see to it, Comrade General. By the way, sir, I had a visitor last night, but I expect you already know that." He had not meant to be sarcastic, but it just slipped out. Patrikeyev's eyes narrowed, and Chernikov could see that the comment displeased him.

"Be careful, Colonel. Do not let your pride get the best of you. Even I have spies watching me and reporting to someone, and those spying on me likewise have spies watching them. It is the Soviet way, and I should not have to remind you of that. You must not take this personally."

"Yes, sir. Forgive me, comrade General. A great deal of my irritation, sir, has to do with the fact that I did not spot Yuri's activities myself. It's very humiliating."

"Never mind, Kolya. So, the legendary Russian bear came to see you last night?"

"Yes, sir. Comrade General Geredin delivered a message to me."

"He threatened you, to be precise. If you dishonor the Soviet Union, he will have you executed. I did not hear that from Sergeant Slavin, by the way—he does not report again until tomorrow. Geredin told me the same thing—about you, that is—at the last Politburo meeting. You may safely ignore his threats, comrade. Be respectful to our dear comrade Geredin, but do not allow him to intimidate you or to distract you from your task. He is a dangerous opponent, but not even Geredin has the political clout to execute a rising star in the GRU who is carrying out a task assigned by the Politburo. Unless, of course, you should fail.

"Now, Kolya, let's talk about what is next for you. The entire Politburo was very impressed with your rapid success on the Kilo project. They are directing that we repeat the project on a much larger scale. Your orders, therefore, are as follows: first, you are directed to construct an interrogation and prison facility forty-six kilometers west of Tara in the Omsk Oblast. Orders will be issued later today attaching an engineering company to your command. They will construct the facility according to your specifications. It must be designed to hold thirty-six inmates, with barracks to accommodate a company-sized security unit, plus comfortable accommodations for visiting scientists and engineers who will assist with the interrogation of prisoners once they have been broken. The facility is not intended to host research; it is for incarceration and interrogation only.

"Second, when the facility is completed, rotating companies of Spetsnaz pulled offline from Afghanistan for rest and refit will be attached to your command for three-month tours to provide security for the facility.

"Third, you will be given a list of ten individuals, foreign scientists and military personnel, against whom you will be authorized to conduct covert kidnapping operations. You will be pleased to learn, comrade Colonel, that this time we will not be using the KGB to do the kidnapping. Two squads of Spetsnaz operators will be assigned to conduct the kidnappings.

"Fourth, you are to conduct preliminary interrogations until an individual has broken and is ready to cooperate. At that point you will call in selected scientists and specialists to complete the interviews on the targeted scientific subjects. You are not authorized to cause the death of any detainee for any purpose; those decisions must be made at the Politburo level. You must have adequate medical facilities to ensure that each subject survives your interrogation techniques.

"Fifth, you are to run the strictest security for this facility. Not only must there be no chance of escape, but not a word of the existence of this camp is to get out. You must impress upon all those who are involved that any breach of security will be handled with summary execution, on the spot. You are authorized to handle this punishment on your own initiative without consulting me. At no time will any prisoner be allowed to leave your facility, unless it is in a coffin.

"And finally, it was the decision of the Politburo that a project of this nature should be run not by a colonel, but by a major general. Allow me to congratulate you on your promotion, *Major General* Chernikov! It is well deserved."

Chapter 5

Oswald Simmons pulled out the third drawer of the large red tool chest standing in his garage, and retrieved several cold chisels, a rock hammer, safety glasses, and a small mineral field test kit containing a Moh's hardness set, a tiny portable Bunsen burner, several small vials of chemicals and acids, and other miscellany. He filled a knapsack with his gear, tossing in several small boxes for sample collection. The tall, curly-haired scientist was wearing a faded pair of blue jeans, hiking boots and a John Denver tee shirt. He could not wait to get up in the hills and do a little rock-hounding. He walked over to the open door of his garage and gazed southwest. In the distance, Long's Peak towered over everything, a glorious spire of gray granite stretching to the heavens. Standing as a barrier between Fort Collins, where Simmons was looking from his garage, and the fourteen-thousand-foot peak were the foothills, the serrated and folded brown and red ridges of sandstone, bearing occasional intrusions of granite, schist, pegmatites, quartz and a host of other interesting minerals and rocks. The morning air had the sort of clarity only observed at higher altitudes in lower humidity, both of which Colorado possessed in unfair abundance.

Simmons was not a geologist, though his undergraduate degree from Colorado State University was in geology. His true love was electrical engineering. While finishing up the details of his doctoral dissertation at MIT, he was teaching at CSU. Known to the faculty and students alike simply as Oz, the young scientist was held in an esteem that varied between awe and amusement. Put simply, Oz was a genius. He was also one of the few scientists in the world working on the physics of producing sub-micron semiconductor structures on the substrate of an integrated circuit. While the technology was a few years away, he was a walking textbook on the subject of integrated circuit miniaturization.

Wednesdays were his day off, and if he was not trout-fishing he was rock-hounding. On today's menu was garnet. Up in the foothills several weeks earlier he'd found an exposed face of schist peppered with perfectly formed, BB-sized garnets, and he intended to investigate it more thoroughly in hopes of finding larger samples of the beautiful, semi-precious mineral. He tossed the lunch he'd thrown together into the pack along with several bottles of water, locked up the house and climbed into his old, beat-up Willys Jeep. A ripe old twenty-eight, Simmons was not married yet—life was simply too much fun for a relationship. Fun for the young scientist meant his lab work, his classes, his dissertation, his Willys, his trout-fishing and rock-hounding and backpacking and—well, suffice it to say that Simmons hadn't been bored since he was twelve years old, and then only for a few minutes.

****

The two men watching Oz weren't bored either. When the scientist had appeared on the Soviet Academy of Science's radar several years earlier he'd been designated as a "person of interest." That interest had morphed into a desire to possess. The two agents were preparing to collect the desired treasure.

****

Oswald pulled onto West Prospect, and enjoyed the bite of the early morning air as he drove west toward the foothills. Turning south on Overland Trail, he passed the stadium where the CSU Rams had accomplished the difficult feat of stringing together five straight losing seasons in the Western Athletic Conference. *We've got to do better this year*, he thought to himself, *certainly can't do much worse*. He didn't notice the black

Chevy Suburban pacing him about a half mile behind. Turning on to Dixon Canyon Road, Simmons drove up the switchbacks and passed Horsetooth Reservoir. Fifteen minutes later he was driving on Buckhorn Road toward Pingree Park. The semi-arid landscape was still green from the late spring rains and the light breeze carried the delicious savor of sage.

Oz shook his head, grinning; he still couldn't get over the fact that he lived in Colorado. Texas Instruments had tried to recruit him when he'd finished his coursework at MIT, but the offer from CSU was just impossible to pass up. It was the difference between Texas and Colorado; a no-brainer, from Simmons' perspective.

Crossing a cattle-guard, Oswald slowed down as the road entered a small range where several hundred cattle grazed. He turned left onto Pole Hill Road and then onto Stringtown Gulch Road. After another three miles he pulled off the gravel road and parked on the shoulder. Grabbing his pack, the professor started up a faint trail to the outcrop he'd run across several weeks earlier.

****

"He's stopped moving. Go left here. HEY! Viktor, watch those cows! We can't afford any accidents." The speaker was a compactly built Ukrainian, a member of a specially trained Spetsnaz unit chosen to infiltrate English-speaking countries. Dmitriy was twenty-five, with the youthful good looks that caused casual observers to underestimate his age. He was wearing jeans, a black tee shirt and a pair of lightweight hiking shoes. For this operation his cover name was "Mike." He and Viktor were posing as G.I. Bill freshmen at CSU.

"Yeah, yeah, I'll watch the cows, *you* watch the direction-finder! And call me 'Tom,' you idiot, not 'Viktor!' If you don't get in character you could blow our cover." Viktor Fyodoryevich Poda was the team leader. He was sporting a navy blue polo shirt, jeans and sneakers. Twenty-eight years old and a muscular six foot two, he was aggressive and generally bad-tempered. A native-born Russian, Viktor was a top-drawer operator who could assume the character of his cover story with the ease of a Hollywood bad boy. With his fellow Spetsnaz he was a pain; when in character he was all sweetness and light. Despite Viktor's surly attitude, Dmitriy loved to work with him. Viktor typically received the most interesting—and dangerous—assignments. Both men spoke flawless English.

"Yeah, and if you don't relax, *Tom*, you'll jeopardize the operation. Don't be so uptight!"

The two had attached a tracking transmitter under the bumper of the Willys and it was leading them straight to Simmons, although the canyons were causing them to lose the signal periodically.

"There it is," Viktor murmured as they came upon the dust-covered jeep. He drove past the vehicle, continued another mile, then turned around and came back. There was no traffic on the rough gravel road, and not likely to be. "Let's do it," he said, as he parked next to the other vehicle.

****

The secure teletype chattered in the watch officer's cubicle, buried within the bowels of the Aquarium. The watch officer, a senior lieutenant, noted that the information originated from the Soviet diplomatic mission in Seattle. After decoding, the message was added to a sheaf of intelligence communications pertaining to "persons of interest." Though the information was considered secret, and any breach would result in a one-way trip to the GRU's own crematorium, it was not considered high-priority traffic. It wound its way through several hands until it landed on the desk of one Colonel Boris Tsvetkov. Tsvetkov was responsible for target selection for Project *Krasnyy Voskhod*, Chernikov's kidnapping operation, and the message immediately grabbed his interest.

2 JULY 1986
SEATTLE, USA, DIPLOMATIC MISSION.

*USAF MAJOR JACOB KELLY
TRANSFERRED FROM EDWARDS AFB,
CA, TO EIELSON AFB, AK, TEMPORARY
DUTY, MISSION UNKNOWN. ARRIVED
F-16C S/N 83149. HIGH SECURITY
NOTED AROUND AIRCRAFT.*

Tsvetkov picked up his phone, and dialed General Patrikeyev.

"Comrade General, I have received a signal of some importance. May I come up to your office, sir?"

****

Clink. Clink. While walking the strike of the exposed layer of schist the month before, Oz had come across a pegmatite inclusion with a particularly large, well-formed crystal of tourmaline. He had then contacted the land owner and secured permission to remove samples in exchange for information about any mineable ore he discovered. *Clink.* One last tap of the hammer on a well-placed cold chisel and the amateur geologist freed the beautiful crystal with a small piece of its host rock from the surrounding material. He hoisted the heavy prize to inspect it more closely. *Lovely,* he thought to himself, *that's going on my coffee table after I clean it up.*

He looked up in time to see two young men walking through the aspen on the trail one hundred feet below him. Sitting down on a rock, he took a swig from his water bottle and waited for the two to traverse the winding switchbacks.

"Professor Simmons!" called one of the young men, flashing a cheerful smile.

Oz observed that both men were well built and carried themselves in the distinctive way of those who have been in the military. The speaker appeared to be the younger of the two and was wearing a black tee shirt. Both were wearing the new style mirror sunglasses. Simmons could see four identical reflections of himself as the men looked at him.

"That's me. What's up?" They had piqued his curiosity, for this was no Forest Service trail and the two were on private property. He wondered who they were and what they were up to.

"Wow, that's a beautiful crystal you've got there! What is it?" The man's curiosity seemed genuine and it caused Simmons to relax his guard.

"Tourmaline. It's an unusually good sample for this area," he said, handing the piece to the young man.

"It's gorgeous!" black tee shirt said, as he inspected it closely.

"Yep, that it is. So, who are you guys and how do you know me?" queried Simmons.

"We're both in your remedial calculus class," replied the older one, who'd been silent to this point. "We recognized your jeep down on the road and just thought we'd stop by."

Simmons was teaching a summer modular class for incoming engineering students who needed a little more work in calculus. It was a large class, but he'd never noticed these two.

"Aren't you two a little old for a freshman class?"

"G. I. Bill. When most kids were going from high school to college, Mike and I went into the Marines. Met up at Camp Lejeune. We both decided to come to CSU when we got out. It feels a little funny, sure, being in class with guys ten years younger, but, hey, at least tuition is paid for! Name's Tom," the older one said, putting out his hand with a warm smile.

Simmons nodded, shook his hand and thought to himself, *so that explains the military bearing. I had these guys pegged.*

"Good to meet you both. Hey, look, I don't want to be a heavy or anything, but this is private land we're on. I've got permission to be here, but it's not my place to give you guys permission."

"No problem, Professor. If it's okay, we'll just watch for a few minutes and then leave."

Simmons went back to work on the schist outcrop, removing the top weathered portion of a small area. The students strolled around the site, examining rocks and talking quietly together. He overheard them decide to walk the length of the outcrop to see if there were any more big tourmaline crystals.

"You go that way, I'll go this way. Ten minutes, and then we'd better head back to the car," Mike said to Tom.

****

General Chernikov had launched Project *Krasnyy Voskhod*, or *Red Sunrise*, with an aggressive schedule of kidnapping hoping to impress his superiors with some quick victories. One of the problems that the kidnapping teams were encountering as a consequence was that the mission planners were not given adequate time to fully investigate the targets. Thus several helpful pieces of information about Oswald Simmons were not known to the operatives: he was fluent in Russian, and he had achieved black belt status or beyond in five different martial arts disciplines.

****

Viktor followed the craggy outcrop until he was sure that the professor could no longer see him. He pulled a small hard case out of his fanny pack and opened it up. Inside was a syringe, several vials, needles, a small bottle of ether and an applicator cloth. Dmitriy was supposed to distract the professor with a rock sample while he came from behind and anesthetized him.

In a moment he heard his companion call out to Simmons. He quickly soaked the applicator cloth with ether. Stowing the hard case into his pack, he began walking toward the sound of the voices.

****

"Valeriy Ivanovich, I've just received intelligence indicating that one of our top targets, Major Jacob Kelly, has been assigned temporary duty at Eielson Air Force Base. He arrived earlier today, flying an F-16 whose tail number identifies it as one of the aircraft assigned to a classified weapons development project at Edwards," stated Tsvetkov.

"You're sure of that? He's actually flying an aircraft used in an Edwards development project?" Patrikeyev asked, surprised.

"The tail number matches, sir."

Patrikeyev swiveled in his chair so that he could see the Khodynka runways in the distance. He pondered for a moment then turned back to his subordinate.

"If that is so, then they're about to run some kind of test regime. General James Franks at Edwards is heading up *Hydra*, the classified project that Kelly's attached to. He'd never let one of his aircraft leave the security of Edwards unless it was absolutely necessary for testing. And if Major Kelly's going to be flying some tests, maybe we'll get an opportunity to grab him."

Patrikeyev paused. He knew, though Tsvetkov did not, that the GRU had an asset in place at Eielson located in the Operations Section. As long as the links in the chain functioned properly Patrikeyev would know of any scheduled flights for Kelly before the major himself did.

"You've done well, Boris. Draft a message to the Cultural Attaché in Seattle. Direct him to keep us updated with any intelligence pertaining to Major Kelly's movements and schedule as soon as he becomes aware of it, until otherwise notified. Inform him that this is a matter of the very highest priority."

"Very good, sir."

****

"Professor Simmons, what's this? I found it along the outcrop," Mike exclaimed. He seemed a little too enthusiastic to Oz, but the scientist shrugged it off as a student's attempt to brown-nose the teacher. He took the rock out of Mike's hand and examined it.

"This is a hunk of pegmatite, Mike. These flat pink faces here," he gestured with his finger, "are crystals of feldspar.

The black, flaky stuff is biotite mica. Well, would you look at this! I've been looking for these! These small red crystals are garnets." He looked up as he dipped his hand into his pocket, going after a small but powerful magnifying class.

It was the motion reflected in Mike's mirror sunglasses that caught Simmons' attention: Tom was coming up rapidly behind him with a hand set to encircle his throat. The professor dropped the rock sample and grabbed Tom's hand as it came from behind, yanking it taut down his torso. He used the other man's momentum and his own hip as a fulcrum, throwing Tom into Mike, both of whom went sprawling into the dirt.

Simmons assumed a fighting stance. The other two men rolled and immediately regained their feet. Mike produced a combat knife from somewhere, which Oz kicked out of his hand as quickly as it appeared. The surprised expressions on the faces of his visitors were quickly replaced by grim determination.

"I think you guys better leave now," Simmons said angrily.

"Not without you, we're not," Tom replied. He was circling to Simmons' right, while Mike stepped lightly to his left. If Oz didn't take the initiative quickly he'd have one opponent in front and one behind.

As soon the knife made its appearance the professor knew this was no sparring match. His life was on the line! If he was to survive this bout his kicks and punches would have to be killing blows. *Time to get down and dirty,* he thought to himself.

He feinted toward Tom and pivoted, anticipating a rush from Mike. But Mike didn't take the bait, putting Simmons out of balance. He barely slipped a brutal snap kick from Tom. Then Mike attacked, striking with the speed of a snake. Simmons parried, grabbing his wrist and throwing him down with a leg sweep. He used his opponent's falling weight to pull himself down into a quick shoulder roll, whirling about and coming to his feet in a single motion. The move had placed both opponents in front of him again. He kicked Mike in the head as the man was regaining his feet, stunning him. For a precious moment that left just Tom.

"You're just making this hard on yourself, Simmons!"

"Actually, I was trying to make it hard on you!" He advanced aggressively to see how Tom would respond. He had to initiate contact before Mike was back in the game. Tom launched a side thrust kick; Simmons twisted inside, Tom's foot just grazing his left ear. Tom was left momentarily vulnerable at close quarters by the miss, and Oz smashed his face with a wicked elbow strike. He swiftly followed up with a right cross, then a snap kick that caught Tom full in the chin. Tom crumpled.

Bang!

The professor whirled around and saw that Mike had triggered a round into the dirt and now was aiming his Beretta 92 at him.

"Stop! Now!" the younger man commanded. Simmons stood trembling, the adrenaline of combat still pumping. "Move over there," he motioned with the gun, "and sit down." The professor shifted as instructed, and sat with his back to the outcrop.

"Put these on," Mike instructed, tossing a pair of handcuffs to Simmons.

"And if I refuse?"

"All the same to me, Doc. CSU will have to hire a new remedial calc prof," he replied, shrugging his shoulders and raising his weapon. He aimed for a spot right between Simmons' eyes. Oz began snapping the cuffs on himself.

"And if I don't refuse?" he asked, as he tightened them.

Mike smiled. "CSU will *still* have to hire itself a new remedial calc prof," he answered, lowering his pistol.

"Somehow, I knew you were going to say that," Oz scowled.

"Tough breaks, Doc."

Thirty minutes later the scene had been sanitized and a very grumpy and sore pair of Spetsnaz, one with a broken jaw, were driving a drugged professor to a rendezvous with a small Soviet Embassy jet on the civil aviation side of the Natrona County International Airport, in Casper, Wyoming.

Chapter 6

Saturday, July 5, 1986: 0540 local
Bermuda, UK

"What are you doing, sweetheart?" Erin Shimonah murmured sleepily, rolling over so she could see her husband.

"Shh. Go back to sleep. I'm just going out for my run," replied her husband, Moshe, as he laced up his running shoes. He was wearing a pair of black athletic shorts and a white tee shirt emblazoned with "Virginia is for Lovers" that he'd purchased during last year's vacation. Completing his outfit was a khaki-colored ball cap bought the day before as a souvenir, that proclaimed "Bermuda: Getting away to it all."

"Honey, we're on vacation! Can't you skip your run today? Come back to bed," she purred. Erin was four months pregnant with their first child. Normally an early riser, she considered it bad form to get up before seven when on vacation. She'd never been able to convince her husband of that perspective.

He leaned over and kissed her, and replied, "I'll be back soon. Go back to sleep. I've got a key with me."

He closed the door to their rented cottage and trotted down to South Road. Jobson Bay extended before him, the turquoise water merging in the distance with the deep purple early morning sky. The sun would not rise for another thirty minutes, but it was already light enough to see easily. An early morning offshore breeze tugged at his shirt, carrying the unique perfume of the sea. Shimonah loved this time of day. From his point of view a pre-dawn, five-mile run was the perfect way to begin his second week of vacation in the paradise called Bermuda.

****

Four years ago Moshe had met Erin, an American, at an archeological dig in the Negev. Shimonah was at that time a lieutenant in the Israeli Defense Forces and his platoon had been deployed to provide security to the archeologists during a time of unrest in Gaza. She had just graduated from Cornell University in Ithaca, New York, with a degree in history. As a graduation present to herself she had signed up for a summer class in Near Eastern archeology conducted on-site at various digs in Israel.

Moshe and Erin had fallen in love immediately. By the end of Erin's class the young IDF lieutenant had proposed and she had accepted. The last four years had seemed like a dreamy, happy whirlwind for her. She'd fallen in love not only with her lieutenant but with his country as well.

Two years ago her husband had been promoted to the rank of captain and the nature of his work had changed. He'd explained to her that his work was now classified and he was unable to discuss it with her or anyone else. They'd moved to Dimona and from there he made frequent trips to Jerusalem.

Before last year's vacation to Williamsburg, Virginia, Moshe had sat down with her at their kitchen table and they'd had what seemed to her an odd conversation.

"Erin, this is our first trip together out of Israel since my promotion. There's something we need to talk about."

"I know. You want me to limit my spending as I get us ready for this vacation. But you know we're going to need some new luggage, honey. What we've got right now is falling apart."

Moshe had laughed. "No, that's not what we need to talk about. But you're right, we *do* need some luggage! Please just leave enough room on the credit card so we aren't stuck in our hotel eating pita bread and drinking water.

"What we need to talk about now, though, is serious. You know that I can't talk to you about what I do, right?"

"I know, Moshe. I'm okay with that."

He nodded. "Thanks, babe. I really do appreciate your understanding. But listen! You must remember this: if anything happens to me when we are traveling, if I have a bad accident, or if I go missing, you must get yourself to the nearest Israeli Embassy right away. Don't go back to our hotel, don't try to pack anything, just get to the embassy as quickly as you can. If we don't have an embassy or consulate, go to either the British or the American Embassies, in that order. Call this phone number," he said, placing a scrap of paper with a number on it in front of her. "Memorize it, then flush the paper down the toilet. Don't write it down anywhere."

"But what—" she began, but he cut her off.

"I can't explain, sweetie. Please trust me. I'm not expecting anything to happen, ever, so I don't want you to worry. But I do want you to have a plan in case something were to happen."

****

What Erin did not know was that Captain Moshe Shimonah was the permanent military liaison assigned to brief the Prime Minister on the progress of Israel's nuclear weapons program. He was chosen not only for his exemplary service in the IDF and his undergrad degree in nuclear physics, but also because no one would expect a lowly captain to fill such a role. In his position he knew everything there was to know about Israel's tactical and strategic nuclear weapons development, production and delivery systems.

And what neither Moshe nor Erin was aware of was that Shimonah had percolated to the top of Patrikeyev's *Red Sunrise* target list, which had been expanded by the Politburo to include those who knew vital military secrets.

****

Erin's eyes popped open to a room flooded with sunlight. She looked at the clock and groaned to herself, *Eight-thirty? I'm wasting my day in bed! What a slug!* She got out of bed and walked into the small kitchenette. With a start she realized that she was alone in the cottage. Moshe had not yet returned from his run. *That's odd. I wonder if he came back and went out again. Or is today the day for his ten-mile run? But he'd be back by now even if it was. Hmm.*

She started the coffee then showered and dressed. By ten o'clock she was worried, but decided to wait another hour before she took action.

****

"Thank you, comrades, for gathering on such short notice," Lieutenant General Valeriy Ivanovich Patrikeyev said. The group was meeting in one of the small, private conference rooms in the Kremlin. His aides had swept the room for bugs before the others arrived, found one, and disabled it temporarily with a compact electromagnetic noise generator.

Seated around him were the five power brokers of the Politburo. Though thirteen men made up the total number, the rest would fall in line with whatever these decided. To his left was Chief of the General Staff of the Soviet Armed Forces, Kirill Yegorov. Sitting at one head of the table was Yuri Rodchenko, General Secretary of the Communist Party. Across from him was the old Russian bear himself, Anatoly Geredin, head of the KGB. Next to Geredin was Valerian Voznesensky, the First Deputy Premier of the Soviet Union. At the far end of the table was the most powerful of the group, Nikolai Kosygin, the Premier of the Soviet Union.

"Before you begin, Comrade General, please give us an update on the progress of the *Krasnyy Voskhod* project," requested Kosygin.

"Certainly, Nikolai Stepanovich. The interrogation facility, known as Prison 87, has been completed. Eight of the ten targets have been apprehended and relocated to the facility, and their interrogation is underway. I anticipate that the last two targets will be captured in the next five days.

"With the exception of Dr. Robert Alton, we have not yet

extracted useful information from the current residents of Prison 87. We expect that the first five to ten days will be necessary for the men to adjust to their new surroundings. Until they grasp how hopeless their situation is they are not generally cooperative. Because of their potential long-term value we try not to damage them physically during interrogation, at least not in ways that would hinder their future usefulness."

"Very good, Comrade General," Kosygin replied. "How is our new general taking to his rank?"

"Quite well, Nikolai Stepanovich. I have known General Chernikov for a number of years and I believe his promotion is well deserved. He is more than competent to hold that rank. He has proven himself worthy as a leader of men in battle during the conflict in Afghanistan." As Patrikeyev said this he noticed out of the corner of his eye a look exchanged by Anatoly Geredin and Voznesensky.

"Have there been any difficulties in the captures to date?" asked Voznesensky, just a little too innocently.

"No, comrade, nothing worthy of reporting," Patrikeyev affirmed.

"No, comrade General?" Geredin asked. "I understand that two GRU operatives came back black and blue from an incident in Colorado, one of them with a broken jaw. Perhaps it was a skiing accident?"

Valeriy Patrikeyev ground his teeth. *How does that man find out everything? We've got a leak somewhere. Must find it!*

"My dear KGB colleague, they completed their mission and brought their target back to us. Yes, they were a little bumped and bruised, but they were successful, nonetheless."

"I see. And how did Colonel Tsvetkov, who is responsible for assembling the dossiers on the targets, miss the simple fact that Dr. Oswald Simmons had attained black belt status in no fewer than five martial arts disciplines? Surely there are records of such activity. I have transcripts of the debriefing of your agents, General, and by their account Dr. Simmons made short work of your precious Spetsnaz until one of them pulled out a gun," Geredin stated, satisfaction spreading over his face.

Patrikeyev realized that Voznesensky had been prepped to ask the question, after which Geredin would administer the *coup de grace*. *Well,* he thought philosophically, *at least I have now verified Geredin's alliance in this group. That's profitable, though it's been embarrassing.* He was on the point of responding, when Rodchenko stepped in.

"That is quite enough, Anatoly. We are interested in outcomes here, not the difficulties along the way. If Tsvetkov failed in his vetting of the targets, Valeriy has compensated for that by sending agents who are sufficiently competent to successfully execute an operation despite inadequate intelligence. I daresay that if we began to investigate your precious KGB we would find similar difficulties.

"Valeriy has been successful. General Chernikov has likewise been successful. That is all we need to know."

"*Da,*" agreed Yegorov, who was the head of the GRU, and who had placed Patrikeyev over the Ninth Directorate. Yegorov had been his mentor and one-time patron before Patrikeyev had joined him in the Politburo. "That is all we need to know," he repeated. "Now can we please get on with it? I have another meeting right after this one."

Kosygin nodded and motioned to Patrikeyev, "Please, proceed."

"Thank you, comrade. I received notice several days ago that our final target, Major Jacob Kelly, has been assigned temporary duty at Eielson AFB in Alaska. Our source tells us that the F-16 he flew from Edwards to Eielson has the tail number of one of the fighters involved in the development project at Edwards. We believe that means that he will be putting the aircraft through a regime of tests.

"The only time that test aircraft have come from Edwards to Alaska was when they were being tested for cold weather compatibility, or when some component of their avionics was being tested for electromagnetic emissions. I am told there is something about a portion of the Bering Sea that makes it suitable for these sorts of tests, some factor regarding the Earth's own magnetic field. In any case, the Americans have on several occasions conducted avionics test flights over the

Bering Sea, usually under strict emission control standards.

"What this means, comrades, is that Major Kelly will be flying without his radar, radio or other electronics active. It's a perfect opportunity to take him, and to set back the Americans' development program in the same blow."

"Are you suggesting what I think you are, General Patrikeyev? Are you considering shooting Major Kelly's aircraft down in order to capture the major?" asked the First Deputy Premier, who had an incredulous expression on his face.

"Yes, comrade Deputy. So long as there are no other American assets in range to detect the attack, that's precisely what I am suggesting."

The momentary shocked silence was broken by the First Deputy's outraged reaction. "YOU WANT TO SHOOT DOWN AN AMERICAN AIRCRAFT OVER INTERNATIONAL WATERS? THAT'S AN ACT OF WAR, YOU MADMAN!" Valerian Voznesensky shouted. The room erupted in a cacophony of voices as the other men objected or sought clarification.

Finally the Premier slammed his hand down on the table and called out sharply, "ENOUGH! Control yourselves, please, comrades! General Patrikeyev is neither mad nor foolish. Let's hear his reasoning before we decide."

"Why would you capture him in this way, comrade General? You are proposing an act of war that carries a serious risk. Why not a simple kidnapping?" asked the Party Secretary.

"A simple kidnapping is not so simple, comrade Secretary. We have had the major under surveillance for three weeks and he presents an extraordinarily difficult target. He spends nearly all his time on base. Whenever he goes off base he is completely unpredictable. For example, if he goes to buy groceries he returns to the base housing by a different route. He establishes no patterns. None of his trips off base, even for similar purposes, ever occur at the same time of day, nor are they ever on the same day of the week, and never to the same destination. In fact, it appears from his behavior that he's had training to spot and elude surveillance. But there's not a trace of such training in his records," said Patrikeyev.

"Have your men been spotted, General?" asked Geredin. "Is his behavior reflecting a suspicion that he is being watched?"

Patrikeyev furrowed his brow and rubbed his chin unconsciously before answering. "We do not think so, comrade. I suppose it is possible, but I know personally the team who are watching him. They are men who readily admit to their mistakes. They have assured me that the caution and care Major Kelly exhibits appears to be a natural part of his behavior and not a result of some specific suspicion.

"Consequently, comrades, we must either remove the major from our list of targets or move against him in an unusual way. It is my estimation that the risk of a kidnapping exceeds that of a careful shootdown."

"Perhaps we should remove him from the list," the Party Secretary suggested.

"The reason he was placed on the list to begin with, comrade Secretary, is because he is working on a project which is rumored to neutralize the Warsaw Pact advantage in armor. If true, that project could be even more dangerous to the Soviet Union than American improvements to its nuclear weaponry," replied General Yegorov.

"How so?" asked Voznesensky.

"Because, my dear First Deputy Premier, the use of nuclear weapons is unthinkable. No matter who would use them first, the Americans or us, the outcome would be utter destruction. Therefore, improvements to nuclear weapons are improvements to weapons that will never be used. On the other hand, the possession of a significant tactical advantage in conventional weaponry, such as the ability to eliminate an opponent's armor without the risk of commensurate retaliation, is an ability that one *could* be tempted to use. It is the one scenario in which the impact of conventional weapons is so significant that they become strategic," replied the Premier, who had commanded the 5th Guards Tank Army during the Second World War.

"That, sir, was my thinking as well," General Patrikeyev said. "We run a significant risk no matter what we do. It is my estimation that a shootdown entails the least risk."

"Don't do this! We must not do this," said Anatoly Geredin. "We are already risking too much. We could humiliate the *Rodina* in the eyes of the world. Let us drop the major from our target list and be satisfied with our current prisoners. I'm an old man, but I'm not a crazy old man. Stop now, comrades, before this madness spins out of control."

"We'll vote," replied the Party Secretary.

The vote was four to two in favor. Geredin's expression was unreadable. But he looked at Patrikeyev as he left the room and raised his eyebrows slightly, as if to say "you'd better not fail."

****

By eleven o'clock, Erin was convinced that something terrible had happened. She rapidly threw her clean clothes into a small carry-on along with their valuables and passports, while she forced back the tears. Grabbing her handbag and the carry-on, she scribbled a quick note and left it on the table in case Moshe returned. Then she exited and locked the cottage.

They had rented scooters at the airport when they arrived a week earlier. She strapped the handbag and small suitcase onto the tiny luggage rack, put on the helmet, and headed for Hamilton. Within a few minutes she was at the center of the small city, between the Parliament building and the Assembly. She spotted a local policeman sitting in his patrol car and motored over to him.

"Officer, can you please direct me to the Israeli Embassy," she asked in a quavering voice.

"There is no Israeli Embassy in Bermuda, Miss," replied the man in the distinctly correct British accent native to the islanders.

"Then can you tell me where I can find the British Embassy," she said, eyes beginning to leak tears.

"Bermuda is part of the British Commonwealth, Miss. We don't maintain an embassy in our own country," the officer chuckled.

She couldn't hold back her fears any longer, and burst into tears. The policeman kindly helped her off of the bike, placed her and her suitcase in his patrol car, and drove her to police headquarters where she filed a Missing Persons report. Sitting in the Police Commissioner's office, she remembered the number that Moshe had instructed her to memorize the year before. With the Commissioner's permission she used his phone to make an international call.

"Hello?" said the voice on the other end.

"My name is Erin Shimonah. My husband is Moshe Shimonah. He told me to call this number if something happened to him. He's missing . . . " The tears started to flow again.

The Commissioner took the phone from her hand, and continued the conversation, "This is Nigel Turner, I'm the Commissioner of Police in Hamilton, Bermuda. With whom am I speaking?"

"Hello, Commissioner. I'm Mr. Tov and I work for the government of the State of Israel. Mr. Shimonah is one of our employees. Can you tell me what is happening?"

Turner related the details of the Missing Persons report, but was not prepared for what followed.

"Commissioner Turner, may I speak with you privately?"

"Yes, of course. Just a moment." He put the phone on hold and had the patrolman help Erin into a waiting room. Then he shut his door.

"I'm back. Mrs. Shimonah is in a waiting room."

"Thank you. Commissioner, I'm afraid I cannot divulge the sort of work that Mr. Shimonah is in but what I *can* tell you is that there is a high likelihood that Mrs. Shimonah is in great danger. Do whatever you have to do, lock her up if necessary, but please ensure her safety. Do not under any circumstances allow her to leave the police station—not for any reason. We'll send an aircraft to pick her up. It's possible that someone will pose as an Israeli agent and attempt to retrieve her from your custody. It's vital that you not release her to anyone but us. Ask whoever comes to pick her up what she found on the day that she met her husband. If she is not satisfied with the answer to that question, *do not* release her to them."

"Should I arrest them?"

"No! Those men are very likely violent professionals. Make no move against them unless you are prepared for a great deal of bloodshed. But there is one thing you can do. Contact every landing strip on Bermuda and have them double-check the tail number and flight plan of every long-range aircraft that leaves the island. Turn that information over to our people when they arrive. That would be very helpful.

"If you need official cover for your actions, Commissioner, your government may call the office of the Prime Minister of Israel and provide them with my phone number. You'll get all the help you need."

****

Twelve hours later Erin was seated safely on an Israeli military aircraft, returning to Israel. With the help of the sympathetic Bermudan police all of the Shimonahs' belongings had been retrieved from their rental cottage. No threat had developed against her, for which Nigel Turner was quite thankful.

The Shimonahs' possessions back at their home in Dimona were being packed up while she was in the air, and would be relocated to a safe house at an undisclosed location in Israel. She would be provided a new identity and would live out the rest of her days—at least until Moshe reappeared, if ever—under the watchful protection of the Mossad. As far as the rest of the world was concerned Moshe and Erin simply evaporated, leaving not a trace. The precautions were necessary. One of the promises made to Moshe during the training for his job as liaison, was that if he was ever captured the Mossad would ensure his family's protection so that they could never be used against him as bargaining chips by a hostile power. They kept their promise.

Chapter 7

Barely above stall speed, the F-16 wallowed through the clear summer night two thousand feet above a moon-drenched Bering sea, three hundred kilometers south of Provideniya. The resulting flight attitude gave USAF Major Jacob Kelly a much better view of the stars than it did of the ocean, but at the moment he had no time for sightseeing. He was conducting a test flight under provisional emission control (EMCON) conditions, which meant that all avionics not critical to flight itself were powered down. His eyes were glued on his instruments as he delicately maintained the near-stall attitude.

This portion of the test flight was designed to establish the baseline of radio frequency radiation emitted by the aircraft's fly-by-wire electronics. The Falcon was outfitted with sophisticated sensors designed to pick up the slightest activity on the electromagnetic spectrum. The sophisticated fly-by-wire system that made the F-16 sufficiently stable for a human pilot was working overtime in the current flight attitude, making minute corrections to Kelly's light touch on the controls, which meant that the flight control avionics were generating as much electronic radiation as they ever would.

Like sound to a submarine, the electronic radiation emitted by a fighter aircraft was a large part of what enabled an enemy to detect its presence. Once he'd completed establishing the baseline emissions, he would activate the experimental ground-attack weapons package carried by the aircraft and repeat the various flight configurations while the recorder captured the added emissions of the weapon and its systems.

Four thousand meters behind Kelly's Falcon, a Soviet

fighter struggled to avoid overrunning the slow-flying F-16. He, too, was flying under EMCON conditions but for different reasons: he was hunting. Like an archer stalking his prey, Captain Vasiliy Ostrovsky didn't wish to advertise his presence —or his intentions. The *Tayfun*, a Soviet *Nanuchka III*-class frigate steaming thirty miles to the south, had the Falcon illuminated on its air search radar and had vectored the Su-15 Flagon into a firing position. Even if Kelly's avionics had been online, he'd not have detected the passive infrared homing lock of the Anab AA-3 missile.

Seconds after Kelly powered up the prototype weapons package a violent explosion rocked the cockpit and the aircraft stalled. The nose pitched down and the Falcon began a slow tumble, end over end. Kelly's thoughts briefly jammed from disorientation and sheer surprise, but years of training quickly took over. While part of his brain fought off mounting panic, the other part began to deal with the situation. Whatever had happened, his sleek fighter now had the aerodynamics of a cinder block. Recovery procedures were not an option; ejection was the solution. He flipped an emergency destruct switch that would turn the top secret developmental weapon and its associated electronics into little beads of molten silicon. Next, his fingers flying over the instrument panel, he brought his radio online to try to get off a distress call. The unmistakeable harsh roar of a jamming signal filled his headphones. *That's odd*, he thought.

For the briefest instant he dreaded what he had to do next. *Bailing out over the sea is mighty inconvenient*, he thought, grimacing, *and I'm a long way from home*. Besides that, ejection was a cross between being shot out of a cannon, and sitting on top of a Roman candle. He was not looking forward to it.

Using both hands to minimize the possibility of injury, he grasped the main handle of the ACES II ejection system and yanked. He was immediately transformed from pilot to passenger. The restraint system tightened, yanking him back into the seat while the canopy blew off. A tenth of a second later a rocket catapult launched the entire seat assembly up its rails and out of the aircraft. It felt like a hard kick in the butt. Another rocket motor ignited to stabilize the pilot in the proper orientation for the parachute deployment.

With a loud *bang!* a mortar automatically deployed the parachute, producing a hard jerk. Yet another rocket motor ignited to separate the heavy seat assembly, now no longer needed. Several seconds later a final explosive charge detached a survival rucksack and life raft from its case in the seatpan and they fell, then were caught up with a jerk, dangling twenty feet below him on a dropline. The tug of the dropline activated an emergency radio beacon. Unfortunately, there were no U.S. forces in range to pick up the signal.

Just like the Fourth of July, Kelly thought. *And now I'm like one of those fireworks that you watch, wondering if it will still be burning when it reaches the ground. Except that there's no one watching me.*

He was wrong, however. He *was* being watched.

****

For a brief second the pyrotechnics lit up the night sky, reflecting like fiery moonlight off the water below. The Soviet fighter circled the scene: to its pilot, Kelly appeared as if he was riding a meteor away from his stricken aircraft.

Vasiliy Ostrovsky felt no elation at what he'd done. It was no accomplishment. It was little more than an aeronautical mugging, and he knew it. He was bitter at having been chosen for this mission. Though the American pilot was an enemy, Ostrovsky felt an odd kinship with him—after all, they were both fighter pilots. It was a brotherhood the fat cigar-smoking men in Moscow would never understand.

His controller's voice crackled in his ears, and he banked the fighter and headed home.

****

As Jake drifted slowly down toward the surface of the water, he mentally replayed his actions leading up to the explosion. *What happened*, he asked himself, *what went wrong?* It wasn't as if one of his armaments had cooked off; the plane was un-armed. *Did the engine ingest a bird and blow up? Or did the installation of the* Hydra *system interfere with some part of the aircraft? And why was I getting a jamming signal out here in the middle of nowhere?*

He looked down at the dark shimmering sea, a thousand feet below. The Bering was very cold, he knew. He was not looking forward to the dunking.

Seconds later Kelly heard the *whump-whump-whump* of a helicopter approaching. *That's convenient,* he thought. *We must have somebody out here. At least I'll get picked up quickly.* But as the chopper passed between him and the moon, he was able to make out the silhouette. *Wait! That's a KA-27, not one of our birds!* In a flash he put it together: the explosion, the jamming signal, and now the chopper. He'd been shot down in peace-time and somebody was coming to collect the goods—or to eliminate the witness! *It's a Russian-built helicopter, but who's flying it? Will it be the North Koreans, the Chinese, or the Soviets?* It was beginning, the pilot decided, to look like a really bad day.

The chopper snagged his chute with a dangling grapnel. As he was winched up to the helicopter, it turned north and ac-celerated. Kelly released the dropline, knowing that it would be safer to get him aboard the aircraft without it. He briefly considered resistance but decided against it until he knew ex-actly what the intentions of his "rescuers" were. It didn't take long to find out. As soon as the crew of the chopper had brought him safely on board, he was shackled under gunpoint, strapped into a seat and drugged.

****

Captain Vasiliy Ostrovsky felt sick to his stomach. There was no pride, no sense of victory or accomplishment in what he'd just done. It gnawed at his conscience. He felt like a crim-inal. He'd jumped an unarmed American fighter and shot it down. Had it been wartime he'd have been elated, but Mother Russia was not at war.

He was relieved when the wheels of his Su-15 fighter

touched down on the runway of Ugolny Airport in Anadyr. He taxied to the hangar and initiated a shutdown. The ground crew positioned a boarding ladder, and the ordnance crew wheeled a cart up to remove the three remaining air-to-air missiles. Ostrovsky raised the canopy and climbed out of the fighter.

"Captain!" the ordnance crew chief called to him, "I thought we sent you out with four missiles. What happened to number one?"

As the captain opened his mouth to respond, a man dressed in the uniform of a major general stepped out of the shadows. Everyone in the hangar ceased their work, and stiffened to attention.

"Sergeant," the visitor said, "Captain Ostrovsky found it necessary to jettison the missile prior to landing. Apparently there was some sort of malfunction. Is that not correct, Captain?"

Ostrovsky saluted the general, and responded, "Yes, sir. I had to jettison the missile, sir. I did not feel it was safe to land the aircraft with the malfunction."

The general looked at the ordnance crew chief and said, "Sergeant, I'm afraid you'll have to write it off your stores." Looking back at Ostrovsky he said, "Comrade Captain, would you follow me please?"

As the two officers walked away the ordnance chief walked over to the leading edge of the empty pylon and wiped his finger along it. He put the finger to his nose and sniffed at the faint, white residue. He murmured quietly to himself, "Malfunction my foot, Captain. You didn't jettison it, you launched it."

****

"You did well, comrade. I will see that an appropriate commendation is placed in your service record," Chernikov said to the pilot.

"I serve the Soviet Union, Comrade General," Vasiliy Ostrovsky replied without enthusiasm.

Chernikov looked at him sharply. *Perhaps he is simply weary or unwell.* "You do not seem excited about your victory, Captain," he suggested.

Color rose in the pilot's cheeks, but he caught himself quickly. It would not do to share his objections with a general. "I . . . am not feeling well, Comrade General, forgive me."

"Of course. Captain, what you have done tonight has given the *Rodina* a great victory over the Americans. You deserve a medal. Unfortunately, we can't reward you in that way because your mission was also highly secret. As I said, I will put an enthusiastic commendation in your file. But if you breathe a word about this mission to anyone, you and your family will be shot. Good day, Captain."

Chapter 8

The tip of his lightweight spinning rod jerked several times as the unseen fish made several passes at his lure. Jake slowed his retrieve, and *wham!* The fish committed and inhaled the plug, tugging mightily on the light monofilament. As it fought against the tension of the line, the fat smallmouth bass leapt out of the water, shaking its head back and forth. Jake carefully played the fish, taking a step to his left as he struggled to keep the bass from gaining the safety of a submerged branch. But he lost his footing in the hip-deep current of the Susquehanna and fell into the strong flow. He managed to hold onto his rod and clambered out of the water and up the bank, laughing at himself. In the confusion the fish had thrown the hook and gotten away.

Feeling a sudden sting on his shoulder, Kelly looked down and observed a horsefly biting him. He tried to swat it but could not move his hands. He felt more water hit his face, and thought, *That's weird . . . where did that come from? I've climbed out of the river.*

****

The doctor pulled the needle out of Kelly's shoulder, turned to Chernikov and said, "He'll come to any moment, sir. Since he's been drugged for so long, he'll be a little disoriented when he wakes up. It will be another hour or so before he's able to make much sense."

"Very good, Doctor. You may leave us now," the general responded. He threw another bucket of cold water on the pi-

lot's face. He was standing in a small, concrete-walled interrogation cell in Prison 87. Shackled to the chair on the other
side of the table was the pilot they'd shot down the day before. Chernikov's dossier identified him as Jacob Kelly, Major,
USAF. In time, Chernikov would learn that there were several
vital pieces of information about the disoriented pilot in front
of him that were not contained in the file. But by then it
would be too late.

The general was anticipating becoming personally acquain-
ted with the American major. Aside from Captain Shimonah,
Kelly was the only other military man kidnapped under his
Red Sunrise program. Chernikov was planning to interrogate
both officers himself. They weren't scientists; he didn't need a
specialist to make sense of their data, as was the case with all
his other prisoners. The military was *his* specialty; in that field
he was the expert. He was looking forward to dragging every
drop of useful information out of Shimonah and Kelly before
the Politburo decided their ultimate disposition. In the case of
these two, when they had coughed up all the intelligence he
was after, their usefulness would be ended. The Politburo's decision would be but a formality. Shimonah and Kelly would be
executed and buried in an unmarked grave. Chernikov was not
so sure he wanted to execute them that quickly, however. Instead, he planned to fish around a bit for any bonus intelligence they might possess. He was confident that he could extract whatever he wanted, eventually.

He checked Kelly's shackles, then exited, locking the door
securely behind him. He'd take care of some matters in his office, and return in an hour.

****

When the cell door snapped shut, Kelly was yanked from
his pleasant Susquehanna dream. He stared dumbly around
the cell as his muddled mind sought to make sense of his surroundings. Slowly his mental acuity returned. He became
aware that his wrists and ankles were shackled. Then it all

came back to him: the explosion, the ejection, the helicopter. He remembered that the airmen in the chopper had been speaking to one another in Russian, and he concluded that he was now a prisoner of the Soviet Union.

He began to analyze why he'd been shot down. *Surely I had not wandered into Soviet airspace? I thought I was well clear of it, but nothing else would make sense. Or would it?* As he reviewed possible explanations, a dark suspicion began to grow. *Maybe it's* Hydra *they're after; somehow they connected me with the project. Or maybe it was not me, but the aircraft itself? I should have had the tail number altered before leaving Edwards.* After considering it for a moment, he was confident that the correct explanation had something to do with the *Hydra* project. That thought led to another: the Soviets had crossed a line when they shot down his aircraft. It was an unprovoked act of war. Consequently they would never admit that it had happened. They could never afford to let him go and would never trade him in a prisoner swap. There were, then, only two ways out of his quandary; one involved a pine box, and the other was escape. *Think I'll pick door two; I'm not really in the mood for dying.*

First things first: where am I? He looked around the cell carefully, but there was not much information that could be gleaned from his surroundings. There were no words, no script, and no markings on anything. The walls, ceiling and floor were dull gray, the color of raw poured concrete without any attempt at aesthetics; he could even see the grain pattern embossed in the concrete from the rough wooden forms used when the cement was poured. The heavy door was metal and contained a small window crisscrossed with a lattice of metal bars welded to the door itself. Other than the window in the door, there was only one other window, also barred. The room was furnished with a heavy metal table and two metal chairs, to one of which he was shackled. *The décor confirms it: the Soviet Union it is. The architecture is unmistakeable. But* where *in the USSR?*

His examination of his surroundings complete, the next step was to take inventory. *What assets are at my disposal? Weapons? Nope. Equipment? None. Supplies? None. Allies? Un-*

known as yet. Okay, I have no assets. Jake thought for a few more moments and then changed his mind. *Yes, I do! I have the element of surprise! There are two important facts about me that show up nowhere on my dossier, unless the Russians know more about me than the Air Force does. First, my captors have no idea that I'm fluent in Russian. Second, they can't possibly know that I have some very special skills. It's not much, but it might help me create an opportunity to escape.*

The jangle of keys behind him alerted him that he was about to have a visitor. He craned his neck around to see who might enter. Unless it was an official from the U. S. Embassy, Kelly figured that his situation was about to go from bad to worse.

****

Major General Chernikov motioned to the guard, who opened the interrogation room door. He walked around the table and sat in the empty chair.

"Good morning, Major Kelly," he said, speaking in Russian. Kelly just looked stupidly at him. He repeated his greeting in English.

"Jacob Kelly, Major, United States Air Force, serial number 227-67-4290," Kelly replied.

Chernikov reached across the table and slapped him hard across the face. "Say, 'sir,' when you address me, Major Kelly!" he said firmly.

"Jacob Kelly, Major, United States Air Force, serial number 227-67-4290, sir!" Kelly repeated.

"That's better, Major." Chernikov reached across the table and slapped him again. "Do they not teach you to stand in the presence of a superior officer?"

"I'm shackled to this chair, I can't stand!" Kelly objected.

The general reached across and slapped him again. Each time, the blow was a little harder. "I can't stand, SIR!" he said, as though speaking to a child.

"I can't stand, sir," repeated Kelly.

"Do we understand one another a little better now,

Major?"

"Yes, sir."

"Good. You will address me with respect at all times."

"Yes, sir. May I ask a question, sir?"

"Of course," Chernikov smiled warmly, "anything. What is it?"

"Sir, does the Geneva Convention permit you to strike a prisoner of war, sir?"

Chernikov slapped him once again. "No, it does not, Major, but we are not at war, therefore you are not a prisoner of war. Nor does the convention allow me to shoot down an unarmed fighter in international waters, yet I have done so. We have no interest in the Geneva Convention here."

Chernikov stood up, walked around the table, and yanked Kelly's chair around so that they were facing each other. Without another word, he began to slap the flier in the face, alternating hands, first with the left, then the right, then the left, and so on. This went on for fifteen minutes, with neither man saying a word. Blood was trickling out of Kelly's mouth and nose when Chernikov finally stopped. He faced Kelly's chair back toward the table, then walked around and seated himself once again.

He studied the pilot's face. There was fear there, but something else, too. The general sensed strength, though he couldn't say why or how he'd picked up on it. It certainly was not obvious. Something deep within him warned that Kelly was a very dangerous man.

Kelly spat out some blood, then asked, "May I be dismissed, sir?"

Chernikov stared at him, admiring his moxie. He smiled suddenly and replied, "Of course, Major. We'll resume this tomorrow." He walked to the cell door, and shouted, "Guard!"

The poorly hung door opened with a protesting groan, and two guards entered.

"Take him to his cell."

****

"What have you got so far, Gene?" General Franks demanded of his deputy. He'd sent Captain Gene Salisbury to Eielson AFB to keep him apprised of the progress of the Accident Investigation Board (AIB) currently looking into the disappearance of Major Jacob Kelly and his aircraft.

"Well, sir, we found a floating debris field along the last known track of Jake's 'refresher' flight. The debris is consistent with what an F-16 might leave behind if it had broken up."

"Any sign of a life raft?"

"No, sir. No life raft, no body. No sign whatsoever that Major Kelly was even able to eject. I'm sorry, sir. I know you were close to the major."

"He was like a son, Gene," Franks said, his voice husky. He wrestled with his emotions momentarily, and then resumed, "What else have you got, Gene?"

"I managed to cop a ride on the P-3 that found the field, so I have my own photos as well as the official ones from the Board. Together there are about sixty pictures, fifteen of the debris field from the air, and the rest are close-ups of the recovered portions. I'll send them to you, sir.

"The AIB has begun its discussions, General. At the moment they are examining Major Kelly's service record, including training and evaluations. They've also requested his medical records. Something that seems very odd to me, sir, is that they are working with legal authorities to get access to his financial records. I'm not sure why this would enter into an accident investigation."

Franks knew why they would request Kelly's financial data. Someone on the AIB must be thinking of defection as a possibility. Though military intelligence, working with the FBI, would push that portion of the investigation forward, the AIB must be taking a chance on finding some low-hanging fruit. The very thought infuriated him. He sighed, and rubbed his forehead. He would bet his life that Kelly would never defect, but the AIB people did not know the flier as he did, and their job was to do a thorough investigation.

"Is this your first AIB, Gene?"

"Yes, sir."

"They are checking into his financial dealings to eliminate the possibility that Major Kelly might have defected with the aircraft."

"What?!" Captain Salisbury shouted. Then he remembered with whom he was speaking, and stammered, "Oh, sorry, sir! That just caught me off guard. Anybody who knows Jake would never even consider such a possibility. It's ridiculous to even think it."

"But the AIB folks *don't* know Major Kelly, Captain, and they have a job to do. Assure them that we will help in any way we can, including with the financial stuff. And, Captain, if you give them a hard time about this they're liable to send your head back to me on a platter. So don't hassle them."

"Yes, sir," came the chastened response.

"Please continue."

"Yes, sir. The Board has forwarded requests to both Edwards and Eielson for all maintenance records on this particular aircraft. They've also brought in a team from General Dynamics that specializes in the F-16C Block 25 aircraft.

"Last of all, General, I should tell you that the meteorological portion of the investigation is complete. All the data for the night in question, sir, July 10, indicate that VFR flight conditions were perfect with unlimited ceiling, unlimited visibility and near calm winds with very little possibility of turbulence."

After Franks had hung up the phone, he stood and moved over to the window overlooking one of Edwards' runways. A pair of F-15s streaked down the runway and lifted off in tandem. The throaty roar of their twin Pratt & Whitney F100 turbofan engines could be heard easily though his office was a thousand yards from the runway.

He had multiple problems. Most important was the life of Jacob Kelly. He loved Jake like a son. The young pilot was what every father would want his son to grow up to be. The second problem was that a complete prototype of the onboard avionics of the *Hydra* weapon system was gone. It had been installed in Jake's Falcon. Thankfully, the most important piece of the system was not; the microcomputer and associated circuitry located in the ordnance itself had not been carried by Jake's aircraft. Franks did not allow that portion of the project to go off base. His third problem was that if Jake was still alive and somehow wound up in the hands of the Soviet Union, China, or the North Koreans, he could compromise the project under extreme torture.

Well, he thought philosophically, *life must go on. Sitting here and weeping will solve nothing.* He considered the immediate implications to the *Hydra* project. He would need a new test pilot who, in turn, would need to get the extra training and experience that Jake had received. The whole project would be set back at least six months, if not a year.

That's why they pay you the big bucks, Jim, he thought to himself, *to fix all these problems without pausing to grieve.*

Franks was a committed Christian and believed in the power of prayer because he believed in an all-powerful God who sovereignly intruded into human affairs. He bowed his head and prayed for Jake.

If Jake had survived the crash, Franks was confident that he was still alive somewhere. General Franks knew something about Major Kelly of which only three other living people were aware. Kelly was one tough operator; he'd been given the tools to survive anywhere. And what would turn out to be providential is that those special skills didn't appear anywhere in Kelly's military records.

****

Major John "Smitty" Smith did not exist. The service records residing in the Air Force personnel database and in too many squeaky-drawered file cabinets were made up out of whole cloth. The financial transactions, the training records, even the initial application to the Air Force Academy were total creations. Smitty had received the most advanced training possible as a Combat Control Team (CCT) operator and he had been deployed on four different CCT combat operations. He was a skilled shooter with multiple weapons, including all common NATO and Warsaw Pact small arms. His hand-to-hand combat abilities were honed to razor sharpness. Smith had received survival training in multiple kinds of terrain. And he had been thoroughly instructed in surveillance and intelligence fieldcraft.

The common thread linking his deployments was the use of the Paveway targeting system. Part of his personal mission, assigned to him by none other than USAF General James Franks, was to become intimately familiar with the problems encountered by troops on the ground in setting up and using the targeting lasers.

Only with this experience would Major Jacob Kelly be prepared to help the *Hydra* project team untangle the many practical challenges associated with illuminating multiple targets in a target-rich environment in an actual combat situation.

Kelly had attempted to convince Franks, unsuccessfully, that he should be receiving double pay since he had a double O4 identity. The creation of the nonexistent Major Smith was an attempt to protect the security of *Hydra* from any foreign operative who might connect Kelly's CCT Paveway missions with the development project.

The upshot of all this was that the guards watching Major Kelly had no clue of his true capabilities. It was an advantage that Kelly was preparing to use.

Chapter 9

The guard released Kelly from the metal chair and then securely shackled his wrists and ankles together. He yanked Jake to a standing position and gave him a hard shove through the door. Kelly was led down a short hall with an interrogation cell on either side, through a steel door into a small area containing a desk and two more guards, who fell into step with them, and then through another steel door outside onto the detention facility's grounds. Blinking in the bright sunshine, Kelly looked about, trying to absorb everything he saw.

In addition to the interrogation building he had just exited, he counted six other buildings within the immediate compound. Five were identical in shape and size, and the sixth was about double the size of the others. All were of the same drab gray concrete construction, and all had bars on the windows.

His chains clinked and rattled as he shuffled between two guards, trying not to trip. Kelly noted that his guards were clothed in a desert-pattern Soviet battle dress uniform. Their posture, gait, physical condition, and alertness were that of well-disciplined troops, not jailers. *What else is going on here?* he wondered to himself. *What is this place?*

His guards paused to speak with several others, and Jake took the opportunity to examine his surroundings more closely. He was standing in an open space that he estimated to be sixty meters by one hundred. It was enclosed within a chain-link fence topped by razor wire. The area outside the fence was patrolled by dogs, and was itself surrounded by a second chain-link perimeter fence, also crowned with razor wire. Both inner and outer fences appeared to be electrified. Jake counted six guard towers equipped with mounted machine guns and spotlights, spaced at intervals around the inner fence. He measured the towers with a grim professional appreciation: they were so situated that there was not a single blind spot in the entire prison compound. Every square inch could be covered by at least one machine gun.

Looking behind him he observed a second compound, also enclosed within the outer perimeter fence. It, too, had an inner fence topped with razor wire, but no guard towers. A five meter walkway, gated on both ends and enclosed on the sides and top with chain-link fencing, connected the two separate compounds. Kelly guessed that the other compound was the administrative side of the prison. He counted six buildings in it, one of which had a smokestack. Three of the buildings appeared to be troop barracks. There was a parking area with a motor pool containing four vehicles, three large URAL-375 trucks and a jeep.

The entire complex was situated within a meadow some three hundred meters square, ringed by a thick forest through which snaked a single gravel road leading up to the main gate on the west side of the administrative compound. Jake shook his head and frowned. Escape was going to be a difficult task, if not impossible.

A sharp shove in the back interrupted his surveillance and sent Jake sprawling into the mud. "Move, American!" He regained his feet and fell into step. They led him toward one of the buildings that he had assumed was a cellblock.

"Any of you guys speak English?" he asked.

Immediately the men yanked him to a stop, and one, wearing the insignia of a sergeant, began to rough him up. They pushed him to the ground and surrounded him, kicking him. The abuse continued for a minute or so, and then they stood him on his feet.

"You're new here, so we'll go easy on you this time, American," said the sergeant in fluent though thickly accented English. "If you talk, we'll beat you. With each infraction the beatings will get worse. There are only three situations in which you may speak. One is if we speak to you first. Second is during meal time. Third is in the interrogation room. If you try to communicate with anyone, us or your fellow prisoners, at any other time, you will be beaten. Do you understand?"

"Yeah, got it," he groaned, checking his ribs and hoping that nothing was broken.

They resumed walking toward the cellblock and Kelly continued to take mental snapshots of what he saw. The guards on the ground in the prisoner compound were armed only with batons. The entire camp had the look of new construction; other than graveled paths between buildings, everything else was just mud. Kelly counted ten prisoners walking about the compound, each dressed in a bright orange jumpsuit. There was a Kamov KA-26 chopper sitting on a helipad outside the perimeter fence. The NATO designation of the helicopter popped into his mind. *Hoodlum. How fitting*, Kelly thought wryly.

His escort took him into one of the cellblocks and handed him over to the two guards on duty. After removing his shackles, they pushed him into a cell and then threw an orange jumpsuit, a change of underwear, and a pair of cheap sneakers and socks at him.

"Put these on." They watched him while he changed, making sure he had no contraband on his person, and then left, taking his clothes and locking the cell door.

After the guards left, Kelly sat on the cot. *Home, sweet home,* he thought, looking drearily about him. As he reviewed all he could remember of the last 36 hours, a deep sense of despair settled over him.

****

Major Kelly lay on his cot, exhausted but unable to sleep. The bulb hanging from the ceiling which had seemed so dim at twilight he now found to be obnoxiously bright. It was too high to unscrew, and there was no switch.

He rolled over, turned from side to side, and finally gave up trying to sleep. He sat up and considered his situation. In the space of a few days he had been reduced from a happy-go-lucky fighter pilot at the top of his craft to the impotent victim of some sort of crazy Sov scheme the dimensions of which he still didn't understand.

Fury overtook him. Filled with rage, he stood up and began pacing about his concrete cage. He abandoned his initial idea of escape as being impossible and decided instead to just kill the nearest soldier as soon as he had a chance. That he would die doing it Jake accepted without emotion or sentimentality; he was going to die anyway, might as well take down several of his enemies at the same time. No sense in delaying the inevitable. It was preferable to the torture he would experience as his captors sought to extract information about *Hydra*.

The thought of revenge calmed him. As his anger subsided he began to calculate the best way to do as much damage as possible before they snuffed his lights out. *They don't know what I can do. Perhaps I can lure them to within reach.* He considered the matter, and then decided he was setting his sights too low. *Maybe I can take out Chernikov. Why settle for killing a couple of sergeants when I can off a Soviet general? Hmm. That's going to be harder, but a lot more satisfying. How can I do this?*

He entertained the idea, mulling over the possibilities. *How can I get an opponent, who's got all the advantages, close enough to get my hands on him? The only way that's going to happen is if he does not consider me to be a threat. I've got to provide him with the illusion of safety.*

And then he had it! The answer was contained in his memories of the *Rumble in the Jungle*, the 1974 boxing match between Muhammad Ali and George Foreman in Kinshasa, Zaire. It was a fight that then nineteen year old Jacob Kelly had watched with relish. Foreman was the world champion heavyweight and an odds-on favorite to win; Ali was the challenger. Many in the boxing world thought that Foreman's raw punching power would overmatch Ali's "flit like a butterfly, sting like a bee" finesse and tactics.

For seven rounds the older Ali had baited Foreman, drawing him in by leaning against the ropes, apparently defenseless, allowing the younger man to pummel him with punishing blows to the body and the arms. But in the eighth round, when Foreman was exhausted from giving his opponent such a brutal beating, Ali uncorked a five-punch combination that put Foreman on the mat long enough to lose the count, the match, and the heavyweight title. It was a strategy that Ali afterwards memorably dubbed *rope-a-dope*.

I'll do a rope-a-dope myself. These troops have no idea that I have trained and deployed with special forces. If I pretend to be a wuss they will disdain me and consider me harmless. They will let down their guard. And then I will strike.

Anticipating his revenge brought a perverse pleasure to Kelly, but it also renewed his thoughts of escape. If he played his cards right, perhaps he could parlay the advantage of surprise into a legitimate escape attempt. Jake decided that his best approach was to present himself as uncertain and fearful. His earlier defiant coolness to Chernikov was a tactical error, but he mustn't compound it by suddenly changing and becoming fearful or Chernikov would smell a rat. Instead he would have to change over three or four interrogation sessions; the general must be convinced that he'd been broken through interrogation. Crucial to Jake's plan was that his captors underestimate him and his abilities. They must be lulled into carelessness.

A new concern emerged. If he was going to escape, he had to avoid any significant injuries. Kelly knew that he would be tortured, but hoped that the really bad stuff wouldn't begin immediately. In any case, he'd have to make the attempt sooner than later.

While he sat thinking he gradually became aware of a quiet puffing and the faintest rattling of a chain at regular intervals. He got off his cot and put his face up to the barred window of his door. The low, muffled voices of the two guards in their office drifted down the hall from the right. To the left he saw another door, but that cell was dark and the pilot figured it was empty. Opposite him was a door just like his, and the cell was occupied. He observed that two hands were gripping the window bars from the inside. From what he could see of the straining fingers and hear of the grunting, he guessed that the inmate across the hall was using the bars on his cell window to do calisthenics. *Great idea*, he thought. *If I'm going to escape, I'll need to stay in top condition.*

He turned around, pushed his back to the door, and grabbed the bars on either side of his neck and did fifty hanging leg lifts. An involuntary groan escaped his lips, as his ribs were sore from the beating he'd received, but he clenched his teeth and worked through the pain. Next came one hundred squats. Then he worked out a way to do something resembling a pull-up by placing his feet against the door and grasping the bars. Not bothering to count, he did those until he couldn't do any more. After fifty single-hand push-ups with each hand, a flexibility routine, and what he guessed was twenty minutes of yoga, he was sweating heavily.

Stripping, Jake took a sponge bath—ice cold—in the sink, then went back to bed and slept like a baby. It became a routine he repeated every night without fail.

Chapter 10

The captives of Prison 87 sat at tables in the building that one prisoner had dubbed the "cafeteria," eating breakfast. They were fed two meals a day and the food was surprisingly good, due to the fact that it was the leftovers of what had been served to their Spetsnaz guards.

Chernikov sought to make this time as pleasant as possible, in contrast to the often brutal interrogations. It was not a humanitarian goal. The general hoped that the prisoners would eventually develop the *Stockholm Syndrome* in which hostages begin to empathize with their captors, reading kind intentions and good will into any actions of their keepers that fell short of brutality. Chernikov intended to parlay such mistaken notions into more successful interrogations, and in the case of the scientists, he desired to turn them to the point where they would resume their research in Soviet labs.

The atmosphere their captors sought to create in the cafeteria was relaxed and unhurried. It was the only opportunity the prisoners were given to talk to one another. The guards who prepared the food remained out of sight in the kitchen and no other Soviets were present. But this was not a humanitarian move, either. The eating space was thoroughly bugged and the conversations reviewed daily for any nuggets of information not gleaned through interrogation. Scientists love to talk about their work, particularly to other scientists. Chernikov was counting on that fact.

Kelly picked up a tray at the cafeteria window, and then looked around the room, deciding where to sit. It was the first day that his keepers had allowed him to eat with the other prisoners. He counted ten other men in orange jumpsuits. Except for two fellows whose faces appeared as his own must, beaten and bruised, the rest appeared to be in surprisingly good condition. He shrugged to himself; he knew very little about the details of interrogation, but he assumed it would get progressively worse.

Jake sat down with the two men with battered faces.

"Welcome to Club Med," said the one next to him. "What's your offense? Murder someone? Break the speed limit? Or just know too much about something valuable?"

"Guilty on the last two," Kelly said with a grin, glad to find that his new companions weren't moping and filled with self-pity. "And I'm seriously contemplating becoming guilty of the first. I guess its the same story for you guys, huh?"

Both men nodded. The one sitting across from him stuck out his hand and said, "Milt Yoder, I'm an engineer for North American Rockwell. I think I must know too much about heavy bomber design. That's what they've been asking about, anyway. What's your name, and what's your secret?"

Kelly shook his hand. The man's grip was hard and calloused, as though he'd been spending more time operating a shovel than a calculator. "John Falcon, USAF," he replied.

Yoder blinked, and paused for the slightest instant. Then he said, "Well, er, Falcon, I'd rather have met over drinks in Seattle. So what brought you to this fine establishment?"

Jake smirked, and replied, "A helicopter brought me here." He turned to the other man and said, "I see they've been trying to rearrange your face, too. Are you here on a tourist visa, or did you come for your health?"

"Moshe Shimonah, IDF. I was vacationing with my wife in Bermuda. One minute I'm out for my morning run, minding my own business. The next minute I'm zipped into a bag with an oxygen mask strapped to my face, flying in the baggage compartment of an aircraft. Or, at least, that's how it felt. I couldn't see anything. I have no clue as to how I got from the beach to the bag."

"Bummer. At least they could have had the decency to pick you up on the way to a root canal or a colonoscopy, or something. Seems to me it's bad form to nab you on holiday."

"No kidding. We'd saved up two years for that vacation."

"Who are the rest of these people?"

"They're all scientists with specialties in one area or another. Each was shanghaied and brought here. Some of the stories are downright interesting. Whoever is behind this crime spree planned it well. Best I can tell, each person here is doing research in a field relevant to Soviet weapons development. It looks as if they were grabbed in order to force them to spill what they know and give the Soviet researchers a cheap leg up."

"Any of them military?"

"Nope. Just you and me, Falcon."

"So," Yoder asked, "why'd they grab you, Falcon?"

"Just good lookin', I guess. Maybe they needed a classy gent to spruce the place up? I don't know, Yoder, maybe it was just my lucky day."

Yoder laughed, "Yeah, right. No, really, what's your area of expertise?"

"I'm expert at blowing other people out of the air, Milt. But this time it was *my* airplane that got wrecked. Other than that, haven't a clue."

"There must be something you know that they want to know."

"Perhaps there is, but it wouldn't be the kind of thing I could tell you about, now, would it?" Kelly said pointedly.

Yoder scowled. "You military guys are all alike," he said. "Shimonah won't say anything either."

"Surely you've had to sign confidentiality agreements, Yoder, especially if you're working on a weapon system. I did, and I take it seriously. So, no, I'm not going to tell you what I do."

"Hey, Milt, you're a civilian contractor working with the military in Seattle, right?" asked Shimonah. The other man nodded. "Then surely you must know that intelligence only flows in one direction: from the civilians to the military. It never goes the other way. Besides, if we told you . . . " he said, and paused.

Kelly completed Moshe's cliché with a conspiratorial grin,

" . . . we'd have to kill you."

"Suit yourself," Yoder frowned. He picked up his tray and went and sat with a different group.

Moshe looked at Kelly with mock surprise, "Was it something I said?"

Jake looked around the room. No one was paying any attention to them. He wrote with his finger tip in the grease on his plate, *room bugged*. Shimonah nodded.

Jake wrote again, *Milt's a plant*. Moshe lifted his eyebrows quizzically, so Kelly stirred his food with a fork, erasing the words as with an Etch-a-Sketch, and then wrote again, *USSR ahead in bombers*. Instant understanding showed in Moshe's expression, and he nodded agreement. The Soviet Union was ahead of or equal to NATO in heavy bomber technology, consequently there was no need for the extreme measures represented by Prison 87.

"I guess Yoder didn't find our company acceptable this morning," Shimonah commented, breaking the silence before listeners might get suspicious.

"Guess not. Who's the guy in chains?" Kelly asked, pointing at one of the prisoners.

"Name is Oswald Simmons, a Ph.D. candidate in Electrical Engineering from MIT. Works with integrated circuit design. He roughed up the goons that snatched him. Scuttlebutt has it that he busted one man's jaw and was well on his way to trashing the other guy when they pulled a gun and ended the party," Shimonah said. "Consequently, they always have his wrists shackled to his ankles, even at night."

"And he's not military?" Kelly asked, impressed.

"Nope. He's a scientist who's spent entirely too much time in the gym. In any event, they keep him all bundled up in case he decides he wants a rematch. He's in your cellblock, by the way."

"Really? I knew there was someone across the hall from me, but this is the first time I've seen his face. Wasn't looking out the door when they came and got him this morning. Anybody else in my cellblock?"

"Nope. Nearest I can tell, this is a new facility and they are still working the kinks out. They've got us distributed just two to a block. Probably making sure all their systems and procedures are working right before they fully populate the place."

The two men spoke quietly, watching the rest of the room. Kelly learned from the Israeli the names, nationalities, and specialties of each of the other men. He committed the roster to memory.

"Why do you suppose that only Milt, you, and I have been worked over? Everyone else looks pretty untouched," observed Kelly.

"Been wondering the same thing. I don't know about Milt," the Israeli said, for the benefit of the eavesdroppers, "but as far as you and me? I think it's because we're military and they figure we might have been trained to withstand interrogation. But the rest of this group will crumble like a house of cards when they start breaking fingers. I'd guess they are trying to turn these guys, get 'em to resume their research in the USSR, causing as little bodily damage as possible. But the Sovs will get rough if they need to, if these guys don't start cooperating," the Israeli said. He added, "I don't think their job is going to be too tough. You could cut the despair in this place with a knife. I think you, Milt, and me are the only ones left with a sense of humor."

"What about us? What about when they break us?" Kelly asked.

Shimonah turned and looked him in the eye, his mouth framed in a sad smile. "When we finally break and tell them what they want to know, we're dead."

****

For reasons of which he himself was not entirely certain, Kelly had decided to introduce himself by his nickname, *Falcon*. He'd earned it from his fellow airmen back at Hill AFB when he'd elected to read the technical manuals one night rather than going bar-hopping with the other pilots. He'd spent weeks mastering arcane details of the F-16 simply out of a passion for the well-designed aircraft. The handle had stuck, and he liked it.

His caution had already provided a payoff. *Falcon* was not the name Milt Yoder had been expecting to hear, and Yoder's reaction had made Kelly suspicious. The man's supposed specialty, his eagerness to learn Kelly's secrets, and the fact that his face was bruised when no other scientist had yet been beaten all suggested to Kelly that the man was an informer.

****

"Good morning, Major. I've prepared a few, ah, treats for you this morning," said General Chernikov. Sitting in front of him was a small, hot soldering pencil, a thin wisp of smoke rising from the tip. Jake groaned.

"I'm going to be inscribing your new loyalty on your shoulders today. On one shoulder will be a little heart symbol, with the name 'Stalin' burnt into it. On the other, the same symbol, with the name 'Lenin.' I will let you choose which Soviet hero gets burned onto which shoulder."

Kelly did not respond. He was sitting in a much sturdier chair that had been bolted to the concrete floor. His limbs and head were securely strapped in place; only his mouth and eyes could move.

"We can avoid the unpleasantness, Major Kelly, if you will simply tell me about *Hydra*. You talk, no pain. You don't talk, lots of pain."

Jake did not respond.

"Major, let me explain the situation to you. No one in the U.S. knows where you are. They think you are dead. When I am done with you, I will kill you. You are not going to get out of this alive. Abandon all hope, Kelly! You are a dead man and have been since your aircraft was destroyed. Nothing can change that."

"Then why should I cooperate with you, sir?" Kelly challenged. "You've just told me that you'll kill me when you've got the information you want. So what incentive is there for me to cooperate, sir?"

"Pain, Major. I have control over how much pain you will feel before you die. I am going to burn you, Major. I am going to write things on your body with a hot soldering pencil. You are going to discover why the religious fools believe that hell is a place of burning fire, for I am going to put you in hell while you are still alive. There are few sensations, Major Kelly, that produce as much pain as a burn. You are going to have burns all over your body in unspeakable places before I am done with you.

"So you have a choice, Major. I can drag out your life in excruciating pain, or you can die honorably, painlessly and quickly as a soldier before a firing squad. You *are* going to die, Major, and you *are* going to tell me what I want to know before you die. Why not avoid the pain? Make it easy on yourself.

"I'd far rather meet you, warrior to warrior, face to face, on the battlefield. But that is not the lot you and I have been given. I have my job as a general in Military Intelligence. You had a job as an American fighter pilot working on a secret weapons development project. Your job ended when you were shot down. My job, my responsibility, has not ended. We want military information. You know this information, and we will have it, and I will inflict whatever pain I must in order to get it.

"I'm not a sadist, Major Kelly, I'm a soldier. I take no pleasure in this unpleasant business. You have my word as a soldier that once you tell us what we want to know, all torture will stop and you will be well treated, with honor, up to the time of your execution which will be as swift and painless as possible."

Jake looked General Chernikov in the eye, faltered, then looked at the floor. He appeared to be considering the general's words, but after a moment replied, "You know as well as I do, General Chernikov, that there is no honor or respect for a traitor. There never is, sir. No deal."

Chernikov stared at Kelly for a moment, shaking his head. Then he walked over to his desk and pulled a small coil of solder out of a drawer. He picked up the hot soldering pencil, walked over to the pilot, and placed the silver end of the solder to the tip of the pencil. A thin wisp of smoke rose as a glob of molten solder formed on the tip of the pencil. Kelly could smell the sweet scent of the rosin. With a gentle flip of his wrist, Chernikov shook the solder onto the back of Kelly's hand.

Kelly cried out as fiery pain shot through the nerves of his arm straight to his brain. He reflexively jerked his hand back, but he was too tightly strapped in. He couldn't move, not even to shake the still-burning solder off of his skin. The smell of rosin was replaced by that of burning flesh and hair.

"What was your job at Edwards, Major?"

"Flying airplanes," Kelly said through gritted teeth.

Chernikov slapped him hard across the face, and reminded him, "Flying airplanes, *sir.*"

"Yes, sir. Flying airplanes, sir."

"Flying airplanes for the *Hydra* project?"

"Yes, sir." Kelly had already decided that he would give on the obvious answers.

"What is the *Hydra* project trying to accomplish with those airplanes, Major?"

"It—," Kelly stopped, purposely tantalizing Chernikov. Jake knew his transition from defiance to cowardly compliance required several sessions in order to be convincing, and somehow he must accomplish it without truly compromising the project.

When Kelly remained silent, Chernikov produced another small molten glob on the tip of the soldering pencil. Kelly shut his eyes, and thought, *So, the rough stuff finally begins. As long as he just burns me and does not break anything, I still have the chance of an escape.*

＊＊＊＊＊＊＊＊＊

That night at supper Milt kept his distance; Kelly guessed the informer was going after easier marks. Kelly was picking at his food when Simmons walked up with his tray and sat next to Shimonah, across the table from Kelly.

"Name is Oswald Simmons, but everyone just calls me Oz. I'm living in the cell across the hall from you." The chains on his wrist rattled noisily over the lip of the table as he put his hand out to shake.

Kelly held up his hands. The burns were ugly and red, the skin raw and weeping. "Sorry," he quipped, "I seem to have lost some skin. Don't think I'll shake. No offense intended. But I am pleased to meet you. Folks call me Falcon."

"Oh, man, what happened to you?" Simmons exclaimed, staring at the ugly burns.

"Same thing that's going to happen to you, Oz. At some point the interrogations become torture sessions, until you give 'em what they want."

"Did you give 'em what they want?"

"Not yet," Kelly replied. "I hope I can hold out. Hey, I understand that you gave your escorts a run for their money back in the States. Congratulations." Kelly noticed out of the corner of his eye that Moshe was writing the words *room is bugged* in his dinner plate with his finger. Shimonah showed it to Oz, who mouthed back, *you're kidding*. The Israeli shook his head no and mouthed, *be careful.*

Oz nodded, then responded to Kelly, "Yeah, well, didn't want to just roll over and play dead. I thought they were just a couple of local thugs. If they hadn't pulled a gun, I'd still be in Fort Collins and they'd be in jail. Or in the hospital. Or worse.

"By the way, Falcon, I understand you were in the Air Force."

"I'd prefer not to use the past tense, Oz. I *am* in the Air Force. I fly fighters. Of all the guys here, I probably have the best story. I was flying along in an F-16 and got shot right out of the sky. Never saw it coming. I ejected and along comes a Soviet chopper, and snags my parachute. Moshe here got nabbed on the beach in Bermuda."

While the Israeli recounted the details of his capture, Oz mouthed to him, *keep talking*. Moshe nodded, and rattled on about the beaches in Bermuda. Mimicking what he'd seen Shimonah do, Simmons wrote on his own plate, *tonight — listen for me,* and looked straight at Kelly. Kelly nodded.

Chapter 11

Saturday, July 12, 1986: 2345 local
west of Tara, USSR

Kelly lay awake on his cot, listening. The guards had changed shifts about an hour ago and Kelly figured it was getting close to midnight. Suddenly he heard a fit of coughing across the hall. Figuring that was the signal he'd been waiting for, he got up, walked to the door of his cell, and peered across the hall. Oz was grinning back at him from his own cell with his finger over his lips. Both men knew that if they made any noise they would receive an immediate beating.

The scientist raised his hand, palm toward Kelly. He opened his hand wide, quickly closed it, and swiftly repeated the action two more times. Then he opened it, paused briefly before closing it, and repeated that two more times. Then he repeated the first sequence and stopped, looking at Kelly as though he expected a response.

Kelly shook his head and shrugged, brow furrowed in confusion, thinking to himself, *What on earth . . . ?*

The other man went through the sequence again: palm opened and closed rapidly three times, opened and closed more slowly three times, opened and closed rapidly three times.

Again, Jake shook his head and shrugged his shoulders.

Simmons repeated the odd gestures in the exact same sequence, only this time he simply continued to repeat the entire series of movements over and over again.

Kelly watched the display. Something in the pattern was familiar. *Three shorts, three longs, three shorts. What the . . . ? Oh, you idiot! It's the international distress signal in Morse code, S-O-S! Wait! . . . This guy knows Morse?*

Kelly held up his own hand, and quickly signed, MY NAME

IS JOSE JIMENEZ, using the catch-phrase that comedian Bill Dana always employed to introduce himself. *Now I'll know if this guy watches late night television*, Kelly thought to himself.

Oz nearly laughed out loud.

Kelly smiled, *Yep, he does.* Then he signed, HOW LEARN MORSE?

EARNED 1-CLASS RAD-TEL LICENSE AS TEEN. WARNING, TOMORROW YOU ARE PUPPET! Oz signed back.

WHAT?

EXERCISE DUMMY FOR GUARDS. SPARRING PARTNER. ONE-SIDED FIGHT. BE CAREFUL. Oz shook his head, and mimicked breaking an arm.

HOW KNOW?

OVERHEARD GUARDS.

IF TALKING ENGLISH, WANTED YOU HEAR. PROBABLY NOTHING. Kelly figured they were just messing with Simmons' mind.

NOT SPEAKING ENGLISH. BE CAREFUL.

YOU SPEAK RUSSIAN? DO THEY KNOW?

YES, NO.

DON'T TELL ANYONE. NOT EVEN PRISONERS. VALUABLE EDGE. Knowing what was being said by their captors, when they were unaware they were being understood and were consequently unguarded in their speech, was an advantage of inestimable proportions. It was something that Oz should not give away under any circumstances, Kelly knew.

OK.

MILT INFORMER. DON'T TRUST. BUT THEY CAN'T KNOW WE KNOW.

HOW KNOW?

HE MADE MISTAKES. WHEN PUPPET?

AFTER BREAKFAST. DON'T EAT TOO MUCH.

ROGER.

****

"Hey, Yankee, I need some exercise. You want to exercise

with me? You want to be my puppet?" The speaker was a lean, wiry soldier who looked as tough as shoe leather.

"Not really," responded Kelly. His guards were escorting him back to the cellblock after breakfast. It was a beautiful, sunny morning, low humidity and cool. Kelly guessed the temperature to be around 60 degrees Fahrenheit.

The soldier grabbed him, spun him around, and slapped him hard across the face.

"Say, 'sir,' when you talk to me, American!" he said, laughing. The other guards laughed, too, and the soldier slapped him again. Kelly's anger flared and he almost lashed back. But as humiliating as it was, he had to present an image of helplessness to the guards. Jake saw this as an opportunity to begin "breaking" and displaying a cowardly streak. It grated mightily on his pride, but he was convinced it was critical for any future escape attempt. But he would, he decided, fight back with his tongue. That they would interpret as mere empty bravado, especially once they saw his cowardly performance in the ring.

"I'll say, 'sir,' to a superior officer, soldier, according to the code of military ethics. But I won't say it to you, Sergeant."

"Oh, this one thinks he's tough, Anton. He will be fun!"

The group pushed him into an area of the compound marked off with four stakes in the ground connected by rope, forming a rough square.

"Here are the rules, American. I can do anything I want to you. You can defend yourself, and if you are feeling lucky, you can fight back. If you step outside the rope, you'll get a beating. You cannot leave the square until I say you can leave."

The prisoners and soldiers gathered around the crude ring to watch the contest. It was an event fraught with danger and opportunity. Jake needed to maintain a delicate balance between playing the incompetent coward, and getting beaten to a pulp. It wouldn't matter how low was their opinion of his fighting ability if he came out of this match with broken bones. That would eliminate *any* opportunity to escape and seal his eventual death warrant.

Somehow he had to stay relatively unscathed without giving too much away. He decided that he could display the rudiments of combat every soldier learns in basic training, but the skills he had acquired and honed in special ops training he would keep under wraps—for now.

The wiry soldier, Anton, took off his shirt, and stepped into the ring. Jake stood in the farthest corner from his opponent, and limbered up, shaking out the morning stiffness. His shoulders and hands burned painfully from yesterday's interrogation session.

Anton motioned him forward, so Jake moved up and stood before him.

"Are you ready, American?"

"Ready as I'll ever be. Can I ask a question?"

"*Da.*"

"How long does this match go on? When do we stop?"

"When I decide to stop, American."

The soldier assumed a fighting stance and began to circle to Kelly's left. He threw some left jabs, testing the range, which Kelly blocked clumsily, leaving his chin open. He knew that a combination was coming, but figured he could take several shots to the head as long as he caught them rolling away. He didn't have long to wait. Anton jabbed with the left and as Kelly blocked it the Russian struck with a lightning-fast right cross. Although he'd been expecting it the punch almost caught him full in the face, but Jake was able to roll back and diminish the impact. Even so, he was knocked off his feet.

He rolled as he fell and just barely avoided a vicious kick. As Jake scrambled to his feet, Anton had a knowing smirk on his face. Kelly figured that the simple stuff, the boxing, was over. From this point it would be combined action.

"C'mon, American. Take your shot. Here's my chin." The Russian dropped his hands and stuck his chin out, inviting the pilot to take a swing at him. Kelly took the bait and moved in with his own combination. Anton slipped the jab, then grabbed Kelly's arm as the American launched a ponderous right hook, and threw him over his shoulder. Kelly rolled as he hit the ground and again avoided the man's dangerous boots. Kelly brought his fists up, but Anton unleashed a snap kick aimed at his chin. Jake barely slipped the kick and again lost his footing.

The soldiers surrounding the ring were cheering, but the prisoners stood in silence, knowing that any sound would bring down a beating on them. The fight went on like this for another five minutes, with Kelly displaying enough fighting technique to be credible, but executing in such a clumsy way so as to be deemed inept by all the watchers, soldiers and prisoners alike. The Soviets began hurling insults. Kelly ignored them and concentrated on protecting his vitals and avoiding broken bones.

"This one is worthless, Anton!" mocked one.

"No wonder they turned him into a pilot!" laughed another.

"My girlfriend could do better!"

"Yes, Boris, but your girlfriend is built like a tank. She probably beats you up every night!"

Kelly decided it was time to show the cowardly streak, and began withdrawing from his opponent, running around the ring in an attempt to stay out of reach of Anton's hands and feet. The soldier chased him for a moment, but quickly tired of it. He motioned to three of his fellow soldiers, and with wolfish grins they stepped into the ring.

A lieutenant who'd been watching called out to the men, "No broken bones, comrades! No serious injuries. The general isn't finished with him. Unless you want to spend this winter in Chersky digging holes in the ice, you'd better be careful!"

The men grabbed Kelly and held him while Anton began to work him over. Somewhere along the line, Kelly lost consciousness and remembered no more.

****

Major General Chernikov stood at his office window, watching the prisoners walk the path just inside the prison compound fence. Even at that distance he could observe their fear: each was walking alone lest they might be tempted to talk and therein earn a beating from the attentive guards. It was like a pathetic little parade, around and around the compound.

He was satisfied, though not pleased, with progress. None of the interrogations had yielded anything of worth as of yet, but among the scientists he sensed the tide was beginning to turn. They were responding readily to simple kindnesses on the part of the guards, and seemed eager to believe that the brief moments of warmth were a sign of common humanity, not understanding that, in reality, it was cynical psychological manipulation of the worst sort.

A knock at the door interrupted his thoughts.

"Enter."

The duty sergeant stuck his head in the door, and said, "Sir, you had asked me to remind you that General Patrikeyev is expecting you to call him this morning."

"Thank you." Chernikov sat at his desk and picked up the phone. Several layers of secretaries later, he was connected.

"Dobryy dyen', Nikolai! It's good to hear your voice."

"*Zdravstvuitye*, General Patrikeyev."

The two men exchanged pleasantries for a moment. Within the dog-eat-dog environment of the GRU, Patrikeyev nonetheless retained a fatherly affection for his protégé.

"Go secure, Nikolai, code of the day."

Chernikov consulted the GRU code book, and punched encryption code 1403 into his telephone scrambler. For a moment a cacophony of whistles and tones sounded in the earpiece as the devices synchronized. Then the tones disappeared and Patrikeyev's electronically massaged voice sounded as though it was coming from a deep well.

"Tell me, Nikolai, how does Project *Krasnyy Voskhod* fare? What is your status at this moment?"

"We have our full authorized complement of prisoners, General, plus one stooge. Both the prisoners and the troops guarding them are settling into their routines, and so far everything is moving ahead smoothly."

"Excellent, General. What is the status of the interrogations?"

"As yet they have produced nothing of value. I'm taking it

slowly, attempting to turn the scientists without creating unnecessary damage or resentment. It will be another ten days to two weeks before I begin the rough stuff on the holdouts. It may not be necessary, however, as I sense that they are all swinging my way."

"Are you being too soft, Nikolai? Are you moving too slowly? At the moment you have a blank check from the Politburo, but that could change quickly if we don't start seeing results."

"Valeriy Ivanovich, I must ask for more time. I am pursuing a course that I believe will yield far greater results than simply breaking bones and pulling fingernails. Are you familiar, Comrade General, with the report that Karlov wrote for the KGB last year on the Stockholm Syndrome?"

"I've seen it, but I have not read it."

"I've read it thoroughly several times, sir, and believe that it's the best approach for this project. I've been attempting to use his techniques. I am convinced these methods will shortly reveal their value here."

"Very well, General Chernikov. I have utmost confidence in you. I will try to keep our political masters happy while you pursue this approach. It might please Geredin to know that we are using a KGB study to inform our interrogations.

"What about the two military men you captured? Are you using the same approach with them?"

"No, sir. I am proceeding with the assumption that they've been trained to resist interrogations. In their case, I have been employing the motivation of intense pain. They've not broken yet, but I'm confident that they soon will. One is already showing the signs."

"Try to break the Jew quickly, General. We need the information he has on Israeli nuclear capabilities before the American president begins the next round of Mid-East peace talks."

****

When he came to, Kelly was lying on the floor of his cell in a fetal position. His face was covered with dried blood, and his body ached all over. Each breath was an exercise in pain. Gingerly he stretched out as much as he could and rolled to his back. His whole body was stiff and bruised. He ran his fingers over his torso, trying to discern any broken ribs amidst all the pain. None were apparent, at least not by such a cursory inspection, but it hardly mattered in his present condition. Any thoughts of escape needed to be delayed while his body healed. Groaning, he rolled onto his stomach, got his knees under him, and managed to crawl to his cot. Soon he was fast asleep.

Chapter 12

Tuesday, July 22, 1986: 1545 local
Edwards AFB, CA, USA

"General Franks, the AIB completed their investigation this morning. You aren't going to like their conclusions." Captain Gene Salisbury's voice sounded disgusted through the phone line.

"Already?" exclaimed Franks with surprise.

"Yes, sir. There wasn't much to go on. The floating debris field added nothing to the investigation, since all the metal pieces of the airplane are sitting at the bottom of the Bering Sea. There was no other physical evidence of the crash to study, aside from a few pieces of insulation, and the odd bladder or tank that retained enough air to remain buoyant."

"So what was their conclusion?"

"General, you aren't going—"

"Just give it to me straight, Gene."

"Pilot error."

"PILOT ERROR!" Franks shouted over the phone. "PILOT ERROR? IDIOTS! That's outrageous! If this had been a new aircraft that might be a typical Air Force butt-covering conclusion, and I could at least understand it. But this is a reliable airplane flown by an even more reliable officer!"

It was not uncommon for general officers to have a temper; patient men don't usually rise to such ranks. But General Franks was unusually distinguished in his capacity to deliver a good, outraged butt-kicking, and his subordinates didn't relish being on the receiving end of it.

"Sir," came Captain Salisbury's voice meekly over the receiver, "I told you—"

"Didn't those clowns seriously consider any other possibilities?" demanded Franks.

"Well, sir, there was a brief consideration of the possibility of defection, but that didn't make it into the final report, nor was any account of those discussions entered into Kelly's service record or the Defense Prisoner of War/Missing Personnel Office database."

"Well, sanity and decency be praised. At least they had the good sense not to accuse the major of stealing the aircraft. Pilot error, my foot! There's something else going on here, Gene, but I've no clue as to what."

"You mean, with the report?"

"No, Captain, I mean with Major Kelly's disappearance. I've got a feeling that it's not over yet. I just can't believe that Jake is at the bottom of the Bering with his airplane. Can't explain it, but that's my suspicion."

"Yes, sir." Salisbury paused for a moment, and then added, "There's no need to notify the next of kin, General. According to the records, no member of Major Kelly's family has survived him."

"I know. I think Jake considered us his family, Gene. This is going to hit Shandra and the boys pretty hard. Hits *me* pretty hard. Ah, well, it's a fallen world, Gene. The only thing certain about this life is that one day it will be over, and we'll all meet Jesus, face to face."

Salisbury didn't know what to say, so he simply responded, "Yes, sir." Everyone working in Franks' unit was aware of the general's religious faith due to the fact that Franks made no bones about it. Captain Salisbury had no idea what his own personal beliefs were, had never stopped moving long enough to think about it. His personal policy was that maybe if he avoided the future, it would never catch up with him.

"Gather the major's personal effects and come on home, Captain."

****

Two nights after his terrible beating in the sparring ring, Kelly started exercising again on a limited basis. Within a week he was back to his full exercise regime. Though there were slaps, kicks, and punches, Kelly suffered no sustained beatings during this time. But Chernikov continued to inflict excruciating burns to his arms, hands, and shoulders. The pain kept Jake focused.

In the meantime he'd been busy. He knew exactly how many steps it was from the cellblock to the inner gate. He'd figured out the guard schedule, which apparently did not vary. He'd observed from his cell window that the inner gate and walkway between the two compounds was left unlocked and unguarded during the midnight and 0400 shift-changes, when all the prisoners were securely locked away. The area was well lit, and the guard tower near the inner gate was relied upon, apparently, to provide adequate security. The precautions were sufficient for broken prisoners who had no thought of escape. But Kelly wasn't broken, and he'd figured a way out.

He'd picked out the day and time for his escape. Both cellblock duty guards on the watch in question were about his height and build, and he counted on using a uniform to get from the prisoner compound into the administrative one. Unfortunately, that was as far as his planning could carry him. He'd tinkered with various ideas for getting through the main gate, but he didn't have sufficient information to make detailed plans. And once he escaped the camp itself, *if* he escaped, he'd be flying by the seat of his pants. He was counting on three guiding principles: seize the initiative, move quickly, and force the enemy to react to his moves.

Kelly had perceived a change in the guards' attitude toward him since his lamentable performance in the sparring ring. They disdained him, and like sharks smelling blood in the water lost no opportunity to abuse him, considering him to be a coward. For his part, Major General Chernikov made no attempt to hide his disgust with the flier. Unfortunately, Kelly's staged display of weakness merely incited Chernikov to be more aggressive with his soldering pencil, as the Soviet was confident that such a coward must soon give up the desired intelligence. Jake knew that he'd be executed and thrown into some muddy hole immediately upon providing what

Chernikov wanted.

His fellow prisoners were sympathetic but kept their distance, as though associating with Kelly would bring suffering upon themselves. Only Shimonah and Simmons continued to eat meals with him, but their pity was irritating to Jake. It was clear that they thought he'd been broken. Kelly's one diversion was the late-night Morse code bull sessions with Simmons, which mostly revolved around talking about movies and TV shows. Thankfully, Simmons never mentioned the debacle in the ring.

While it rankled his pride to be considered a coward, Kelly knew that the two essential conditions for his escape had been established. No one considered him to be a serious threat, and he had received no broken bones nor major injuries.

Chapter 13

Saturday, August 2, 1986: 0145 local
west of Tara, USSR

"Hey! HEY! I'm tired of this! LET ME OUT OF THIS STINKIN' HOLE!"

Kelly grabbed the metal drinking cup they'd given him, and rattled it noisily on the bars of the window in his door. By the pilot's guess, it was probably around 0200 in the morning.

"HEY, YOU SOVIET PIGS! I'M TALKING TO YOU! LET ME OUT OF THIS PLACE!"

Oz appeared in his cell door window across the hall and frantically motioned for Kelly to settle down and be quiet, but it was much too late for that. Jake clanged his cup on the door, and made as much racket as he could.

"SHUT UP, YOU STUPID AMERICAN!" barked the approaching guard. "I'm going to beat you to a pulp if you don't be quiet!"

Kelly ignored the warning, and continued to rap his cup on the door. Both guards stood outside his cell and shouted at him to shut up and go to bed.

"You want another beating?" threatened one of the guards.

"You aren't man enough to do it," Jake boasted, taunting them, but as soon as they began to unlock his door, he backed up and cowered in the far corner of his cell. Oz watched from across the hall, sadly shaking his head.

The two guards opened his cell door, and stood observing him with contempt.

"You're nothing but a cowardly dog! You're pathetic! How did you even get into the military? I will honor a fighting man, enemy or not, but you are no fighting man," one of the soldiers growled. He spat at Kelly with disgust.

Moving into his cell, the guards each pulled a baton from their belt to pummel him into silence. But coaxing both guards into his cell while the self-locking door stood wide open was the centerpiece of Kelly's plan. Jake played his role to the hilt, cowering in the corner and clutching the blanket from his cot, a terrified expression on his face. As the men stepped within reach, though, Oz observed a wicked smile crease the pilot's face.

With blurring speed Kelly threw the blanket over the guard on his left, then snap-kicked the one on his right, connecting with his chin and staggering him. Jake pivoted back to the first guard, who was still untangling himself from the blanket, and jabbed a quick, ranging blow with his left. He followed with a devastating uppercut, snapping the man's head back. Shifting his weight with the fluid grace of a dancer, Kelly broke the guard's knee with a sharp kick. The man screamed in pain, and collapsed on the floor.

Jake whirled and faced the second guard, who was still shaking off the kick he'd received on the chin. Kelly launched another snap kick, but the man blocked it and responded with a kick of his own. Jake tried to slip the blow but wasn't fast enough. He took it on the chin while falling away, tucking into a backwards roll, putting distance between him and his attacker. As he sprang to his feet he tasted blood and chipped teeth.

The guard circled warily, not keen to renew contact. But his eyes betrayed him, flickering involuntarily to the cell door, telegraphing his intentions. He broke for the door but Kelly anticipated his move and lunged, tackling him. They rolled on the floor, grappling and punching. Jake head-butted him twice, smashing the man's nose. The guard cried out, and when he drew his hands back to protect his face, Kelly slammed his head down on the concrete floor again and again until the man was lifeless.

Groaning in pain, the second guard was frantically trying to drag himself out of the cell. Jake scooped up one of the dropped batons, and brought it down with such force that he broke the man's neck.

He stood trembling, his system still coursing with adrenaline. Less than thirty seconds had elapsed since the guards entered his cell. Kelly checked each for a pulse, but both guards were dead. He regretted the kills, necessary though they were. He had not started this fight but he was going to do whatever was required to finish it.

Oswald Simmons looked on from his cell, his mouth open in an incredulous expression. He began to sign in Morse, but Kelly stopped him, "It's just us, Oz. You can speak now."

Simmons blinked, and replied, "Oh, right. Hey, wow, what . . . ? How . . . ? What got in to you, Falcon?" he exclaimed, looking at the two soldiers sprawled on the floor. "I saw you in the sparring ring and you were a world-class pansy. What—?"

"That was a setup. This was the sting. Had to make 'em think I wasn't a threat."

"Must have worked," Oz observed dryly. "Now what?"

"Gonna check out and find a different hotel. Don't care for the amenities here, nor the attitude of the staff."

"Need some help with your luggage? Take me with you! I can be handy in a scrap."

"No can do. All I'd be doing is putting your life in danger. Besides, I have no idea what I'm going to do once I get beyond the main gate. In fact, I haven't even figured out how to *get through* the gate. But I'm going to get out or die trying."

"Look, Falcon, my life is forfeit anyway. They'll never let me go, so what difference does it make if I die here or die making a run for it with you? And it's a matter of national security, because sooner or later I'll break under their interrogation. I don't want the Soviets to gain the ability to miniaturize the electronics in their weapons, which is my specialty. I'd rather go out like Bonnie and Clyde than spill my guts under interrogation."

"No! I can't take you."

"If you think you're going to walk out of here when the shift changes, dressed in one of those uniforms, you might want to remember that they are expecting *two* men to leave this cellblock, not just one. Not sure how you plan on accomplishing *that* by yourself, comrade," Oz finished, speaking in perfect Russian.

Kelly smiled and replied in equally fluent Russian, "I've got two hours to kill before the next shift change. I'll think of something. By the way, your Russian is great."

"C'mon, how about it? Take me with you!"

"Nope. Sorry. Don't really know you, Oz, don't know what you can handle. If I'm going to get out of this mess in one piece, I've got to travel fast and light. You'd just weigh me down. And if it's just me, I won't have to vote over decisions; I can just follow my own instincts without getting into an argument."

"Listen to me, Falcon! I can fight hand to hand as well as anyone we might run into. I can speak virtually flawless Russian with a native accent. And I promise to follow your lead without question. Besides all that, I can give you something you really, really need."

"What's that, Oz?"

"That second uniform, like I said! If only one man leaves this building they're going to want to know why. Every eye in every guard tower will be on you. Somebody will be checking on you before you get to the first gate, and then your escape will be over before it even gets started. But with me you'll at least have a chance! Take me with you!"

"You hook your wagon to mine, you could die. You know that, don't you?"

"Death I don't fear. The torture from these interrogations I do fear. As far as I'm concerned, Falcon, it's a win-win. I've got nothing to lose."

"When the shift changes, Oz, I have to kill two more men. Before I get out the main gate, the body count could go north of half a dozen. Can you handle that?"

"I've never killed before. I don't like the thought of it. These soldiers are simply following orders coming from way above their pay grade. But I know I'm in a fight for my life. It's six of one, half dozen of the other as to whether these characters have committed the crime of kidnapping or an act of war. Either way, any damage I do is going down as self-defense in my book. When they put my life on the line, they put their own there, too. So I won't be using sparring ring kicks and jabs, I'll be aiming to kill."

Kelly studied the other man, considering his request. Two men had a better chance of escaping the prison than one. But once beyond the prison fence one man would probably survive more easily than two. *One problem at a time*, Jake thought to himself.

"Welcome aboard, Oz. Let me find the key, and I'll spring you."

As Kelly searched the bodies of the guards, looking for the key, Simmons had some questions of his own.

"I knew our fighter jocks were good, Falcon, but I didn't know they were *that* good at hand-to-hand stuff. You'd have put ground-pounders to shame with the moves you used on these two. Are you sure you're not really a SEAL just pretending to be an Air Force pilot?"

Kelly chuckled, and admitted, "Well, I *was* in the Boy Scouts."

"Somehow I don't think that explains it."

"I guess we all have our secrets, Oz." He straightened up, frustrated, having checked the pockets of both corpses without finding the cell key. "For crying out loud! Where is that stupid key? Here, I found this, it probably goes to your shackles." He tossed a small key to Oz, who deftly caught it and unlocked his own shackles. "But neither of these two are carrying so much as a key ring."

"I can see why you need me for this little operation, Falcon. Did you try your door?" he asked, pointing at the clearly visible key and its dangling ring, still inserted in the lock of Kelly's cell door.

"Listen, propeller-head, at CSU you might have been a genius, but here you're just muscle. I'm the brains of this operation, so don't push it," Kelly groused, as he unlocked Simmons' cell. "Grab those batons, we're gonna need 'em."

Chapter 14

Saturday, August 2, 1986: 0345 local
west of Tara, USSR

Yevgeniy Lebedev and Anton Kuznetsov walked out of their barracks and stood looking at the night sky. It was 0345 hours. Cassiopeia was climbing in the eastern sky. Perseus was also rising in the east, but closer to the horizon. Tendrils of fog wavered above the dew-drenched meadow below the perimeter fence toward the east. The faintest hint of an aurora made the northern sky shimmer with an uncertain green glow.

"It's a shame these yard lights blot out the stars, Anton. I was raised on a *kolkhoz* about 75 kilometers south of here, near Reshetnikovo. There wasn't any light pollution on the farm there, because there wasn't any electricity nearby," the heavy-set soldier said, chuckling. "You could see every star."

"Every star, Yevgeniy? Every star?"

"*Pravda!*" the young man insisted, "Every one. I used to dream that they were all mine."

"I had no such dreams," said Anton. "I grew up on the streets of Leningrad. My father was a drunk. There was no time for dreams in my life," he said bitterly. "The army is my dream and my family." He looked up at the sky and cursed. "You couldn't see the stars in Leningrad where I lived. We were too close to the Admiralty shipyard. It was illuminated day and night. There were no stars in my night sky, Yevgeniy." He looked at his watch, and saw other soldiers moving toward the inner gate. "It's time for our shift. *Poshli.*"

The pair walked through the unsecured walkway between the administrative and prison compounds. It was bathed in cold, white light. They trudged toward their assigned cellblock, talking quietly. Searchlights played silently over the ground, directed by alert guards in the watchtowers. There was little sound: the crunch of their boots on the gravel path, the muffled hoot of an owl back in the forest, and the low murmur of the conversation of guards being relieved.

Yevgeniy entered the cellblock. He looked about the small guard office with alarm. No one was there, and the iron door to the prisoner section was standing open.

Anton shouldered past him and called, "Hello?"

"Back here," came the response out of the prisoner section. "One of the prisoners is causing trouble, and needs to be taught a lesson. Come on back and take over. We want to get back to the barracks and go to bed."

Anton unclipped his baton and stepped through the door, followed by Yevgeniy. As soon as Yevgeniy had passed through the doorway, Jake stepped from behind the heavy steel door and smashed a baton down on Yevgeniy's head. With the speed of a striking snake, Kelly snapped the soldier's neck with a second blow. The man was dead before he hit the floor.

Anton wheeled to face Jake, turning his back on the open cell door. Oz sprang out and crushed the soldier's skull with a single strike. Anton collapsed in a heap. Neither body so much as twitched. Turning about, Simmons vomited into the cell.

"You okay, Oz?"

"Yeah," the scientist answered grimly. He wiped his mouth on his sleeve.

"You sure he's dead?"

"Oh, he's dead all right. His head looks like he stopped a truck with it. Oh, dear God in heaven, forgive me!"

"Look, if you can't do this, I can make it look like it was all me. I doubt they'll punish you for something that happened when you were locked in your cell."

"Nope. I'm good. In for a penny, in for a pound. They started this fight, we didn't. There's a lot more at stake here than just you or me. Let's do it. Just pardon me if I barf every once in a while."

"Just don't puke on me, okay?"

Each quickly changed into a uniform and pulled their caps down low on their heads.

"You ready?" asked Jake. Oz nodded.

"Showtime," replied Jake, stepping through the door into the pale brightness of a searchlight that had stopped on their door.

Oz stepped out behind him and closed the door. The two began walking carelessly toward the connector to the administrative compound. The light followed them halfway and then resumed its search pattern, the operator apparently satisfied.

****

The passage through the walkway was uneventful. The other guards coming off their watch had already returned to the barracks. Kelly had feared that he would be recognized if he had to mix with the other guards, but the delay in their cellblock solved that problem without raising suspicion.

Jake pictured the escape as taking place in four distinct phases. First, he must get out of his cell. Second, he had to get from the prison compound to the administrative side without being re-apprehended. Third was escaping from the administrative compound to the outside, and last was escaping the Soviet Union itself. *Two down, two to go*, he thought to himself as he cleared the connecting walkway.

"Comrade, let's enjoy one last cigarette before we turn in, eh?" he called out in Russian, loud enough to be overheard, quiet enough not to draw more than passing attention.

"*Da*," replied Oz.

They strolled over to the motor pool, and leaned on one of the vehicles, smoking and talking. At first their conversation was loud enough to be overheard, but they gradually toned it down. Within a few moments, the guards in the towers were ignoring them.

"Okay, here's what's next," Kelly whispered. "The building behind you is the physical plant. Through my cell window I've observed that the telephone and power lines from outside the camp enter it. We've got to get in there, cut the communications lines, disable the power lines, and kill any backup generators we find. If we can cause any kind of explosion or fire, all the better."

"Why go to all that trouble, Falcon? Let's just hot-wire one of these vehicles and crash through the gate!"

"No, we've got to cut their power and communications in order to have a fighting chance. We need to buy at least thirty minutes, or they'll just nab us down the road a ways. Besides, with those .50 cals and spotlights in the guard towers, we wouldn't even make it to the gate. Got to kill their light, and the only way to do that is kill the power. They won't risk their own men by firing blindly into the dark. At least, I hope they won't."

"Well, then, we should also disable the other vehicles so they can't chase us. Thankfully, the chopper's not here, so we don't have to worry about trashing it."

"Right," agreed Kelly.

"Then what?"

"Beats me. I'm just making this up as we go along."

"You sure know how to give a guy confidence."

The best way to proceed, Kelly decided, was to act as if they knew exactly what they were doing. He threw his cigarette to the ground, tamped it out, and said loudly to Oz, "The lieutenant ordered me to take a look at it when I came off duty. Come along, give me a hand."

The two men walked over to the entrance of the physical plant building. Oz fervently prayed that the door would not be locked. Then he began thinking about the complications that would ensue if anyone else was inside the building, and he added that to his prayers, too. But within seconds, they were inside the building and it was indeed empty. Several bulbs hung from their wires throughout the space, providing weak illumination.

"Is this the only way they know how to do lighting?"

"Really. Maybe they should have kidnapped someone from Home Depot!"

A large diesel generator was directly in front of them, mounted in a shallow concrete pit designed to keep any oil or fuel leaks from the main floor. Down a dim hall to their left was a large boiler room, and a garage-sized door through which coal was brought to feed the boiler. Off to their right was a workbench and tool area.

On the wall directly to their right, neatly identified with Cyrillic script, was the demarcation point for the communications lines, and just beyond that was the main power panel with the feeds coming in from the grid.

The pilot began to trace the lines from the main panel to the generator, muttering to himself. Oz pushed him aside.

"This is my specialty, flyboy. You take inventory of whatever we can use in here, and I'll figure out how to kill their communications and power."

"Works for me, propeller-head. Just don't write a dissertation on it. We've got to be going back through that door within five minutes, or someone's liable to get suspicious."

Kelly quickly searched the entire building, and then returned to Oz, who was busy at the tool bench.

"What did you find?" Oz asked.

"Oh, nothing much. Just keys for their entire fleet of vehicles out there, several five-gallon jerry cans of gasoline, a rope, some bottles, and rags. How 'bout you?"

"Figured out how to kill their main power. That'll be easy. And if we cut these two lines it will bring down all their landline communications."

"How about the generator?"

"It doesn't kick in automatically. Someone has to come in here and start it. So I simply clipped all the fuel lines with this," Oz said triumphantly, holding up a large pair of diagonal cutters. "It's not going to be running anytime soon. And if we don't get out of here pretty quick, we're going to be swimming in diesel. Someone is bound to smell it before long."

"Excellent! Here's the plan. We're going to commandeer two trucks, one of the URAL-375s out there, plus the little UAZ-469. Then we—"

"Wait, wait, speak English."

"No way, man, we might be overheard!"

"No, that's not what I meant, Falcon. I don't know what all these truck number things are. Give it to me plain."

Kelly paused for a moment, and then said slowly, "I'm going to drive the big trucky, and you are going to drive the little jeepy. I will go first, and with my big trucky I'll run over the guards, trash the guardhouse, and punch through the gate. You will drive your little jeepy through the big hole I make in their gate, and follow me down the road until we are out of the line of fire of those guard towers. We'll leave my big trucky in the middle of the road, set it on fire, and then go merrily on our way. In your little jeepy. With me driving. How's that for a simple plan?"

"Sounds like a military guy thought of it, with all the death and destruction."

"I'll take that as a compliment."

"You shouldn't, flyboy. Let me propose a much simpler plan . . ."

****

Kelly had to admit it: Simmons' plan was excellent. It took them about three minutes to put the pieces in place. Using a pail and the rags Kelly found, Oz poured about two inches of diesel fuel into the pail, over the rags. Kelly threw one end of the rope over an overhead steam pipe, and tied it to the pail. He hoisted the pail about six feet above the floor and secured the rope around a leg of the workbench. Then they overturned several cans of gasoline, and the flammable liquid began pooling on the floor. After snipping the communication wires, they tossed a match into the pail, and yanked the main power switch.

The camp plunged into darkness, and even from within the physical plant building they could hear shouts around the camp. They slipped out of the building and crept between the vehicles. Very quickly, either the flame in the pail would burn through the rope, sending the pail tumbling to the gasoline-soaked floor, or the gasoline vapors would rise to the level of the burning rags in the pail. One way or another, there was about to be a conflagration.

Kelly wormed beneath the vehicles, and snipped the fuel lines of each except for their getaway jeep. Returning to the driver seat, he crouched down and waited. Oz was folded up on the floor in back. Over at one of the barracks he heard what must have been an officer giving a command to start the generator. Here and there flashlights were winking on.

Suddenly they heard the pail clatter to the floor, and with a violent *whump* the windows and doors blew off the physical plant. The blackness of the night was chased away by angry orange flames, jetting from every window and door. Shouts of *OGON', OGON',* filled the night and men poured forth from all the barracks.

When the confusion grew to a fever pitch, Kelly leaned out of the jeep window and bellowed in Russian, "SAVE THE VEHICLES!" He turned the key, and the little UAZ-469 roared to life. He slowly picked his way through a surging mass of humanity, some with buckets, some with fire extinguishers, and drove over to the main gate.

"Open the gate!" he shouted at the guards on duty.

"What's the password?" challenged the senior enlisted man, keeping half an eye on the fire.

"How should I know what today's password is, you idiot? We haven't been briefed yet! I'm not even supposed to be on duty until the morning watch! Lieutenant Suvarov ordered me to move the vehicles outside the fence before the fire burns them up, so that's what I'm doing. Now are you going to open the gate or do I have to go find an officer to order you to open it?"

The soldier looked back at the rapidly growing flames, shook his head and ran to open the gate. Kelly drove through, and kept right on going.

Chapter 15

Saturday, August 2, 1986: 0420 local
west of Tara, USSR

Oz climbed over the passenger side seat and buckled himself in as Kelly negotiated the rutted mountain road, driving as fast as he dared.

"Where are we, and what's next?" Simmons asked.

"No idea and haven't a clue," Kelly replied. "I'm guessing that we have maybe two hours before word gets out of our escape. Unless they have a battery-powered transmitter, there's no way the camp can communicate with the outside world. The most important thing at the moment is to get as much distance between us and them as possible."

The night was pitch-black, starry but moonless. Judging from the constellations, Kelly figured he was traveling due north. After about five kilometers the rutted trail ended at a larger, graveled road. Kelly came to a stop and looked both ways. To the right, the eastern horizon was slightly brighter, as though from the lights of a city. The western horizon was as dark as the zenith. Jake weighed their needs. They needed information and supplies, and these would be available only where there was a population. It was a risk, but nonetheless, Kelly turned east.

"The way I figure it, Oz, we've got to ditch this jeep somewhere they won't find it. Then we need to come up with civilian clothes. The next order of business is to find out where we are. We'll also need to work out food, travel, and possibly identity papers. Somehow we've got to get into a friendly consulate or sneak across a border.

"One more thing, Oz. From here on out, we speak only Russian—even when we're alone. I want you to forget you ever knew English. If you stub your toe I want you to say 'ouch' in Russian. Got it?"

"*Da!*"

****

Major Roman Romanovich Nikitin glumly watched the raging inferno that once was Prison 87's physical plant. Shortly after the camp lost power the fire broke out. Nikitin suspected that it began with someone's attempt to start the backup generator, though he had not yet questioned his men. In any case, the fire was impossible to fight by any means at hand. The few fire extinguishers they possessed were now empty and useless. Without electrical power the camp's well pump was inoperable, thus no water was available. The telephone lines were connected to the outside world through the physical plant, consequently they had no communications. The keys to the motor pool were also located in the burning building. By the time someone had thought of hot-wiring the vehicles they were fully enveloped in flames, thus they had no transportation.

This is probably my career going up in smoke before my eyes. I did nothing to cause this, I have no tools to fight this, but none of that will matter to the powers that be. I'm in command, therefore I'm responsible, and Chernikov is going to need a sacrificial lamb. Baaah.

"Major Nikitin, I think we must have one vehicle available to us." The speaker was Senior Lieutenant Suvarov. His face was grimy and blackened with soot and his uniform singed in spots from his attempts to fight the blaze.

"What?"

"Sergeant Bok is in charge of watch duty on the main gate at this hour. He just sent one of his men to inform me that, based upon my orders to save the vehicles, they let the UAZ through the gate shortly after the fire began."

"That was good thinking, Suvarov. Take the jeep and go into Tara to inform General Chernikov of our status. Go yourself, don't send anyone else. Tell him that we have no means of fighting the fire, no water, and no communications.

Request all assistance immediately."

"But, sir, I gave no such order. And the driver didn't know the gate password."

"Who was the driver?" asked the major. He rubbed his rusty-colored hair with a grimy hand.

"Bok's man didn't know who it was. Their company just arrived last week and they don't know the men in the other units yet."

"No matter. It's a mystery we can figure out later. Probably one of the enlisted men taking initiative when everyone else was milling about in a panic. Take the jeep and inform General Chernikov immediately."

"Yes, sir."

****

The dark forest fell away, and several hundred meters ahead there appeared a few dim lights. The road surface improved, a clear sign that they were approaching a town.

Kelly reminded Simmons, "Remember, Oz: we belong here. We're attached to the military camp ten kilometers behind us. We've no reason to be nervous."

"I'm good, Major. Don't worry about me."

Not a soul was stirring as they pulled onto a dark street with a few dwellings on either side. They continued until they arrived at an intersection where a small sign proudly proclaimed "Timino."

"My knowledge of tiny Russian cow towns isn't too good. Does 'Timino' ring any bells for you?" asked Kelly.

"None. Wait, Falcon . . . looks like there's a sign with an arrow another hundred meters ahead. Let's check that one out."

Kelly pulled forward until his headlights illuminated the sign. "Bingo! Tara! I overheard Chernikov speaking to one of his lackeys, and the name 'Tara' came up in that conversation. I think that's where Chernikov stays on the nights when his helo isn't parked at Club Med. Does the name 'Tara' get your geographical juices going?"

"Nope. Never heard of it."

"What good is a propeller-head who doesn't know anything? I thought you were working on a doctorate at MIT!"

"Easy, flyboy. You want to know the inter-electrode capacitance of two pure silver traces separated by 10 microns, I can tell you. But if you're looking for a guided tour of the smallest towns in the Soviet Union I'll have to confess ignorance. Besides, it's you Air Force guys who've targeted everything in the USSR. Surely this town is on your target list?"

"Nah. Biggest thing 'round here is probably the outhouse, and we don't target those. Don't want to create a biological hazard." Kelly turned in the direction of the arrow and accelerated.

"Whoa, cowboy! I thought you said that Tara is where the evil General Chernikov lives! Don't we want to go the other way? Didn't you want some distance between us and the bad guys? We are trying to escape, after all."

"Relax, Oz," Kelly said confidently, "it's the last place they'll look!"

****

The blaze had spread to the pile of lignite, but there was not much chance it would spread any farther, and there had been no additional explosions in the last half hour. The heat radiating from the conflagration was intense, and without water or fire-fighting equipment there was nothing anyone could do. So, except for protecting the other buildings, Nikitin had ordered the men to stand down.

"Major Nikitin, I've sent out three details and they have searched the entire perimeter and as far as five kilometers down the road. There's not a sign of that jeep," Suvarov reported wearily. Suvarov was Major General Chernikov's aide de camp, and served as Major Nikitin's assistant when the general was not on site.

The major seemed not to have heard. He was standing,

hands behind his back, watching the fire burn. His face, illuminated by the flickering light, was set in a stony mask.

"Sir?"

"I heard you, Lieutenant. Recall your squads. Major General Chernikov should be here at 0600 if he sticks to his normal schedule. By the time we could get a runner to a telephone in Timino, he'd have already left his quarters anyway.

"Pass the word: all three company commanders are to form their men up and take roll call. I want a complete list of the injured and missing in fifteen minutes. Ensure that the identities of those on watch duty at the gate, guard towers, and each cellblock are visually verified.

"Have the kitchen detail use their field equipment to prepare breakfast immediately. The whole camp is already up, might as well feed them.

"And please inform Captain Gromyko that I wish to see him immediately in my office. We'd better establish a detailed chain of events before the general arrives."

"Yes, sir."

****

"Good morning, General Chernikov," said Staff Sergeant Yuri Slavin cheerfully, as he held open the door on the Zil for his superior.

"Good morning, Yuri," Chernikov replied as he entered the vehicle. He began to peruse the stack of morning briefings that his bodyguard had placed on the seat.

Slavin shut the door, walked around the car and slid behind the wheel. About one hundred feet down the street, a man who'd been lounging against the side of a building smoking got into a car, which pulled out and followed Slavin as he drove the four kilometers to the helipad.

"You're being watched, General."

"I know, Yuri. Spotted them already, idiot KGB goons! For all their subtlety they ought to simply wear a sign saying, 'Big Brother's watching you!' I also have acquired a new neighbor in the flat above me, moved in last week. He always seems to be home when I am; never goes out, no known means of support. I hope our own men are not this obvious, Yuri."

"So do I, sir," the bodyguard said with a chuckle.

The pilot already had the blades spinning when Chernikov and Slavin approached the chopper from behind. They strapped in and the pilot lifted the craft into the air, pivoted, and began flying west toward Prison 87.

After a moment, Yuri pointed out a black, oily pillar of smoke rising in the distance, and shouted over the clatter, "What's that, sir?"

"Somebody's tractor must have cau—wait! My word! That's us, Yuri, that's the prison! Pilot," Chernikov barked, "Contact the prison on military frequency 34!"

The pilot adjusted a knob, spoke into his microphone several times, and then shouted back over the noise of the engines, "No answer, sir."

"Never mind, we'll be there in a minute."

****

The sun was peeking over the horizon when Kelly's jeep crested a small hill and started down the gentle grade, headed southeast. A large town spread out in front of him, smoke rising from several dozen chimneys. The red hue of sunrise shimmered on a wide river that looped lazily on the north side of the town and stretched out of sight to the southeast. Morning fog hung over some fields to the south. Had it not been for the circumstances, Jake would have stopped to enjoy the beautiful, peaceful view.

"Wake up, Oz. We're here."

His companion sat up and stretched, yawning. "Where's 'here?'"

"Beats me, but I think it's time to ditch our ride. I suppose this might be Tara in front of us, but whatever it is, it's big enough to serve our purposes."

"Think we can scare up some coffee?"

"That sorry question doesn't even deserve a response. You want to make me really unhappy, just throw in a comment about bacon and eggs."

A path on the left disappeared into the thick pine forest. Kelly turned onto the trail and drove until they were out of sight of the road. Spying a thicket, he maneuvered the vehicle into the densest part of the bramble. The two men spent the next twenty minutes dragging branches and dead falls over the little UAZ-469, and carefully brushing out the tracks where they left the highway.

"Nobody's going to find this. We might even be able to come back and use it again," said Oz hopefully.

"Not a chance. It'll take 'em a while, but they'll find it. They'll post a surveillance unit here, and we'd never see 'em. They'd nab us and put us back in the pokey. We're not even gonna come within a klick of this thing, ever again.

"C'mon, pardner. Time to do a little surveillance of our own. We need to grab some civilian clothes and some food. Word's going to get around fast if folks see a pair of soldiers out for a stroll. We need to blend in."

The unmistakable sound of a chopper sent the two men scurrying for cover beneath a large silver fir tree. Kelly located the aircraft: it was a Hoodlum with an attached crew pod, and it was heading in the general direction of Prison 87. "If that's Chernikov's chopper, then this must be Tara," he remarked to Simmons. "In a town this size, I can't imagine anyone other than the military having a Kamov."

The cover of the forest enabled the two men to get closer to the north side of the town without being seen. They found a dilapidated barn with a collapsed roof and decided to hole up until nightfall, figuring that the risk of getting caught stealing clothes in the daytime was just too great.

****

Duty roster in hand, Sergeant Andrei Yakimov was inspecting the watch party at each cellblock, since Nikitin had insisted on a visual verification of the companies' roll call. The sergeant was in a foul mood. Breakfast had been a disappointing affair and he was irritated by the knowledge that until power was restored, his unit's assignment to Prison 87 was turning into more of a field operation than the rest and refit it was supposed to be. They'd been pulled off the line in Afghanistan just three weeks prior, after a grueling and bloody tour. The whole unit was on edge, and now this.

He opened the door of cellblock 5, and looked in. The small guard office was dark and empty, and the steel door into the cell area was wide open. *That's odd*, he thought. He unclipped his baton and put the clipboard down on the desk.

"Hello? Hello? Anton, are you there?"

There was no response. The tough veteran stepped lightly to the right side of door and peered into the darkened hall. The doors of the first cells on the left and right were both open. In the gloom he could just make out a pair of bare feet sticking out of the one on the left. He shifted silently to the left side of the door to get a different view before entering the space, and spied an orange jumpsuit wadded up on the floor. *Uh-oh. Better not go through this door without backup.* Yakimov was in his tenth year in the elite Spetsnaz and reputed to be the toughest NCO in the company. But he'd not survived four tours in Afghanistan by taking stupid and unnecessary chances. He backed out of the building and called to three more men.

Together they reentered the cellblock. They found four dead men, all fellow soldiers from their own company. After quickly searching the remainder of the building, they examined the bodies of their comrades, two of whom were stripped naked.

"Get Lieutenant Suvarov here, *now!* And bring a flashlight!" Yakimov snapped at one of the men. He knelt beside the body of Sergeant Anton Kuznetsov, his best friend, a man who had joined the unit on the same day he had. It was too dark to see much, so he ran his fingers lightly over his friend's head and neck. There was a little matted blood in his hair from a brutal wound to his skull. *A baton, I'll bet.* He felt himself switch into combat mode. Grief could wait. A cold fury washed over him, and he was ready to kill.

****

The sky had brightened enough so that flashlights were no longer necessary in Major Nikitin's tiny office in the administrative building of Prison 87. Standing before him were Lieutenant Suvarov and Sergeant Yakimov.

"Report!" he snapped.

"Sir, all troops are accounted for but—" began Suvarov.

"Ah! You found the jeep?"

"No, sir. Major Nikitin, we have four fatalities, all in cellblock 5. And both prisoners are missing."

For a moment Nikitin was silent. Yakimov noted that the major's face had turned white; whether from rage or shock he could not tell. Then, in a steady voice the major asked, "What about injuries?"

"Each of the four appear—"

"*No*, Lieutenant! I asked for a full report on each company! We'll deal with the fatalities in a moment. We can do nothing for the dead, but I need to know what sort of medical assistance is necessary for the living."

"Yes, sir. First Company reports four dead, and no injuries requiring medical attention. Their cohort was posted at duty stations when the fire broke out, and was not involved fighting it. Second Company reports twenty-two casualties: five troopers with third-degree burns requiring medical evacuation, and seventeen with second- or severe first-degree burns. Third Company reports eleven casualties: all cases of second-degree or severe first-degree burns. Each company brought their own medical field equipment, so we should be able to handle everything but the third-degree stuff. But we will need about 150 more doses of antibiotics, and extra bandages and dressings. No officers were injured in any company.

"All of the Urals have been destroyed by the fire, and we now believe that the UAZ was stolen; in any case, we have no

vehicles. No other damage to either compound has been reported, and all fencing is intact. All prisoners are accounted
for and in lockdown, except the two escapees from cellblock
5."

"That would be Simmons and Kelly," observed Nikitin.

"Yes, sir."

"Now tell me about the deaths."

****

The Kamov settled onto the helipad.

"Stay here and don't shut it off," Chernikov directed. The
pilot nodded and throttled down to idle. Chernikov grabbed
his briefcase, and clamped his hat firmly on his head as he and
Slavin ran out from under the still-spinning rotors.

Major Nikitin and Lieutenant Suvarov were waiting to
greet him. Even as he was running up Chernikov was shouting to his second-in-command, "What's happening here, Major? Quick now!"

"Sir, we have an emergency situation. The fire you see has
knocked out our power, water, all communications, and has
destroyed all of our vehicles. We have thirty-seven casualties,
including four fatalities. There are five troopers requiring medical evacuation as soon as possible. And sir, we have two escapees."

Chernikov grimaced. The news could not have been worse.
"What have you done so far, Major Nikitin?"

"The prisoners are in lockdown, and all the troopers have
been armed." Even as he voiced the words, Nikitin felt keenly
the feebleness of his answer and the inadequacy of his actions. And yet the situation was still unfolding, even now, and
his responses had kept pace with each new development. He'd
nothing of which to be ashamed, but he braced himself for
the reaction he knew was coming.

"What? That's IT? That's ALL you've done?" rejoined the
general, raising his voice.

"Sir, the situation began about two hours ago when we lost

power. At the time we assumed that the outage was on the grid, not local. An explosion and fire in the physical plant followed, not five minutes later. We initially believed that the fire had broken out during an attempt to start the generator. All our efforts at that point were directed at controlling the fire. None of us had any reason to suspect that this was connected with an escape attempt. It is only in the last twenty minutes that I have learned of the escape. The integrity of the prison compound has been maintained at all times."

"The integrity of the prison compound was maintained at all times, you say, and yet two men managed to escape? How can you make such a statement?" Chernikov was shouting at his subordinate.

"Sir, if I may?" interjected Lieutenant Suvarov.

"Speak!"

"Sir, though we do not yet know how, the prisoners in Cellblock 5 managed to overpower and kill their guards sometime during the midnight watch. They then killed the new watch party that came on duty at 0400, took their uniforms, and walked to the administrative side of the facility without raising an alarm, since they appeared to be part of the midnight watch going off duty. Somehow they started the fire, then tricked the guards into opening the gate under the guise of moving the motor pool away from the fire. According to Sergeant Bok, the watch detail at the gate reported that the driver was uniformed, spoke flawless Russian, and claimed to be acting under my orders. We are guessing that the second man was hidden on the floor of the back seat."

"But how could two—two *scientists*, for crying out loud, overpower a pair of my commandos, let alone escape their cells? We designed these cells so that they could be unlocked only from the outside. Even if a prisoner managed to get hold of a key, the lock was impossible to reach from the inside. And the doors are self-locking: if they swing shut, they lock. So the only way for a prisoner to get out is if *both* guards enter the cell, leave the door open, and are overpowered by the inmate. And you know, Lieutenant Suvarov, it is a violation of my express orders for *both* duty guards to *ever* enter a prisoner's cell!"

"Yes, sir, I know. Nonetheless, that appears to be what happened, sir," replied Suvarov.

Chernikov forced himself to calm down. He knew his soldiers were good men; if he flew into a rage no one under his command would ever dare to take initiative again. He admitted to himself that Nikitin had taken the only steps available to him, and he realized that the information he was hearing was almost as new to his deputy as it was to himself.

"Cellblock 5, you say? That would be Simmons and Kelly," Chernikov observed.

"Yes, sir."

"Somehow Simmons must have gotten out of both his shackles and his cell, killed the guards, and freed Kelly. That just does not seem possible," mused the general.

"Actually, sir," replied Nikitin, "it appears that the opposite occurred. The corpses of both men assigned to midnight watch were found in Kelly's cell, not Simmons', and it does not appear that they have been moved."

"But Major Kelly possessed neither the skills nor the aggressiveness to kill two of my best Spetsnaz. He has demonstrated that in the sparring ring as well as in interrogation."

Suvarov spoke up again. "Sergeant Yakimov has a theory about that. He's been observing Major Kelly ever since he was brought to the camp, and he believes the man has had some sort of specialized military training in the past. It's Yakimov's opinion that what happened in the sparring ring several weeks ago was a bit of theater on Kelly's part, designed to deceive us. He thinks that Kelly taunted both guards into his cell, and they felt safe enough to enter, believing the major to be a coward."

"What evidence does Yakimov offer for this idea?" asked Chernikov, dubiously.

"None, sir. He just calls it a 'soldier's intuition,' sir. He claims that one special forces operator can recognize another. And the bodies of both guards *were* discovered in Kelly's cell, sir."

Chernikov nodded, and then began issuing a series of orders to recover the situation and hunt down the escapees. By the end of the day, a temporary generator was providing power and water, and the telephones had been reconnected. The following day the connection to the power grid was restored. Within a week, a new physical plant building would be under construction.

Chapter 16

Their first foray into Tara proved to be quite useful. Jacob Kelly and Oswald Simmons managed to steal a small chicken, and some rather unremarkable but warm work clothes from a clothesline. They verified that the town was indeed Tara and that the large river was the Irtysh, even though neither knew where on a map either would be found. Quite unintentionally they also located the helipad where Chernikov's helicopter was parked. With the addition of the work clothes to their small wardrobe, they would feel safe walking in the town in the daytime.

"They will be searching for us soon, you know," remarked Oz as he listened to the chicken sizzling over a slow roasting fire. They had returned with their prizes to the fallen-down barn. In one corner, situated under a part of the roof that still provided shelter, there was an old fire pit that now hosted a cheery fire. Evidently the deserted site had been used by vagrants before them.

"Oh, I expect that they had squads out shortly after dawn, trying to pick up our trail. In fact, tomorrow we need to move to the south side of town. Won't do to stay in one place too long," answered Jake. "I wouldn't be surprised if this spot is swarming with troops tomorrow afternoon, at the latest. When we leave tomorrow, we need to brush out any evidence that we've been here."

"That's why you insisted we pluck the chicken down by the river!"

Jake grinned and nodded, "You're learning."

"Who are you, Major? You seem to know about a lot more than just F-16s."

"Told you. I was a boy scout growing up. Now, why don't you tell me how in the world you learned that perfect Muscovite accent?"

Simmons shook his head. "Are you kidding? Why should I tell you about me when you won't tell about yourself," he replied, frustrated that Kelly wouldn't answer basic questions about himself. "Thought you were an Air Force pilot, but the way you've carried yourself today makes me wonder if you're not actually something else. It's irritating to get brushed off every time I ask you a personal question."

Kelly poked the fire with a stick before answering. "Oz, I really am a major in the Air Force and an F-16 test pilot. But I'm also something else for the Air Force, and I am prohibited by an agreement I signed from talking about it. I can't tell you because I gave my word to never tell anyone."

"Oh, I've got it. If you told me, you'd have to shoot me, right?" queried Oz, raising an eyebrow in mock suspicion.

Jake smiled. "Something like that, I guess."

"Okay, Mr. Mysterious. You can keep your secret. I suppose I can answer your questions without violating national security, as long as you don't ask me about things like embedded microprocessors, clock frequencies, or application-specific integrated circuits.

"As far as my Russian goes, I'm self-taught. Didn't have much difficulty with my high school math and science classes, so dad gave me a copy of Solzhenitsyn's *One Day in the Life of Ivan Denisovich* when I was a freshman and challenged me to read it. I was bored, getting into trouble—"

"Wait! You read Solzhenitsyn as a freshman?" Jake said with admiration. "Really? I was reading Marvel Comics when I was a freshman. What year was that?"

"'72."

"Wow. So, what does Ivan What's-his-name have to do with your knowing Russian?"

"The copy dad gave me was in Russian. I had to learn the language in order to read it," Oz said, grinning sheepishly.

"You're kidding!"

"Nope. Learned it, loved it, and began to devour

everything I could get my hands on regarding Russian culture. Studied a year at the Leningrad State University during my undergrad program, where I fell in love with a girl from Moscow."

"So that explains the accent," said the pilot. Oz nodded. "So what happened?" asked Kelly.

The other man paused, and looked away. "She developed spinal meningitis three weeks before the end of the spring semester. It was not properly diagnosed until it was too late. She died within a month," he said softly, his voice husky. "I was devastated."

Kelly nodded, not knowing what to say. "I'm sorry."

They sat in silence for a few minutes, until Simmons stirred again. "Yeah. Me, too." He cleared his throat. "That was six years ago. It was really the loss of my girlfriend that drove me to Christ."

"What do you mean, 'drove me to Christ?' What's that supposed to mean?" Kelly wasn't sure he liked the direction the conversation was taking. It wasn't that he was an atheist, it was just that he'd never had much use for religion and he preferred that people kept their religious thoughts to themselves.

"I guess God uses different ways of drawing people to Himself. I had no idea of what's really valuable in life until I experienced a significant loss. It wasn't until I was grieving about my girlfriend that I realized that my own life had no inherent purpose; there was no 'cause,' if you will, larger than myself and my own pleasures.

"Anyway, I knew there had to be something more. So I began reading, searching, and really observing life for the first time. It was like being adrift in an ocean amidst all the flotsam and jetsam of life, with no fixed point of reference, and not realizing that it was all in motion, that it was all going somewhere. When I dropped an anchor, so to speak, I began to see that everything was shifting and changing around me, flowing with the current, and I didn't like where that current was taking me.

"That's when I picked up a Bible and started to read. What I read there made sense of my life and what I was seeing around me. After studying it for several months I realized that I'd been searching for Jesus Christ all along, or rather, He'd been searching for me."

"So you got religion. But you're a scientist, right? How do you reconcile science and religion? Doesn't the one kind of eliminate the other?"

Simmons laughed. "Not at all. Science deals with the measurable, the observable, the repeatable. It's not competent to deal with the supernatural, which, by definition does not follow natural laws.

"Knowing Christ made me love science even more, because now I know the Author, the Creator! Mathematics and physics are among the most elegant works of art in all of life! They're beautiful. God is the great Artist, and He paints by numbers! It's a mathematical universe, and it makes sense because it's designed by a God who makes sense.

"There's no conflict for me. I can't wait to get back to my work at CSU and my students and my laboratory. When I found Christ, science came alive and I became alive at the same time. It was like going from black and white to color."

"Can we please talk about something else—anything else?"

Simmons laughed again. "Sure Falcon, whatever you want to talk about."

"Why are you laughing?"

"Because nearly everyone I tell about Christ responds the same way you just did: 'can we please change the subject!'"

"I'm not surprised. Religion is a very private matter."

"Well, I don't agree, but I'll respect your opinion on that point. Now, how are you going to get us out of this mess, and back home?"

"Me?"

"Well, yeah. Do you see any other military guys close by with 'special secrets?' After all, I'm just a helpless civilian. Aren't people like you supposed to rescue people like me?"

"I think you have me confused with Captain America. Anyway, I don't think you're going to like the rest of my plan."

"Why not, Captain America?"

"Because it involves breaking into Chernikov's quarters here in Tara."

Simmons rolled his eyes and groaned. "You're right. I don't like it. And why do we need to go into the fox's lair?"

"Because we've got to have detailed maps. The Soviet Union is not like the United States, where any guy off the street can stop into Kmart and buy a Rand-McNally road atlas. But Soviet general officers carry a travel kit that always includes a complete, non-classified map set of the USSR. We're going to lift Chernikov's map set, and anything else of value in his apartment."

****

Lieutenant General Valeriy Ivanovich Patrikeyev slammed the phone down, seething with rage. He'd just taken a call from Major General Chernikov and learned of the escapes of two Prison 87 inmates. Patrikeyev was unable—and unwilling—to believe that two prisoners could escape from a GRU facility guarded by dogs, a double set of electrified fencing, and three companies of Spetsnaz. It was a major embarrassment. Surely there was some laxity in the administration of the prison, some explanation that would make sense.

Patrikeyev was not concerned that the two would successfully escape the country. The nearest friendly border was India, well over twenty-six hundred kilometers south of the facility, on the other side of the rugged Hindu Kush mountains. The fugitives would have an easier time flying to the moon.

No, sooner or later the two would be apprehended. What really bothered the general was that he was going to have to cooperate with the KGB. Surveillance on all embassies and consulates at which the two might conceivably find sanctuary would need to be doubled or tripled. The number of agents assigned to the Trans-Siberian Railway would need to be beefed up, in addition to that of airports and bus stations in the Omsk Oblast. This sort of police action was clearly KGB turf. The GRU would lead the search for the escapees, but the cooperation between the two agencies would have to be extensive.

Under no circumstances could Simmons or Kelly have any contact with foreigners. If the GRU technology-harvesting operation became public knowledge, the damage to the USSR on the world stage would be incalculable. It would also place his own head on the chopping block.

Angry though he was, Patrikeyev didn't allow his anger to interfere with clear thinking. He wrote up a directive giving General Chernikov wide-ranging authority to commandeer and employ any military assets deemed necessary to locating and capturing Simmons and Kelly.

The general massaged his temples, trying to forestall a headache. He was reaching for the phone to order tea when it rang.

"General, Comrade Geredin is holding for you on line one." Patrikeyev swore vehemently, then apologized to his secretary and ordered his tea before picking up the call.

"Patrikeyev here," he barked.

"I assume that you'll need my help, General," said the head of the KGB, dispensing with faux pleasantries and small talk.

The head of the GRU's Ninth Directorate squeezed his eyes shut. He didn't want to answer, but his silence would make Geredin's victory complete. It galled him to know that Geredin had probably been informed of the escape before he had. The old KGB bear probably even knew that Chernikov had just called.

"Of course I will require the KGB's assistance," Patrikeyev replied easily. "We are, after all, playing for the same team, Anatoly, are we not?"

"You tell me, Valeriy. *Krasnyy Voskhod* is under your stewardship, and yet what just happened could result in a deep humiliation for Mother Russia. It was a foolish gamble to begin with, and this escape has exposed it as such."

Patrikeyev bristled, "I will not have my loyalty to the State questioned by the likes of you, Anatoly!"

"And how would you describe 'the likes of me,' Valeriy? Never mind! We haven't the time to trade insults. For the sake of the homeland, I offer the assistance of the KGB. What is your plan for recovering the fugitives, and what can we do to assist you?"

****

"Can't we just find a consulate somewhere?" asked Simmons. The two were discussing various ideas to complete their escape.

"No! Think about it, Oz. We have information that implicates the Soviets in kidnapping eight scientists plus two military officers, and making an unprovoked attack on an unarmed American military aircraft. There's no way they will let us get within a klick of a consulate, and they certainly aren't going to allow us to make our way to the U.S. Embassy in Moscow. They'll be expecting us to try. They'll have snipers posted at every possible location. Even if we did manage to get onto friendly diplomatic ground, they'd arrange a 'terrorist attack' on it just to ensure that we, and anyone we with whom we've had contact, die."

Simmons nodded, "I see what you mean."

"I think our best bet will be to get to a port city and either stow away or pass ourselves off as merchant marine seamen. One of the Black Sea ports, Odessa or maybe Sevastopol, would work, or maybe Nakhodka on the Sea of Japan."

"Let's try for the Black Sea, Kelly. At least if we get there and the shipping thing does not work out, we might be able to sneak across several borders and wind up in Turkey or Greece. But we'd never get across the North Korean border, even if we wanted to."

"Sounds good. Black Sea it is. Now we just need to find out where we are!"

It took another day, but the two were finally able to locate Chernikov's apartment building. They planned to figure out his apartment number in the afternoon, when the general would be at the prison camp. If it wasn't possible to break in without drawing attention they'd have to make other plans.

Chapter 17

Sunday, August 3, 1986: 1040 local
Tara, USSR

"Are you sure this is a good idea, Falcon?" Simmons asked. Sauntering into General Chernikov's flat wasn't quite the scientist's idea of an escape.

"*Da*. Relax, Oz. We'll have the advantage of surprise. And right now he's convinced we are on the run. He's going to be locking down all the transportation centers and sending patrols out in an ever widening radius from the prison. I can guarantee you he's not waiting for us to come through his front door."

"Well, I'm convinced we ought to be on the run, too, so that's something Chernikov and I agree on."

The two were walking into town, clothed as rough laborers. The only part of the costume that did not fit the picture was their shoes. Each was wearing a pair of military-issue boots that they had lifted off the guards in the prison. They'd made an effort to rub mud and sand over the black boots to scuff them up and take the shine off, but the high quality foot gear was still at odds with their worn clothing.

Kelly stopped and turned to his companion. "Tell you what, Oz. We'll call this little operation off if you can produce for me detailed maps of where we are, and detailed maps of where we need to go. Can you do that? No? Didn't think so. We've got to have those maps, and Chernikov's apartment is, at present, the only place I know of that we can find 'em."

"But this is Sunday. He's probably going to be home."

"I know. It's a risk. But if he is home and we pull this off successfully, it will probably give us a twenty hour head start before anyone knows. I'll bet his driver won't be looking for him until tomorrow. On the other hand, if we hit his apartment during the day, when he's gone, we'll only get an eight hour start, max, before he comes home and finds that we've been there."

"You're the boss, boss. But if we get nabbed, you're going to hear 'I told you so' from me until you're sick of it!"

They were a block from Chernikov's apartment building when Kelly spotted two men sitting in a black Lada sedan. His pulse quickened, and he murmured to Simmons, "Don't look now, but there are a couple of goons watching the building in that black sedan. Ignore it and act normal." He knew it was too late to run. But the men in the car ignored Simmons and Kelly as they walked by, causing the pilot to chuckle once they had passed out of earshot.

"I'd sure love to know what's so funny, because right now I'm sweating up a storm," said Oz. "I thought you said this would be the last place they'd look for us," he added, as they walked past the apartment building.

"Never thought I'd see it with my own eyes," Jake said, "but I just did."

"What are you talking about?"

"You know that special training I can't talk about? Well, they told us that the KGB and the GRU hate each other's guts, and they spy on each other. I didn't believe the instructor then, but I do now. The gorillas in that car? They aren't looking for us, Oz, they're spying on Chernikov. Unbelievable."

"So who are they?"

"Well, Chernikov must be GRU because he's military and the GRU is basically military intelligence on steroids. That means our friends in the car are probably KGB."

"What now, Captain America?"

"Keep walking, propeller-head. Too many eyes on the place today. They won't be on surveillance when he's at the camp, so we'll come back tomorrow. There goes our head start, right out the window."

✱✱✱✱✱✱✱✱✱

Sure enough, the surveillance team was gone when they came back the next day at mid-morning. The two stood outside and examined the five-story apartment building. It was unremarkable in appearance and architecture. Like most Soviet buildings, heat and hot water was provided from a central facility that serviced the whole area. Large insulated pipes ran along the ground from the heating plant several blocks away, rising up to cross the street above the height of traffic, and then descending and disappearing behind the apartment building at ground level.

"Chernikov is probably in a ground floor apartment," said Oz, looking at the building.

"How do you figure that?"

"Learned it when I was in Leningrad. The ground floor apartments are coveted because the water pressure is higher and the hot water warmer."

The two men entered the building and stood uncertainly for a moment in the lobby area. The *dezhurnaya*, a concierge with the authority to deny them entry, stood up and came from behind her desk. She was a large, hard-looking, officious woman.

"*Dobryy dyen'*, said Kelly pleasantly.

Frowning, the woman asked flatly, "What do you want?"

So much for charm, Jake thought. "I'm looking for Major General Chernikov's apartment."

"Papers, please," she snapped, holding out her hand. The way she spat out "please" made it an empty formality.

"I—I don't have them with me," Kelly said.

"Then you'd better leave," she said. She returned to her chair and glared at the two until they left the building.

"Wow. Wouldn't want to meet her in a dark alley," said Oz .

"You said it," agreed Kelly. "Come on. Let's see where those pipes go."

They followed the steam pipes around the rear of the building. The pipes entered the building through an opening in the foundation. A rusty door stood next to them. Kelly guessed that it was an entrance to a maintenance area, and he tried the door. It was locked, but the whole door handle and lock assembly were broken, and it opened with a slight tug.

"Don't look around," he whispered in Russian. "Just look like you know what you're doing." He walked through the door with Oz on his heels. They entered a large mechanical room containing a mass of piping, pumps, valves, and conduits. Over the hum of an electrical panel they could faintly hear the familiar sounds of a large apartment building: a door slamming, a baby crying, a muffled voice calling out, the heavy bass beat of music.

Kelly saw a door in the wall opposite him, and figured it must lead into an interior hallway. He opened it quietly and found that it did indeed open into a corridor. The pilot peered down the passageway in both directions. At the far end to his left was a door separating the hall from the lobby area.

No sooner had both men entered the hallway than a thick-set *babushka* wearing a colorful red scarf and an unpleasant expression came through the lobby door and started down the hall. She carried a canvas bag of brown-wrapped packages, and she walked as though arthritic in the hip. As she limped slowly past, eyes averted, Kelly could smell the pungent odor of cheese, and guessed that she was carrying her groceries.

"Comrade, can you help us?" Kelly asked.

She turned around in the act of opening her door, her expression full of suspicion. "What do you want?" she asked.

"We are trying to surprise General Chernikov. We both served with him in the Army several years ago, and we heard he was in town. We know he lives in this building, but we don't know which flat," answered Kelly, with what he hoped was a disarming smile.

She studied them intently for a moment, then said, "Number three," and entered her apartment, closing the door behind her.

"Told you it would be first floor," whispered Oz victoriously.

Despite the fact that he was sure the general was not home, his heart was pounding when he rapped on the door. Down the hall he heard the click of a door opening quietly, and knew that the old woman must be watching them.

"He's not there," she called down the hall. "He leaves early every morning."

"Ah. *Spasibo.*"

"*Pozhaluysta.*" She shut her door.

With a slight movement of his head, Kelly motioned that Oz should follow and the two left the building through the maintenance area. "We're attracting too much attention right now," he muttered once they were out of earshot. "Too many eyes on us. There's no way we could break in without being caught. We'll have to come back tonight and put the general out of commission so we can search his apartment."

"You're not going to kill him, are you?"

"Are you kidding? There'd be no quicker way of getting an entire army after us than assassinating a general. No way. We'll just knock him on the noggin, tie him up, and take what we need. But one day," he said, stopping to look Oz in the eyes, "once we are safely back in the States, I *am* going to come back over here on my own time, drop off the radar, and then, yes, I'll find him and kill him. I will take revenge on him for what he has done."

****

The KGB surveillance team they had spotted the day before was nowhere to be seen when Simmons and Kelly came back around nine-thirty that evening. They entered through the maintenance area again, not wanting to try their luck bluffing their way past the formidable *dezhurnaya* or whoever might have replaced her. The faint throb of a disco beat pounded from somewhere on a floor above, while the angry words of an arguing couple provided background noise on the first floor.

"You ready?"

Oz nodded, so Kelly tapped lightly on the door. There was no response so he knocked a little louder. He heard the dead-bolt sliding back, and watched the door handle. As soon as it began to turn he launched himself into the door, slamming it open and throwing Chernikov back onto the floor. Oz followed him in and quickly shut the door, being careful not to make any additional noise.

Chernikov tried to roll to his feet, but the furniture got in the way and he stumbled, falling back to the floor. Kelly managed to kick him in the solar plexus with a followup to the groin before the former Spetsnaz could get sorted out, and by then it was too late. A savage chop to the neck rendered him unconscious. It was over in fifteen seconds, and the faint rumble of disco never lost a beat.

****

In apartment 13, one floor above Chernikov's, Agent Ilya Dubinin sat down with a fresh cup of tea that he'd just brewed. He noticed that the reels on the sound-activated tape recorder were turning. *Perhaps the good general has just flushed the toilet,* he thought to himself as he picked up the headset to listen. For a moment, he heard nothing but some scrabbling sounds, and then he heard a voice he did not recognize say in Russian, "Found it, Oz. Here are the maps, a pistol with plenty of ammo, and a duffel bag we can use. There's even a pad of forms for issuing orders and requisitions. What have you come up with?" A different voice said, "I've sacked some food. And his wallet was chock full of rubles. Payday must have been pretty recent."

Dubinin called to his partner, Pavel Lyubov, "Pavel, come listen to this! Somebody has just rolled the general. Should we go down there and put a stop to it?"

"It would blow our cover, Ilya. We'd have a hard time explaining how we knew. Spying on the GRU is one thing. Getting *caught* spying on the GRU is another. It doesn't matter that we've been *ordered* to spy on Chernikov—if we get caught we'll be disavowed. You know that Geredin wouldn't save us from the fallout."

"*Pravda.* On the other hand, if the general is seriously injured or killed, and we don't try to help him, there's not a spot cold enough on the planet for the KGB to send us."

Pavel sighed, "True. Better to err on the side of caution. Get your weapon. Let's go down and see what's going on."

****

Chernikov's apartment had proven to be a gold mine. Jake and Oz each had a duffel bag over one shoulder, and were preparing to leave when the door burst open and the two KGB agents sprang in, weapons drawn. Neither American stopped to think, each simply reacted, but Kelly's reaction was borne out of combat experience whereas Simmons' reflected the dojo.

Jake jumped to one side, throwing off the aim of his opponent. But Oz stepped straight forward to close the range and launched a snap kick. The aggressive movement was all the warning the agent needed. Ilya fired an instant before Simmons' foot knocked the gun out of his hand, breaking the agent's wrist.

The bullet caught the scientist in the left shoulder, breaking his clavicle. The impact threw him, and he landed on top of the still-unconscious Chernikov.

Lyubov fired at Kelly and missed. Jake kicked the gun out of his hand, then tackled him, knocking over both agents. For a moment Lyubov and Kelly wrestled violently on the floor, throwing wild punches, until they each regained their feet. Dubinin was scrambling for one of the guns with his remaining good hand, but a vicious kick from Kelly snapped his neck and the agent collapsed. Kelly scooped up the gun and trained it on Lyubov. With a scowl, the Russian slowly raised his hands, chest heaving from the exertion of the fight, blood trickling from his nose.

"Turn around and put your hands on the wall," Kelly barked. When the agent complied, Kelly smashed the butt of the pistol down on his head, and the man slid down the wall, unconscious.

Jake looked around and saw Simmons, and for the first

time it registered that the scientist had caught a slug. He crouched down beside the fallen man, gently probed the back of his shoulder for an exit wound. Kelly breathed a sigh of relief: it was a close thing, but the projectile missed his friend's carotid artery by a good ten millimeters

A curious, fearful face peeked in the door, and Jake shouted, "Stay away, get away! Go, get a doctor!" The face disappeared. Kelly helped the tall scientist up from the floor and laid him on the couch.

Working quickly, he fashioned a bandage that slowed down the blood flow from Simmons' shoulder. Jake was torn; he didn't know whether to run or stay. At any moment more people were going to burst through that door, and Jake had no desire to injure non-combatants. But he couldn't leave Simmons.

"Go, Falcon, go! Get out of here. Go while you still can," Oz insisted. He saw the uncertainty on the pilot's face. "Look, we knew this could happen. I knew it could happen. One way or the other I'm going to be okay. Either the Sovs patch me up and throw me back in that prison, or I die and go to be with the Lord. It's going to be okay. But you've got a chance to run, Falcon. Do it! Go! Get back to the States and tell 'em what's going on over here! NOW MOVE!" With his last bit of energy, Oz shouted in Jake's face.

Jake stood up, shocked. He picked up both duffels, and looked back at Oz. Simmons grinned at him and said, "You are one bone-headed stick jockey. Now get your butt moving." He held his right hand out, and Jake shook it, grinning back at him.

"Okay, propeller-head, I'm leaving. But I'll be coming back, and when I do I'm going to bring some of my buddies with me. It might take me a year. If they relocate you somewhere, Oz, be sure to leave a forwarding address."

Jake collected all the weapons from the floor, and stuck the extras in his duffel. Waving one of the pistols, he moved out into the hall. Oz heard him shout, "Back, everybody get back! Somebody go get a doctor!" Then he heard the door of the maintenance area slam. He clutched the makeshift bandage on his shoulder, and breathed a prayer for his friend.

****

Falcon ran out of the building, a heavy duffel bag over each shoulder. He slipped the pistol into his waistband and covered it with his shirt. Suddenly he knew what do to. Setting a brisk pace, he ran the four kilometers to the helipad.

Crouching in the shadows, he surveilled the area. After ten minutes he located two guards in the darkness, one next to the chopper and one patrolling the perimeter. Every two or three loops around the helipad, the men would switch places.

For a moment he considered how he could finesse an approach, but then decided it would take too much time. Brute force it would have to be. He crept around to the darkest part of the perimeter, and lay in wait behind a bush for the patrolling guard. As the man came past, he smashed the butt of his pistol on the soldier's skull, and caught him before he fell, laying him softly on the ground. He wrestled the man out of his field jacket, took his cap, and slung the soldier's AK-74 over his shoulder. It was not much of a disguise, but it would do in the dark, allowing him to close the range with the other guard.

He dropped his right arm, concealing the pistol behind his leg, and walked toward the other guard, who at first ignored him, not sensing any danger. But something about Jake's stride alerted him and the guard called out, "Pyotr? Is that you?"

Kelly aimed his pistol at the guard and commanded, "Lay your rifle on the ground, and don't make any fast moves." The soldier gingerly pulled his assault rifle from his shoulder, holding it by the strap, but then whipped it around on its sling, catching Jake in the side of the head with the butt. Stars exploded in Kelly's eyes, and he struggled to retain consciousness. He started pulling the trigger on his semi-automatic pistol, firing three, then four times. He felt blood trickling down the side of his face, and he fell, lapsing into unconsciousness.

It was the cold dew on the grass that brought him to. He

groaned, and felt dried blood caked on the side of his head, then remembered what had happened. His head was throbbing as he staggered to his feet. He collected his pistol, and wondered how long he'd been unconscious. He grabbed the wrist of the body of the soldier and checked his watch, and then decided to take it.

His dizziness subsided, though the pain did not. After slapping a fresh magazine into his pistol, he trotted over to the edge of the field, recovered his duffel bags, and returned to the helicopter. As he had hoped, it was unlocked. He climbed in and turned on the map light. He had to locate himself, and come up with a plan.

Within a few minutes he'd found Tara on General Chernikov's map set. He sat back for a moment, thinking. Even though he had to get moving before the next shift of guards arrived, he now had the valuable asset of the helicopter and he didn't want to waste it. He'd get just one hop out of it and he had to make it count.

Nakhodka would be his destination, he decided, rather than the Black Sea ports. Because it was farther and a more difficult journey, they would not immediately suspect that he'd go there. He examined the maps again. Omsk was 215 kilometers south-southwest of him, and the Trans-Siberian Railway (TSR) went through the city. The eastern terminus of the railway was Nakhodka.

He knew from his briefings that the KA-26 had a range of about four hundred kilometers. He plotted a southeasterly course that would leave him near the railway when the chopper ran out of fuel. If everything worked just right, he'd put about 250 miles between him and General Chernikov in a little under three hours, and then maybe he could hop a train.

Chapter 18

The eastern rim of the horizon was becoming visible when Kelly began to think about landing. Based on his flight time and the status of the fuel tanks when he left Tara, the pilot guessed that he had about 20 minutes of fuel remaining. He was exhausted: trying to stay below the radar without crashing into the darkened terrain below him had made it a very tense flight.

Kelly swung south to find the TSR. Before he ditched the chopper he wanted to pinpoint the location of the rails. It was his ticket east, or so he hoped.

The TSR is one of the longest railroads in the world, originating at the picturesque Yaroslavsky Station in Moscow and stretching nearly fifty-eight hundred miles east to link up with the port city of Vladivostok on the Sea of Japan. Crossing seven time zones and an entire continent, it's actually a network of railroads linking Russia to Mongolia, Manchuria, China, and North Korea. A sturdy traveler can board the train in Moscow, and get off in Pyongyang, if he doesn't mind sitting for nine days. Beijing is another stop in the web of rails branching off in dendritic fashion from the main route. The railway was built between 1891 and 1916, and one of the major engineering challenges was bridging the numerous mighty rivers that have, for centuries, carried Siberia's goods. The TSR carries around 30% of Siberia's freight, and is one of the most heavily traveled rail corridors on the planet.

After about five more minutes flying due south, Kelly picked up the gleam of rails reflecting the headlight of a westbound locomotive. His mission accomplished, he banked the chopper and flew northeast over an uninhabited, darkened landscape.

Fifteen minutes later he landed the KA-26 in an isolated meadow, surrounded on all sides by thick forest. Out of habit he did a complete shut down, then thought again and left all the avionics running so that the battery would drain. Jake shouldered his duffel bags, and began striding steadily south southeast.

****

Oswald Simmons was led by three guards into Major General Chernikov's office, where he was shoved into a metal chair. His shoulder was bandaged, and the wound seemed to be healing rapidly. Oz had no complaints about the medical care he'd received. *Apparently*, he thought, *they still consider me a valuable resource. I haven't even been beaten since the escape. Not yet, anyway.* His hands and feet were again shackled, as they had been prior to the escape.

Chernikov ignored him, working with his secretary on a small pile of paperwork. Intruding through the open window were the sounds of construction, as Prison 87's physical plant was being rebuilt on the foundations of the original building. Simmons' guards stood impassively on either side of him at full attention. Oz remained silent, not wanting to provoke Chernikov's mercurial anger.

"At ease," the general barked. The guards on either side relaxed slightly. "Dismissed," he snapped a moment later. The three troopers left the room, shutting the door behind them. After another five minutes of low conversation that had to do with repairs to all the damage the two escapees had wrought, the secretary, who was himself an enlisted Spetsnaz, gathered up the paperwork and left the office.

"Ah, Professor Simmons," Chernikov began pleasantly, "how is the shoulder this morning?"

"Fine, sir. The care I have received from your men here has been quite good. I have no complaints. Thank you for asking. And how is your neck, sir?"

"Stiff and painful, although the bruise is disappearing." Chernikov's good humor evaporated like rain on a hot summer sidewalk, and Oz observed the general's face darkening. He prepared himself for the rage that was sure to follow.

"Between you and Major Kelly, Professor Simmons, you've killed six of my men in the last week, and caused severe burns to another two dozen. You've also killed a KGB agent and wounded another. You've made my men and me look bad in the eyes of my superiors." Chernikov came around his desk and stood in front of Simmons. He drew his pistol. "I'm not entirely convinced I should allow you to live, Professor. You've given me nothing of value and you've cost me a great deal. Why should I let you live, Professor Simmons?"

Okay, Lord, if this is it could we just cut to the chase? Would You please make him put the bullet right between my eyes? I really don't want to lose fingers, toes, knees or elbows. "Well, General, my mom would probably appreciate it if you didn't kill me. That's one reason."

"I'm not in the mood for humor, Professor," Chernikov snapped. He checked the safety on his weapon, then began to pistol-whip the scientist. After three or four minutes of abuse, the flesh on Simmons' face was torn badly and bleeding profusely.

As blood ran down Simmons' neck and stained his orange prison jumpsuit crimson, a thought began to form in his mind. *Give him what he wants. Tell him what Falcon's plans are, because I know Falcon has already changed his plans, anticipating that I'd be interrogated. And cooperating is not a bad idea. I followed numerous false leads when I was working on integrated circuit miniaturization. Why don't I just lead their researchers down some of those same blind alleys? It will provide the appearance of cooperation without giving them anything truly valuable. If I drag it out long enough, perhaps the situation will change. Maybe we'll be rescued or ransomed.*

He nodded his head, eyes averted, and whispered, "Okay, General. You win."

"What?"

He raised his head, putting an expression of misery and guilt on his face. "You win, General. I just can't take this. I'll tell you anything you want to know. Please, just don't hit me again."

Twenty minutes later, while Oz was getting his face patched up, orders were going out to army and KGB units between Tara and the Black Sea port cities to set up check points at all the transportation centers, and to quarantine the foreign consulates in all the affected cities.

****

For the next two days Kelly walked east, staying in the forest, keeping the train tracks visible several hundred yards off to his right. Numerous trains passed, going in either direction, but always moving much too fast to hop. Halfway through the second day after ditching the helicopter he'd still seen no sign of human habitation, other than the railroad tracks.

He felt a sprinkle on his neck and looked up. The weather was closing in with a lowering sky and a chilly rising wind. He decided to stop for the day and seek shelter; getting wet in this country was to be avoided if possible. To the north he could see a craggy hill rising several hundred feet, with a sheer rock face. Heading for it, he scouted the base and located a cave-like indentation in the rock. There was plenty of overhang under which to keep dry, so he dropped his two duffel bags and proceeded to build up a stock of firewood. Though he had some canned food from the raid on Chernikov's apartment, Jake didn't want to use it until he had to. The rain hadn't begun in earnest yet, so he decided to spend the rest of the afternoon hunting for game. He felt sure that he was still too far from any dwellings for the report of the rifle to be heard.

By late afternoon he'd bagged a small doe, and by the time darkness had fallen he had a cheery fire going in his shelter with both haunches of the deer roasting over it. A single crack of thunder announced the arrival of the storm, and shortly after a cold, steady rain began to fall. It remained dry under the overhang.

It was the first time since escaping that he had the time

and inclination to go through the loot they had taken from Chernikov's flat. Jake spread the stuff out, intending to reduce his travel load to a single duffel bag. Initially, he decided to keep the money and maps, several changes of clothes, the uniform he'd used to escape from Prison 87, a pair of boots, heavy coat and gloves, the pad of forms on which Chernikov wrote orders, a combat knife, several pistols with ammunition, and a shoulder holster. A dozen or so cans of food were keepers. What he wasn't sure about were more clothes, a second heavy coat, another pair of boots, and the two AK-74s he'd taken from the helicopter guards.

He pulled one of the pieces of venison off the fire, cut off a hunk, and sat eating his supper while he mentally sorted out what to keep and what to ditch. After finishing supper, he disassembled the rifles, then repacked both duffels, putting an AK-74 into each. He'd decided to keep everything. What he didn't need himself, he might be able to sell or trade for something he did need, like coffee, a coffee pot, and a water container. A sheet of plastic or a tarp would be helpful, too.

****

A long freight rumbled by on the westbound tracks, the heavy coal cars rocking ponderously and click-clacking as they crossed a joint in the rails. From his vantage point Kelly could hear occasional snapping and popping as the pantographs on the locomotives contacted the electric wires above the railway.

He picked up his duffel bags, and resumed walking east. By midmorning he was seeing more roads, and even occasional traffic. Knowing that he would look far more suspicious trying to keep to the dwindling forest, he abandoned the woods and walked along the highway. It turned out to be the M51 federal highway.

He hadn't been walking along it for more than thirty minutes when a large eighteen-wheel end-dump filled with sugar beets passed him and pulled off on the shoulder several hundred meters ahead. The driver climbed down from his cab and walked around the truck, checking the tires. When he was done with his inspection he leaned against the truck and watched Kelly approaching on the other side of the road. The man was dressed in rough work clothes and an old pair of black combat boots. He was short, powerfully built, clean-shaven, and bald, with a wind-burnt face. Kelly could see some tattoos on his forearms. He guessed the man to be in his forties.

"Where you headed, soldier?" the man asked in a friendly tone.

"East," Kelly replied.

The man's eyes narrowed a bit. "Where east, comrade?

Kelly kicked himself. *This is the Soviet Union, Jake! People don't just wander here!* He visualized the map in his mind, and then said, "Novosibirsk, or just above it, actually. I mustered out a few weeks ago. How did you know I was a soldier?"

"Saw your duffel bags. They're military issue. What unit were you with?"

"106th Guards, Airborne Division. We were in Afghanistan when my enlistment was up, so they shipped me home. They gave me enough money to get home, but a week ago I got into, well, a little game of chance in Omsk, and I, well, I lost all my money," Jake said, hoping that the expression on his face was sheepish. "So I've been walking and catching a ride here and there ever since."

"106th? No kidding. I served in that unit up until ten years ago. Is Colonel Chernikov still around?"

Oh, great, Kelly thought, *now I've stepped in it*. "*Nyet*, not anymore. He got bumped up to military intelligence some time ago. I hear he's a major general now. Current commander is Colonel Ustinov," Kelly lied. He said the first Russian-sounding name that came to his mind.

"Ustinov? Never heard of him! What unit did he come from?"

"Uh, beats me. None of us had ever heard of him either. But then, colonels and majors were too far above my pay grade for me to know anything about them. All I know is they give the orders and we obey."

"*Da,* you got that right. Well, comrade, I can't let a brother soldier walk to Novosibirsk, not when I'm taking this load of beets there. If you want a ride, get in."

"*Spasibo.* I really appreciate it!" Kelly walked around and climbed into the passenger side of the cab.

The driver got the truck rolling, and shouted over the rattling growl of the diesel, "Name's Ivan. So what's your name, and what's in Novosibirsk?"

"I'm Dmitriy. My family works on a farm about ten kilometers north of Novosibirsk."

"I know the area south of the city like the back of my hand, but I've never been on the north side." Jake breathed a sigh of relief, but it was short-lived, for Ivan continued, "Tell me all about your family and your farm."

"I, uh," Kelly stammered, "I'd love to tell you about my family. But, uh, you go first. I want to hear about your family, and your time in the 106th."

Luckily for Kelly, the gregarious trucker loved to talk and with a little prompting whenever Ivan started to wind down, the pilot managed to keep him talking for the next 230 kilometers.

****

"One more time, please," requested Geredin, as he sat in his office on the third floor of the Lubyanka in Moscow. His aide rewound the tape, and after queuing it to the proper place he pressed *Play.*

> *Go, Falcon, go! Get out of here. Go while you still can! Look, we knew this could happen. I knew it could happen. One way or the other I'm going to be okay. Either the Sovs patch me up and throw me back in that prison, or I die and go to be with the Lord. It's going to be okay. But you've got a chance to run, Falcon. Do it! Go! Get back to the States and tell 'em what's going on*

> *over here! NOW MOVE! . . . You are one bone-headed stick jockey. Now get your butt moving.*
>
> *Okay, propeller-head, I'm leaving. But I'll be coming back, and when I do I'm going to bring some of my buddies with me. It might take me a year. If they relocate you somewhere, Oz, be sure to leave a forwarding address . . . Back, everybody get back! Somebody go get a doctor!*

The KGB director rubbed his chin. "What do you make of that?" he asked his aide.

"Pretty obvious, sir. He intends to blow the whistle on this GRU fiasco, if he's able to escape the country. The rest of it, about getting his friends together—just hot air, Comrade General."

The head of the KGB sat thinking after his aide left. Geredin doubted very seriously that Kelly would be able to escape the country. But if by some chance he was able to slip through their fingers, Geredin would see that the major was assassinated as soon as he arrived in the USA. And perhaps he would take out Chernikov, for good measure. *That would discourage other lunatics from launching such damaging projects*, he thought.

Chapter 19

Kelly looked down from the pedestrian overpass at the huge Inskaya marshalling yards. Brightly painted locomotives, rusty hoppers, gondolas and boxcars, flatcars filled with who-knows-what, tankers and other rolling stock trundled busily beneath him. It was the largest rail yard he'd ever seen, and he hoped it would be his ticket east.

South of the yard was a large forested park several kilometers wide. It was largely undeveloped, and Jake had located an untraveled portion and set up a hidden camp. He intended to spend several days watching the trains and getting a feel for the ebb and flow of rail operations. The last thing he wanted to do was hop a train that would take him somewhere he didn't want to go.

****

The alarm clock jangled. Anatoly Geredin groped for it, managing to shut off the alarm just as his phone rang. Uttering a few well-chosen epithets, the old man answered the phone.

"Geredin. Speak."

"General Geredin, this is your four AM wake-up call," said the pleasant voice of the female duty officer at the KGB's Moscow office.

"Thank you, Tamara," he replied, and hung up the phone. For a moment he lay in bed and took inventory of his latest aches and pains. The dull ache in his lower back was there, and his right hip hurt, a casualty of arthritis. He rubbed his left shoulder, and found to his satisfaction that it was not aching. It would be a good day, he decided.

Throwing back the covers, the elderly head of the KGB stumbled groggily to the bathroom to begin his morning ablutions. He noted with approval that his aide had hung a freshly laundered uniform on the clothes hook the night before.

The first indication that something might be wrong was when the aide did not show up with his morning tea while the general was shaving. *Perhaps his alarm malfunctioned*, he thought. *I'll growl at him to keep him on his toes. But he's a good and faithful man, so I won't be too hard on him.*

His impatience grew, however, when the customary cup of tea had not shown up by the time he finished dressing. Geredin left his bedroom and descended the stairs carefully, favoring his bad hip. There were no sounds of anyone else stirring, but the kitchen light was on. He limped into the kitchen and was startled to find Lieutenant General Valeriy Ivanovich Patrikeyev sitting at his table, sipping a cup of tea and reading the morning edition of *Pravda*.

"How did you get in here?" roared Geredin, trembling with a combination of rage and shock.

"Your back door," replied Patrikeyev calmly, pouring the shaken Geredin a cup of tea and pushing it across the table to him.

"But my men—"

"Are all trussed up and pleasantly sleeping in your outbuilding, General. Please sit, Anatoly, you'll aggravate your hip if you continue to stand. I took the liberty of fixing some tea. I hope you find it to your satisfaction."

Geredin sat heavily, disconcerted. "But how . . . ?" He didn't finish, and dismissed his own question with a wave of his hand.

"Really, General Geredin, the KGB is not the only service that knows how to carry out a clandestine operation. Penetrating your security was child's play. I wanted to have a private chat with you, and that's why I did not use the front door, so to speak."

Geredin nodded and sipped his tea, getting his irritation

under control. He was flustered, but he was not about to allow this GRU officer to know.

"Well, Valeriy, you seem to have my undivided attention. Tell me what's on your mind."

"Lay off Chernikov."

"He's a fool, Valeriy! Project *Krasnyy Voskhod* is a disaster, a fool's errand! And he has bungled the management of it, allowing Major Kelly to escape. If Kelly is able to get word out, Mother Russia will be humiliated in the sight of all nations."

"I admit, Anatoly, mistakes have been made. But we have also had great success. The new propeller on the Project 877 submarines is a testimony to that. Kelly will be recaptured, I have no doubt of that. But your threats and intimidation do not help. Chernikov is not going to be able to focus on what's in front of him if he's always looking over his shoulder."

"His bungling is inexcusable. The GRU will embarrass us all!"

"And how about the KGB bungling, Geredin? Your men were spying illegally on a general officer attached to the military intelligence directorate of the General Staff of the Soviet Army! What's worse, they allowed General Chernikov to be beaten and robbed, right under their noses. Four of your men, two inside and two outside, were holding guns on Kelly and could not stop him. You wish to talk about bungling, General? Fine! Let's begin with the KGB!"

"Are you worried about your golden boy, General Patrikeyev? Does he need a protector?" needled Geredin, trying to change the subject.

Patrikeyev's face was red with rage as he stood up, but his voice was controlled, just above a whisper, when he responded. "A protector? Do you jest? The man is a veteran of Afghanistan! Let me tell you something, General Geredin! If your boys get in Chernikov's way, he won't need my help, he won't ask for my help. Some of your people will simply disappear."

"Are you threatening me, or the KGB, Valeriy?"

"Wouldn't think of it, Anatoly. Well, I'm afraid I've got to get back to work. I enjoyed our little, ah, chat. And thanks for the tea. You'll find your bodyguards tied up in the back shed. They should be waking up anytime. I'm sure they'd appreciate some help." Patrikeyev started for the back door.

"I'll have my driver see to it," Geredin grumbled as he stood up.

"Oh, that's another thing," General Patrikeyev said as he stood in the open door. "You're going to need a new driver this morning. Your regular man slipped on a patch of ice and had to be taken to the hospital."

"It's summer, Valeriy, there is no ice."

"That's right, Anatoly. There is no ice," Patrikeyev replied with a smile that would have looked natural on a shark. He closed the door and disappeared into the early morning gloom.

****

It took several days, but Major Kelly finally located the local watering hole where the railroad workers gathered for drinks at the end of their shift. It was a noisy tavern north of the yard across the street from the main gate. He had figured that the best way to overhear talk of train destinations and learn on which tracks eastbound consists were built would be to hang around the workers and keep his ears open.

At four o'clock in the afternoon the massive steam whistle located above one of the yard control towers hooted, and workers began streaming toward the north entrance gate on the boulevard. Kelly merged with the crowd and crossed over to the *Nochnaya Smena*, the bar appropriately called the Night Shift. As he opened the door he was assaulted with the smell of heavy cigarette smoke and beer, and the raucous sounds of boisterous conversation. The conversation stopped briefly as the other patrons turned to stare at the newcomer. Like any tavern in the world located next to a major industry, it functioned as a meeting place for the locals; it was their turf. Visitors were looked upon as intruders.

Jake ignored the cold stares, elbowed his way to the bar,

put down twenty kopecks and ordered a beer. The barkeep slid a tankard full of the foamy beverage over to him, glaring at him balefully. "*Spasibo,*" Kelly acknowledged, ignoring the hostility. He looked about and found an empty booth from which he would watch the door. After a few minutes the buzz of conversation resumed and he thought that he had been forgotten. But when a burly fellow walked up to his table and demanded he leave, he realized he was mistaken. Big, bald, and sporting a gold earring and a gold-capped tooth, the bouncer was wearing the dirty overalls of a rail worker who'd had a long day. Kelly observed enough knife scars on his face to know that this was not the fellow's first dance. Conversation stopped again and Kelly perceived that the rest of the room had an idea of what was about to happen. *At least, they think they do*, he mused.

"Do you work in the rail yard," the man asked coldly.

"*Nyet,*" Jake replied.

"Raised here?"

"*Nyet.*"

"Then leave. This place is for locals and rail workers. Get out."

Jake almost replied, "It's a free country," but caught himself. Instead, he looked the stranger up and down contemptuously and then replied, "*Nyet.*"

His opponent shrugged, reached down and grasped the front of Kelly's shirt and yanked him up. *Bad move, Kojak.* It was clear that the brawler was accustomed to winning by intimidation and wasn't expecting resistance. Rather than trying to break free, Jake used the man's own motion and force to draw him in. A knee to the groin and a sharp jab to the kidneys when the man doubled over put the bouncer on the floor. Jake leapt, poised to crush the man's neck with his boots, but purposefully stepped aside at the last instant. It was obvious to everyone watching that he'd pulled up short of putting the fellow in the hospital, or worse.

He reached down and helped the man up, seating him on the other side of his booth, then called out to the bartender, "A beer for my friend, and something salty to go with it."

Conversation slowly resumed around the smoke-filled room, though the other patrons stole occasional sideways glances at Kelly's table. The pilot sensed the confrontation was over, for now.

"That was a neat piece of work," the would-be bouncer grudgingly admitted after downing half his beer.

"You weren't expecting it," said Kelly. "If you'd been ready, we'd probably still be throwing punches."

The other man nodded. Then he said, "This bar is where the rail yard workers gather. It's for us. We don't like snitches or secret police, political officers, or government officials. If you belong to any of those groups, finish your drink and leave. If not, you can stay as long as you behave yourself and mind your own business."

"Wait a minute, comrade. I just put you on the floor without so much as getting my hands dirty. Now you're threatening to throw me out again?"

"You did pretty good against me. How do you think you'd do against the house?"

"Ah. I see your point. Well, as a matter of fact, I don't much care for the four groups you just named either. I'd just as soon stay clear of 'em myself."

"You on the run?"

"At the moment I'm seated," Kelly replied with a smile.

The bald man stared at him for a moment. Kelly knew he was being evaluated. Gold-tooth finally came to a decision. "Keep your secrets. As long as I vouch for you, comrade, no one here will bother you." He stood, slapped Kelly on the back as if he were an old friend, and then wandered off into the cigarette haze. Jake knew that the back slap was a signal to the rest of the patrons that he'd passed the test.

For the next several days he visited the bar, eavesdropping on conversations among the weary yard workers. He learned on which tracks the eastbound consists were built, as well as the westbound. He also discovered that there was a special section devoted to shipping bound for the eastern seaports.

****

The dying embers of the campfire glowed a dull orange, like a faint beacon in the gloom of night. A wisp of smoke rose into the sky, merging with the overcast, through which the moon occasionally peeked. The wind carried a muted rumor of the rail yard several kilometers to the north as night trains moved along the rails to their far-off destinations.

Snap! The breaking stick sounded like a pistol shot in the dark forest. There was a muffled curse, and the four shadowy figures froze. After a moment the four resumed their stealthy approach toward the fading orange coals. They split up and quietly encircled the campsite. In another ten minutes they were standing about the fire ring staring at the embers, and swearing bitterly.

"Wonder if someone warned him," said one.

"It's possible. The men at the bar have warmed up to him the last few days," replied Pyotr Fedin. Fedin was a KGB stooge who frequented the tavern across from the rail yard. He was a dirty, slovenly man whose two passions in life were vodka and trains, in that order.

"How would the men at the bar know, Fedin?" queried Stanislav Emsky, the chief railroad bull for the Inskaya yards and a local KGB official. Emsky was a compactly-built man with broad, muscular shoulders and a handlebar mustache. He wore a black bowler hat, a fancy he'd acquired from having seen a western movie featuring turn-of-the-century railroad detectives.

The three looked at Fedin.

"Wait a minute, comrades! I haven't said anything to anyone!"

"Really?" Emsky asked, glaring at the frightened man.

"Really! Think about it! You know how they are: if those men knew I worked for you, they'd kill me! And if I double-crossed you, you'd kill me! I have every reason to keep my mouth shut, comrade, and no reason to talk," Fedin insisted.

Emsky stared at him for a minute, and a cruel smile formed on his lips. He nodded, "You're right; if you double-cross me you'll simply disappear, Pyotr, and no one will ever find your remains."

Fedin stared at the fire for another moment. Then a thought came to him. "I'll bet a bottle of vodka that he's hopped the westbound freight. This afternoon he was asking about westbound trains. I heard Oleg mention the weekly coal train bound for Odessa, and he seemed very interested."

"Could be. That train pulled out two hours ago," observed Emsky, checking his watch. "Is it non-stop?"

"Oh, no. It stops in several places. Omsk is the first," Fedin replied. The man was a slob, but he had the schedules of the regular trains committed to memory.

"Pasha," Emsky said to his deputy, "contact the Omsk office. Have the train stopped and searched. And send a message to Major General Chernikov. The description of this bum fits the man on the bulletin. Tell him we might have a lead. Oh, and Pasha, double the security on the entire rail yard for the next week."

"Yes, sir, right away."

But it was too late, for at that moment Kelly was hidden in an empty eastbound boxcar, five kilometers distant, accelerating away from the sprawling Inskaya marshalling yards.

****

Sam Bergman studied the small pile of translated intercepts and groaned. Most of them were probably trivial, but if they had reached his desk it was either butt-covering or because some propeller-head in the NSA thought they might have sufficient import to be examined by the next guy up the food chain. Bergman was considered a top-drawer analyst at the CIA regarding Soviet intelligence and counter-intelligence. Therefore he received a great deal of meaningless material for review, mixed in with the important traffic.

The way butt-covering worked in the intelligence community was quite simple: if you weren't quite sure of the significance of an intercept, you passed it up the chain. If it was 1645 hours, and you got off at 1700, and you still had a stack of intercepts to review, you passed them up the chain, too. It was like a sophisticated game of hot potato: when the music stopped, you didn't want an important intercept to be languishing on *your* desk.

Bergman had never been a believer in butt-covering. As a consequence, he often stayed at his desk for long after-hours, examining SIGINT that others below him should have filtered. And if something was passed along from his desk further up the chain, it was considered to be PRIORITY traffic.

He ran one hand through his jet-black hair, while reaching for his ubiquitous bag of red licorice with the other. Bergman weighed in at 190, while registering an average 5' 10" on the height chart. The thirty-three year old didn't worry about his licorice diet: between weight-lifting and running his body was constantly craving more calories. When in his twenties and still single, Bergman had not minded being married to his work. When he passed thirty he began to wonder if perhaps life involved more than the CIA. But he hadn't found a woman who could compete with the thrill of reading the mail of the Soviet top brass.

He examined the prologue attached to each message. They were coming from source *Leaning Tower*. He knew from past experience that information from that particular source was invariably reliable, although not always significant.

Sixty minutes and ten intercepts later he'd seen a pattern. There was a lot of GRU traffic coming in and out of Omsk, which was in itself not odd. Even though Omsk was not an intelligence hotbed, there was a huge military-industrial complex in the city. Much Soviet armor was produced there, including the T-80 main battle tank. But these intercepts concerned what appeared to be some sort of search, as well directives to strengthen the security presence along railroads and even at consulates in various large cities. And in one of the intercepts there was a tantalizing name: the codename for Nikolai Pavlovich Chernikov. The officer was known to be a rising star in the 106th Guards. But Chernikov had dropped off Sam's radar for almost a year. He'd been in Afghanistan and when his unit was pulled offline the man had disappeared.

There were rumors that he'd been recruited into the secretive GRU. Until now his name had not reappeared on the intelligence grid.

Bergman thought for a few moments. *Omsk . . . Chernikov . . . .* He reached for another piece of licorice and considered the connection. The officer had been involved in numerous armored operations in Afghanistan, maybe he'd been attached to the tank production facilities in Omsk for some reason. *That makes sense.*

But Sam didn't know what to make of the intercepts regarding a search. Perhaps a soldier or an officer from Chernikov's old unit had gone AWOL, and the powers that be were wondering if Chernikov had seen him. But that explanation seemed a bit of a stretch. Mystified, Sam placed the intercepts in his safe, and headed for home.

Chapter 20

"I said, 'Wake up!'" The railroad detective nudged the sleeping figure in the ribs one more time with his boot as he shined his flashlight on the hobo's face. He wasn't prepared for what happened next.

With lightning speed, the prone figure grabbed the heel of his boot with one hand and smashed his knee with the other. Screaming in pain, the detective fell. A karate-chop to the side of the writhing officer's head rendered him unconscious.

Kelly jumped to his feet, grabbed his two duffel bags, and leapt out of the door of the empty boxcar. He was still disoriented from having been woken out of a deep sleep. He found himself standing in a large rail yard about ten tracks in width, bathed in electric lights and filled with busy workers. Drawn by the sound of the scream, some of the workers began to run towards him.

Adrenaline took over, and the pilot began sprinting northwest, away from the pursuers and toward the darkest part of the landscape. His boots grated on the gravel as he struggled to keep his footing on the uneven ground. Between the rails, the ties, the ballast and his bags, he was having a rough time of it and stumbled twice. The raised ground of the rail facility gave way to lower, marshy terrain.

Kelly looked back. The pursuit had stopped and he could see rail workers gathering around the boxcar he'd just abandoned. Gaining the forest, Jake ran until he was well out of sight and then changed directions, heading east.

What's wrong with you, Jake? You almost got caught back there! He was disgusted with himself for sleeping so deeply that he hadn't even been aware that the train had come to a halt and his car had been uncoupled.

After a few moments of trotting, he emerged from the forest at a road already busy with morning traffic. He crossed the road and strolled nonchalantly onto a street lined with apartment buildings. It was a familiar scene repeated daily all across the globe, no matter the language or location: a town waking up and going to work at the beginning of a new day. Men dressed in rough clothes carrying lunch pails. A *babushka* toting empty bags, headed for market. Children walking to school. *What town is this?* he wondered. *Better find a spot to check my maps.*

He walked another mile, passing stores and a small factory. No one paid him any mind. At an intersection Kelly turned south and crossed the railroad tracks. Lining the road were large buildings that he guessed housed the local government. Among them was the post office, bearing the name Glav-pochtamt Birobidzhan. *Okay, so I am in Birobidzhan. Where's that?*

He kept walking and soon came to a beautiful park nestled along a river. It was still very early and except for an old wo-man feeding pigeons the park was deserted. He sat on a bench where he could see anyone approaching and gathered his thoughts. He needed to find food, he needed shelter away from curious eyes, and he needed to plot his remaining route to the port city of Nakhodka, where he hoped to slip aboard a Japan-bound freighter.

He studied his maps. By following the route of the TSR, he quickly located Birobidzhan. East of him about 160 kilo-meters was Khabarovsk, a large city. *An easy five-day trek*, Kelly decided. *Better walk it. Don't want to press my luck by hopping the train again, at least not here.* Though he was confident that the railroad detective didn't get a good look at him, it was too big a risk. As long as Chernikov did not receive any sighting re-ports east of Omsk, Kelly was sure that the general's search would concentrate on the Sevastopol area on the Black Sea, seven thousand kilometers to the east. The pilot was counting on Oz to give up that piece of information under interroga-tion.

From Khabarovsk the port city Nakhodka was another seven hundred kilometers south. His route would skirt the Chinese border. Kelly grinned. If luck stayed with him, in just another month or so—even walking—he could be in a position to stow away on a freighter to Japan. He could be back at Edwards by the first of October. He decided to set *Edwards by October* as a goal. For the first time, he felt deep within his heart that he really was going to make it!

****

Maxim Lebed grimaced in great pain as his broken knee was being set. He'd not allowed them to administer the intravenous sedative yet, for there was one task he had to do.

"I know I've seen that face, Comrade Olenev. I got a good look at him before he attacked me."

"Might it have been on the bulletin we received late last week about the deserter?"

Patrikeyev and Geredin had agreed together to create a cover story for Major Kelly's escape. They could not very well tell the rank and file GRU and KGB officers that the object of the manhunt was an escaped American Air Force pilot. They knew by now that Kelly had a Soviet battle dress uniform that he'd taken off of the guard he'd killed, a member of the 106th Guards Airborne Division. They also knew that he spoke fluent Russian. So they wove a cover story certain to fire up the troops. Jacob Kelly they renamed *Yakov Sokolov*, or Jacob Falcon, having learned from their informer that Kelly was calling himself "Falcon." Yakov Sokolov, the story went, was an AWOL soldier from an army infantry unit who had raped and then murdered another soldier's wife. Patrikeyev advised against identifying which unit Sokolov had deserted, so that no one would be able to check out the story.

With such a story to inflame the troops, there wasn't any member of the Soviet Army, intelligence, or police services who wouldn't shoot to kill Sokolov, if so commanded. Kelly's picture with a warrant for his arrest had been distributed the length of the Trans-Siberian Railway, and to every administrative center and police station where he might conceivably appear.

"Sokolov?"

"*Da.*"

"It's possible."

Olenev left the room for a moment and made a call to the local KGB office, directing them to bring a photo of Sokolov immediately to the hospital.

Within a few moments the attacker's identity was confirmed: Yakov Sokolov had been seen and was somewhere in the vicinity. Thirty minutes later, the KGB units between Omsk and Sevastopol were told to stand down. GRU troops standing by embarked on air transports headed for Khabarovsk where they would be loaded onto vehicles and driven to Birobidzhan. In addition, a detachment of KGB officers with dogs trained to track fugitives was en route from Khabarovsk.

****

"You lied to me, Professor Simmons." *Slap!*

Oz tasted blood. One of his front teeth had been driven through his lip from the force of Chernikov's blow.

"I did *not* lie!"

Slap! "I did not lie, SIR!"

Oz shut his eyes and nodded his head, trying to ignore the pain and the blood dribbling down his chin. "I did not lie, sir," he dutifully repeated.

"Oh, but you *did* lie! You said that Kelly was heading for Sevastopol. We've found him in precisely the opposite direction, Professor, at Birobidzhan. I don't like being lied to!"

"But sir, I did not lie. May I explain?"

"Please do."

"Major Kelly and I *did* decide to go to Sevastopol. We figured it had the best opportunities to get across the border. If he's changed directions it's because he knew you would interrogate me. I had no way of knowing that he would change plans. Sir." he added, quickly.

Chernikov stared at him for a moment, then walked back to his desk chair, seating himself. "You know how he thinks, so where is he going now?"

"I would assume, sir, that he is still going to escape by stowing away on a freighter. He's probably headed for a port city somewhere on Siberia's east coast."

Chernikov nodded, apparently satisfied. "Then please, my dear professor, forgive me for striking you," he said magnanimously, "I believe you did tell me the truth after all."

Simmons nodded, and then decided to make the stakes a little higher. He smiled at Chernikov, and said, "You won't catch him, sir. You know that, don't you?"

The Soviet frowned. "Of course we will catch him," he scoffed. "Whatever do you mean by that?"

"No, sir, I don't believe you will. Major Kelly is more than just a pilot. He's had some sort of specialized training. I've seen him in action. I asked him about it and he refused to discuss it with me. All I can tell you is that he's good, perhaps the best, and you've no one that can match him. No, General, I do not think you will catch him."

"Take him away," Chernikov barked to the guards who were standing by. He sat deep in thought long after Simmons had been removed, considering what the scientist had said.

****

Jake stole a melon and several ears of corn from a garden adjacent to the forest. Retreating into the woods, he ate the corn raw, devoured the melon, and then set off with a long stride toward Khabarovsk. It was not until several hours later that he first heard the dogs and realized that he was in big trouble. He began to trot, hoping to maintain a lead over his pursuers while he figured out what to do.

Coming to a small stream, he splashed into midstream and then headed downwind, south, for a mile or so in the water.

When he emerged, he decided to do what he'd been avoiding; he had to lighten his load. He quickly transferred the most valuable items into a single duffel bag. The remainder he jammed into the other bag. He wedged the duffel with its castoffs into the crook of a fir tree, high up. It would drive the dogs nuts, and delay his trackers another ten or twenty minutes. Now encumbered by only one bag, he jumped back into the stream and waded for another mile before he splashed back out. A quick change into dry socks, and he was off again with a fast jog to the east.

After several kilometers, he came to a heavily traveled gravel road that wound to the east through low, fir-covered hills. Jake jogged alongside the road until he heard a truck approaching from behind. It was a flatbed semi, fully loaded with logs. Kelly stepped into the center of the road, and flagged it down.

A grizzled man peered down from the dusty cab. "What do you want?" he growled, "I've got a load to deliver!"

"I need a ride," Jake said.

"Doesn't everyone," the driver muttered. "I don't take riders, comrade."

"You do today," replied Jake coldly, as he pulled the pistol from the waistband behind his back, and leveled the weapon on the driver.

"You're not going use that thi—"

His sentence was cut off by the bark of the pistol as Jake shot a hole in the roof of the cab from where he stood.

"You were saying?" the pilot asked.

"Get in," the trucker fumed.

Kelly walked around the cab and got into the passenger side. "I don't know where you were headed, but now you're headed to Khabarovsk."

The driver glared at him for a moment, then got the truck rolling. "Better not fall asleep," he said to Kelly, "because first chance I get I'll kill you."

****

"We lost him, sir. He was pretty tricky, tried to throw the dogs off by walking in the stream. For a while it worked, but they found his scent again. We trailed him to a road, sir, before we lost the scent again. If I'm reading the signs right, from the look of footprints in the dust I'd say that he hitched a ride with a truck headed east."

"Well done, Lieutenant. Return to Khabarovsk. That's where he's going, I think. Your report has added confirmation to what I already suspected."

Chernikov contacted the Khabarovsk KGB headquarters and directed them to set up roadblocks west of the city. Then he redirected all his GRU assets between Omsk and Birobidzhan to converge on Khabarovsk.

****

"Would I be right if I guessed that these guys are looking for you?" the trucker chuckled. Up ahead was a roadblock, and the traffic was lined up approaching it. Every vehicle was being searched thoroughly.

"Turn the truck around, now!" Jake commanded.

"And just how am I supposed to do that? This is a two-lane road with narrow shoulders, and marshy ground beyond on both sides. I'm hauling a full load of timber on a 25-meter trailer. And I've got traffic behind me. I couldn't turn around on this road if it was four lanes wide and I was the only vehicle on it!" The man laughed unpleasantly.

Kelly knew the man was right. He gathered up his duffel bag and slipped out of the door. He walked toward the rear of the line of traffic, hoping that the troops manning the blockade would not notice him. But it was not to be.

"*Stoy!*" The shouted command was accompanied by the sound of running feet and the chambering of rounds in weapons. Looking over his shoulder, Jake saw four soldiers running after him and guessed that there might be several more on the other side of the line of traffic. The way the men were carrying their weapons and the expressions on their faces told him that this was not a time to press his luck. He stopped and turned around, waiting for them to catch up.

"Please drop your bag, comrade, and put your hands behind your head," commanded a lieutenant, holding him under the muzzle of an assault rifle.

Kelly complied, and two soldiers stepped up to frisk him. They located the pistol tucked into his waistband, and a combat knife strapped to his shin, a trophy that Kelly had lifted off of the guard at the helicopter several days earlier.

"You are *Yakov Sokolov?*" the lieutenant inquired, when the soldiers had turned up no identification in their search of his person and his duffel bag.

For an instant Kelly was confused by the question, and then he realized what Chernikov must have done. He laughed out loud and responded, "Sure. I am Jacob Falcon. And why are you taking me into custody? What have you been told?"

"You are wanted for rape and murder, Sokolov."

"Would you like to know who I really am?" Kelly asked bitterly. "I am Major Jacob Kelly of the United States Air Force. I have been shot down illegally by your country over international waters and kidnapped, by the order of Major General Nikolai Chernikov of the GRU. And if you value your life you'd best not tell Chernikov what I just told you, otherwise you'll probably just disappear and your wife and children will never see you again."

The men stared at him. When he repeated the same words in English, the lieutenant paled. "You speak English?" he asked.

"Of course I speak English. I'm an American."

"You liar!" shouted one of the soldiers. "You are a deserter, a murderer, and a rapist!"

"Have it your way," he replied in English. He held his wrists out in front of him, hoping that they would handcuff him with his hands in front, but no such luck. One of the soldiers jerked his arms behind him and snapped the cuffs on, then shackled to his feet. The length of the chain on his ankle cuffs was about two feet, which barely allowed him to shuffle as he moved.

"Take him down to KGB headquarters in Khab'," the lieutenant directed. Kelly was led over to a black VAZ-2103 four-
door sedan. The soldiers placed their rifles in the trunk with
Kelly's duffel bag, though each retained a side arm. They
shoved Kelly into the driver's side rear seat. One sat next to
Jake, another sat in front with the driver. The lieutenant waved
them through the roadblock, and they turned east toward
Khabarovsk.

Kelly sat uncomfortably with his arms behind him. A wave
of weariness and fear washed over him. He couldn't bear the
thought of returning to the prison camp. He'd probably be
shot this time. Glumly staring out the window as the Russian
forest passed by, he was out of ideas. Up until now he'd had a
fighting chance, but not anymore. They knew he was a skilled
fighter. They knew he could speak Russian. He no longer had
an edge and he was out of options.

Chained as he was eliminated fighting as a possibility. Besides, there were three of them. He might be able to briefly
subdue one man, but the other two would be more than
enough to handle him, shackled as he was. About the only way
out of this situation was if they got into an auto accident and
everyone got hurt except him. *An auto accident . . . hmm.* He
shifted positions, and the shackles on his feet rattled slightly.
He leaned over and stared at them, and the chain connecting
them. He had plenty of leg room, as the driver was short and
had adjusted his seat forward.

And then Kelly figured it out. It was so simple. And it
might work. He would attack the driver and cause an accident.
The men in the car were not Spetsnaz and he was counting on
them to make a fatal mistake, rushing to the aid of the driver
instead of going for their side arms.

Jake considered his situation. He himself could die, or be
seriously injured even if he was successful. On the other hand,
if he did nothing and was shipped back to Chernikov he was
certainly a dead man. The gloves would come off and he'd be
interrogated with a combination of chemicals and brutality.
He'd tell them everything involuntarily, and then he would be
eliminated.

What's there to lose? he thought. *Either I'm dead, or I'm dead. Think I'll pick an option that does not involve me being tortured or spilling my guts.*

The highway they were on had become a paved road some fifty kilometers back, when he was still in the truck prior to the roadblock. The driver was maintaining about 95 kilometers per hour, Jake observed, and there was no other traffic in sight. He waited until they were approaching a curve to the left, wooded on both sides of the road. *It's now or never.*

He groaned and hunched over. "My stomach," he moaned.

"You better not throw up in this car, comrade!" the soldier sitting next to him warned.

"No, no, it's not that. I've got an ulcer," Jake muttered. Mollified, the guard left him alone.

Jake leaned back and slouched down in the seat, as though it eased the pain. As soon as he felt the car enter the curve, he drew his knees to his chest, raised, then extended his feet, and with the momentum flipped the chain on his ankle shackles over the neck of the driver in the seat directly in front of him. The entire maneuver took little more than a second. He yanked his feet back, and began a sawing motion with his feet, dragging the chain back and forth across the neck of the driver. Within two savage strokes, the chain was cutting through flesh and tissue, and blood was everywhere.

****

Sam Bergman rounded the corner, his house in sight about one-quarter mile down the road. He was sweating profusely in the humid, northern Virginia air and was completely gassed from his five-mile run, but he coaxed his thirty-three year old body into a near sprint anyway. *Leave it all on the field, Sam, don't take any of it with you to the shower,* he admonished himself. He passed his driveway, and checked his chronometer. *Still not good enough!* There was a buddy he wanted to beat in the next 10K, but he was still a long way from being fast enough.

Sam walked up and down the street for several moments,

cooling down, then entered his house. After a long hot shower followed by bacon and eggs, he was ready to head for the Firm for another day of *Spy vs Spy*.

A new batch of intercepts was in his inbound safe when he arrived at the office. *More SIGINT originating from General Chernikov,* he observed, *he's one busy man.* As he read through the transcripts, his brow furrowed. Two motorized rifle regiments without their vehicles were being air-transported from Sevastopol to Khabarovsk. *That's five thousand men, for crying out loud.* They were to pick up motorized transport in Khabarovsk. Their vehicles would follow on the TSR. Sam scratched his head and leaned back in his chair. *Hmm. Whatever it is, it's so urgent that the men aren't even traveling with their equipment.* With a start he remembered that not seventy-two hours earlier the same units had been moved *to* Sevastopol. *What's going on?*

He read the rest of the transcripts carefully. One regiment was to proceed from Khab' to the southern portion of the Primorsky Krai, with elements deployed in every port city and rail junction. The other regiment was to be split up between Khab' itself, points west to Birobidzhan, and points north. And there was more about a search for a soldier named *Yakov Sokolov.* The troop movements all concerned finding and capturing Sokolov.

Whoever this guy is, he must have kicked over a real bee's nest, Bergman thought. *Glad I don't have half the Red Army chasing me.*

He considered the matter, and then decided to open an incident folder on the troop movements in his personal files. Whenever Bergman encountered bits and pieces of intelligence that seemed to be related, and yet did not warrant a full write-up to brief his superior, he would start a file on it. He was not permitted to keep actual intelligence materials in his files, but he could cite their catalog numbers and journal his thoughts about the matters. More than once, he'd uncovered matters of major significance, merely because he'd been the only one with the prescience to connect seemingly unrelated threads of intelligence.

He wrote two requests to be added to the day's message

traffic. One was addressed to the station chief in the Moscow embassy, the other to one of the CIA's data storage research assistants. He wrote the same message to both:

> *Need all extant records on living Soviet citizens named Yakov Sokolov who are currently enlisted or under commission in the Soviet Army. Also need latest records on General Nikolai Pavlovich Chernikov, GRU, including current assignment and whereabouts. Low priority. Respond to Samuel Bergman, Counter-Intel Analysis Office, Soviet Desk.*

This calls for a cup of hot chocolate before I start journaling, he decided. He shoved the material back into his inbound safe, locked it, and headed for the cafeteria.

****

Pandemonium ensued, with all the guards shouting and the car swerving. The driver's hands involuntarily left the wheel and went to the chain, trying to pull it away from his ruined neck. The other man in front was trying to help him. The guard sitting next to Kelly was pulling on Kelly's knees trying to stop the sawing motion. In his panic he was inadvertently working against the men in the front, tightening the chain around the driver's neck. As Kelly had predicted, no one went for their weapon; they were all intent on restoring control to the driver.

The car careened off the road and slammed into a tree, impacting on the left front bumper which then spun the vehicle to the right. It flipped over and rolled several times, coming to rest on its wheels. Jake's slouched, legs-up position protected him from the initial impact, which drove him against the soft back of the seat in front of him. The front seat brackets snapped, with the result that the driver was crushed against the steering wheel. The passenger in the front had been ejected from the car when it rolled. The guard in the seat next to Kelly had gone through the windshield when the car hit the tree.

Jake groaned. It took a moment to gather his senses and orient himself. He was lying on the floor in the back, pinned between the back and front seats. Somehow in the wild twisting and rolling of the vehicle, his ankle chain had become disengaged from the carnage in the front seat. After several moments of struggle he managed to get off the floor and regain the back seat. His hands were still manacled behind him. Carefully he worked his wrist chains down past his bottom and threaded his feet through them, ending up with his hands in front of him. A few good kicks opened the passenger-side door, and he was free of the wreck.

He realized he was trembling, and knew that as soon as the adrenaline stopped pumping he could go into shock if not careful. Jake searched the bodies of the other men and located the key to his shackles. He also found a numbered, military-issue rail pass in the pockets of one of the men. It was good for unlimited travel on the TSR through September. *Apparently*, he thought to himself, *they are using the TSR to move the troops that are hunting for me. I'll bet that for time's sake they don't check individual papers when they see one of these military passes. Could come in handy.* He pocketed the pass, as well as all of the cash that each man was carrying.

After freeing himself from his shackles he began searching for his duffel bag. The rear trunk had sprung open at first impact, and its contents were scattered around the forest. It took ten minutes, but he finally located it.

Kelly surveyed the accident scene. The car had come to rest far enough from the road that it would not be easily seen from it. There were no skid marks to indicate where the vehicle had left the road. The forest was thick enough that a search by air would reveal nothing. It would take his pursuers time to figure out what had happened—time Jake planned to use wisely.

The major took one last look at the bodies, and found

himself sickened by what he had done. These men had no responsibility for Kelly's capture. They had not abused him. They'd simply followed orders, believing that what they were doing was right. Under other circumstances they could have been his friends. It was one thing to kill an enemy in a shooting war. It was something else entirely to kill in this fashion. The body count was mounting, and Kelly was getting sick of it.

Chapter 21

It was a pleasant mid-August day. The railroad platform in Khabarovsk streamed with people coming and going, women in colorful scarves, men in dark suits, others in rough clothing, lots of uniformed soldiers, and, as always, the ubiquitous police presence. The people Kelly found to be beautiful, wonderful, fascinating. The railway station itself lacked imagination, smacking of standard utilitarian Soviet architecture with all the panache of a '60s era Trailways bus station, something one might find in downtown Detroit.

Early that morning outside the city, he'd had a chilly sponge bath in a creek, and then clothed himself with the battle dress uniform he'd taken from the guard at Prison 87. He was badly bruised in several places from the auto accident, but the bruises were hidden by his clothing. With his rail pass and his command of Russian he felt confident that by afternoon he'd be on a train to Nakhodka. *Edwards by October* seemed a real possibility.

He bought some bread and cheese, and a bottle of beer, and sat eating with his head down as he watched the people go by out of the corner of his eye. The passers-by kept their faces averted, avoided all contact, and kept conversations with companions to a minimum. The major's CCT training had taught him to blend in with the host culture when he was downrange, and the last thing he wanted to do was stand out. He checked his watch; the train to Nakhodka would arrive in ten minutes, and be on its way in forty-five.

Soldiers carrying their gear began to fill the station, standing around the platform in little knots, talking loudly to one another as a band of brothers will do, laughing, joking, complaining. He noticed that it was on the platform for Nakhodka that they were gathering. Kelly stood, picked up his duffel, and walked to the northwest end of the platform, not wanting to mix with the men. His cover would be blown immediately if anyone asked him what company he was in. He hadn't a clue what unit this was, who their commanding officer was, or even where they had just come from. He wouldn't be able to fake it.

Looking around, Kelly came to a decision. The risk today was just too great. He'd come back tomorrow. He turned around, and found himself staring into the face of Major Roman Nikitin, Chernikov's aide-de-camp. Recognition flickered in Nikitin's eyes, and a sardonic smile crossed his face.

****

It was 0715 in Prison 87's time zone, and Chernikov sat at his desk nursing a cup of tea. The reconstruction of the camp's physical plant was complete. The replacement generator they had ordered was scheduled to arrive tomorrow morning. The routine had returned to normal, for the most part.

Project *Krasnyy Voskhod* was again demonstrating its worth. The scientist who'd been involved in the breakout, Oswald Simmons, was becoming cooperative. A small team of physicists were being flown in to interview him on Thursday. Robert Alton was continuing his work, and even beginning to take pleasure in the thought that his skills were considered so valuable that he'd been kidnapped for them. He'd requested a personal computer, which would be provided. The German biologist, Karl Willets, was showing signs of cracking also.

Even if all we attain are two or three more successes, Chernikov mused, *the Politburo will be pleased. As long as we find Major Kelly. We've got to reel Kelly in before he becomes a danger and an embarrassment to the program.*

He'd dispatched Major Nikitin to coordinate and liaise with him on the manhunt. When Nikitin had received the assignment, his crestfallen face told Chernikov that he considered the job to be punishment for the American pilot's escape.

Chernikov had placed his arm around his subordinate's shoulders and explained, "No, Roman, you don't understand. I'm getting you away from here to protect you. If the Politburo drops a hammer on me, everyone close to me will suffer. If you are away in the field you are not as connected and therefore not as stained as I am. Besides, I have no one who will prosecute this search so effectively as you."

It was true. Nikitin was leaving no stone unturned, and responding rapidly to all reported sightings and leads. He deployed his troops skillfully, and dealt with logistics responsibly. Nikitin took the initiative and was a creative thinker. And he'd just found his man.

****

"Why, Major Kelly! How convenient it is to find you here! Certainly saves me the trouble of moving all these men south to Nakh—"

A kick to the groin and a chop to the back of the head as the man doubled over put Nikitin out of the fight. The officer to Kelly's left made the mistake of going for his side arm. A lightning-fast jab broke his nose, and when he crashed to the concrete floor a concussion was added to his troubles. The white-faced officer to Kelly's right raised his hands in surrender and got away with nothing more than a hard side kick to the ribs, which broke two of them and cartwheeled the hapless fellow over a bench.. It all happened so fast that no one shouted to raise the alarm until Jake was running down the tracks, headed west.

"AFTER HIM! IT'S SOKOLOV!" shouted the officer with the broken ribs, grimacing with pain. The peaceful platform was transformed to bedlam as several dozen soldiers began racing after the fugitive. The enlisted men's weapons were secured for traveling, so at least no one was taking any shots at him.

Jake's options narrowed rapidly. To his right was a line of stationary boxcars. Even as he sprinted down the graveled railbed the leftmost tracks were filled by a fast-moving inbound passenger train. He was trapped! There was nowhere to go but forward, and he'd be in plain sight for several hundred meters. The men behind him were gaining on him; he could hear their booted feet grating on the gravel.

Running out of possibilities, Kelly skidded to a stop and darted between two boxcars on the right. He immediately found that he'd leapt out of the frying pan and into the fire! He had happened onto an overpass where the railroad crossed over the highway, and was pinned in less than a meter of space between the boxcar and the raised side of the railroad bridge. He heard breathless shouts and the scuff of boots behind him.

Below him were the busy southbound lanes of the M58; a steady stream of traffic disappeared beneath the overpass. An end-dump filled with sand was just passing under him, followed closely by another semi. Jake vaulted the side, and found himself hurtling through space. The truck was moving faster than he realized, or the drop was farther, but he remembered thinking, *I'm going to clean miss this stupid thing, and wind up getting smashed to a pulp by that second truck!*

****

On the other side of the world, in northern Virginia, it was 8:30 PM on Sunday evening and Professor Bill Jenson was working on a bowl of chocolate ice cream while he indulged in a favorite activity: reading the *Chronicle of Higher Education.* Although there was an undisclosed side to his life and career of which very few people were aware, in his public life Jensen was a full Professor of Political Science at Georgetown University. He loved the academic life and enjoyed the intellectual rigor of the campus. He loved to teach.

The professor finished his bowl of ice cream and stared at the clock. It was only 8:30 PM, but he'd discovered that by going to bed early and getting up at 4 AM, he had four hours to work uninterrupted before the start of the official workday. He was busy developing a graduate-level course entitled *Nixon and China: Breakthrough or Capitulation?* and he needed those hours for reading the available literature on the subject.

He set his empty bowl in the sink after fighting back the urge to have a second, and put his magazine on the back of the couch as he passed by, heading for the bathroom. He didn't hear the glossy journal slide off and fall between the sofa and the wall. Jensen would wonder for weeks what had happened to his magazine, which would not be found until long after, when the Jensens moved into their next home.

It's a pity, for Professor William Jensen might have seen a brief article on page 47 describing the inexplicable disappearance of ten academics, all of whom were leaders in their fields, fields which were closely related to militarily useful technologies. Had Jensen seen this article and taken it to his *other* place of business, it might have prevented some of the deaths and heartaches that were now destined to occur in the next eighteen months. All of which just goes to show that sometimes the most useful intelligence is right under our nose.

****

At the last possible moment the trucker hit the brakes as traffic ahead of him slowed. It saved Jake's life. With a sickening crack, Kelly's upper right arm struck the top of the tailgate of the end-dump as he fell into the truck. The sand cushioned his fall, and though he was otherwise uninjured his right upper arm was broken.

Hot on his heels, several troopers arrived at the edge of the bridge in time to see him land in the truck, which then disappeared beneath them. They turned about and raced back to the train station to report and to receive the orders to quarantine the area, orders that they knew would be issued.

The trucker had no idea that he had a fugitive riding in his load. Several blocks later he turned right on *Ulitsa Nekrasova,* and the train station passed from sight. When the truck came to a stop at the next intersection, Jake vaulted from it with the duffel bag slung over his shoulder, clutching his right arm. His sudden appearance in the middle of a busy street startled the drivers around him, and several laid on their horns. Stopping oncoming traffic with a raised hand, he raced to the passenger side of an orange ZAZ-968M Zaporozhets. He yanked the door open, and jumped in.

"DRIVE!" he shouted.

"Who are you? Why are you in my car? Get out! Get out!" the woman behind the wheel screamed at him.

Kelly roughly grabbed her shoulder with his one good arm and pinched the nerve until she cried out. "I said, 'drive,' and I mean it! Shut up and drive! *Now!*"

Squeezing back tears, the woman clenched her teeth and drove. She was moving in the opposite direction the truck had been going. When they got to the intersection of the M58, Kelly shouted, "Left! Turn left here!"

Sirens were coming from the direction of the train station, once again in sight to their right after she made the turn. Several police cars forced their way through the intersection ahead of them and raced off in the direction of the truck. Kelly kept his head down.

The woman continued north, back under the same overpass Kelly had just jumped off, but now moving the opposite direction. The sound of the sirens gradually faded. When Kelly looked behind them he saw no pursuit.

"They are looking for you, aren't they?" she accused.

He turned back to the driver and apologized, "Yes, they are. I'm so sorry, ma'am, to involve you in this. Please, please, don't be afraid, you are in no danger from me."

"Tell that to my shoulder," she sniffed angrily.

"Forgive me. I didn't know how else to get you moving. If you go another couple kilometers north, you can let me off and I won't trouble you any longer."

"Are you Sokolov?"

He looked at her, shocked. "How do you know that name?"

"We all know it. We know what you did! It's been all over the news. Are you going to rape me and murder me, too?" she challenged.

"But it's not true! None of it is true! It's a cover story to hide what they are really doing. None of this is what you think! Oh, good grief! Never mind. Just—let me out here."

"Isn't your name Yakov Sokolov?"

"*Nyet!*" Jake snapped. Frustrated by the situation and irritated by the throbbing pain of his broken arm, Jake switched to English, "My name is Jacob Kelly. My nickname is Falcon. If you put my first name with my nickname, and say it in Russian, you get," and here he switched back to Russian, "*Yakov Sokolov.*"

She pulled onto a side street and stopped the car, then turned and asked him, "You speak English?"

"*Da. Sokolov* in English is 'Falcon.'"

"I know what it is," she replied in perfect English. The panic she had felt when he had jumped into her car was draining away. She put her face in her hands for a moment, collecting herself. *If he wants out of the car, he must not be planning to hurt me*, she thought. She looked up and examined her passenger. *He must be a soldier, though; he's wearing a uniform.*

Switching back to Russian, she asked, "You are in the military, though, aren't you?" gesturing to his clothes.

"*Nyet!* Well, yes, actually. I am in the military, just not *your* military. These clothes I stole."

Her eyes widened, "What do you mean you're not in *my* military?"

"I'm an American, a United States Air Force officer."

"Right. And I'm Solzhenitsyn's grandmother."

When Kelly did not respond, she realized that he wasn't joking. "You're serious, aren't you?" Kelly nodded, and she followed up with another question, "Are you a spy?"

"*Nyet!* I was captured and brought into this country against my will. It was an act of war. Very few people in your country know about it, and the powers that be want to keep it that way. That's why they've concocted this cockamamie story about *Yakov Sokolov* and a rape and murder. I'm the victim of, well, I'd guess you'd call it a kidnapping."

"Excuse me, but *I'm* the victim of a kidnapping!" she snapped.

"No, you aren't. In the good old US of A we'd call this a carjacking, not a kidnapping. Actually, I'd prefer to call it 'bumming a ride.' In any case, I will leave you now. Thanks for your help. I hope your shoulder is feeling better; it was not my intention to hurt you." Kelly reached across with his left arm to open his door, and then grabbed the duffel bag and got out of the car.

"Wait!" she said, noticing the way he was holding his right arm. "What's wrong with your arm?"

"I broke it escaping from the soldiers at the train station."

"What will you do?"

"Splint it, I guess, and try not to make it worse. Then I've got a long walk ahead of me."

"You probably did not know this, Mr. American Air Force Pilot, but you can't *walk* back to America." The trace of a smile was teasing the corners of her lips.

My word! She's beautiful! he thought as he studied her for the first time.

"Oh, I know," he replied carelessly, "I'm going to swim *that* part. I've got to get to the seashore first, though. And that is a long walk."

They both laughed. She pursed her lips and thought for a moment. "Get in," she said finally, "this time it is not a—a carjacking, this is a kidnapping. Your second one today. Now *I'm* kidnapping *you*. I'll take you to my community. They will fix your arm and decide what to do with you."

He bent down and looked in the car at the young woman. "Ma'am, there's nothing I'd enjoy more than a car ride with a beautiful woman. But the people chasing me want to recapture me, and failing that, they will kill me. They won't care who gets hurt in the process. If I go with you, I will put you and all your loved ones at risk. I can't do that. I've already been the cause of enough deaths. I'm not going to add yours to my tally. But thanks, anyway." He shut the door, picked up his bag, and began to walk down the street.

Where to, now? he thought to himself. *I've got to fix my arm, and lay low. Within a few days I'll need food. Wonder if I ought to go north while I heal?*

The orange Zaporozhets pulled up alongside of him with the window rolled down. She leaned across the seat and said, "Please, Jacob Kelly, get in. I'll take you to my community. You'll be safe there."

"You are very kind, Miss, but like I said, bad things happen around me and I would not want to be responsible for any harm coming to you—"

"Please *shut up and get in the car,* and let me explain something to you!" she demanded. Her eyes flashed with momentary irritation. Falcon thought it made her even more beautiful. He opened the door and crouched to hear what she had to say, but did not get in the car.

"Jacob Kelly, my community is what you in America would call . . . ," she paused, brow furrowed, "ah, under . . . earth?"

"Underground?"

"Yes, that's it. We are an underground logging community. We have an, ah, *arrangement* with the local head of the Communist Party and as long as we make our quota no one comes to bother us. We not only deal in the legitimate market, but we sell our lumber on the black market, too. So you see, Jacob Kelly, we don't want any entanglements with the police or the KGB either. You will be safe with us. The decision will belong to the whole community, of course, but we can at least set your arm and let you stay until it heals."

As Kelly looked at the young woman, trying to decide what he should do, he felt the weariness of the past several weeks settle on his shoulders. He was exhausted emotionally and physically, his arm was throbbing with intense pain, and he had no other options. He threw his duffel bag in the back, sat heavily in the seat, and said, "What is your name? Who should I thank?"

Her eyes laughed as she said, "Galina Toporova. My name is Galina Toporova."

"Galina? That was my mother's name. *Bolshoe spasibo,* Galina."

She smiled as she pulled away from the curb. Jake closed his eyes and within minutes was fast asleep.

Chapter 22

Monday, August 18, 1986: 1335 local
Khabarovsk, USSR

Galina Toporova avoided the main roads as she picked her way carefully through the city, steering clear of the areas in which the KGB typically set up roadblocks when they were looking for someone. With several years of experience navigating the metropolis while transporting contraband, it wasn't too difficult. Finally she was on a small, two-lane highway headed south. After fifty kilometers or so, she would turn east toward the rugged Sikhote-Alin mountains.

When she felt that she had driven beyond the range of any reasonable search, she began to relax and consider what she had just done. She was harboring a very hot fugitive, one that some very powerful people were trying to recapture. Although she had no idea what the fuss was all about, her own sources had informed her that several elements of a motorized rifle division had been mobilized to assist in the recapture of the exhausted man sleeping in the seat next to her.

Galina glanced at the man. He'd called himself Jacob Kelly. The news media was calling him Yakov Sokolov. By one account he was a murderer and a rapist. In his own words he was the victim of some crazy plot. She shook her head. Sorting out the truth was going to be difficult, but she knew she'd already decided to believe Kelly over the official story line. Her mind had been made up when he'd let her go and walked away from the car. He'd have never done that had he been the criminal he was reputed to be.

Why am I even bothering with this man? Why am I helping him? This is not my affair. Naught but trouble can come of it! Even as she considered this she knew that it was the voice of Boris, her brother, speaking in her mind. Boris was a good man, the best brother a girl could ever have. But he was imminently practical and somewhat unimaginative. The equations in her brother's mind all revolved around the functional: survival and sustenance. They had a community with ten families to maintain. They were already operating beyond the far edge of the law. Though the authorities had been persuaded—bribed was a better word—to look the other way, interfering in the affairs of the State regarding the Sokolov matter would be unforgivable and catastrophic if it should become known. *Whoever this man really is, I need to manufacture a new identity for him.*

****

One hundred and forty kilometers later, the little Zaporozhets was toiling through the curves and grades of the Sikhote-Alin mountains. Galina decided to stop at a little diner in Sidima where they could get a bite to eat and she could gas up the car.

"Jacob Kelly," she said. She was afraid to shake him, knowing that soldiers sometimes react violently when awakened with a touch. "Jacob Kelly!" she said, louder.

His eyes popped open and for an instant he looked wildly about. "What! What?" He shook his head to clear the cobwebs. At that moment the throbbing pain in his right arm reasserted itself, and he grimaced. "What are you doing?" he asked warily.

"We are going to get something to eat, and then we need gas."

"No. Gas first, then eat," he insisted.

"Why? What does it matter?" she asked stubbornly.

"It will matter a great deal if we have to leave in a hurry!"

She shrugged, and drove over to the pump. She presented her papers and petrol coupons to the attendant. They sat in silence while the man filled the tank.

Forty minutes later they were back on the highway, which had become a graveled road with deep ruts. From the looks of it Kelly surmised that it was frequently used by heavy trucks.

"Where are we going?" he asked.

She looked at him and then resumed studying the road ahead of her. "I am taking you to my village. We are a community of dissidents, outcasts, and misfits who are trying to remain under the government radar. We have a timbering operation, and just enough official sanction that we can buy what we need and sell what we cut. The head of our local administrative district knows where and who we are, but he has found it profitable to leave us alone. That could change at any time, however, so we make sure we don't give him a reason to change his mind. Given the circumstances, you present a dangerous threat to our operation. I don't think you should stay any longer than it takes to heal your arm.

"In the meantime you're going to need an identity and some sort of cover story. I don't want anyone to know who you really are; I'm hoping I'll forget it myself."

Kelly thought for a few moments, and then said, "I am Sergei Primakov from Birobidzhan. I'm a, uh, farm worker and I've run away from our *kolkhoz* because I hate farm work. I've managed to get all the way to Khabarovsk, looking for something else to do. I was jumped in the city by a bunch of men who stole my things and broke my arm. You saw the attack and had pity on me and picked me up. I don't trust anybody, so I don't talk about myself."

Galina thought for a moment, and then agreed, "That will probably work. Do you have civilian clothes?"

When Jake nodded, she added, "With that story, you'll have to get rid of your duffel bag." She thought briefly and then said, "I think I know just where you could hide it."

"I'll need it when I move on. Will I be able to get to it without your help?" She nodded, so Jake said, "Okay, I'll change when we get there."

When they were but a few kilometers from the village, Galina pulled over and Jake changed into his rough civilian clothes. She led him down a narrow path to the fallen-down ruin of a cottage, and he hid the bag in the rafters under a section of the roof that was still intact.

****

The sun was on the western horizon when Galina left the main road, turning onto a deeply rutted dirt road that wound into a steep-sided valley. A kilometer later the little orange Zaporozhets pulled into a large clearing that occupied the whole valley floor. Ahead of him Kelly could see a small sawmill with a large mound of sawdust. Next to it was a large building with a pair of stacks, a wisp of smoke curling up from one and steam rising from the other. To Kelly's left were several neat piles of uncut logs, around which were parked various pieces of heavy equipment. Ten or so modest but neat homes were situated on the right.

"This your place?" he asked.

"Home, sweet home," she replied.

"Where is everybody?"

"Supper, probably," she said. She checked her watch and added, "They knocked off for the day about an hour ago. Tonight you'll stay with my brother and me. You can sleep on the couch, and we'll get that arm fixed up. Tomorrow you move in with Filipp and Yulian, where you'll stay until you're ready to leave. Tomorrow morning I'll introduce you to the group and give you your work assignment."

"Work assignment?"

"We don't have any tourists here, Mr. American Air Force pilot. You've still got one good arm and I intend to put it to work. Besides, it will hurt your story if you don't get right to work."

"Are you sure this will be okay with whoever is in charge?"

"Boris and I are in charge. If I say you stay, you stay. But that also means when I say you work, you work. And—when I say you go, you go." She parked the car, and led him into one of the homes.

The house was constructed from poured concrete walls, with rugs and other fabric hangings covering the interior walls and floor. It was simple and comfortable. As they entered the home, Kelly hungrily inhaled the welcome aroma of what he guessed was a potato and onion stew, combined with a spice he couldn't identify.

A male voice came from another part of the house, "Galya?"

"It's me," she responded.

"You're late!" A tall, muscular man came around the corner, wiping his hands on a dish towel. He had bushy black hair with a beard to match, and was clothed in a worn but clean pair of overalls. He made no effort to hide his surprise and irritation as he saw Kelly standing in his living room. "Who are you?" he demanded. Without waiting for an answer, he turned to Galina and asked, "Who is this? Why have you brought him here?"

Kelly interrupted and suggested, "Would you like me to step outside, so you two can talk privately?"

"*Nyet!*" answered Galina.

"*Da!*" grouched the man.

"*Da,*" conceded Galina. "Let me talk to him."

Kelly stepped outside but could still hear the raised voices arguing within. After ten minutes the front door opened and the man stepped out. "Go inside," he commanded coldly, "I'm going to get the doctor to set your arm."

Light was fading as Jake reentered the house. Galina was standing with her back to the door, hands on hips, shaking her head. As he came in she turned around and stared at him. Her face was flushed and she was still angry. With a clipped voice she said, "You'll stay until your arm is healed, then you have to leave. I had to tell Boris who you are; I never could lie successfully to my brother—he knows me too well. But he has agreed to allow you to stay, temporarily."

In a moment Boris reentered followed by an older man carrying a black bag. Boris pointed to Jake and said to the other man, "There he is, Sevastyan." The newcomer was a solidly-built man with a gold tooth, a prominent hook nose that must have been broken in some fight long ago, and a completely bald head. He had a pair of intense, brown eyes, and heavy, black eyebrows. He reminded Kelly of a sixty-year old Telly Savalas.

"Take your shirt off, comrade, and let's get a look at you."

Kelly struggled, one-handed, with the buttons until Sevastyan finally helped him, gently removing his shirt. On Kelly's left forearm was a distinct USAF insignia tattoo. On his right forearm was the squadron insignia for the 34th Fighter Squadron with a small American flag underneath it.

Sevastyan stared at the tattoos, stood up, and backed way. "Who is this, Boris? He does not appear to be a farmer from Birobidzhan." Sevastyan's tone of voice carried a gentle rebuke.

Galina stared at the tattoos and said quietly, "I told you he's telling the truth, Borya."

"What's going on here?" the older man asked again, his voice trembling slightly. "And what are these?" he demanded, pointing to the ugly red scars on Kelly's shoulders, one saying "Lenin" and the other "Stalin."

"I was tortured by the GRU. General Chernikov burned those onto my shoulders several weeks ago, when he was trying to make me talk." Kelly's shoulders slumped and he shut his eyes, slowly shaking his head. His luck had finally run out, and he felt that the situation was on the verge of deteriorating rapidly. *There's not a whole lot I can do about this. And no lie I can dream up fits as well as the truth. Maybe I'd better just trust these people. I'm already at their mercy, anyway,* he thought. He looked up at the three who were still staring at his tattoos, and said, "I guess I'd better tell you the whole story, although it would be better for you if you didn't know anything." For the next ten minutes Kelly related the whole tale, beginning with the shoot-down and ending with his close brush with Major Nikitin in Khabarovsk.

"Remarkable," Sevastyan responded when Jake was done. "And what are they doing with all those scientists?" he asked.

"Filling in the gaps in Soviet research. I would imagine that each of the men they kidnapped has crucial knowledge in a specific area needed by Soviet weapons development."

"And what about you? You're not a scientist, you're a pilot. Why did they capture you?"

"You'll understand if I don't answer that question."

Boris asked, "How do we know if any of this is true? How

do we know this is not just some wild lie? Maybe you *are* the murderer Sokolov!"

"You're looking at the evidence! I don't know what else to tell you. How long do you think a Soviet soldier would last in the ranks with these tattoos? Do you think I got these tattoos and burn marks and a broken arm just for grins and giggles?"

"I speak perfect English, because I *am* an American," the major insisted. "I didn't force Galina to bring me here; she was free to go. I was walking away when she came back after me and insisted that I come here.

"And when was the last time you can recall that an entire division of troops was mobilized to track down a deserter, even if he did commit rape and murder? Does that make sense to you?"

The three Russians stared at him for a moment. Boris finally spoke, but this time his voice had no tones of hostility or suspicion, "Alright. You can stay until your arm heals. But we stick with the story that Galina told me first, about the farmer Sergei Primakov. No one here must know any different; some might be tempted to turn you in. And for crying out loud, keep your shirt on! I don't want anyone else to see those tattoos."

Sevastyan knelt down and began probing the bone in Jake's upper arm with experienced fingers. Jake winced. With a wolfish grin Sevastyan spoke as he worked, "I am Sevastyan Zavrazhny. I was in the Soviet Navy for twenty-three years. I was sworn to kill all enemies of the State, especially Americans. I was a corpsman, and now these people call me 'Doctor.' I'm not really a doctor. But you may relax, Major Kelly. I don't think I will try to kill you at the moment, and most people don't die of a broken arm."

When he had completed his examination, Sevastyan said, "You have a mid-shaft fracture of the humerus. It feels like a clean break. Unfortunately we do not have access to an x-ray machine, so I can't verify my diagnosis. The bone appears to be broken in place, so there's no need to set it. I'll put a splint on it and immobilize it. You'll be in a sling for four weeks, and unable to use the arm for eight weeks. In twelve weeks you should be as good as new, if you behave yourself."

"*Spasibo*, Doctor," Jake said.

"You're welcome, *Sergei*," he replied with a mocking smile.

****

The work crew gathered in front of the mill, as they did every morning, to receive the day's work assignments. Boris stood on the flat bed of the logging truck and spoke to the group of men standing about on the ground.

"This here is Sergei Primakov. He's taking a break from his *kolkhoz* in Birobidzhan. He was mugged yesterday in Khab', a bunch of hooligans stole his clothes and papers and money, and gave him that broken arm," Boris said, pointing to Jake's immobilized right arm. "Galina happened to run into him in town. She's a sucker for hard-luck cases, bought his sob story, hook, line, and sinker, and brought the poor puppy home."

At that the men guffawed and elbowed each other in the ribs. Jake flushed with anger but restrained himself and pasted a tight smile on his face. He hated feeling helpless, but knew that he could not acquit himself well in a fight, or in anything else at the moment. He'd have to bide his time, then maybe he'd get a chance to put this young Paul Bunyan in his place.

"Comrade Primakov will be working in the office with Galina until his arm heals enough to bring him out into the yard, and then we'll see what he can do.

"Okay, today's work assignments: Sevastyan, you need to go to the Japanese consulate in Khab' today and get that contract signed for ten thousand board feet of lumber. Don't let them play hardball on the price: they need the lumber more than we need the business. You can take the Zaporozhets into town. And I'll have a list of parts for you to order. I busted a hydraulic line on the front-end loader yesterday, and it's going to be useless until it's fixed. That's what I'll be working on.

"Isidor, you, Filipp and Prokhor put the skidder on the lowboy, and go pick up all the stuff you felled yesterday south of Sidima.

"Yulian and Koloda, help Grisha run that pile of fir through the saw mill. We need to get it in the dryer before September, if it's going to be ready to plane down next spring.

"Let's get to it."

****

"You smell better than you did yesterday. You must have had a bath last night," said Galina matter-of-factly when "Sergei" entered the office.

"Well, good morning to you, too."

She stopped what she was doing and turned to face him. "I'm sorry. I guess I've picked up some bad habits working around men all the time, trying to keep my distance."

"Well, perhaps you haven't noticed, Miss, but I've not made a pass at you, and I'm not planning on doing so. So you'll forgive me if I keep *my* distance from you!"

Galina's face flushed with anger and she snapped, "Please *do* keep your distance! Besides, my brother beats anyone who comes within ten feet of me. Now enough of this talk!"

"Hey, I'm not the one who started it in the first place. You did. Now, maybe you could tell me what I'm supposed to be doing in here."

"That box of papers," she said, pointing at a large cardboard box that Kelly had assumed was trash, "contains orders, payments, and letters from customers. They need to be placed into the proper file folders in that file cabinet. No matter how hard I try to train him, Boris is not a businessman. He just throws stuff in that box and I have to deal with it later."

"Businessman, contracts, orders, customers. That all sounds so, so, *American*, so capitalistic. Are you sure you guys are really communists?"

"America didn't invent business, Sergei. I imagine businesses run much the same all around the world. But I guess we are rather unusual, by Soviet standards. We here actually do make a profit. The head of the Communist party in this krai is on the take. After we provide the official quota of lumber, he allows us to sell whatever else we can cut to Japan. He takes twenty percent of the sales, we get to keep the rest."

"But I thought Soviet industry usually missed the centrally-planned quotas."

"That's typically true. But when we get to keep the profit we work harder and we work longer hours. This mill is currently producing 130 percent of our annual quota. Business is good."

"I thought you said this is an underground community. If you are meeting a State quota, how 'underground' can you really be?"

"Much in Russia is not as it seems, Sergei. We do have an official quota, but neither our community nor any of our heavy equipment is on anyone's books, anywhere. There is no official oversight of our community. We receive no visits from Party officials. Our quota is strictly local, and what we produce is added into the production from all the timbering operations in the krai, effectively padding the numbers. Moscow has no idea we even exist. Because of our lumber production, this krai is one of the few districts in Siberia that actually meets or exceeds the wood products quota each year."

"You mean, it's like, Moscow gives a quota for ten sawmills, not knowing that Khabarovsk Krai actually has eleven?"

"Something like that, yes."

"But, Galina, isn't there a great deal of danger to you and the others if this whole scheme is discovered?"

"Of course. But we have a source in the KGB main office in Khab', and several years ago we were told that someone very high up had given an order that we were not to be interfered with. No one knows who or why, or how long this favored status will last. But that's life. Nothing is certain. We'll enjoy the ride as long as it lasts."

With his one good arm, Kelly tugged the box of papers over to the file cabinet, pulled up a chair, and began the boring job of filing. As Galina moved about the office working on other projects, the scent of her perfume permeated the room and Jake found himself staring from time to time. For the second time in two days he was struck by the beauty of her face and form. He was also attracted to the fact that she was no shrinking violet, and seemed to be able to hold her own no matter what group she was in. She had a femin—*Wait a minute, Jake! Don't go there! Don't even begin to think that way!* he told himself.

****

Bergman's fishing expedition had produced one important piece of information. The CIA Station Chief at the Moscow embassy had made discrete inquiries and learned that there were eight Yakov Sokolovs in the Soviet military, all of them accounted for. And yet the search in the Far Eastern High Command was continuing. Major assets had been deployed and someone was spending a lot of money moving troops and equipment. *All to search for a man that does not exist,* Bergman mused. *Interesting. I wonder what's going on? Did someone go rogue, and they're trying to reel him in? Was there an assassination we haven't heard about, and they're trying to nab the perpetrator?*

His quest for information on Chernikov turned up nothing he didn't already know. Chernikov's present location and assignment was unknown. The best information available suggested that when his unit was taken offline in Afghanistan, he followed Patrikeyev into the GRU. Since then, no other information had become available. *That by itself is unusual,* considered the analyst. *The dearth of intelligence might suggest a lockdown of info; maybe he's working on a black project.*

Sam scribbled a few more notes, and added them to the file folder he was building on the unexplained troop movements. He felt certain that sooner or later a piece of intelligence would crop up that would begin to connect the dots.

****

For the next three weeks Kelly performed menial clerical labor in the office. Although it was frustrating and boring, he wanted to make a contribution to his upkeep so he kept at it without complaint.

Slowly his arm healed. Sevastyan kept a close eye on it. Kelly found the older man to be friendly, and a great conversationalist. Whenever they were alone the two compared notes about the respective military services, swapped stories, and asked about each other's families and backgrounds. Though Jake never told his friend anything militarily useful, he felt that the man was trustworthy. He looked forward to his checkups, if only to have some time to talk.

Thrown together for three weeks with Galina, his admiration for her had grown as well. Though she possessed a sense of humor, she was quite serious-minded and rather intense. Galina had a short fuse, and the pilot began to learn to read her moods. Somewhere along the way, flying in the face of all his best judgment, he found himself being drawn to her. He loved her moral strength and courage and her ability to deal with a business, making rapid-fire good decisions.

Like that of her brother Boris, her hair was jet black; but while his was curly hers was long and straight. She kept it braided in a thick rope that was usually pinned up on top of her head. Her eyes were black, well set in a broad face with high cheekbones. Both she and her brother were dark-complected, offspring of a Ukranian father and a *Nanaitsy* mother. Her wide smiling mouth, set with perfect teeth and full lips, fascinated him and he carried on conversations with her just so he could enjoy watching her face. Galina was tall and slender, proportioned in such a way that Jake had to work at not staring.

As a thinker, she was well informed but very opinionated. That there might be shades of gray or middle ground was a possibility she had little use for; Kelly usually found her at one pole or another regarding most of the issues they talked about. The longer he worked with her, the more beautiful she appeared to him. It was becoming, for him, a problem.

****

"So, why have you never married? Couldn't find anyone to put up with you, or what?"

She looked at him with an expression that communicated patient disdain, and responded, "Now, why on earth would I ever want to marry? What *possible* advantage would there be for me to marry? I *already* have to take care of my brother and several other of the men on this site, who wouldn't have enough sense to come inside if it were raining cinder blocks. Why add a husband to that mix?" She shook her head like it was the dumbest question she'd ever heard, and turned back to the report she was working on.

Okay. That went nowhere, Jake thought to himself. The calculator wasn't working, and he had its parts spread all over the desk in an attempt to fix the paper-feed mechanism. After several moments of silence, a curious voice came back at him. "What about you? Why haven't *you* ever married?" *Two can play at this game, sweetheart; perhaps you ought to sit down.*

"What makes you think I'm not?"

"*Oh!* . . . I—I just assumed that you weren't. I mean, I didn't see a ring or anything."

Kelly grinned to himself. It was the first time she'd been flustered in three weeks. He wondered if he could take advantage of it.

"A ring? Were you looking for a ring?" he asked innocently.

"*Nyet!*" she snapped, "Of course not! What a stupid question!"

"Actually, I've got twelve children. They—"

"Twelve children? That's ridiculous! You're not old enough to have twelve children."

"Two wives," Jake explained, enjoying her consternation. "I've got two wives."

"Is that even legal in the United States?"

"No. But they're in different cities. Nobody knows." He turned his back on her and resumed working on the calculator.

She stared at his back for a moment, and then muttered, "You don't have two wives. You don't have any wives."

Jake just chuckled.

****

Galina pulled a thick black sweater over her blouse. Carefully she arranged her braid on her head, and pinned it in place. Examining her face in the mirror, she expertly added the tiniest, subtle bit of makeup, and an extra splash of perfume. *Why did I do that?* she asked herself. She stared at herself. *You know exactly why you did that, girl. Quit pretending. You're falling in love with him. And there is absolutely no future in it, and you know it.*

She walked into the office and looked about. There was no one but Boris.

"Where's Sergei?" she asked, fighting to keep the tone of disappointment out of her voice.

"Sergei," Boris said, drawing out the name to emphasize its falsity, "is working with the mill crew today. Sevastyan cleared him for heavier work last night. He's not ready for the timber crew yet, but he's getting there."

"Oh," Galina replied airily, as though it didn't matter. But it did. Major Kelly's improving arm meant the day was drawing near that Boris would make him leave. She wasn't ready to see him go.

"Be careful, sister."

"I can't imagine what you are talking about," she said, flipping through a stack of orders.

Boris walked up behind her, and gently turned her around, and gave her a big-brother hug. Despite her steely demeanor, a couple of tears escaped her eyes.

"You know exactly what I'm talking about, Galya. You can't fool me. You're falling in love with that man. It's been written all over your face for the last three weeks. You are tormenting yourself, little one; there can be no future for you with him. He's an American fugitive who's trying to get home. You are, well, you are my little Siberian princess, and you'd never be permitted to go to America. Our government wouldn't allow it." He felt her shoulders shake, and held her gently.

The care of his sister had fallen on Boris early in life. Their father had died in unknown circumstances serving the Soviet Union when she was one and he was six. Their mother died when Boris was fourteen. Always big and strong for his age, Boris had managed to keep the two of them together by working at a man's job from his early teens.

At critical turns in their lives help had always arisen from unexpected quarters, and Boris had wondered if they were being watched and taken care of from a distance. But no one had ever approached them or identified themselves as a benefactor, so for Boris it was an unresolved question.

He had gone straight into factory work, working at the T-72 main battle tank production plant in Omsk, where they had been living since the death of their father. She had gone to the university in Moscow, getting a degree in Mathematics. After she had been teaching for several years in Omsk, the two had received permission to move to Khabarovsk, where she resumed teaching while he worked in the rail yards. He eventually fell in with Sevastyan, who talked him into starting a timbering operation above Sidima. Not only were the necessary permits issued, but the head of the Communist Party in Khabarovsk Krai had loaned them a skidder and flatbed, in return for a percentage of profits. That was five years ago. Because they were able to operate both on and *over* the edge of legality, the business had blossomed and become very profitable. Japan's voracious appetite for lumber had given them a ready market for anything above their quota. They were successful beyond Boris' wildest dreams.

He was a careful and attentive big brother, protecting Galina from men, some rich, some powerful, some both, who would have used and abused her. One man had managed to get beyond Boris' protective presence, and wouldn't take *"nyet"* for an answer. Boris had happened to walk in when the man, having failed in his propositions, was on the verge of forcing her. The fellow was fortunate that his next ride was to the hospital and not the morgue.

Boris patted her gently on the shoulder and said, "I've decided to allow him to stay through the winter."

"You what? You never discussed it with me!" She pushed

away from him and glared at him through teary eyes.

"Now quiet down. I never discussed it with you because you were no longer able to give me a wise answer about it. You would have answered from your heart, not your head. Now shush, Galya," he admonished when she began to protest again. "You know I'm right. Anyway, I did talk it over with Sevastyan and we agreed there's not much chance he'll be spotted among our crew. If he works hard I'll let him stay through the winter and he'll leave when he's ready in late spring."

She absorbed his words and knew he was right. The flash of anger drained away and she admitted, "Thank you, Borya. I'm glad he *is* staying. I want to enjoy every moment of his remaining time here."

"Be careful, Galya. It would kill me to see your heart broken."

"I'll be careful. If it is supposed to be, it will be. Somehow I know that."

Chapter 23

Wednesday, September 24, 1986: 1315 local
west of Tara, USSR

General Nikolai Pavlovich Chernikov, commandant of Prison 87, director of the GRU project *Krasnyy Voskhod*, stared at the picture in the dossier. The man in the photo was staring at the camera, a confident grin on his face. *Who are you, really, Major Kelly? You are just a pilot, are you not? My men are Spetsnaz. How is it that you have bested me and my men in every encounter except the very first when we shot you down?* The face in the picture seemed to say, *You won that first encounter only because I wasn't looking.*

He was jarred from his thoughts by the impatient jangle of the phone.

"Chernikov."

"Sir, General Patrikeyev is on the line for you."

"Put him through, please."

After a few seconds, he heard the voice of his mentor at GRU headquarters, "*Dobroye utro*, Nikolai. Go secure, please."

Chernikov engaged the scrambler, waited for the whistling sounds to end, and then responded, "*Zdravstvuytye*, General. What can I do for you, sir?"

"An update on the manhunt, please."

"Well, sir, there's not much to report. Since Kelly escaped from the train station in Khabarovsk last month, we've not had a single sighting report. With the KGB's help, we located the truck the major jumped into. It was delivering a load of sand to a construction site. The site, the sand pile, everything there was carefully searched. There was not a scrap of evidence that Kelly had ever been there. The theory now is that he exited the truck before it got to its destination."

"It's been a month, General! By now he could be anywhere. He could even have escaped the country."

"It's possible, but we don't believe that's the case. Major Nikitin believes he is still in the Khab' area, sir."

"On what grounds?"

"Up until the train station, we'd run across Kelly's trail multiple times, every couple of days. Nikitin believes this is an indication that our search techniques and security measures are effectively countering the major's attempts to evade detection. So if he's dropped off the grid, it must be because he's gone to ground and quit moving—otherwise we'd have spotted him again. As Nikitin quaintly puts it, 'a bear that stays in his cave leaves no tracks.' Major Nikitin believes that Kelly is still within 50 kilometers of Khab'. And I think he's right."

"I'm getting a lot of pressure from the Kremlin, Nikolai. Geredin is agitating for 'shoot on sight' rules of engagement. The others are beginning to see it his way. And they have a point: if Kelly escapes, the damage to our country will be incalculable."

"Sir," Chernikov began carefully, "Major Kelly remains an extraordinarily high value intelligence target. He's just as valuable now as he was the first time we captured him. We need to know what he knows about the F-16 project. Please, give me more time! We can reel him in. We've had a few bad breaks, but we will catch him."

He heard Patrikeyev sigh over the phone. It was an odd sound that the scrambler did not handle well, coming across as more of a drawn-out squawk. "General Chernikov, I have expended what little political capital I have on you and project *Krasnyy Voskhod*. My future, not to speak of yours, is now wholly dependent upon this endeavor. I will hold the wolves off as long as I can, Nikolai, but you'd better produce Major Kelly. And you probably need to look to your own security."

"My security, General Patrikeyev?"

"*Da*. You know that I'm not going to make a move against you, Nikolai. If I am dissatisfied with your performance, I will simply reassign you. But there are other people, important people, who will not forgive you if you fail."

"I assume you are speaking of General Geredin."

"Da."

"Very well, General. I will look to my safety and the safety of my people. We are, after all, Spetsnaz. Comrade Geredin and his KGB stooges might find it a little more difficult than he imagines to take me down."

"Do not underestimate him, Nikolai. He's a wily old bear, and I have already poked him in the eye once, and that makes him an angry, wily old bear."

"Yes, sir. I will be careful. Now, General, I have an idea for the next phase of our search. I would like to propose a major 'troop training exercise,' for asymmetrical urban warfare. I am suggesting that we launch a house-to-house, village-to-village search beginning at the extreme south of Primorsky Krai and moving up north into Khabarovsk Krai. Every soldier will be issued a large, laminated photo of Major Kelly. We will couple the search with actual training in techniques for hunting down armed and dangerous fugitives. We can bill this as a training exercise for tracking down Afghan insurgents."

"You are trying to flush him out of his hiding place?"

"Yes, sir, and to drive him north, away from the seaports and transportation centers. It will become more and more difficult for him to hide and survive if there's nothing around him but the Siberian taiga. As a precaution, I will leave significant detachments at every port and rail center, just in case he manages to slip through the net and head south."

"This is a good plan, Nikolai. I will contact the Far Eastern High Command for their approval, and ask for an infantry division to be temporarily attached your command, General Chernikov."

****

Kelly was covered in sawdust when the work day was over. He had been working with the saw mill crew for the past week. His arm was healing, but he was not yet able to use it for heavy work. Sevastyan wanted him to wait for another four weeks before he put much stress on the bone. His present work was like physical therapy: he was using a full range of motion, but without heavy stress.

He found himself loving the work and the rough men alongside of whom he was working. The smell of fresh cut timber was like perfume. The mud and dust and sawdust of the yard, the blue sky above, and the fall colors, were glorious. If he had not been a fugitive, and had not longed for his own homeland, he'd have been happy to stay the rest of his life. The dark Siberian taiga was a place of beauty and mystery; it drew him in some inexplicable way.

The culture of his Russian friends was growing on him, too. There was a coarse good humor about them. They had a passionate love for the *Rodina*, for mother Russia. In the underground community led by Boris and Galina, there was a friendly openness and hospitality he'd not seen in the cities. *Perhaps it's because they're getting to know and trust me*, he pondered.

He found a note pinned to his bunk: *Please come dine with me tonight. Galya.* He sniffed the paper; there was the faintest hint of her perfume on it. He knew he should not be forming an attachment; there was no hope of a future in it. But her beautiful eyes were like dark pools, and when he looked into them he felt as though he was falling in. He was helpless.

While he waited his turn for the tub, he informed his roommates, Filipp and Yulian, that he wouldn't be eating with them.

"No? You have special plans, Sergei?" asked Yulian, winking at Filipp.

"Uh, the boss has asked me over," he replied, hoping they would assume it was Boris.

No such luck. Yulian whistled and Filipp smiled knowingly. "The boss? The big ugly one, or the gorgeous one?"

Kelly laughed, "I'm going to tell Boris you said that. He might want you to explain in detail exactly what you meant."

"Oh, no, no, no! You don't understand, Sergei. It's not me that should be afraid of Boris—it's you! He's very protective of his sister."

"I never said it was his sister who invited me," Kelly protested.

"Oh, it's her, alright. Boris left for town at noon, and he's not expected back until late tonight."

Jake grinned sheepishly, "I think I'm more concerned about my safety around her than I am around him. Have you ever been the target of her wrath?"

Both Filipp and Yulian laughed. "Who hasn't?" Filipp said. "She's a little spitfire. I've seen her back Boris down. I wouldn't want to tangle with her."

****

When Kelly walked into Galina's home, the table was set for two, with candles. He realized that the setting was an open statement about how she felt toward him. And he felt the same way toward her. He shut the door behind him, his mind filled with a thousand questions. He was drawn to the woman with an attraction that went far beyond mere sensuality. He loved everything she was, from the tough, competent exterior complete with snarky comments, to the way her eyes laughed when she teased him. *But there's no future for us, not with her trapped here, and me in the USA. Should I run now while I still can? Should I just leave? I'd rather die than break her heart.* He hesitated, uncertain, torn.

"Sergei?" Her voice floated around the corner, from the kitchen.

"It's me," he answered.

"Well, don't just stand there, you lazy oaf! Come in here and help me."

He was afraid to move, for his next action would set the course of his life; he knew that with clarity. He was rooted to the spot, savoring the fact that she had declared her intentions, but unsure if he should respond in kind. *I cannot break her heart.*

"Are you deaf? Your arm is still healing, I know, but surely you can peel potatoes?"

He didn't answer, but stared at the candles flickering on

the table that had been set so carefully. So . . . lovingly. *If I don't run right now, the only thing left for me is to commit to getting her out of the USSR, and home to the States—whatever it takes. There's no other option. If I return her affection, I cannot, I will not leave her here forever. I will not break her heart.*

She appeared around the corner and saw him staring at the candles as though mesmerized. She walked up to him, tilted her head and said, "Jacob? Is something wrong?"

He looked into the dark pools of her beautiful eyes, and fell in.

Chapter 24

Sam Bergman was late getting to his office. An early morning staff meeting in the building's auditorium about changes to CIA employee benefits had been stupefyingly boring. He'd managed to sneak out without being noticed. He knew all the HR employee benefit claptrap was important, but he wasn't interested. He would still want his job even without benefits and at half his current salary; he loved what he did. *Let the bean counters do their thing, and let me do my thing; just don't waste my time.*

It was against regulations, but he had a small, personal coffee pot in his office. He loaded the filter up with a dark Italian roast, and opened his inbound document safe while the coffee perked. The transcript of an intercept caught his eye. An entire Soviet infantry division had been moved to Primorsky Krai to engage in a training exercise: a house-to-house search. The odd thing is that they were searching every single house in the populated areas. Already the dragnet had moved from the southern tip of the krai, up to the closed city of Vladivostok, all the way over to Nakhodka, and every coastal city in between. It was billed as an urban warfare exercise designed to instruct troops how to identify and locate insurgents hiding out in the general population.

Maybe. But I don't think so. Something else is going on here. I just don't know what.

Bergman poured his cup of brew, filling his small office with the aroma, and shuffled quickly through the rest of the transcripts. Several had to do with the logistics of the troop movement and the chain of command pertaining to the exercise. The rest were unrelated.

Just in case they might be related to the others, he pulled out the personal file folder he'd been keeping on the unusual troop movements between Omsk and Khabarovsk. He wrote a précis of each intercept, attached its document file number and put the personal file away. *Something's cooking in the Soviet Far East; I just can't put my finger on it. Yet.*

****

"Do you enjoy games?" Galina asked Kelly. They had cleared away the dishes, and Boris was sitting in the corner, smoking a pipe and reading. Not only had Boris acquiesced to their growing relationship, much to the surprise of the couple he had given his blessing.

"I do."

"Then let me teach you how to play *Chapayev*. It's sort of like your checkers, just with a Russian twist," she said with a mischievous twinkle in her eye.

"How so?"

"You don't capture your opponent's pieces by jumping over them, as in checkers. You capture them by knocking them off the board."

"That does sound Russian," Kelly agreed with a chuckle.

They had played halfway through the first game when Boris got to his feet, tossed his book onto the chair, and said, "Sergei, do you feel ready to work with the timbering crew? That's where I really need you."

"I do. Sevastyan cleared me for heavy work on Friday, says my arm is completely healed. I need to do something to rebuild the strength in it. I'd love to work on the timbering crew."

"I'm not sure how long we'll be able to cut before the snow gets too deep, but in any case, you can start tomorrow. I'll go tell Isidor." Boris pulled on his coat and stepped out into the cold night.

After they finished their game the two sat for a long time, talking. They had talked about their families, their childhood memories, and sundry topics when Galina asked, "Do you believe in God?"

Jake shrugged his shoulders, and replied, "I don't know. I don't think about it much. How about you?"

"I'm an atheist, but I think about it a great deal," she said.

"I'm an agnostic," he said. "I just don't get into religion all that much. God might exist, he might not. Doesn't really matter to me."

"You're kidding?"

"No, I'm not. Why? What's wrong with that?" he asked, surprised at the fervor of her response.

"That is absolutely the dumbest thing I've ever heard," she accused.

"What's dumb?" he asked, confused.

"That it does not matter to you whether or not God exists. That's stupid!" she insisted, eyes flashing.

At that moment, Boris returned. He sensed the tension in the air and stood watching the two.

Jake ignored him and looked at Galina, mystified. He liked her combativeness, but he wasn't sure he liked this. "Wait a minute! You just said that you're an atheist. How in the world can you call being agnostic dumb? You've already decided that God does not exist. I've just punted on the question. I'm more open-minded than *you* are. How does my response qualify as 'the dumbest thing' you've ever heard? I don't get it!"

"The question of God's existence is the single greatest question of life, Jacob. I don't believe he does exist, but if he does, it matters more than anything. If God exists, it changes everything. How can you say that it doesn't matter?"

Boris looked at Jake and rolled his eyes. With a wry grin he shook his head, turned around and left the house.

Jake stared at her, stunned. "What on earth are you talking about, Galina?"

"You can't avoid the question of God, Jacob. It matters, and because it matters, it's foolish to just 'decide not to decide.' You're not being open-minded when you do that, you're being intellectually lazy. You just said a few moments ago, 'I don't think about it much.' But you should! You should think about it all the time, until you can assert firmly, 'God does not exist,' or until you come to believe that he does. And if he were to exist, that raises a whole host of issues."

Kelly looked at her, the attack so utterly unexpected he hadn't a clue as to how to respond.

"Jacob, it's like this: if there is no evidence for God, there's even less for demigods, or super-humans, or divine beings that are somehow halfway in between. As a mathematician, that's an improbability so great to my mind, it does not even bear investigation.

"So what are we left with? Either an all-powerful, creator-God exists, or there's no God at all. If a God worthy of the name exists, he created everything. There is, after all, the fact of our existence, a fact which must be accounted for somehow, either by natural processes, or by a creator.

"Jacob, think about this: if we were created by natural processes—hydrogen, so to speak—then *nothing* really matters. We construct our own personal meaning and morality the best we can, live our meaningless lives, and then we are gone, having left no more of a mark than a mosquito does when it collides with a tree. We're gone, and after a generation or two, no one remembers, no one cares.

"On the other hand, if we were made by a creator-God, then he is the one who designed us and owns us. It would be reasonable to assume that he would have intentions as to how we are to live. Consequently, if he exists, both genuine meaning and morality also exist. He is the one to whom we will one day give account and who will one day dole out reward or punishment according to whatever measure he has determined. In other words, if God *does* exist, *everything we do* matters.

"So your agnosticism is foolish, Jacob, because you don't search out and come to a conclusion on the single greatest question of existence. You don't really care whether God exists. That's philosophical Russian roulette, because it matters a great deal whether or not he exists." She stopped and took a sip of her tea.

"Hold on just a minute!" Kelly objected. "I think the pot's calling the kettle black! You're right—I have not spent *ten seconds* thinking about whether God exists and I don't intend to. I frankly don't care. But how is that any different from you arbitrarily deciding that he *doesn't* exist? How is your uninformed decision that he does not exist superior in any way to my uninformed decision not to waste time thinking about it?" Kelly asked, somewhat heatedly.

"It's superior because I have spent a lot of time studying the issue. It's *not* an uninformed decision," she replied.

"What do you mean?"

"I mean, for example, that I have studied a number of the eastern religions, I've also worked my way through Islam, the Greek mystery religions, and the various earth religions and I have rejected them all as improbable. I've just started on Judaism and Christianity. When I'm done with those, I'm pretty much finished. At that point I can conclude that God does not exist, and I won't spend another second thinking about it or worrying about it. But I won't be trapped in the blatantly dangerous and illogical position of admitting that he *might* exist, but if he does, his existence *does not matter*. As far as I am concerned, that's a philosophical irresponsibility."

"So you're trying to prove whether or not God exists?" asked Kelly.

"No; as a mathematician I don't believe such a proof is possible. But I am trying to establish probabilities. I'm asking the question, 'which model of existence and beginnings, between atheism and the teachings of the various religions, best accounts for life as I know it?'" Galina corrected.

"So what have you come up with?"

"I told you: I'm an atheist at present, and expect to be one when I am done. But I will be an atheist who has examined the evidence; I will be an *informed* atheist."

"But that's a foregone conclusion. Scientific evidence will never support the idea of the existence of God. So we are back to square one; like I said: it's a waste of time," asserted Jake triumphantly.

"You're not listening," she said patiently. "I'm *not* examining scientific evidence, and besides, you're wrong about that, too. Examining *scientific evidence* to settle the question of God's existence is a fool's errand, a category error of the worst sort. Science deals with natural phenomena, natural cause and effect. Science is by nature and definition, materialistic. It is not *competent* to answer questions concerning God, who is by definition *super*natural if he exists at all.

"The evidences that I am examining are the teachings of the various religions about beginnings and life. The religions I have rejected, I rejected because *their teachings* simply do not stack up to life as it is or their historical claims don't match the historical record."

Jacob Kelly had never given much thought to what he believed about ultimate questions, and he now understood that this lovely woman was rebuking him for that thoughtlessness. He had decided not to decide about what she claimed was the single most important fact of life: the existence of God. It was something he'd have to think about—but not right now.

Chapter 25

Friday, November 28, 1986: 1325 local
above Sidima, USSR

Light snowfall came to the Sikhote-Alin mountains in early October, but a rare November storm brought heavy snows to the region. News reports were calling it a "fifty-year storm." A brief warming spell followed, creating lots of mud. Boris and Sevastyan continued sending out timbering crews, trying to extend the harvesting season as far as possible. But the temperatures finally dropped again producing a hard freeze that would persist the rest of the winter. When the work-crews experienced several minor accidents caused by icy conditions the community decided to end timbering operations for the season after one last day of cutting.

Prokhor drove the flatbed into the yard loaded down with large, fat logs for the mill. Filipp, Yulian, and "Sergei" followed the semi into the yard in a pickup truck. Isidor guided the tracked material handler to the side of the truck and began unloading the logs and stacking them in the yard.

Boris walked up to the side of the flatbed, clipboard in hand, and began estimating the board-foot content of the load. Galina stood in the office door observing the men process the last logs of the year. It had been a profitable harvesting season, and the entire community was excited about their growing prosperity.

As Filipp watched the first log being lifted off the truck, he noticed that the side supports were coming up with it. Boris was studying his clipboard, and was not aware of the danger he was in.

"STOP! *STOP!* ISIDOR! *NO!*" Filipp shouted, waving his hands trying to draw the operator's attention, but Isidor could not hear him above the din of the machinery. As soon as the side supports were lifted clear of their channels there was nothing to hold the logs in place. They began to tumble off the truck onto Boris. From the direction of the office came a piercing, anguished scream that rose above the noise of the machinery.

Jake had been watching Galina, and had not seen Boris. Burned into his mind forever would be the slow motion image of her growing horror as the logs rolled, helter-skelter, off the flatbed. As she dashed toward the truck, her face contorted by fear and grief, Jake realized something terrible was happening. He sprinted toward her, intercepting her before she could get close to the truck.

"NO, NO, NO!" she cried, beating him on the chest. Jacob held her tight with one hand, and pulled her head to his chest, covering her eyes with the other. Then he turned and looked at the jumbled mass of logs. Sticking out from under the pile was a pair of legs. He recognized Boris's boots.

Men were running from all over the yard to help, and Isidor began carefully removing the logs with the material handler, trying not to cause any further movement on the pile that could worsen the situation. The men worked carefully, but everyone knew that they were retrieving a body, not rescuing a person.

Galina collapsed in sobs, and Kelly picked her up and carried her into the house.

****

How desperately he wanted to comfort her, to make the pain go away, to say something, anything, to assuage her grief. But he could not. There was nothing that could be said, as far as Jake was concerned. Boris was gone, and that was that.

But still there was the strange compulsion to say something. Kelly had noted for years, had become cynical about it, how people who had not claimed to believe in God or in life after death suddenly became quite certain that the deceased still existed somewhere, that they were in a "better place" or somehow "better off." It was a well-intentioned deception. They wanted to believe it, they wanted the bereaved to take comfort in it, even if nothing in their lives or their belief systems prior to the tragedy gave any credence to such a belief.

Others who had rejected belief in God because they felt it unscientific, Jake noted, nevertheless in the face of death suddenly professed at least a temporary belief in some sort of ambiguous unscientific spirituality, saying things like "her spirit is still with us," or "I feel his presence," or "she remains alive in our memories." *Not in any objective sense*, Jake thought sadly. *Boris is gone. All he was has been wiped out, erased as though the world never knew him. There is no sense whatsoever in which he, in his self-conscious personality, is living or aware. All our platitudes are so self-serving*, Jake thought. *He's alive in our memories. Really? Lot of good that does him.*

Kelly was determined not to yield to the temptation to offer a well-intentioned but false platitude, and was quite sure that Galya would call him on it, anyway, if he did. So, he said nothing. But he was there for her, and that was what mattered. He was there to support, to serve, to do whatever needed to be done. But he would give her no false comfort. "His spirit is here with you," is a warm sentimentality, but in the end it means nothing when what you need is a good hug.

****

The color and joy was gone from her life. Galina functioned on automatic for the next several weeks, feeling nothing and trying to avoid thinking about the loss of her brother. Sevastyan stepped forward and took the leadership of the community, a necessary move that found approval among everyone, including Galina.

Jacob Kelly's arm was now fully healed, and he began an aggressive regime of exercise to regain operational fitness for the next portion of his escape. Word-of-mouth gossip filtering up from the south made it clear that he would have no luck traveling to Nakhodka, or any other port when the winter was over. A military training exercise had literally taken over the whole of the Primorsky Krai and was moving north, soon to reach the Khabarovsk area. Rumors spoke of assault-rifle-toting soldiers guarding the seaports, airports, and rail centers.

This left him without a plan. He wasn't sure what to do now that the southern route was completely closed. He couldn't head back west: the distances were so immense that he knew he would be identified and recaptured at some point. That left but one option: northeast. But aside from a few villages and small towns scattered across the landscape, the far northeastern expanse of Siberia contained few resources and still fewer transportation options, other than his own two feet.

Except for the Bering Straits, he mused. At their narrowest point there was not but fifty miles separating Siberia from Alaska. *I wonder if I could steal a boat?* One day in January, he mentioned the idea to Sevastyan.

"That would work, Sergei. An ocean-going kayak is what you need." Sevastyan never called him by his real name, fearing that he would slip up when others were around. "The whole Chukchi Peninsula is populated by Yupiks and other indigenous tribes. They all fish, and all the coastal villages have ocean kayaks. And they're no friend of the Sovs.

"When I was in the Navy, one of my tours of duty was up around that whole coast. There is very little government presence up there in the villages, although you will need to stay clear of larger towns, like Uelen. You'll also want to stay clear of the Diomedes. There are very sensitive surveillance stations on those islands, and they might pick you up even in a kayak, if you get too close.

"Your best option, Sergei, would be to launch from the north shore. The Siberian Coastal current will take you east until it hits the north-bound Bering Slope current. That current will set you to the north, away from the Diomedes. Ice could be a problem; September will be your best bet. The ice pack has receded farthest north by early September."

And so it was settled. Kelly spent the rest of the winter laboring on the timber crew, rebuilding his strength. Every spare moment, with Sevastyan's help, he was collecting hard-to-find maps and equipment. The older man had a source in Khabarovsk, and though it came with a price, Kelly was able to obtain military-grade expedition gear, such as good boots to replace his worn ones, a camouflaged backpack, tent, and mummy bag, and other items as well as clothing. He also secured a pair of snow shoes, since he would be leaving when the northlands still had deep snow on the ground.

The money to outfit him came from what Sevastyan and Galina had saved from their timbering profits. The plan was that Galina would drive Kelly as far north from Khabarovsk as she could, and that he would walk from there. The target date was Sunday, May 3.

"I will come back for you, Galina. Somehow I will bring you to the United States, and when I do, I will make you my wife." They discussed plans of how she might be able to escape, and made arrangements for her to leave word of her whereabouts if she was no longer in Sidima when Kelly returned for her.

****

The winter passed slowly. Though timbering operations had ceased for the winter, the dryer and the planer shop were busy, and they accumulated stacks of finished lumber ready to ship in the spring.

Galina refused to speak of Boris' death. Whereas she'd previously had great confidence in her intellectual ability to think her way through religious and philosophical matters, that confidence evaporated with Boris' death and she refused to deal with it. It was clear she was having a hard time living with her own worldview, which provided her no hope and no means of thinking of Boris in any sense other than a momentary meteor on an otherwise empty, black sky. Jake continued to provide her with quiet strength, and the tragedy made the bonds between them even stronger.

Though time may have stood still during the slow winter

months for the logging community above Sidima, it was not standing still for General Chernikov. His soldiers were beating the bushes, moving north through Primorsky Krai, trying to flush the quail. In January they passed into Khabarovsk Krai, looking for their quarry, and in April they were getting close to Sidima.

Chapter 26

It had been five months since Boris's untimely death. Galina was finally able—and willing—to talk about her brother. His death had strengthened her, and she had refused to succumb to bitterness or self-pity. The heaviness that had settled over the tiny village in November and December had lifted, and they were looking forward to a new season of harvesting timber. Everyone had remained busy over the winter months in the dryer and planer shops, and there were piles of finished lumber ready to ship. "Sergei" had become as natural a part of the community as Filipp or Isidor, and no one thought of him as temporary.

The telephone rang in the office and Galina answered it. Sevastyan continued working on a quote he had to deliver to the Japanese consulate later in the day. Her tone, however, made him stop and pay attention, and he listened with growing apprehension to her side of the conversation.

"When did you find out? . . . *Da* . . . *Da* . . . Do they suspect that he is here, or is this just part of the larger search? . . . Oh, good, that's a relief. When are they supposed to be here? . . . Uh-huh. . . . They have his picture? Then Sevastyan and I are finished. Someone is bound to talk, for sure. Will I be able to stay with your sister? . . . Thank you! I expect I'll be there in the next several days. Listen, control of the operation will pass to Grigori. No one here knows anything, other than Sevastyan and myself. Hopefully they will not take vengeance on the innocent. . . . *Nyet* . . . Ivan, thank you for everything. I know that this phone call puts you at risk. You probably just saved our lives. Tell your sister I will be coming. . . . *Da.* . . . *Poka.*"

She hung up the phone, pale and trembling.

"What is it, little one?" Sevastyan asked, already guessing.

"That was Ivan at the KGB office in Khab'. The searchers will get here today, in about two hours. We have to leave, Sevastyan. We are finished here. Both of us know who Sergei really is, and the State is not going to forgive us for giving him sanctuary. If we stay, we put the others at risk." She began to weep. "I'm so sorry, Sevastyan. This is your home, too. And now my actions have ruined your life. You're losing your home, and everyone here is losing you. You're our doctor. It was you and Boris who started this camp, and now it's all coming apart and all because of me."

The old man crossed the room and took her in his arms. He pressed her head against his chest as he stroked her hair, and said quietly, "Some things are worth doing, little one, no matter what the cost. What you have done for Major Kelly was worth it. You were righting a wrong, and you'll hear no regrets and no rebuke from me.

"And do not worry about me, little one," he said with a smile. "This is only one of several operations I've started. I have a place to go. It is a foolish bear that has but one den.

"Come. We must hurry."

****

The workers gathered around the flatbed truck on which Sevastyan was standing. From where Galina was positioned she saw the mound of Boris' grave with its marker, far behind Sevastyan, at the edge of the clearing. Knowing that she would be leaving her brother's grave, never to return, made her begin weeping once again.

"Within the next hour and a half, government troops will be arriving here," Sevastyan began in his clear, powerful voice. "They are searching for a fugitive. These are the ones who've been searching throughout Primorsky Krai, and now they are here. Unfortunately, Galina, Sergei and myself have had some contact with the fugitive and we don't wish to be questioned by these soldiers, so we are leaving. We will not be coming back. Grigori, I am leaving you in charge.

"When these searchers come answer their questions honestly; lie about nothing and you will probably be okay. They might hang around for several days, but I suspect as long as you tell the truth you will have nothing to fear. Do not lie to protect us—they will know you are lying.

"We have counted it a privilege to be your friends and comrades. I wish you the very best. Grigori, the keys to everything are in the office. Someone may have my house and Galina's house. We cannot stay to say personal goodbyes. It is vital to our safety that we leave now. May God be with you all."

****

The little orange Zaporozhets was loaded to the gills when they finally pulled away from the fallen-down cottage where Kelly's duffel bag and new backpacking gear had been stored. The snow was still thigh-deep and Kelly's pants were wet and cold when he returned to the car.

As they turned north on the M60 to head for Khabarovsk, a military convoy pulled off at the intersection and deployed to set up a checkpoint. If the threesome had been five minutes later they would have been caught.

On the south side of Khabarovsk, Galina let Sevastyan off at a friend's house. She got out and hugged him, and Kelly embraced him as well. But there was no time for extended goodbyes and soon the little orange car was picking its way through the city, headed north.

Three hundred kilometers later, as dusk was approaching, Galina entered a line with other vehicles, waiting to drive onto the auto ferry at the Amur River at Komsomolsk.

The ferryman approached the car and said, "Papers, please." She passed over her identification, and he studied it with the boredom of one who was looking forward to getting off work. His eyebrows went up, impressed, when he saw that she was the director of a timber collective.

After returning her papers he asked, "What is your purpose in crossing the river today, Comrade Toporova?"

"I'm evaluating a stand of timber farther north, to see if it's worth harvesting."

"Very well. Your papers, please," he said, pointing to Kelly.

Feigning impatience, she snapped, "He's an employee, and he's with me. Don't waste my time!"

The ferryman shrugged, and went on to the next car.

They crossed the river without further incident. Galina drove for several more hours, then she pulled off the road and they slept in the car.

****

The phone jangled on the desk of the old spy. He grumbled, then picked it up.

"Speak."

"Please go secure."

The old man grumbled again, set the scrambler and replied impatiently, "Speak!"

"Yes, sir," the man on the other end responded nervously. "We've a lead on Major Kelly, sir. He spent the winter with a logging operation in Khabarovsk Krai."

"Well, go on."

"It was a logging operation above Sidima, sir."

The old man felt his chest pounding and massaged it with his free hand. "Not that operation?"

"Yes, sir. *That* operation."

The old spy's heart sank. "Oh, no! Did they pick anyone up?"

"*Nyet.* The agent in charge did not find it necessary. Everyone cooperated freely, on the spot. Apparently Major Kelly left with two others an hour before the troops arrived. The loggers identified Kelly from the photographs and said that he was traveling under the name Sergei Primakov."

"And the girl?" asked the old man, holding his breath.

The voice on the other end of the phone hesitated. "I'm

sorry, sir. She was one of the two that left with Kelly."

The old man slammed his hand down on his desk and cursed.

"They put out a description on her and the car. Roadblocks are being established everywhere. If she is still on the road, they'll snag her soon, sir. What are your orders?"

The old intelligence officer thought for a moment and then said, "She's to be put in a detention cell and isolated. We want to know everything she knows about Kelly. She can be interrogated, but I will tolerate no physical torture. I'll personally kill anyone who puts so much as a bruise on her. I expect you to make that clear to the local head of the KGB in Khabarovsk."

"Yes, sir."

"Prepare papers for her, permitting her to cross into China. I want the Chinese government to issue her a *Certificate of Permanent Residence of Aliens* card. The KGB resident in Beijing can handle that. The girl will not be allowed to reenter Russia. She has placed me in a situation where I have no choice. It's the only way I can protect her now."

****

Galina pulled over to the side of the road. There had been no traffic for the past fifty kilometers. One hundred meters ahead of the car was the Amgun River. She looked at Kelly and a tear rolled down her cheek.

"This is as far as I can take you. The road gets rougher from here and I don't want to risk the ferry. It's pretty unusual for them to have civilian traffic beyond this point."

He reached across and gently brushed the tear away with his thumb. "Galya, give me three years. If I survive Siberia, somehow, some way, I will get you to the United States. If you've not heard from me by the first of May, 1990, then you'd better move on with your life. If I've not contacted you it will be because something will have happened to me."

"Three years, Jacob Kelly. You have my word."

"I hate goodbyes. I'm not going to do a long goodbye." He leaned over and kissed her, and whispered, "I love you." He got out of the car and pulled his pack and gear out of the back seat. He strapped on the snowshoes and wrestled into the heavy pack. Clumping around to the driver's side, he leaned over and she rolled down the window. He kissed her again and asked, "Are you familiar with Orion, the hunter?"

"The constellation? *Da*. It was the first one Boris taught me to identify."

"It will be our constellation. When I look up at Orion, I will know you are looking at him, too. Whatever miles separate us, we can at least have that together."

"But what if it's cloudy?" she asked, weeping softly.

"It won't always be cloudy, dear Galya," he said, gently wiping the tears from her cheeks. "When you look up at night and see the hunter, know that somewhere I am seeing the same stars and thinking of you."

"I love you, Jacob Kelly."

"And I love you, dear Galya. I will come for you."

He kissed her again, and clumped off into the woods.

****

Kelly's goal was to make at least thirty kilometers per day. Sevastyan had guessed that it probably would work out to more like fifteen, because of the wet terrain. The Siberian Far East is riddled with rivers, lakes, and marshes. Sevastyan had warned that it would be his greatest problem. There were no bridges, few roads, and no railroads that he would encounter. Every river would present its own problem for crossing. The solution they had come up with was for Kelly to spend up to two days looking for a dry way to cross the wider rivers. Failing that, he would swim the river. He was packing an air mattress as floatation for his pack and gear, and a thermal dry suit to keep him from hypothermia. It had been prohibitively expensive, but Sevastyan had insisted on paying for it. Kelly often wondered who Sevastyan's contacts were in Khabarovsk but knew better than to ask. He suspected that most of the gear was stolen Soviet military property. *If that's the case*, he thought, *so much the better!*

He followed the course of the Amgun River as it wound north and east, looking for a boat or any means of crossing. The snow was around four feet deep, and the snowshoes were a necessity. Within an hour he was beginning to sweat, so he stopped and removed several layers, then walked until dusk.

Jake set up a snow camp that night, resolved to swim the river on the morrow if no other means of crossing presented itself. As the temperature dropped, he was thankful that the old Navy corpsman had helped him collect expedition gear. It would make the difference between a long, tough trek and a miserable, perhaps impossible one.

****

"Papers, please," insisted the ferryman at Komsomolsk. The man Galina had encountered yesterday was nowhere in sight. "What is your purpose for crossing the Amur today, comrade?"

"I am returning from evaluating timber. I am the director of the Sidima Timber Collective," she said as she handed him her identification.

He examined her papers, then returned them to her and waved her onto the ferry. After a thirty-minute trip across the river the ferry docked on the opposite side and the cars began rolling off. When it was her turn, she drove the Zaporozhets off the boat but was immediately stopped by a uniformed officer. As he walked around to her door a car pulled in front of her, blocking her way.

"Please get out of the car, Comrade Toporova," the officer asked politely.

"What is this about, officer?" she asked.

"Routine matter, ma'am. We just have some questions for you. Please get out of the car." Several other uniformed men walked up and one opened the door for her. She got out of the car, and immediately they slapped a pair of handcuffs on her and hustled her over to a waiting Zil. It was the last time she ever saw the little orange Zaporozhets.

****

It was late evening when Galina arrived at the KGB headquarters in Khabarovsk. She was searched thoroughly, along with her few possessions from the car, and then locked in a cell in the basement of the building. It was dank and dark, and smelled foul. There was nothing in the cell, no bed, no chair, just a bucket in the corner for her toilet, and that was it. She curled up on the floor and cried herself to sleep.

****

"Oh, you poor dear!" the matronly woman cooed when she opened the cell door and observed Galina on the floor. She bustled in with an air of command and snapped at the male guards accompanying her, instructing them to bring a bed and chair right away and *why weren't those things moved in here for the poor girl last night? Men! Heartless animals!*

Galina was stiff and cold and felt dirty. She slowly got up from the floor and the woman led her to a well-appointed bathroom with a shower, leaving her with a towel, a bar of soap and some of her fresh clothes recovered from the car. Galina did notice that the woman locked the door when she left, emphasizing the fact that she was, after all, a prisoner of the KGB.

****

It was the snow that saved him. A low pressure cell over the Shantar Islands in the Sea of Okhotsk was scooping up ocean moisture. High pressure over Yakutsk brought arctic air from the north and the two systems collided, forming a major storm and dropping three feet of snow on the northern and central portions of Khabarovsk Krai. The storm lasted for four days. While it did not slow Kelly down at all, as he had to use his snowshoes anyway, it did keep all helicopter-borne troops on the ground. By the time the snow stopped falling, Kelly was eighty kilometers north of his starting point and the tracks were completely obliterated by the snow.

****

The key rattled in the lock and the cell door swung open. Galina was sitting on her bed reading a copy of *Pravda* that she'd been given earlier in the day. The matron stood in the door with a large suitcase. She placed it in the cell.

"You are being released today, Comrade Toporova. You'll need to clean up and change. I brought your things."

Thirty minutes later she was being escorted to a waiting black Zil, suitcase in hand. The driver took her luggage, placed it in the trunk, and then opened the door for her. She entered the car and found an old man sitting in the vehicle.

"How are you, Comrade Toporova?" he inquired. "Have you been treated well?"

"Very well, comrade. I'm afraid you have me at a disadvantage, grandfather. I do not know your name."

"Indeed, daughter, and my name shall remain unknown. Here," he said as he handed a folder to her. "Inside you will find train tickets to Beijing, a passport, and documentation that will allow you to live in China for the rest of your life. There is also one thousand *yuan*. It should be enough to allow you to become established and find work.

"You must never return to the *Rodina*, Galina Toporova. You will be arrested at the border if you attempt to do so. You will be safe so long as you remain in China. There are several large communities of Soviet expatriates in China, including in Beijing, so you should not find life abroad intolerable."

Galina was surprised by the turn of events but didn't respond, suspecting a trick. She took the folder and examined its contents as the Zil maneuvered through midday traffic, heading for the train station. The KGB had never been known for exercising compassion, and yet she felt sympathy from the old man seated opposite her. On the other hand, she knew that if this was not a ruse of some sort, with the present turn of events she would never see Kelly again. He wouldn't know where to look for her. A tear rolled down her face.

The old man observed her and said somewhat defensively, "You know, comrade, we could have killed you. We could have tortured you for every last bit of information about Major Kelly. But I saved you from that."

"Why?" she demanded, hiding her surprise that the old man knew Kelly's real name. No other interrogator had used any name other than Sokolov with her.

"Why?" He was taken aback by her question. "Why? What about, 'thank you, comrade, for saving my life?' Should you not express gratitude? Or relief?"

"I am most grateful, comrade, of course. You have saved my life—thank you. But the KGB doesn't do good deeds for the sake of compassion. Why am I being released? Is this a trick? Why wasn't I tortured?"

The old man sighed. He turned and looked out the window for a moment as the Khabarovsk cityscape raced by. Finally, he agreed. "*Pravda*. You are correct, comrade: the KGB does not do compassion. *I* am doing this. There will be no record of it on KGB files when I am finished."

"But why?"

He studied her for a moment without responding and then said, "Thirty years ago your father saved my life. We were on a clandestine operation in Syria, and things went awry."

"My father didn't work for the KGB! He was a diplomat," Galina interrupted. "That's what mother always told us."

"Your mother told you that because that is what she was told. Your father was part of a diplomatic mission, yes, but he was the KGB resident in the embassy in Damascus. He was my superior, and my very good friend.

"One night we were tasked to retrieve one of our men who had been captured by an Israeli Mossad unit operating just across the border. We got into a firefight and your father was hit. We were on the verge of being captured and he sacrificed his life to save mine, allowing me to get away. I promised myself, in honor of his memory, that I would never permit his children to suffer if I could do anything to prevent it. That," he said, motioning to the folder, "fulfills my promise.

"At the station two men will meet you and escort you to Beijing. They will return; you will not."

Chapter 27

Tuesday, September 15, 1987: 2215 local
west of Magadan, USSR

Major Jacob Kelly looked morosely at his fire, shaking his head. Five months had passed since leaving Sidima, and he was only now drawing near to the city of Magadan. *One hundred and fifty days*, he thought to himself, *and I've only got about one thousand miles to show for it*. He shouted a curse into the night, and gave full sway to the rising anger he felt. He stood up and kicked his fire, scattering sparks and burning sticks. He picked up his pack and threw it, shouting and cursing.

What with the swampy, marshy terrain, the rivers, the late spring snows, trying to stay out of sight of searching Soviet troops, having to hunt for food and jerk the meat to keep it from spoiling, and dealing with the occasional bout of dysentery, he'd not been able to make near the mileage he and Sevastyan had calculated. He guessed that though he was walking close to twenty miles a day, he was averaging only six or seven miles per day toward his destination. He'd never seen terrain like the Russian taiga. Though he enjoyed its beauty, he just really wanted to get home. Now it was mid-September and Kelly knew that he'd have to spend another winter in Siberia. It was not something he was excited about. He had decided a week ago that he would get past Magadan and then look for a place to hole up for the winter.

His self-control returned and he walked about his campsite, putting out the smoldering embers he had scattered in his rage. The major found his pack in some underbrush where he'd slung it, recovered the items that had fallen out of it, and then prepared for bed.

****

He doused his fire, did a cursory job of eliminating the obvious signs of his stay and then swung his pack onto his shoulders. He shifted the load, buckled his waist belt and set out with a long, ground-covering stride. He knew he was getting careless. He considered that thought as he walked along.

I've had four brushes with searchers since April and I've been lucky every time. But they know where I'm headed now. All they need to do is get in front of me and set up a cordon and they'll have me. It's been a month at least since I've seen a chopper. I wonder why?

****

"He's going to be passing near Magadan, General. I've got the entire 106th deployed in a line forty kilometers long. We've been in place for two weeks and each unit has scouted the ground around them to identify likely routes. He won't get past us," stated Major Nikitin.

"Why have you not caught him already, Major? This manhunt has gone on too long," said Chernikov.

"The terrain here is very difficult, General. There are plenty of places to hide. We've never been able to spot him from the air. He hears the choppers when they are coming, and hides. So we don't have quite the advantage you might think.

"We initially underestimated his rate of progress and were constantly deploying behind him. We'd find signs of where he had been. Then we'd overestimate, and deploy too far in front of him, and he'd see our helicopters and go a different way. We've been leapfrogging one another this way all summer long. But in the last month it has become obvious to me that he'll be passing close to Magadan, so I deployed the entire division way out in front of him and then grounded all the choppers. He'll have no warning this time. He'll walk right into our lines."

"Very good, Major. Inform me as soon as you make contact."

"General, I am assuming we are still operating on a shoot-on-sight footing, as you ordered in June. My troops have been instructed that those are the rules of engagement. Is that still your wish, General Chernikov?"

Chernikov thought for a moment. *Nikitin is on the ball. He's learned from the mistakes he's made. Perhaps it is time to roll the dice again.*

"You are confident that you will catch him this time, Major?"

"Positive, sir. We know how he operates, we know where he's going and we're waiting for him this time, sir. He's in the bag, General."

"Very well. Let's change the rules of engagement, then. Attempt to capture him alive, but if it seems he is getting away, then shoot to kill."

"Yes, sir! I serve the Soviet Union, Comrade General!"

****

Major Kelly's eyes popped open. It was the dark gray of early morning before the horizon had brightened enough to loan light to the world below. Jake groaned, sat up and began struggling out of his warm mummy bag. For the hundredth time he thought of Sevastyan and breathed a word of thanks that the old sailor had had good contacts, and had been able to help him accumulate such excellent gear.

He dressed and then started a tiny fire, just enough to warm water. As he gnawed on a piece of jerky, he boiled a cup of water and prepared to use his last tea bag. In the distance he heard the sound of a single engine airplane, the propeller biting the cold morning air. He quickly doused his fire. All his gear was under the tree and he wasn't too concerned about being spotted, but felt it best not to take chances. The sound grew until he could tell from the change in pitch that the aircraft had passed. He searched for a moment, then found it. A biplane, headed south, was silhouetted by the growing light in the eastern sky. It was an Antonov An-2, known to NATO forces as a Colt, one of the finest utility aircraft in existence. Kelly looked admiringly at its simple, clean lines. Slow, stable, capable of short field takeoffs and landings, the An-2 didn't even have an advertised stall speed. It was rumored to be able to fly at speeds as slow as 30 knots when empty.

Jake watched the aircraft disappear to the south, and scratched his chin. *What's that guy doing up here? Oh, I know. I'll bet he's a fish spotter for the Magadan fishing fleet. Sevastyan mentioned the large fleet they have up here.*

For the next two days as he made his way east Kelly saw the red biplane as it went out in the morning and came back in the late afternoon. He compared his map with the direction of flight and figured that the aircraft was based at the Magadan airport. From the length of time on station indic-ated by when it left and when it returned, the major guessed that it had been fitted with extended fuel tanks.

Chapter 28

Friday, September 18, 1987: 1840 local
west of Magadan, USSR

Kelly waited hidden under the bole of the fir tree, examining the small river in front of him. He carefully scanned the opposite bank from upstream to downstream, over and over again, for any movement or patch of color or shadow that was out of place. Nothing. He examined the far bank again. And again. As dusk was falling, he made his move.

He stepped out from under the shelter of the tree and down into the shallow watercourse. The rocks were rounded from wear, but not slippery. Jake splashed across the stream.

He was heavily bearded and his hair had grown long. He'd learned from his special operations training that self-discipline was crucial to morale on long trips downrange, so he'd been bathing every night that water was available and he'd kept his clothes clean, washing them by hand. His beard and hair, however, he had allowed to grow out to give him options for changing his appearance as necessary. His military-grade combat boots were holding up well, but the rough clothes he was wearing were beginning to tatter and fray.

He crossed to the other side and was clambering up the gravel bar when he realized that he was looking straight into the muzzle of an AK47, held by a grinning, camouflaged soldier. The man's face and hands were painted in a forest green pattern, as was his BDU.

"Hold it right there, Sokolov," the soldier said.

Jake grinned back at the man and said, "Where did you come from, comrade? I never saw you and I've been looking for the last forty-five minutes." Jake's assault rifle was hanging over his shoulder by the strap and he was wondering how he could get it into action without getting shot to pieces.

"Oh, I've been watching you watching out for us. Could not move a muscle, didn't want to give away my position. Good thing you moved when you did, 'cause I was getting a cramp in my foot.

"Now, you just take that automatic weapon off your shoulder very carefully, very slowly. You make one false move, comrade, and I'll drill thirty neat little holes in your hide."

Kelly took the strap of his rifle in two fingers, gingerly disentangled it from his shoulder, lowered it to the ground and then stepped back from it.

"Very good. Now put your hands behind your head and let's move."

Kelly put his hands behind his head. He'd mounted the holster for the pistol he'd stolen from Chernikov behind his head at the level of his shoulders for this kind of situation. It was attached to the pack frame, between his back and the frame, and so could not be seen unless Kelly removed the pack. When the soldier motioned to Kelly with the muzzle of his assault rifle, pointing it in the direction he should walk, Jake grasped the butt of the pistol, drew it and shot the man between the eyes. He scooped up his own rifle and dashed madly back across the stream. He heard voices of surprise up and down the stream, and a few shots buzzed over his head.

Kelly scrambled up the bank on the west side of the stream and disappeared into the heavy forest, running west as fast as the heavy, ungainly pack would allow. He heard the sounds of pursuit, many feet splashing across the stream.

Hoping to throw off the pursuers, he angled northwest, ran flat out for ten minutes and then headed due west again, jogging. His mind was racing even as he himself was running. *That guy was waiting for me, and from the sound of things, he had a lot of buddies waiting with him. How did they know? Actually, how could they not know, since they've been tracking me for weeks. It wouldn't be too hard to extrapolate where I'm headed.*

It also rattled him badly to realize the man had been virtually in the open, but his camo was so good that even with careful surveillance, Kelly had missed him. *These guys are sharp,* Kelly thought. *If I get out of this scrape, I'll be lucky.*

Soon it was too dark to travel any farther, but the darkness is what helped Kelly to escape. The entire night was spent creeping and hiding in the woods. He could hear men all around him, searching. He knew they were trying to flush him like quail, forcing him to give away his position. He crept silently into a thicket, and stayed put.

Finally, about midnight, the men grew weary of their search and withdrew to the east. Kelly dozed for several more hours, then woke up and listened. The night sounds were normal, which would not be the case if men were moving about nearby. He sat up, mounted his pack, and began to walk carefully north-northwest, navigating by Polaris. The night sky was brilliantly clear; the stars were pinpricks of light in a cold black background. He located Orion as he walked, and thought of the girl he'd left behind. *I love you, Galina.* The waning moon was but a sliver, yet it provided sufficient light for careful headway. A loon's cry floated over the night air, and he heard a pack of wolves somewhere to the north, baying at the moon.

It was a good time to think. He guessed that a surveillance line had been established that probably went all the way to the sea, several kilometers south. How far north the line might extend he had no idea. He realized that his opponents had been counting on surprise; that would explain the elaborate camouflage of the soldier he'd run into earlier in the day. That would also explain the lack of helicopter movement. The troops did not wish to expose their position by air traffic.

But the situation had changed and so their tactics would change. Kelly pondered on that. First, they had lost the advantage of surprise. Each side knew the other was close. He could now expect helicopter-borne troops to be deployed at first light, as well as helicopter-based searches. Second, it was more of a police operation than a military one. He could not analyze their strategy by any known Soviet doctrine of warfare. Third, he posed no danger of attack. They risked nothing by thinning the troops out to cover more ground. And he had no heavy weapons with which to threaten vehicles or aircraft, a fact they would use to their advantage.

Perhaps *he* could use that fact to create an opportunity. *They are not expecting me to attack. They are expecting me to run. How can I turn that to my advantage?* As he pondered the problem, he realized that human nature was his greatest ally. People generally saw what they expected to see. Perhaps he could take the initiative and use surprise to work in his favor.

He considered the matter and slowly a plan formed in his mind. It would take some scouting and some preparation, but it just might work. And if it worked, it would give him a boost beyond the present lines.

He heard the sound of the red Colt, and realized that daybreak was near. He found a thick fir tree and hid underneath until the biplane had passed by, heading south for another day of fishing. In a flash he realized that the solution to his larger problem was staring him in the face. That red Antonov, outfitted with oversized avgas tanks, might get him home before winter set in!

****

Major Kelly spent the day dodging searchers and helicopters, but managed to scout the area sufficiently to set up his plan. He woke up around four the next morning and carefully shaved his head and face, removing his beard completely. He changed into the carefully preserved battle dress uniform he'd taken from the guard the summer before. Then he built up his fire to slowly consume a stack of green pieces of wood that would give off smoke, strapped on his pack and headed east.

Kelly traveled about two miles to a clearing he'd located the previous day and hid his pack at the edge of the meadow. He walked back west a mile or so and hid, waiting on the east side of another meadow closer to his campsite. Somewhere in the distance he heard the red Antonov An-2 headed south for another day of directing fishing boats. *Luck to you*, he murmured, *and luck to me.*

In the distance he could see a thin wisp of smoke rising

from his campfire. It was only a matter of time now. Twenty minutes later he heard the *whump-whump-whump* of an Mi-2 Hoplite helicopter. He breathed a sigh of relief: a small chopper was an easier target.

The helicopter settled in the meadow and two troopers jumped out and assumed a defensive stance. They were followed by six more soldiers who disappeared into the woods at the far end of the meadow, headed in the direction of Kelly's fire. The pilot shut down the engine and the rotors slowly spun down. Once the patrol had left, the two men guarding the chopper relaxed somewhat and the pilot emerged. The three lit cigarettes and stood in the early morning sun, talking and laughing.

Kelly waited about ten minutes, and then decided, *Show time!*

"*Zdravstvuytye!*" he shouted, emerging from the edge of the forest into the clearing and striding toward the men standing by the helicopter. His hands were empty and his assault rifle was slung over his shoulder. He noticed that he was dressed in a slightly different uniform than that worn by the men he was approaching. *Even better*, he thought.

"*Zdravstvuytye!*" he repeated, "We need some help!"

"Halt!" shouted the two guards, leveling their rifles at him. The pilot just looked on with curiosity.

Kelly ignored the commands and continued to stride toward the men, talking all the while. "We've had a problem," he said. "Our captain slipped this morning and hit his head on a rock. He's still alive, but unconscious. Our medic says we've got to get him to a hospital as soon as possible."

"Why didn't you just radio in for transport?" asked the pilot.

"He had the radio when he fell. Something must have broken when it hit the rocks, because we can't get anything out of it now."

"What unit are you with?" asked one of the guards.

Kelly drew himself up and put as much arrogance into his expression as he could manage, "I'm afraid I cannot tell you, comrade. It's best you don't know. No one is supposed to even be aware that we are here, but we're not about to let our commanding officer die on this little goose chase."

"What do you mean we can't know, comrade? *We're* Spetsnaz! *We* are special operations. Who the devil are you?"

"I know perfectly well who *you* are," Kelly snapped. "But only General Chernikov himself has authorization to tell you who *we* are, soldier. As I said, you're not even supposed to know we are here." Jake turned to the pilot, "You've got a choice. You will fly this aircraft for me voluntarily and airlift my captain to a hospital, or you can do it at the point of a gun and then spend the rest of your career training recruits. So what will it be?"

At that the two guards began to raise the muzzles of their rifles toward him, and Kelly reached out and pushed the nearest gun down toward the ground. He said in an icy tone, "You'd better think twice, soldier, before you point that weapon at me." The two soldiers looked at each other in confusion, shrugged their shoulders and relaxed their weapons.

The pilot took one last drag on his cigarette, threw it down, stamped it out and said, "Okay, let's go get him. It won't take that long. Magadan isn't twenty minutes by air. Do you need them?" he asked, motioning to the two guards.

"No. Our own guys will load him. Besides, you need these two here to let your patrol know what's going on if they return before you do."

The pilot nodded, satisfied, then asked, "Where is he?"

"In a clearing about two klicks east of here." Kelly walked around the chopper, and got in the right side, and put on the headset. The pilot climbed into the left side, and started the engines. When they were in the air, he said, "I'd better notify my command."

"No, we're not going to do that."

"What?" he said, and looked over at Kelly. Kelly was holding a pistol on him.

"I said, 'We aren't going to do that.' Now you just put this bird down nice and soft in that clearing and don't even think about touching the radio."

"Suppose I don't," the pilot replied calmly.

"Then you are a dead man," Jake answered easily.

"If I'm a dead man so are you, comrade. We're what, five hundred feet in the air? You need me to pilot this thing," the pilot said with a triumphant grin.

"Are you always this stupid, or is it just because you haven't had your coffee yet? Why on earth would I steal a chopper if I couldn't fly it? Why don't I just shoot you full of holes and push your carcass out the door? I don't need you, comrade. You're in the way. So you pick. Land the chopper or you're a dead man."

The grin faded from the man's face and he carefully set the helicopter down in the meadow indicated by Kelly.

Once the rotors had spun down to an idle, Kelly apologized, "This is going to hurt, but it's a lot better than being dead." He clubbed the pilot in the head with the butt of his pistol.

Jumping out, he carried the limp man out of range of the rotors, grabbed the pack that he'd hidden earlier in the morning, and took off. Reaching over the instrument panel, he snapped off the IFF transponder and stayed below the level of radar.

Thirty minutes later he'd located the Magadan airport. He flew the chopper back into the woods, landed it in an isolated clearing and shut it down.

Chapter 29

Friday, September 18, 1987: 1630 local
Magadan, USSR

Kelly picked his way carefully through the thick woods and found that he could get close to some hangars on the northwest side of the airfield without danger of being spotted. While he waited for the red airplane to land he busied himself improving his hiding place, dragging brush into place and weaving it together to create a blind of sorts.

Four hours later, as it was getting dark, he was rewarded with the now-familiar sound of the red Colt. He watched the pilot set it down neatly on the runway and then taxi to the fuel pump. The man shut off the engine, refueled the plane, and called to some workers in the nearest hangar to help him push it to the tie downs. A few minutes later the lights around the hangar went out and the men jumped into a truck and left.

Darkness fell and the runway lights twinkled in the distance, shimmering from the heat waves rising from the still warm tarmac. The rotating beacon on top of the tower made its regular circuit, and Kelly could see the silhouettes of several men in the tower. Somehow the familiar routines of aviation made him feel at home. The runway lights remained on, and Kelly guessed they were waiting for some late arrivals. A twin-engine turboprop landed at around 2050 and then a mid-sized commercial jet around 2200 hours.

After everyone had deplaned and the baggage had been handled, lights around the airport began to wink out. By 2300 the only light remaining was the rotating beacon. Even the runway lights had been extinguished.

Jake continued to watch, observing the night-time security patrols around the airport. He noted that a jeep with two men in it made a check around the hangars every hour, while a second jeep continuously drove the perimeter at slow speed.

He slept in his blind during most of the next morning, but woke in time to see a convoy of troops on the highway south of the airfield heading west into the hills. Evidently the chopper he'd shanghaied had been spotted, and patrols were now searching the area. He was forced to stay inside his blind during all of the daylight hours, and several times searchers had come within a hundred feet of where he was. He knew he'd be in deep trouble if they brought a canine unit to search for him.

That night he observed that security had been tightened appreciably at the airfield. Now two military guards were posted at the hangar, relieved every four hours. The pattern of the mobile patrols remained the same, although instead of two men in each jeep there were now four. Kelly watched all night, surveilling the patrol patterns and schedules and then crept back into his blind to sleep again as dawn approached.

For the next three days the major continued his surveillance until he was confident that he understood all the patterns. Finally he began to plan his next step. He would make his move just before dawn on Thursday morning, September 24.

****

Two squads of soldiers sat in the Zil 131 as it bumped over the rough road. It was time to change the watch at the Magadan airfield and other points near by. At each location, two to four men would jump off the truck, and the guards they were replacing would climb aboard.

The last ten men got off at various places around the airport, and then the truck trundled back past the tower, through the main gate, and headed west for their bivouac. The soldiers going off-duty filled the twenty-minute ride to the camp with standard fare for foot soldiers: grumbling and rumors.

"C'mon, Sarge, who is this Sokolov, really?"

"You've been briefed, Rudin. He's a rapist and a murder, a

private that deserted an infantry unit stationed in Omsk. That's all they told me, and that's good enough for you."

"What unit, Sarge?"

"Not a clue."

"Exactly!" Rudin crowed. He was an *efreitor*, one notch above a private. "Don't you see? They aren't saying what unit he's with so this cockeyed story can't be verified. Or falsified, for that matter."

"What are you ranting about now, Rudin?" asked a soldier seated across from him.

"All I'm saying is that we've been fed a load of manure with this Yakov Sokolov business. They aren't telling us the truth."

"When has an officer ever told the enlisted ranks the truth, Rudin?" the sergeant asked. "You'd better shut up and keep your thoughts to yourself, unless you want to spend some time cleaning latrines."

"We're not going to catch this guy if they don't tell us the truth, Sarge. I was talking to one of my buddies in 143rd Guards Motor Rifle Regiment yesterday. He was with the squad that Comrade Sokolov rolled when he grabbed that helicopter last week, west of Magadan. My buddy talked to the chopper pilot. Sokolov *flew* it, Sarge! How many enlisted men do you know that can fly a helicopter?

"And the chopper pilot had talked to the boys in Khabarovsk who had run into Sokolov a year ago. Apparently they cornered Sokolov at the train station. He trashed three officers and escaped from about forty soldiers in broad daylight. This guy is leaving a trail of bodies across Siberia. There's rumors that he's been captured several times and fought his way out of it each time."

"Shut your pie hole, Rudin, before I do. If you tell anymore of these ghost stories, I won't be able to find anyone to pull guard duty; none of these ladies will want to leave the camp."

****

Kelly was concealed in a drainage ditch next to the road when the perimeter jeep passed. Picking up his pack, he raced lightly to the edge of the hangar, and squeezed between two fifty-five gallon drums. The hangar patrol jeep drove across the tarmac, shining a light on the tied-down aircraft. Once it had moved to the next hangar, Kelly crept to the north corner of the building, pulled out the combat knife he'd taken off of the helicopter guard what seemed a lifetime ago in Tara, and waited.

He heard the footsteps coming and tensed. The guard rounded the corner and Kelly rammed the knife right into the man's throat. Jake caught him as he collapsed without making more than a gurgle. Kelly felt sick; there had been too much killing already and there would be more bodies before it was over. He was sickened by his own brutality. Yet faced with next-to-impossible odds, he was convinced utter ruthlessness was essential to his escape. He found some faint comfort in the fact that the man was a soldier and not a civilian.

Jake straightened up and slung his rifle over his shoulder in the same manner the guard's had been. He adjusted his own beret to the same angle. Leaving his pack, he walked confid-ently around the corner. The other guard would be circling the aircraft, and in the low light would not see anything different in Jake's bearing. He would see what he expected to see: his fellow guard.

Jake walked his prescribed route, turned on his heel, and headed back to the corner of the hangar. He calculated that in two more circuits he and the other guard would pass within arm's length.

Sweat was rolling down the small of his back. For the first time since breaking out of the prison compound he had a realistic chance of escaping, of going all the way. He could not face the thought of being recaptured. That red biplane probably had enough fuel to take him all the way to Uelen, or close to it. There he would steal a kayak, and this time tomor-row night he could be paddling to Alaska!

He passed the guard and nodded. So far, so good. He saw the headlights of the perimeter jeep, far away on the other side of the airport. The hangar jeep had stopped at the main commercial hangar belonging to Aeroflot, as they normally did. They would be there for another ten minutes, checking out the huge building.

At the corner of the hangar he turned on his heel again. Final pass. He walked the normal route, down the side of the building to the door leading into the office, past it, to the far corner of the hangar. When he got there, he turned about and found himself looking right into the face of the other guard, a grim soldier who said, "You're not Vasiliy!" and pulled the trigger on his AK47.

Jake threw himself to the side and drew his pistol as he did. A bullet grazed his torso as he went to the pavement. He rolled and fired, again and again, four shots, then five. Three of them found their mark and the other soldier fell dead.

The shots echoed around the buildings. Jake knew he had mere seconds to act. He broke into the hangar office, kicking the door in with his foot. He turned on the lights and located the keys to the An-2, hanging on a rack on the wall. Extinguishing the lights, he stepped out of the office and smashed the light bulb outside the office door with the barrel of his AK47, adding to the darkness of the night.

The hangar patrol jeep was already racing his way, the perimeter patrol jeep had farther to travel. Kelly hid behind a drum and let the jeep get right up to the hangar, then unloaded his magazine into it. The men in the vehicle never had a chance. The jeep careened into the large hangar door, crashing through it. They must have run into something, Kelly figured, because the inside of the hangar exploded into flames.

Ramming a fresh magazine into his rifle, Jake ran down to the corner and retrieved his pack, then raced to the aircraft. He unlocked the cabin door and threw his pack inside.

"Sorry, old girl. No time for a preflight now!" he said. "You'd better be in top form, or you and I are going down together."

Rather than untying the tie-downs, he slashed through them with the knife. The perimeter jeep was racing across the tarmac, still several hundred yards away. The glare of the raging fire in the hangar would prevent them from seeing what he was doing in the darkness. Finishing his preparations, he strapped his backpack securely into the right-hand seat, then exited the plane and melted deeper into the shadows.

The perimeter guards made a far more cautious approach than had the hangar patrol. As the jeep raced up to the hangar, the three passengers each rolled out at different spots and took up positions behind cover. The vehicle skidded to a stop and the driver bailed out and took up a position behind the jeep itself.

Four guys, Kelly thought to himself. *This is going to be difficult. And who knows how fast they'll get reinforcements. If nothing else, this blazing hangar is going to draw a crowd.*

****

"Okay, Sam, I think that wraps it up. Have you got anything else for me?" The speaker was Chuck Donnely, Sam Bergman's supervisor at the CIA. It was just after noon on Friday, September 18, at Langley. The two men were finishing up their weekly meeting, in which Bergman summarized the intelligence he'd been analyzing for the past week.

"Do you remember those troop movements I've been telling you about for the last twelve months? Well, everything has concentrated around Magadan.

"We've been able to ascertain that the story the rank and file are being given is false. It's some wild tale about one Jacob Sokolov, who is reputedly a deserter, a murderer, and a rapist. It looks to me like they are trying to capture someone; I just don't know why."

"But you think it's important?"

"I do. They are consuming a huge amount of resources moving those soldiers all around. I wouldn't be surprised if the Far East High Command has already expended their gasoline allotment for the year."

Chuck stared at Sam for a moment, wondering if he

should say what he was thinking. "Sam, is it possible someone is pulling your chain?"

"You mean disinformation? Something like *Operation Fortitude* from '44, masking the intended Normandy landing by using fake radio traffic to get the Germans thinking Calais?"

"Yeah, something like that," Donnely affirmed. "After all, we've never tasked a bird to take a peek. We don't know if there really are troops around Magadan, or just some clown on a radio. It's never been considered important enough to verify."

"It is possible. The Sovs are masters at disinformation, and if that's what's happening, I bought it hook, line, and sinker."

"You wouldn't be the first, Sam."

"But why would they pull a rhubarb like that to begin with? What's their point?"

"Nuts, I don't know. Could be to see if we're listening, maybe to spot leaks in their security or communications. Could be to test a new scheme of disinfo to see if it works. Maybe they're hiding something really important, wanting us to watch the left hand while the right one picks our pocket."

"If it's disinfo, Chuck, it's the best I've ever seen. No, something about this feels real."

****

Staying low, Kelly withdrew to the north corner of the hangar then circled around the back side. The fire had not yet breached the back wall, so he was still cloaked in darkness as he peeked around the corner. The jeep was thirty meters away, headlights pointed in the opposite direction. Kelly had a perfect shot at the tango hiding behind the jeep, whose attention was drawn to the front, not the back, of the hangar. Jake triggered a burst, and the man slumped to the ground. Crouching down, Kelly ran to the jeep and laid flat on the tarmac. Peering from under the vehicle, he searched for the other men. A movement illuminated by firelight caught his eye and he located another hostile hiding behind a drum at the south wall of the next hangar over. Sirens began to wail in the distance.

He felt his pockets and counted three more magazines. *I'll just have to make 'em count*, he thought. In a prone position, he settled his sight on the edge of the barrel, guessing it was 30 meters away. When the man leaned around the barrel to search for Kelly, Jake squeezed off a three-shot burst and the man fell over, sprawling on his face in the flickering light. *Two down*, Jake thought.

Return fire came from the other hangar's door, and Kelly had to scramble behind the jeep's wheel to avoid getting hit. He rolled back and put a short burst through the door, then rolled behind the wheel again. Another long burst came from the door. Kelly could hear the slugs whiz by like angry bees. As soon as the firing stopped, the major leapt up and retreated back around the corner of his hangar, figuring that the guy had to change a mag. As Kelly rounded the corner he collided headlong with the fourth hostile, who was trying to flank him.

Both men fell, but Kelly sprang to his feet first. A quick kick to the head of his opponent put the fellow back on the ground, and Kelly kicked him again, smashing his head against the hangar wall. The man went limp. Kelly scooped up his weapons and tossed them into the field, then continued back around the hangar. Heat radiated from the walls, as the inside of the building was now fully involved in flames. Kelly peered around the north corner, from where he'd begun his assault several moments earlier. The remaining hostile was approaching the jeep warily, weapon at the ready, apparently thinking that his last fusillade must have taken Kelly out. Jake stepped around the wall and triggered a long burst, killing him.

With his opposition wiped out, Jake raced for the An-2, jumped into the seat and initiated the engine start-up sequence. The engine coughed once. Kelly tried again. "Come on, baby!" he shouted.

In the distance several fire engines and emergency vehicles, sirens blaring, roared through the airport gate and onto the tarmac down by the tower. Kelly was out of time. He pumped the fuel syringe several times, pushed the starter switch again and the engine sputtered, backfired noisily, then caught with a throaty roar. Jake stood on the brakes and slowly increased the throttle. There was no opportunity to run through the magneto, pressure, or vacuum checks, or even to allow the engine to reach operating temperature. It was now or never. He released the brakes and the Colt began to roll. Kelly didn't even know which way the wind was blowing. He just jammed the throttle to the stops and pointed the aircraft in the direction that gave him the greatest straight distance of paved flat surface.

The emergency vehicles raced past him, blurred faces looking through their windows with amazement as the Antonov, without any lights, roared down the taxiway and lifted into the night sky.

If the FAA had seen that, I'd never fly again, Jake thought to himself as he banked to a heading of 195 degrees true and began to scan his instruments. Leveling out at fifty meters AGL (above ground level), he throttled the powerful radial engine back to allow it to come to operating temperature a little more slowly. He looked over his right shoulder. The burning hangar was lighting up the early morning sky like a beacon.

After trimming the aircraft for straight and level flight, the major turned on the cabin lights and briefly inspected the situation in the cargo space behind him. Three large fuel tanks had been built in to the cabin. A crude panel on his lower left contained gauges for the three tanks and switches for an auxiliary fuel pump. The gauges all read "full." He turned off the cabin lights and concentrated on the scene in front of him. He was coming up on the Magadan harbor. The city lights twinkled below him. He roared over the harbor at low altitude making plenty of noise and hoping that when his pursuers pieced together their data, they would conclude he was making for Japan.

Jake pulled up on the stick. The peninsula that formed the southern arm of Magadan's natural harbor was coming up, and he had to raise his feet to get over the hills that crowned it. Once well clear of the land, he'd turn north-northeast and make for the center of the landmass that terminated in the Chukchi peninsula. He planned to skirt the north side of the Kolyma mountain range in an effort to avoid being spotted by radar or human observers. As far as he knew, the portion of Siberia over which he would be flying was desolate.

He fought the urge to simply continue south and try for the Japanese island of Hokkaido. Several factors argued against that course. He was not entirely sure of the fuel consumption of the Colt. If he got it wrong he'd have to ditch in the Sea of Okhotsk, and he had no emergency gear. Secondly, that body of water was the virtual bathtub of the Soviet Pacific fleet: he imagined that it would be crawling with military assets. He'd be spotted well shy of his goal, and then it would be all over. *No, I've got to make for the Bering Straits and scrounge a kayak. According to Sevastyan, a kayak won't be hard to find. All they've got up there are a few fishing villages, anyway.*

A few moments later, flying at a mere fifty feet above the cold waters of the Sea of Okhotsk, he made a broad sweeping turn to the left and settled on his new course of 30 degrees true. Maintaining a low altitude to stay under Soviet radar, he followed the Ola River into the interior. The blazing yellow orb of the sun was beginning to rise off his right wingtip as he disappeared into the dark canyons of the Ola.

Chapter 30

Major Roman Romanovich Nikitin strode into the building he had commandeered as his temporary headquarters. A highly disciplined individual, the major enjoyed getting to work before his staff. He felt it was necessary lest he be overtaken by events each day. But nothing had gone right for him this morning; he'd overslept, hadn't had breakfast, and was fighting off a foul mood.

"Good morning, Sergeant. Any news?" he asked the noncom who had been manning the communications gear since midnight.

"No, sir. It's been a quiet night. I put a fresh pot of cof—" He was interrupted by the telephone. "Excuse me, sir," he said apologetically as he answered the call.

Nikitin walked into the other room and poured himself a cup. In recent weeks he'd acquired a taste for strong coffee over the traditional tea, and his headquarters personnel tended to cater to his whims.

"Sir, it's Captain Yelagin, up at the airport. He says there's been an attack. He needs to speak with you urgently," said the sergeant.

"An attack?" asked Nikitin. He stepped over to his desk and picked up the phone. "Report, Captain, please!"

"Sir, about forty-five minutes ago both the interior and perimeter security patrols responded to gunshots coming from a hangar on the northwest side. Both patrols were ambushed, and the hangar was set on fire. We've got seven dead soldiers, sir, and three more who are badly injured."

Nikitin sat down slowly and put his coffee cup on the desk. He massaged his temple with one hand as he asked, "Do we have any idea what is behind this? Is this . . . ," he hesit-ated, as the lie was getting rather threadbare, "Sokolov?"

"I'd say so, sir. And it appears that our comrade Sokolov can fly fixed wing aircraft in addition to choppers, sir. Evid-ently he is a multi-talented soldier," he added somewhat sar-castically. "In any case, fire crews who responded to the blaze report that an aircraft without running lights took off as they arrived. It was an Antonov An-2, sir. The airport manager says that it belongs to the fishing fleet. And Major, he says that a year ago the aircraft was fitted with extra internal fuel tanks to extend its range."

"If the aircraft was fully fueled, what would its range be?" Nikitin asked.

"It was fully fueled, sir. The man here says that they topped off the tanks every evening when the Antonov re-turned, and that with full tanks, it has a range of three thou-sand kilometers."

"Which means it could get to Japan or Alaska," Nikitin muttered to himself.

"Sir?"

"Nothing, Captain. What direction was the aircraft going when last seen?"

"South, sir."

"Thank you, Captain. Please prepare your men for trans-port. Spread the word to the other captains. I think we are done in Magadan." He hung up the phone.

South. That means Japan. As he considered this, he re-membered hearing an aircraft go over at low altitude while he was dressing. *That makes sense. He's trying to stay below the radar. It's Major Kelly, for certain.* He picked up the phone to dial Chernikov. As he did, he glanced at his watch; it was 0730. It would be 0230 in Tara. *Sorry, General, he thought. And you will not like this news.*

****

It was clear to Major Jacob Kelly that flying to the extreme northeast Siberian coast was not going to be a simple exercise in straight-line flight. He'd never studied the geography of this portion of the Soviet Union, but was rapidly discovering it to be filled with high mountain ranges, deep canyons, and winding rivers.

Flying at a safe altitude would be dangerous. He'd be very quickly picked up by radar, and he knew that Chernikov would have him shot down—again—without a second thought. Only this time there was no ejection seat and no chopper waiting to pick him up. He would die, as would all the inmates at Prison 87, without anyone ever knowing what had happened.

But flying the terrain—his only chance of survival, really —had dangers of its own. A lapse of concentration could be fatal at such a low altitude. And he did not know the terrain. He had no idea upon entering a canyon whether it would gradually rise to a saddle between peaks, or end in a cirque, a high hanging valley which would not give him any flight room to climb beyond its walls. He was also ignorant of the flight characteristics of the Antonov. It was a very sturdy, stable aircraft, but he did not know its rate of climb or how it handled at higher altitudes. And if he tried to follow the winding rivers, a twelve hundred mile flight would quickly become two thousand miles or more.

He took another look at the fuel tanks behind him and made a best guess at what they contained, and what his current fuel consumption was. He decided that he probably had sufficient fuel to increase his speed for the margin of safety the faster flight speed would provide. He firewalled the throttle once again, and the biplane accelerated from 120 to 160 miles per hour. The added speed would give him better climbing characteristics if he got into trouble. He'd just have to keep a sharp eye on the cylinder head and oil temperatures.

Jake decided to continue to hold a very low altitude, but fly as direct a route as possible. Whenever practicable he would skirt the mountain ranges. If that was not possible, well . . . maybe he'd learn how to pray.

****

All his dreams lately had been bad ones. The insistent ringing of the phone next to his bed was actually welcome, as it yanked him out of the latest dark phantasm. He was dreaming that the Politburo had condemned him, and he was being strapped into a wooden coffin to be sent alive into the incinerator at the Aquarium.

He sat up and fumbled in the darkness, knocking the phone off its stand with a crash. Cursing, General Chernikov turned on the light and located the receiver.

"Chernikov."

"Please go secure, Comrade General."

The voice was Nikitin's, and Chernikov knew he would not be calling at this hour unless it was an emergency. "Just a moment," he said. He got down on his hands and knees, and finally located the scrambler, which had tumbled under his bed. He returned everything to his nightstand, hit the button on the scrambler, waited until the whistling ceased, and ordered, "Report."

"General, I believe we have made contact with Major Kelly once again."

"You 'believe?' You are uncertain?"

"Sir, the only men who actually saw him are dead. But I am quite confident it was him."

"Dead? How many?"

"Seven, sir, and three wounded. He also burned down a hangar at the Magadan airport, destroying three more aircraft. And it appears he stole an Antonov An-2 and flew it out of the airport. Emergency crews report seeing the Antonov take off as they came on the scene."

"He's got an airplane now? My word, Major, this just goes from bad to worse! Does anyone have any idea of how much fuel this aircraft had, or what sort of range it's got?"

"It's the fish-spotter for the Magadan fishing fleet, sir. It was fitted with extended-range tanks, and they were full. The airport manager says that he should have a range of three thousand kilometers."

"Three thou—he could get to Japan on that! Or Alaska!" Chernikov exclaimed.

"It's definitely Japan, sir. Multiple witnesses now confirm hearing him pass overhead here in Magadan, and we're south of the airport. And those reports are confirmed by those who saw him take off. He banked south as soon as he got in the air.

"And that's why I'm calling, General. I need aircraft and air-search capability. While I am keeping our land forces here on alert on the off chance that it was not Major Kelly, it is my belief that this is no longer a land-search operation."

There was silence on the other end of the phone. For a moment Nikitin thought the connection had been lost. "Sir?" he said.

"Major Nikitin, I'm pulling you off this operation. Brief the commanders of all the deployed units. I'll call General Kapustin of the Far East Command, and turn the remaining land-search operation over to him. You arrange air transport back to Khab' and then take the train back to Omsk. I'll have someone pick you up."

"You're relieving me, sir? But—"

"NO BUTS," Chernikov roared, his temper at an end. "You have had multiple contacts with Kelly, and have missed him every time! We could have outfitted an air cavalry brigade with all the men he's killed and equipment he's stolen! The best I can say for your performance on this mission is that you have at least kept us apprised of his whereabouts, though it's always been after the fact. I am relieving you of your command, Major!"

"Sir, in all fairness," Nikitin objected, "none of us knew what Major Kelly's capabilities were. There is not a hint in his dossier that he could handle himself the way he has. He's had us all fooled, including you, sir, with all due respect."

Chernikov sat heavily on his bed. "I know, Roman, I know. He's the one piece of Project *Krasnyy Voskhod* that's gone badly. But it is time you learned the political realities of high command. You have made me look bad to my superiors. I will be punished. But you also will be punished, more severely than me. If I am removed, there is no one in place to protect you.

"Therefore, I have to relieve you of command, Roman, in order to remain in control of the situation. I have no other choice. If I fail to remove you it makes me look that much worse. But yanking you just might save me. And if it saves me, I can save you. I've asked you to come home on the train because it gives me several extra days to retrieve the situation," Chernikov explained wearily.

"But what about the air search, General?"

"It's no longer your concern. You are relieved, Major. Please brief the other commanders and return home as I have requested."

"Yes, sir."

****

Chernikov hung up the phone. He badly wanted to get a cup of tea or, better yet, a shot of vodka, before he made the phone call. But time was of the essence, he could not delay. He dialed the number for Lieutenant General Valeriy Ivanovich Patrikeyev.

He explained the situation and, as he expected, Patrikeyev received the news with even more anger than he himself had displayed.

"I cannot simply give you command of an air wing, General, I think you know that. I will make some calls and do what I can," said Patrikeyev coldly.

Thirty minutes later Patrikeyev called back. "Major General Lukyanov is head of operations of the First Air Army, headquartered in Khabarovsk. He has the authority to assist you. You may ask for the help of his air assets, you may not demand that he provide them, nor will you have any operational control over them. You should get one of your people to the airbase there to liaise directly with you; it will simplify communications." What Patrikeyev didn't say in order to save face for the Air Force, was that Lukyanov was told that he will cooperate or he could consider his career to be over.

Chernikov dialed Nikitin's headquarters.

"Change of plans. Get yourself to the airbase at Khabarovsk immediately. Report to General Lukyanov, and set up a secure link between the operations center there and me. You have no authority, you are to liaise only. Time is of the essence."

Forty minutes later, two Beriev A-50 AWACS (Airborne Warning And Control System) aircraft took off from Khabarovsk and lumbered over the Sea of Okhotsk. The first plotted an intercept course for the Antonov, based upon its take-off time, best speed, and probable course to Japan. The second loitered off Sakhalinskiy Island as an insurance policy. Each crew lit up a circle of ocean 430 kilometers in diameter with their powerful Liana airborne radar system. Two pairs of Mig-29 fighters were placed on alert at the base in Khabarovsk, ready to launch as soon as the Antonov was located.

****

Kelly had no airman's charts to assist him as he flew. None of his other maps were helpful for much more than saying, "Go that way." As a consequence he was mostly flying by dead reckoning. He clawed over a granite-topped range, and settled back down into a canyon with a rushing cataract beneath him.

The day was beautiful and cloudless. He could not imagine a more remote, untamed setting than that scrolling past on the ground beneath him. It was like ten thousand square miles of Colorado, completely undeveloped, unspoilt and uninhabited. The colors were fantastic as the members of the birch family on the slopes below were clothed in their fall colors of radiant gold, the firs dark forest green, and the rock of the peaks ranging from black, to gray, to dull red. For the first time he realized what a treasure the Siberian Far East was. If he'd had his fly rod he'd have been tempted to put the plane down and catch dinner.

The flying was exhausting. At the low altitude he was maintaining, even a second's drowsiness or inattention would mean instant death. Though he needed to stay below the minimum altitude for radar detection, he wondered if he was signing his own death warrant. A dangerous downside to flying so close to the ground was that he couldn't see very far, which meant that he would have very little time to react to obstacles and problems.

The canyon flattened out, and the cataract became a slow, meandering stream. A moment later, Jake was passing over a large, lazy river of which the stream was but a small tributary. He looked down on the multiple channels, separated by white sandbars and wet, marshy islands.

He scanned the instrument panel. So far the oil and cylinder head temps were remaining at reasonable levels. He turned his eyes back to the terrain ahead of him just in time to see a large, twin engine turboprop rising from the forest on his left. He whipped the little Antonov in an eighty-degree bank to the right, while the pilot of the turboprop veered to the left. The turbulence from the larger aircraft shook the biplane.

Kelly's hands were trembling as he guided the Antonov in a full three-sixty and got back on course. By the time he'd come around the other aircraft was half a mile downrange. Climbing to one hundred meters, he looked to his left and spotted the airfield and a small town beyond it. He descended back to fifty meters, trimmed the aircraft again and then took his hands off the yoke and rubbed his face, trying to settle his nerves. *That was close. Too close! And now they know where I am. It's just a matter of time before some hotshot fighter jock is on my tail. Stupid fighter jocks!* His lips curled up in a wry grin. *I should know.*

****

Oleg Fukin received takeoff clearance from the little tower in Omolon, throttled up the turboprops, and released the brakes. His Antonov An-24 was filled with Pacific Fleet naval staff. They had flown into the remote town for some uninterrupted planning, but it appeared that most of their planning must have occurred during moose hunting or late night drinking sessions. It was a hard-drinking crowd. He hoped that they were a hard-fighting crowd, too.

The aircraft accelerated smoothly down the runway. Fukin rotated the nose and lifted off. He grimaced: he'd used almost all of the runway. *Must be all that moose meat in baggage*, he figured. As he cleared the trees he reached for the lever to retract the gear. When he looked back up, there was a small red biplane entering his flight path from the right.

He yanked the yoke to the left, putting the An-24 into a steep, climbing bank, and braced for impact. None came, but shouts from the passenger compartment came beating through the cockpit door, though it was shut. Those sitting on the left side of the aircraft were angered by the unexpected move, but those sitting on the right side, having seen the oncoming airplane through their windows, had cried out in terror.

His copilot had been adjusting the radio to the proper ATC frequency and had not seen the near collision. He looked up, "What the . . . ?"

"You nearly had an An-2 sitting in your lap, Vlad. Some dumb fool cut right across the departure pattern! Nearly hit us! Take the yoke for a moment, will you?" Fukin pulled out his handkerchief and wiped his face. *That was close*, he thought.

Thirty-five minutes later they were in controlled airspace, and he reported the near collision with a red Antonov An-2, flying at fifty meters AGL. And twenty-five minutes after that, the A-50s orbiting over the Sea of Okhotsk were recalled to Khabarovsk, and another was launching out of Petropavlosk-Kamchatsky. Two Mig-29s were put on alert at the small airbase in Provideniya.

****

Kelly pushed the An-2 hard, and he pushed himself as

well. Weaving in and out of canyons, staying low, and running the engine as fast as he dared, it was an intense race. The prolonged concentration gave him a headache. He was making about 150 miles per hour by his calculations, but the need to follow the terrain was adding immeasurably to the length of the flight.

Finally, around 1500 hours, he saw the Chukchi Sea shimmering in front of him. It was time to run for Uelen. Banking east, he followed a shallow river into a canyon, and began what he felt was his last leg of the journey in the air. The mountains grew higher around him, and he put the Antonov into a climb. After another 30 minutes of climbing and snaking back and forth, the land fell away in front of him, and he found himself looking at a lush, green tundra plain stretching away as far as the eye could see, cut in numerous places by small rivers emptying into the Chukchi Sea, once again visible on his left. The vista was beautiful beyond description; he'd never seen such a sight. But he also felt very exposed crossing this great, flat space.

He observed as he flew that he was getting set to the south. The ripples on a small pond he was flying over told him that there was a strong wind out of the north-northwest. Low on the horizon and far to the north heavy clouds could be seen building.

****

"We've got him, but we've barely got him," the radar operator said.

"Where is he?" asked the mission commander. The pilot was holding the big A-50 in a race-track pattern about one hundred kilometers north of Egvekinot. Stretching out far below and to the north was the same tundra plain that Kelly had been admiring.

"Target is seventy kilometers out on a bearing of thirteen degrees. He's about fifty meters AGL, and doing about three hundred kilometers per hour. He must have quite a tailwind. I think I've actually been watching him for about ten minutes, but I had a hard time picking him out from the ground clutter."

"Are you certain?"

"Positive, sir. It's the right size, the right speed, and the right place."

"I can confirm that, sir," the pilot broke in, "I've got a visual of a small red aircraft on the given vector. It's the right size for an An-2."

"Excellent! *Molodets*, Yuri!" the mission commander said to his radar operator. "Okay, Pavel, radio it in, and get instructions."

****

Kelly felt distinctly uncomfortable. He knew his luck had to be running out. Now that the terrain was less demanding he was able to give some attention to scanning the sky above. After ten minutes, he saw a silvery body glinting in the sun, far above him.

Could be a neutral, he thought to himself. *Does not have to be a hostile.* He continued watching the aircraft. He could make out no details, it was too high and far away. But the reflection of the sun off its fuselage made it easy to see. If it was a "neutral" it would be going somewhere. If it was a hostile, it would be loitering.

It was loitering. Kelly knew that they'd finally figured out his intended destination. And if that was an A-50, what he called a Mainstay, he was also sure they were tracking him right now. *The radar in those babies is better than ours for picking targets out of ground clutter.*

Searching the horizon, Kelly spotted some hills in the distance to the southeast. He made a quick decision and jammed the throttle to the firewall. Banking, he raced for the scant safety offered by the low, rolling range. *It's gonna take me about twenty minutes to get there. I expect it's gonna be close.*

****

The Mig-29 turned and lined up with the centerline on the runway. His wing man was awaiting his turn on the apron off to his right. Captain Mikhail Zykov smoothly pushed the throttles to full and the twin Klimov RD-33 turbofans spun up, the jet blast blowing away some bits of trash that had been lying on the end of the runway. Zykov released the brakes and the fighter surged forward like a runner off the starting blocks. Halfway down the runway he rotated and the powerful jet screamed into the sky.

He orbited, waiting for his wing man to take position, then the two fighters streaked north.

"Control, this is flight Alpha Xray one. You should be seeing us, bearing, ah, bearing one-four-zero, about three-five-zero klicks."

"Affirmative, Alpha Xray one. We are tracking you on bearing one-three-eight. Target is at your bearing three-three-zero, distance three-zero-zero kilometers. Altitude five-zero meters AGL."

"Roger, Control. Copy target bearing three-three-zero, distance three-zero-zero klicks. Say again altitude, Control."

"Alpha Xray one. Target altitude five-zero meters, AGL."

"Does he have wings or wheels, Control? I thought the target was an aircraft."

"I think he's trying to hide, Alpha Xray."

"Roger that."

****

Bergman studied the intercepts. *Hold the phone, Josephine! What's this? A general recall?* All the infantry units involved in the search around Magadan were being told to stand down and return to barracks.

The CIA analyst sat back in his chair and stared at his ceiling, thinking. *Wonder if Chuck was right? Maybe the Ruskies were pulling my chain. We've gone from an alert status to "head for the barn." Why? What am I missing?*

He checked the time stamp on the intelligence. It was just a few hours old. The orders came from the Far East High Command. *Somewhere along the line the chain of command changed. Wonder what that means? Beats me. Well, Ivan, I think you win this round. I've no clue what you're doing.*

Sam made several notations in the file folder he'd been building, and then returned it to the "Interesting, but no idea what it means" section of his file cabinet. *Well, that case is closed.* But he was wrong.

****

Kelly glanced at the map, then at his watch, and did some mental calculations. He guessed that fighters would scramble out of Provideniya. They should be on top of him any moment. If they got to him before he got to the hills, he was finished.

****

The base commander at Provideniya hung up the phone. He'd met Chernikov once before and had been impressed with him. Apparently the man had considerable clout, or perhaps a powerful patron, to be able to give directives across commands as he did. Well, no matter. He was glad to give his troops some action. Base duty took the edge off.

"Captain Shubkin! Round up a squad of seven men, plus Lieutenant Tselner. Have them properly armed. I want them on the tarmac in a fully fueled and armed Crocodile, rotors spinning, inside of thirty minutes."

****

"I lost him." The radar technician adjusted several dials as the A-50 continued to orbit.

"What?" the mission officer asked, surprised.

"He made a beeline for the hills. Once he gets into a canyon, sir, even a shallow canyon, the ground clutter gets too confusing. The Liana can't pick a small target out of that, sir."

"Stay on it, he can't hide in those hills forever. As soon as he passes that estuary to the east, everything flattens out again."

"Yes, sir."

****

Kelly watched the cylinder head temperatures. He didn't like what he was seeing, but he figured the engine could hang in there long enough. He checked his watch, and noted that it was 1635 hours. Roughly four hours until sunset. He needed to land before dark.

He banked hard left, as the canyon branched, and then carefully followed the river below as it wended its way through flower-speckled tundra meadows. The ground gradually rose until finally he reached the headwaters of the stream and then passed over a shallow saddle between two rounded hills. Far above him, two new silver streaks appeared. *Fighters*, he thought. For the next twenty minutes they milled about overhead, and he knew they were searching for him. Apparently the Mainstay had lost him in the ground clutter. He grinned and patted the Antonov on the instrument panel. "Hang in there, old girl, we're almost there!"

Jake clung tenaciously to the ground and continued to work his way east. Finally he saw that he had arrived at the base of a large estuary where the hills flattened out. Fifty miles or so in the distance, he could see more small mountains. *Can I get there before these fighter jocks shoot me full of holes? Tally ho!*

****

"GOT HIM, sir!"

"Position, comrade! What is his position?"

"Uh, bearing 133 degrees, range to target sixty-two kilometers. Altitude, twenty meters AGL."

"*Spasibo.* Give me a vector for the fighters; put it on my screen.

"Alpha Xray one, this is Control. We have acquired target, bearing your position four-five degrees, range to target three-zero kilometers. Target altitude two-zero meters, target course eight-zero degrees, speed two-five-zero.

****

"Target in sight. Whoa, what do we have here, the Red Baron? What are your orders, Control?"

"Alpha Xray, weapons free. Engage and destroy."

"Copy that, Control, weapons free. Engage and destroy."

Captain Mikhail Zykov pushed his nose over and rocketed down toward the red Antonov at 960 kilometers per hour. He brought his fighter as low as he dared, roaring past Kelly just thirty meters above him, followed closely by his wing man The Antonov shuddered from the pressure wave of the two fighters screaming by at such proximity.

Zykov pulled up and around to the left, climbed to five hundred meters, and circled around behind the Antonov for another pass. He armed a single Molniya R-60 heat-seeking missile and screamed down once again, waiting to hear the lock tone in his headset. In a flash he had passed the slow-moving aircraft. Having overtaken the biplane too quickly for the seeker-head to acquire the target, he circled around again. He slowed his approach to 650 kilometers per hour. Still no tone.

Zykov tried one more pass at just above stall speed before he realized the Antonov with its front mounted radial engine didn't produce a sufficiently distinct heat signature for his Molniyas. "Control, this is Alpha Xray one. I just learned something."

"Share it with us, Alpha Xray."

"If we ever go to war with somebody whose air force is

made up of Antonov An-2s, there's no point in loading up heat-seekers. They can't even see it. I don't have any radar-homing ordnance loaded, either. Guess I'll have to splash this guy the old fashioned way."

He armed his Gryazev-Shipunov 30mm cannon, and lined up for another pass at 960 kilometers per hour. The red bi-plane was jinking and bobbing as it raced toward another range of hills east of the estuary. Zykhov triggered a burst, missing completely. He'd never led an aircraft flying as slow as the Antonov and he could see from his tracers that he'd shot way ahead of it. By the time he'd adjusted, he'd streaked past the An-2 again.

****

"What are you waiting for?" Jake growled. He felt like a target in a shooting gallery where the triggerman couldn't de-cide whether or not to fire. The Mig raced past him three or four times, enough for Jake to identify the ordnance hanging off the jet's hard points.

"Aphids. Poor sucker! You'll never pick up enough heat off this old engine to lock those AA-8s on to me. You'd have better luck locking 'em on to Chernikov's soldering pencil. Or his mouth, better yet. Hope they didn't arm your cannons, or I'm the poor sucker," Kelly shouted up to the pair of fighters orbiting overhead. He started jinking the aircraft, trying to cre-ate a difficult target. The first canyon was opening up just a few kilometers away. It might not save him, but it would make the fighter pilots' job more difficult.

The cannon shells ripped up the terrain in front of him as the Mig shot and missed on another pass.

"Uh-oh. Looks like I'm the sucker!"

****

Zykov called to his wingman, "Can't take this guy by get-ting on his tail. Got to be an oblique shot. Like this. Follow me."

Zykov rolled over in a dive from one thousand meters up, and used his air brakes to keep his speed down. He sighted on the Antonov and triggered off a burst. Two rounds went into the right wing. He pulled out, and his wing man followed suit, but with clean misses.

****

Kelly felt and heard the rounds strike the wing, but the shells passed right through the thin metal without detonating. It didn't seem to affect the Antonov's flight at all. He grinned, and wished he had a leather cap, goggles and scarf. *If I'm going to go down, at least I can do it in style*, he thought. But he knew his luck was running out.

Finally he gained the canyons again and clung to the bottoms, flying as low as he dared. Although it did not prevent the oblique-angle attack of his adversaries, the terrain kept them from coming in too close.

The engine coughed and skipped. He checked his instruments and saw that the cylinder head temps were pegged. It wouldn't be long before the engine would seize, and he'd be done. He hadn't given any thought to landing the plane. There was no place suitable. The tundra was soft, like peat moss. If he tried to put the aircraft down the wheels would sink and he'd pitch-pole.

The rattle of another hit brought him back to the present, and he thought, *One thing at a time, Jake, one thing at a time. Worry about landing when the plane won't go any farther. Boy, if my flight instructor heard that, I'd never get to fly again.*

He smelled avgas. *Oh, no, one of the tanks has been hit.* He waggled the rudder and checked six. No trailing flames or smoke. *Not yet, anyway. Those cannon rounds are punching through this thing like paper. Good thing they aren't exploding. Advantage, me.*

Jake looked up and located his tormentors. They were high above, diving on him again. He waited till he saw the cannon wink, pulled hard right, then banked left into a narrow valley opening up. The cannon shells zipped through the soft tundra until they struck bedrock several feet down, blowing small craters in the ground. The soil and humus tossed up by the explosions made it difficult to see as he passed through the flying debris.

Jake saw one jet streak to the south, and figured that his cannon must have jammed. *One down, one to go.* Kelly smelled smoke and looked behind him. The tail of the aircraft was wreathed in flames. "Hold together, baby, just a little longer!" he shouted.

He cleared a small saddle at the head of a canyon, and once again a wide, flat vista opened before him. The sea was not six miles away. A stiff breeze was blowing off it, buffeting the red biplane, and the storm clouds were moving closer. Jake flew down the gentle slope and headed for a shallow river that meandered through the grassy plain below him. He was completely exposed, and steeled himself for the end that he knew was coming. He was out of luck, out of options, out of time. *And I'm so close,* Kelly thought, tasting bitter disappointment. He looked up in time to see the Mig-29 Fulcrum starting another dive.

****

Chernikov sat at his desk, signing supply requisitions and handling mundane administrative tasks, a necessary evil of being in charge. It was midday, and he was thinking about having the sergeant on duty get him a lunch tray from the prison camp kitchen. A knock on the door interrupted his thoughts.

"Enter," he called.

The camp's chief interrogator came in with a big smile on his face. "Comrade General, I have some great news. Another holdout broke today—Doctor Cranmer. I'm putting together a group from the Academy of Sciences to begin debriefing him on his carbon fiber technology.

"And I've just gotten a call from the director of the integrated circuits laboratory in Omsk: the information that Dr.

Simmons provided looks very promising in the initial tests. A team of physicists is arriving today to review the lab results with him."

Chernikov's intercom buzzed. He picked up, and the duty sergeant informed him that he had a call waiting from Nikitin. He dismissed his interrogator after congratulating him, and then took the call. It was more good news: Kelly's aircraft had been spotted and was being engaged.

He dialed Patrikeyev to give him an update. It was the first time in several months that he had encouraging tidings to pass along.

"General Patrikeyev, I finally have some good news for you. Please go secure, sir."

The head of the GRU's Ninth Directorate engaged his scrambler, and then replied, "It's about time, Nikolai. What have you got?"

Chernikov shared the status updates on the scientists, and then added, "Even as we speak, Valeriy Ivanovich, a pair of Migs is engaging Major Kelly. He's way up northeast on the Chukchi Peninsula with nowhere to land. Even if he got on the ground somehow, he's got nowhere to hide. I fully anticipate having either him or his body in custody within the hour."

Patrikeyev breathed a sigh of relief. He'd been under intense pressure, and his credibility in the Politburo had been strained to the breaking point. But Chernikov's report would reverse that completely. The value of the technological advances would far outweigh the missteps.

"This is good news, Kolya. With these breakthroughs the Politburo will renew its support for *Krasnyy Voskhod.* And as for Major Kelly, kill him."

"But, sir—"

"Kill him, General! No 'buts!' I don't want any chance that he might yet escape. No arguments, do you understand? Kill him! That's an order, General!"

****

The aircraft shuddered as the 30mm cannon rounds tattooed holes through the main fuselage. One round hit the engine and detonated, blowing oil everywhere. The propeller clanked to a stop. Kelly could barely see through the windscreen. His airspeed began to drop. There was nowhere to put the aircraft down along the broad tundra bank of the river he was flying over. He checked his airspeed: still one hundred kilometers per hour. Jake lifted the nose to bleed off the speed. He remembered reading somewhere the Antonov could fly as slow as forty-eight kilometers per hour. Just then the plane was rocked by another wind gust, and Jake grinned. *I'll bet the wind is blowing that fast.* He continued to lift the nose, and the Antonov slowly settled.

When it touched down, it still had a ground speed of ten miles per hour. The wheels promptly sank into the tundra, and the plane pitch-poled, flipping over on its back. Jake was slammed against the instrument panel, opening up a large gash in his forehead.

With a mighty *whoosh*, flames overtook the Antonov. Jake released his seat belt and dropped to the ceiling of the aircraft, now the floor since it was upside down. He kicked out the window, grabbed his pack from the other seat, and crawled out of the wreckage.

Dazed by the blow on the head, he was bleeding profusely. Nonetheless, his survival instinct took over and screamed *HIDE!*, penetrating the red misty fog that was threatening to obscure his thinking. He stumbled over to the only contour in the spongy ground, the river, dragging his pack behind him. The shallow, wide brook, crystal clear, had carved through the tundra down to the underlying bedrock. The bank was easily six feet above the river bed and there were lots of overhangs where the tundra had been undercut but had not collapsed.

Jake tumbled over the edge with his pack, crawled under an overhang, and passed out.

****

"Control, this is Alpha-Xray two. Target is destroyed and in flames. Returning to base."

"Roger that, Alpha-Xray. Good job."

The controller at Provideniya advised the A-50 to get a precise fix on the wreckage, and then return to base as well.

It took an additional thirty minutes for the communication to wend its way up the chain and then back again, but orders came down to recover the body of the pilot of the Antonov An-2. That job was given to the squad waiting in the Mil Mi-24. The chopper lifted off and raced toward the location of the downed plane.

****

Dusk was coming. The sky was a brilliant orange as the sun sank into the west. There was no sound but the gurgling brook and the occasional snap of the fire as the Antonov burned to ashes.

The cold water on his legs brought Jake back to consciousness. He pulled himself out of the water, retrieved bandages from his pack, then bathed and bandaged the wound on his head. He was careful to leave no litter or other sign of his presence.

Tonight was the night. Tonight he would leave Soviet soil. Finally! He pulled the dry suit out of his pack and put it on, knowing that he'd probably have to move fast when he got to the coast. He was just stowing things in his pack when he heard the *whump-whump-whump* of a fast-approaching helicopter. Strapping on his pack, and being careful to stay hidden under the overhang, he began trotting downstream. He'd seen signs of a small village on the coast just before getting shot down. On the map it was called Chegitun. Perhaps he'd find a kayak there.

As the chopper came over the hills behind him he rounded a bend in the stream, and was hidden from view. Trotting steadily downstream, headed for the sea, Falcon vanished into the Arctic gloom.

****

Kelly looked out on a tiny anchorage protected by a breakwater. He could hear waves crashing on the shore beyond the anchorage. The salty, stiff breeze in his face carried moisture, and the stars to the north were blotted out by the oncoming clouds. He paused and examined the southern sky, looking for Orion. The Hunter had not yet risen and he turned back to the sea, disappointed. *But I am thinking of you, Galya. I will return.*

He walked down onto the gravelly beach. A row of six kayaks were laying upside down, well above the high tide mark.

"What do you do here?"

Kelly whirled about, drawing the pistol from the holster behind his head. Standing in front of him in the faint light was a man of squat, powerful build. He was unable to make out facial features.

"I only wish to leave," he responded. The man did not appear to be holding a weapon.

"To where?"

"Across the sea. I want to go home."

"Alaska?"

"America."

"The Sovs look for you." It was a statement, not a question.

"Yes, they do. I do not wish them to find me. I was brought to this country against my will. I escaped from them, and I want to go home."

"Not many escape from this place."

"But I will."

Ignoring Jake's pistol, the man walked past him down to the row of kayaks. "You were going to steal a kayak?"

"Yes. I'm sorry. I have no choice."

The man paused, as though thinking. Then he looked up. "Come. You must eat first. You have far to travel and a storm is rising. I have a thick stew I will share with you. And then I will give you a kayak."

"I thank you, but there is no time. The soldiers are searching for me. I must leave now!"

"There is time. The Sovs went the wrong way. They are checking out a village east of here. It will take them an hour or so. My son will watch for them, and warn us before they come close." The man began walking up the beach toward a cluster of homes. Kelly shrugged his shoulders, then followed.

The path led to a group of a dozen or so houses, built into the side of a hill. Kelly followed the man into one. An oil lamp guttered in the breeze as the door was opened. Hand-woven tapestries covered the walls, with lots of red and black colors. The aroma of a meat stew filled the air. A black-haired woman sat at a rough table, nursing a baby. Another child was playing in the corner. The man spoke in a language Jake could not understand, to a boy that appeared to be in his early teens. The youth looked at Kelly, then nodded and left the house.

"My name is Umqy. I am of the *Lygoravetlat*, the Sovs call us the Chukchi. This is my wife, Gitingev. Welcome to our home." The man had a flat face and nose, with oriental features. His eyes and hair were black, and he had a brown, weather-beaten complexion. He was wearing clothes made from animal hides, and knee-length moccasin-boots.

"Thank you, Umqy. I am Falcon. Why are you helping me, when your government is trying to capture me?" Kelly took off his pack and leaned it against the wall.

"We don't recognize the Soviet government. We don't recognize any government except our own tribal council. The Sovs come here once a year, and demand a quota of firs. Sometimes we provide them, sometimes we don't. Sometimes we just ignore them. They can't exactly threaten to send us to Siberia," the man chuckled.

The man dished up stew for everyone, and they sat at the table eating. The spoons were carved from bone, the bowls were wooden. Kelly felt like he'd stepped back in time. Umqy was very knowledgeable about his people's history, and told Kelly about the Chukchi wars with first the Czar and then the Soviets.

"I can't pay for your kayak, but you may have anything in

my pack you wish."

"I do not ask for pay. I am the village kayak maker. I will make a new one. As for your pack, you must take it all away. Nothing of yours can be found in my home. It would be our death warrant."

At that moment, the boy burst through the door and spoke excitedly to his father. Umqy stood up. "You must go. The soldiers are approaching. Take the path to the beach. The nearest kayak is yours. May *Kutkha*, the Raven, go with you."

****

"No *body*? What do you mean, 'There was no body'?" Chernikov barked into the phone.

"The soldiers searched the wreckage, several villages and the entire surrounding area. There was no sign of him," Nikitin clarified.

"You're telling me that Major Kelly has escaped?" Chernikov screamed into the phone. "After all this, after a year of cat and mouse and near misses, he's GONE???" Chernikov slammed down the phone in a rage, and threw the instrument across the room.

Oz Simmons was sitting on a chair outside Chernikov's office, chained hand and foot, waiting for a team of Russian physicists. He overheard the clamor and shouted conversation on the other side of the door and grinned.

****

Jake retrieved everything from the pack that he wished to save, and then filled it with rocks and zipped up the pockets. He stepped into the kayak and balanced the pack in front of him. After drawing the skirt tight, he paddled out to the breakwater and sank the pack.

He was by his calculations slightly over one hundred miles from American soil. Both the current and the wind favored him. It would be hard, but he was getting used to doing hard things. Without a second thought or a look back, Falcon paddled into the growing storm.

FALCON RISING

C. H. COBB

Available in December, 2013, in time for Christmas!

Major Jacob "Falcon" Kelly is a man without a country. The Russians want to kill him. The Americans think he's a traitor. Recently escaped from the USSR, yet facing arrest if he contacts American authorities, Kelly has no place to go. He knows that a KGB agent working undercover in the USAF will track his every move if he surfaces. Kelly possesses vital information that needs to find its way to the right people, but he doesn't know who to trust, or where to turn. Caught between Soviet assassins and the American intelligence services, Jake must run for his life!

Please help independent authors

Independent authors usually don't have someone managing their book's publicity plan or marketing. We don't have the support of an organization getting our novels in front of retailers who will carry them in their stores. Other than what marketing efforts we can cobble together on our own, we have only one source of publicity that can encourage others to buy our books, and that's you, our readers.

Your word-of-mouth recommendation, your Facebook comment, your tweet, your Amazon or Goodreads review is likely the only way an unknown author will get the word out about his or her book.

Let me hasten to admit that the reader is certainly under no obligation here. If you don't like the tale, or if the editing was sloppy, the cover or packaging amateurish, then by all means don't encourage someone else to read it. The last thing the independent publishing movement needs are products that fall short of genuine quality.

Even if you think the product is the best work since Bunyan's *Pilgrim's Progress* or Tolkien's *Lord of the Rings*, you still aren't obligated. Art doesn't create a debt or obligation on the part of the viewer. You're free to enjoy it and walk away. Artists take that risk when we create our work.

But if you find a tale you like and you'd like to read more by that author, give him or her a hand by letting your friends and loved ones know where they can get a good story. Post a review, mention it on Facebook, send a few emails, tell a few friends. Once the word gets out, a good story will sell itself; but getting the word out is the challenge. Thanks for your help!

About the Author

Chris Cobb's resume reads like a patchwork quilt. He's driven a forklift, worked as a technician doing component-level repair on digital circuitry, been a programmer-analyst, a data-center shift operator, taught high school science and mathematics, and been an Information Technology Director at a graduate school. Most of his career he's been a pastor.

He lives with his wife, Doris, in western Ohio, and is presently the teaching pastor at Bible Fellowship Church in Greenville, OH. They have three adult children, and two fine sons-in-law and daughter-in-law, all of whom are actively engaged in the arts at some level.

Chris received Jesus Christ as his Savior in 1974, and seeks to incorporate a biblically faithful worldview into everything he does, including his writing.

You can find Chris on Facebook, or find additional works by him at chcobb.com.

www.ingramcontent.com/pod-product-compliance
Lightning Source LLC
Chambersburg PA
CBHW070117120726
47909CB00002B/639